THE BLOOD OF KINGS

TINTAGEL BOOK I

M.K. HUME

THE BLOOD OF KINGS

TINTAGEL BOOK I

headline
review

First published in 2015 by
HEADLINE REVIEW
An imprint of HEADLINE PUBLISHING GROUP

1

Cataloguing in Publication Data is available from the British Library

ISBN 978 1 4722 1580 2 (Hardback)
ISBN 978 1 4722 1579 6 (Trade Paperback)

Typeset in Golden Cockerel by Avon DataSet Ltd, Bidford-on-Avon, Warwickshire

Printed and bound in Great Britain by Clays Ltd, St Ives plc

HEADLINE PUBLISHING GROUP
An Hachette UK Company
Carmelite House
50 Victoria Embankment
London EC4Y 0DZ

www.headline.co.uk
www.hachette.co.uk

This book is dedicated to my friend, Pauline Reckentin, with my love.

Years ago, when I belonged to her writing group, Pauline swore that I would *go off like a rocket* when I eventually forced myself to write a novel. I may not have imitated a space-ship or exploded like a fire-cracker, but Pauline always believed in my ability, even when I expressed my personal doubts, which was often! For her faith and her trust in me and her unconditional love which overlooks my manifold flaws, this book is dedicated to her.

M. K. Hume
June 2015

ACKNOWLEDGEMENTS

Thank you to all the people who bring my books to life. You never get enough of the credit, but you are responsible for ensuring that my frail offering actually sees the light of day. I am always impressed by the improvements to the manuscript once the editorial staff begin to work their magic. Thank you, people.

My editor, Clare Foss, and my agent, Dorie Simmonds, have always given me great support and I thank them both for their patience and forbearance. I offer them a special vote of thanks for this manuscript because a major computer disaster added a bit of drama to the production of the novel. I was beginning to think the fates were conspiring against me.

One of the truly nice things about completing a new novel is seeing what the cover is like. My guesses are always so far off the mark that I've decided to just sit back and watch with amazement. My best wishes go to those involved in its creation.

My thanks also go to my friends and family who make my life so much easier. Thanks go to my sons, Brendan and Damian, for their assistance. Lots of love to both of you.

M. K. Hume

DRAMATIS PERSONAE

Adwen ap Rhys	King of the Dobunni Tribe.
Ael	One of three young brothers in Aquae Sulis who insult Princess Endellion.
Aelheran ap Einion	King of the Silures Tribe. Father of Ardunn. Father-in-law of Prince Cadal of the Dumnonii Tribe. Married to Queen Aoifi.
Aeneas	The Greco-Roman hero who founded Rome.
Aeron ap Iorweth	A prince of the Silures tribe. He is the son of Iorweth, Lord of Caerleon. He is also the nephew of King Aelheran of the Silures Tribe. He becomes the suitor of Princess Endellion.
Ambrose	Bishop of Mediolanum (Milan), Italy.
Aoifi	Queen of the Silures tribe. Wife of King Aelheran.
Ardunn	The new young wife of Prince Cadal, elder son and heir of King Caradoc. She was the granddaughter of the king of the Silures tribe.
Bauto	A general in the service of Theodosius, Emperor of the East.
Bleise ap Bladud	King of the Belgae tribe.
Boudica	Queen of the Iceni tribe who led a revolt against the Roman occupiers of Britannia.

Cadal (Prince)	Eldest son of King Caradoc. Married to Ardunn of the Silures tribe.
Cadoc (Prince)	Second son of King Caradoc. Married to Guenor of the Atrebates tribe.
Caradoc ap Ynyr	King of the Dumnonii tribe.
Caradoc Major	Grandfather of Caradoc Minor, King of the Dumnonii tribe.
Cessus	Roman scout killed at the Outlaw Ambush at Vindo Cladia.
Chronos	One of the ancient Greek gods. Better known as *Father Time*.
Conanus	See Kynan ap Meriadoc.
Decius	A decurion. Aide and personal servant to Flavius Magnus Maximus.
Drustan ap Drust	The son of the Lord of Portus Adurni. An aide to Fiachna ap Tormud, King of the Durotriges tribe in Venta Belgarum.
Elen	The beautiful daughter of King Meriadoc of the Ordovice tribe.
Elphin	An outlaw leader in southern Britannia.
Endellion	The daughter of King Caradoc and Lady Saraid, the Wise Woman of the Red Wells.
Ercol	Dumnonii scout killed at the Outlaw Ambush at Vindo Cladia.
Felix	Felix Marcus Gallus. Roman Magistrate of Aquae Sulis.
Fiachna ap Tormud	King of the Durotriges tribe.
Fortuna	The Roman goddess of fortune.
Gethin ap Gwaun, Prince Gethin	The son of Gwaun ap Mairtin, King of the Atrebates tribe.

Glanmore ap Niall	Courier in the service of Emperor Magnus Maximus.
Guenor	The young wife of Prince Cadoc, younger son of King Caradoc. She was the daughter of King Gwaun pen Mairtin of the Atrebates tribe.
Gwaun ap Mairtin	King of the Atrebates tribe.
Hibernians	The native tribesmen of Ireland.
Horatius	A Roman centurion who successfully defended the bridge over the Tiber River during a period when Rome was under attack from Lars, the King of the Clusiums, in the sixth century BC.
Huw	One of Caradoc's woodsmen who is wounded by a wild boar.
Iorweth	The brother of King Aelheran of the Silures tribe. He is the husband of Eavan and the father of Prince Aeron. He is also related to Llew, King of the Dobunni, by marriage.
Kynan ap Meriadoc	Son and heir of King Meriadoc of the Ordovice tribe. (Also called Conanus by Maximus.)
Livia	Daughter of Felix Marcus Gallus, Magistrate of Aquae Sulis.
Livinia	Wife of Felix Marcus Gallus, Magistrate of Aquae Sulis.
Llew ap Adwen	King of the Dobunni tribe. The son of King Adwen ap Rhys.
Llian	Queen Llian. Wife of King Llew ap Adwen of the Dobunni tribe.
Lorn	A warrior in Maximus's personal guard.

Macsen Wledig	The Celtic name for Flavius Magnus Maximus.
Marcus Licinus	Marcus Gallenus Licinus. The magistrate in Aquae Sulis.
Marcellus	Scribe and personal assistant of Marcus Licinus in Aquae Sulis.
Marcellinus	Maximus's brother. A commander in Maximus's army.
Marcomer	A leader of the Franks during the late fourth century. He fought against the forces of Magnus Maximus.
Maximus	Flavius Magnus Maximus. A Roman tribune who is second in command to Theodosius, the Roman governor of Britain. He eventually becomes the governor of Britannia and, ultimately, becomes the Emperor of the Western Empire in Rome.
Meriadoc ap Nyall	King of the Ordovice.
Mithras	The Roman god of Soldiers.
Picts	The native population of Northern Britannia.
The Red Dragon	King Arthur.
Rowen ap Aidan	An aide to King Caradoc of Tintagel.
Saraid	The Wise Woman of the Red Wells. A white witch and a notable healer.
Sion Cripplefoot	Steward in the court of King Meriadoc of the Ordovice tribe.
Sorcha ap Sion	King of the Regni tribe.
Tegan Eurfron	Queen of the Dumnonii tribe, and wife of King Carodoc. She is the mother of Prince Cadal and Prince Cadoc.

Theodora	Roman wife of Magnus Maximus. Lives in Augusta Treverorum, Germany.
Theodosius	A Roman governor of Britannia in the fourth century. He was a kinsman of Flavius Magnus Maximus.
Trefor	A hunt-master in the service of King Caradoc.
Varrus	A courier sent to Caradoc by Maximus during the campaign in Italia.

MAJOR ROMAN SETTLEMENTS
IN BRITAIN (c. 360AD)

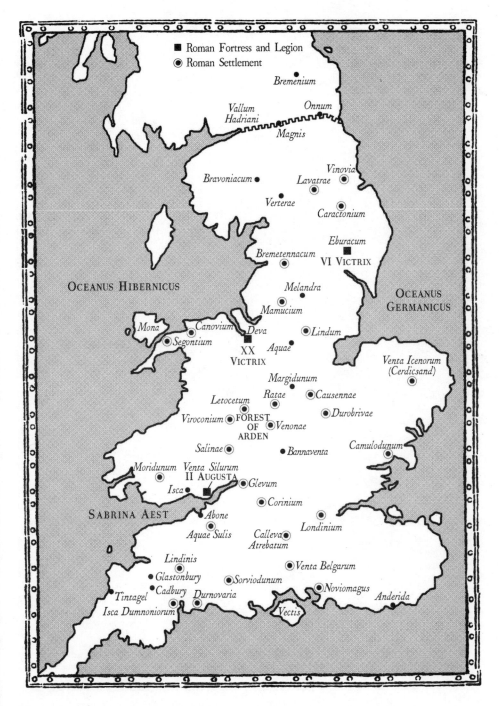

■ Roman Fortress and Legion
◉ Roman Settlement

Bremenium

Vallum Hadriani

Onnum

Magnis

Vinovia
Bravoniacum
Lavatrae

Verterae

Caractonium

Eburacum
Bremetennacum
VI VICTRIX

OCEANUS HIBERNICUS

Melandra

OCEANUS GERMANICUS

Mamucium

Mona
Canovium
Deva
Lindum
Segontium
XX VICTRIX
Aquae

Venta Icenorum (Cerdicsand)

Margidunum

Letocetum
Ratae
Causennae

Viroconium
FOREST OF ARDEN
Venonae
Durobrivae

Salinae
Bannaventa
Camulodunum

Moridunum
Venta Silurum
II AUGUSTA
Isca
Glevum

SABRINA AEST

Corinium

Abone
Londinium

Aquae Sulis
Calleva Atrebatum

Lindinis
Venta Belgarum

Glastonbury
Sorviodunum
Tintagel
Cadbury
Noviomagus
Durnovaria
Anderida
Isca Dumnoniorum
Vectis

BARBARIAN ATTACKS ON ROMAN BRITAIN (C. 383–410 AD)

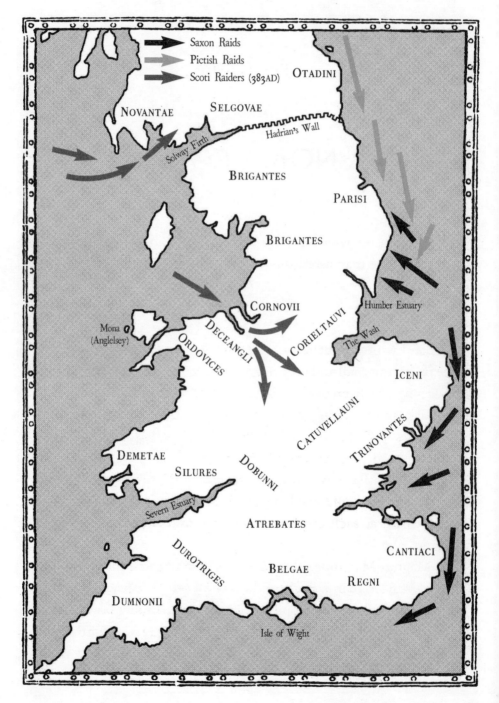

Saxon Raids
Pictish Raids
Scoti Raiders (383AD)

OTADINI

NOVANTAE   SELGOVAE

Hadrian's Wall

Solway Firth

BRIGANTES

PARISI

BRIGANTES

CORNOVII   CORIELTAUVI

Humber Estuary

Mona
(Anglelsey)

DECEANGLI

ORDOVICES

The Wash

ICENI

CATUVELLAUNI

TRINOVANTES

DEMETAE

SILURES   DOBUNNI

Severn Estuary

ATREBATES

CANTIACI

DUROTRIGES

BELGAE   REGNI

DUMNONII

Isle of Wight

PROLOGUE

A NOBLE ROMAN

The reason why we have two ears and only one mouth is that we may listen the more and talk the less.

Zeno of Citium, *Lives of the Philosophers*

A fitful winter light fell on burnished iron helms, breastplates, coats of ring-mail and gleaming swords and spearpoints. Without warning, the Roman *cataphractarii* swept out from the margins of a dark and dripping forest and struck the line of Hibernian warriors with the force of a giant hammer. The superbly trained horses used their sharpened hooves to pound the enemy into the mud until the world was filled with wild Hibernian screams, crushed flesh, wild-eyed steeds and straining men who hacked and thrust at each other in scenes reminiscent of the Christian Hades.

Magnus Maximus grinned with a flash of teeth that was more of a grimace than a smile. This was war and it was all he knew. Yet it accorded him no pleasure and *bugger-all satisfaction*, in the crude description of his manservant, Decius, a hard-bitten decurion.

'For Rome!' Maximus thundered, and heard his call answered, raggedly at first, but then repeated from three hundred disciplined throats. 'For Rome!'

Rome was a city that most of them had never seen; nor would they choose to, even if the chance was offered. But the name still conjured up the familiarity of centuries of rule, of unimaginable power and of deep-rooted corruption under the white marble.

'For Rome!' Maximus bellowed again and slashed down at a leering Hibernian face.

The general kneed his horse to the top of a small rise from where he could survey the battlefield and make a cold and calculated assessment of the conflict's progress. His horse took the climb in its stride, for this particular bay gelding was a superb specimen of horseflesh, one that had been raised on the sweeping plains of Maximus's homeland in the province of Gallaecia in Hispania. Maximus had been born in the wide, spreading estates of Count Theodosius the Elder, his kinsman and the patriarch of their family. As a notable soldier and an aristocrat, the commander scorned to use the hardy hill ponies of the Britons, for the indignity of his feet dangling only inches from the ground offended his sense of self-importance.

In truth, Maximus cared more for the welfare of his horse than he did for most of his men. To his experienced eye, the Eagles were not what they once were, although the Roman cavalry could still be classed among the cream of Britannia's military might.

The Britons are the only tribes in these lands who use horses, Maximus thought sardonically. Yet the other barbarians shun the use of beasts in battle, and reject anything that takes attention away from their own personal heroism.

In the chaotic scene below him he immediately recognised

the core of order and planning that lay beneath the messy detritus of violent death. The cavalry had done well, even the Britons who were all hair and talk. He was satisfied, for he could rid himself of the irritating Hibernians, at least for a time. His kinsman and commander Theodosius would be pleased. Maximus turned in the saddle and pointed his sword towards the dimness of the forest.

The tribune's gestures became sweeping and decisive, as his sword tip was now pointed directly at the melee below the elevated knoll where his horse was standing so alertly.

'For Rome!' he howled, until the wind plucked at his voice and carried it into the tree line.

In answer to his call, a cohort of Roman infantry marched out of the woods in crisp and menacing formations. They moved purposefully towards the enemy with their shields overlapping to provide protection to their comrades, while their short stabbing spears bristled outwards like the spines of primeval beasts.

Maximus allowed himself a smile of satisfaction. Even after fifteen years of war, the tribune could still feel a visceral thrill as his legionnaires bore down on their enemy at an unhurried pace as inexorable as the death that would claim so many souls.

The same breeze that fluttered the standard of the boar and made the eagles appear to dance at the top of their tall poles lifted Maximus's scarf, scarlet for practicality, that he had knotted around his throat to protect his skin from the cold and abrasive iron of his cuirass. This particular Roman was large for his race; men from Hispania tended to grow tall and lean. His profile was sharp and aquiline, while his features were as elegant as a beautifully smithed knife blade, and as masculine as the frozen face of the god, Mithras, who silently overlooked his altar. His hair was so dark that it shone like the breast of a raven. Despite having been shaved by Decius at noon, a blue shadow was already beginning to cover his cheeks and chin. A pair of heavy black brows formed a ridge above a pair of sharp brown eyes. A single clean scar had caught the edge of his mouth on the right side to give every smile a sardonic twist. It added gravitas to one who was very young to have attained his high rank during a short career, although his peers realised how resentful he was of the slow pace of his climb through the ranks.

The Roman troops had reached the edge of the knoll when Maximus gave an order that instructed the *cataphractarii* to vacate the field. His eyes passed regretfully over the fifty or so wounded men, but perhaps the strongest of them would survive the ministrations of the field surgeons. With a shrug, Magnus consigned the Roman wounded to the mercies of their own particular gods, for the subtle deities Fortuna and Mithras between them ruled the battlefield.

He had sent the heavy cavalry in first to test the Hibernians' mettle, despite the fact that they were usually employed to mop up the battlefield, after the initial attacks by the infanteers were unleashed. The unexpected tactics had proved highly successful.

An order from a half-dozen bronze horns sounded from the lines. Spears were thrown and, for a moment, seemed to blot out the sun in a rain of iron. The Hibernians raised their shields to trap the spearpoints and protect their bodies from the deadly hail, before they were forced to cast down the shields with the long spear shafts embedded in them, rendering them useless. Maddened and frustrated, the Hibernians charged towards the Romans while screaming to their gods.

And now, the first lines of Roman infantry marched onto the field for the final kill. In parade-ground straight ranks, they met the Hibernian warriors with a phlegmatic lack of emotion. Killing was their business.

Spears made short work of those inexperienced barbarian warriors who were slow to raise their shields. And, now that so many of the impatient Hibernians were dead or wounded on the battlefield, their bodies were trampled into the mud by the metal-studded sandals of the Roman infantry. With swords drawn, the Roman ranks began to inflict the real carnage.

Maximus's legion had recently been issued with the newer, longer form of the gladius, a weapon that had been redesigned to suit the taller generations of Roman soldiers and barbarian *comitas* who were serving the empire. Already its power and efficiency in close-quarter fighting had given the Spanish gladius a reputation for inflicting mayhem.

'The Hibernians rarely run, Decius. It's a strange trait of the northern barbarians and I wonder why it's so?' Maximus asked his fellow officer who had made his way up the knoll and was now standing beside his master with his sword drawn and ready. Maximus, focused on the butchery below him, never bothered to turn his head away from the action.

'Like most barbarians, they're judged to be courageous or cowardly by their individual actions on the field. Like those blue bastards from the land of the Picts, the Hibernians will always refuse to retreat, unless they have a leader who displays a modicum of common sense. Retreat is always regarded as cowardice.'

'So I thought. A leader's role is to win, but it's pointless to succeed and yet have so few men survive the battle that the leader can't defend what's been taken. Watch! I'll wager that these fools fight to the last man.'

The decurion grinned widely and exposed two browning

canines. 'Perhaps the journey to reinforce Deva won't be quite so harrowing from now on.'

'Let's finish it then! Sound the attack signal and we'll unleash my dogs of war.'

Maximus was prepared to allow the men a little fun now that they had turned the tide of battle. His infantrymen had demonstrated their discipline and martial skills, so the time was right to crush the Hibernians with tried and tested tactics.

'Let the enemy have a taste of Hell,' Decius ordered a boy with a long brass horn who had joined them on the knoll. Above the din of battle, the horn's peal was more the howl of an alien beast than a musical note. Suddenly the Roman infantry changed direction as they followed the tactical instructions of their centurions. In some cases the middle of the line seemed to collapse, so the Hibernians screamed triumphantly and charged into the gap in the retreating line. Then, as if by sorcery, the Hibernians found they were surrounded when large squads of Romans suddenly enveloped them. The small, dark men from the Middle Sea carved the Hibernians up like raw meat.

Decius's grin was even wider now and he wished he could stand on the line with his comrades. Still, serving as Maximus's personal servant had its uses.

All over the field, men fell and died. The Hibernian lords gnashed their teeth, tore at their beards and demanded more and more heroism from their beleaguered men. Meanwhile, the tribune's attention drifted away from the battle. The contest was unequal now, and the numerical advantage held by the Hibernians had been neutralised. Maximus began to lose interest in a struggle whose outcome he had considered inevitable from the very beginning.

'How well did the Britons fight, Decius? Were they useful? They boast enough for ten of our best veterans – but do they possess the necessary martial skills?'

Decius spat a large globule of phlegm onto the dripping grass and cast a jaundiced eye towards a miserable sky.

'I've been in this pimple on the arse of our world for twenty years, master, so I know the Britons and their ways as much as any outsider can – especially the ladies, if you take my meaning.' He chortled, but the commander looked increasingly weary, a sure sign that he was irritated.

'The Britons are strange people with their heathen gods and sacred trees. We removed the Druids, root and branch, but there's a streak in their souls that turns them into nasty enemies, even for professional armies like ours. They'd be good friends though, if we were sensible enough to mix with them and earn their respect. If we could mould their warriors into a manageable whole, they'd march into Hades for us and not give a damn at the cost. They don't realise their own strength, master, and I've sometimes felt that even the Great Caesar might have failed against them, if they'd been united.'

'Heresy! If any man but I were to hear such sentiments, you'd be considered crazed – or a traitor!' Maximus laughed to show he meant no threat. 'But I agree with you that they're odd and difficult to understand. I'm in receipt of an invitation to travel into the south-west to consult with the King of the Dumnonii tribe, if this war with the Hibernians ever ends. I've never seen the south-west of Britannia.'

'Well, master, them's the oddest of the whole lot. The land down there is warmer and more pleasant than elsewhere on the island. Sometimes, the sun's been known to shine all day.'

Both men laughed and stared ruefully at the slowly darkening sky. Below them, the Romans were slaughtering the badly wounded enemy warriors without quarter.

'It would definitely be a good enough land to start with for any Roman commander with ambition,' Decius added, and the pair smiled with a mutual understanding.

'I hear tell the south is a place of great standing stones and sheer cliffs that overhang the wild western ocean. Many folk in that land say there are drowned cities under the waves, so you can hear the bells ringing when the sea is turbulent. There have been nights when I could have believed in that Wilde Hunt of theirs, and the notion that trees can come to life and smother men with their branches and roots.'

'That's an interesting tale, Decius,' Maximus sneered. 'I never took you to be a credulous man.'

'Not I, master! They're just stories that are passed around the fire pits when there's not much else to do. It would be best that you went there, my lord, and saw the place for yourself.'

'I intend to, Decius, for you've begun to whet my appetite. I've heard that the Dumnonii king is called the Boar of Cornwall. That's propitious, don't you think, since the emblem of our own legion depicts the boar?'

'Aye! I've been told that Caradoc's been named for a black beast that harrows the earth with its giant tusks.' Decius couldn't resist one last reference to the supernatural.

Maximus cuffed his servant lightly with one idle hand and kicked his horse into movement. Below them, the cavalry were dragging away the bodies of the dead and preparing them for the funeral fires once the enemy corpses had given up every item of value. Still more of the warriors carried away living Romans or wounded Britons, while the dead were laid out according to their rank and the century to which they belonged.

As they worked, so too did a clerk and a scribe who were already recording the names of the dead and the wounded onto short scrolls that would be placed in the archives of the legion. As always, the Roman war machine rolled inexorably onwards.

The night came and, with it, the inevitable scavengers.

Maximus's Journey
into the South

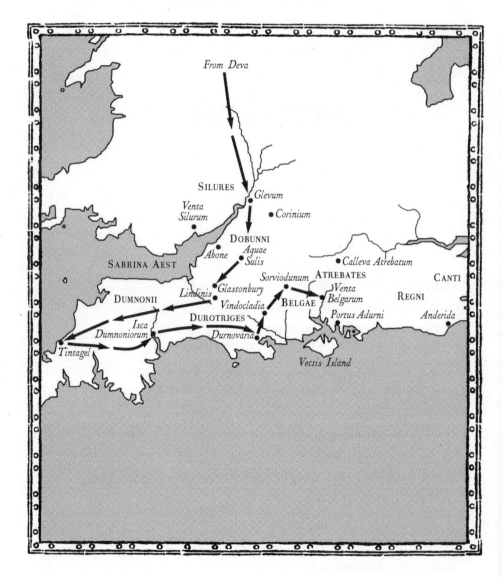

From Deva

SILURES
Glevum

Venta Silurum

Corinium

DOBUNNI
Abone *Aquae Sulis*

SABRINA AEST

Calleva Atrebatum

Sorviodunum ATREBATES CANTI

DUMNONII *Lindinis* *Glastonbury* *Venta Belgarum* REGNI

Vindocladia BELGAE

DUROTRIGES *Portus Adurni* *Anderida*

Isca Dumnoniorum *Durnovaria*

Tintagel

Vectis Island

CHAPTER I

STRANGE BEDFELLOWS

May truth be embodied, strong with life.

The Gathas Yasna

Magnus Maximus, tribune of the Twentieth Legion of Deva, rode over a treeless hill to gasp at the sheer enormity of the wild scene that spread out before him like one of Chronos's jokes.

Time had stood still in this ancient land; it had even defeated Rome's power to civilise, so Maximus was left speechless by the dizzying impossibility of Fortress Tintagel.

The Hibernian raiders had eventually been herded back to their boats and pursued over the Mare Hibernicus to their boggy, rain-drenched homes like a pack of mongrel dogs. Maximus knew they would return, for they would always lust after the riches of Britannia.

Meanwhile, the legion at Eburacum on the east coast of Britannia had driven the Picts back beyond the Vellum Antonini, leaving the Otadini tribe to hunt down any stragglers who were discovered along the escape route. During the uneasy peace that followed, Maximus had begged leave of his commanding officer

1

in Deva to make a diplomatic visit to the court of King Caradoc in distant Tintagel. Maximus had convinced Theodosius that a treaty with the Dumnonii tribe could be advantageous to their mutual security, mainly because this tribe occupied vast lands and lived cheek-by-jowl with the other tribes that inhabited the south. No major Roman garrisons had been constructed in the southern lands, where the Dumnonii were the strongest fighting force of all. Isolationist and self-sufficient, they could become a valuable ally – or a dangerous enemy.

Theodosius had agreed, albeit reluctantly. Many of the older officers, the Duces, had spoken disparagingly of Magnus Maximus, a commander who was altogether too popular with his men and was likely to order the most peculiar strategic formations in battles involving his fanatically loyal troops. His detractors cited his use of *cataphractarii*, the Roman heavy cavalry, at the beginning of the recent battle against the raiders from Hibernia. The young commander's tactics had proved successful, but Maximus's critics were offended that this young officer refused to follow the old traditions. And so, when Theodosius had asked why Maximus had chosen to do this, the senior officers at the conference had almost salivated in anticipation of the embarrassment that would be inflicted on this ambitious young tribune.

Maximus had responded by thanking the great man for bothering to notice the limited strategic capabilities of a relative newcomer. Theodosius was amused by this humble response, for he was aware that this young Spaniard had no such flaws. Interested, he waited patiently for the answer.

'The Hibernians aren't entirely stupid, master, and they know how we fight. After all, we've been trouncing them for years. The landscape at the battlefield offered no advantage to either of us, because it was as dry as the earth can get in this countryside in winter. I decided to break their hearts and be done with it. They knew what to expect from our infantry and were forming up to embrace our warriors with flanking attacks, so I let my *cataphractarii* destroy a large part of their force while they were vulnerable. You'll have to own that my tactics worked rather well and they kept my casualties to a minimum.'

Theodosius had nodded in agreement. 'And would you use your heavy cavalry in the same way on the next occasion you're engaged in battle?'

'How can I know, master? I've not seen the landscape, so I'd consider any commander to be a fool if he made strategic decisions from a pre-ordained scroll. I begrudge losing any of my men because it takes so long to recruit replacements and train them to reach my standards.'

Theodosius laughed then and gave permission for the young tribune to make the journey to the land of the Dumnonii. As he left the commander's lodgings, Maximus heard a howl of protest from one of his opponents inside the conference room.

'You've rewarded that Spanish bastard for his impertinence, master. That young man has ambitions beyond his birth and, as he advances, he'll rise to strike you down. Kinsman or not!'

Theodosius's response had been hard and sharp.

'Then he'll serve me well as he climbs to the top of Fortuna's Wheel. It's far better for me that my officers think on their feet than sit on their collective arses. Which sort of man are you, Crusius?'

And so, with his body servant, Decius, and guard of twenty cavalrymen, Maximus left Segontium on a predictably gloomy day. As usual, rain dripped out of a grey sky. Across the Menai Straits, a narrow ribbon of sand revealed Mona Island, a landmark that loomed darkly out of the choppy sea. As usual, Decius regaled anyone who would listen with tales of the genocide of the Druids and their children, all of whom had been slain pitilessly by legionnaires until the waters of the straits ran red with the blood of innocents.

'The gods say that such actions must be paid for, even if they are necessary,' Decius stated as he rubbed his chilled fingers together and gloated at the various expressions of doubt, suspicion, fear and dread on the faces of the incredulous cavalrymen. Only one horseman among the ancillary troops travelling with the cavalcade, a Brigante, had the temerity to face Decius with an expression that was studiously blank. This particular soldier was far too wise to embarrass a veteran, so he kept his tongue between his teeth.

For an instant, Maximus remembered what Decius had said about the Britons being odd, but then he pushed the thought away. The people of Britannia had been civilised and imbued with Latin culture so, with luck, they were less likely to fall prey to the wights and ghosts of their barbarian past. Those Britons who had been educated were expected to worship sensible gods and to dress, wash and comport themselves like real people.

The journey into the south had taken less time than Maximus expected, for they followed the arrow-straight Roman roads leading to Glevum. The cavalcade passed through the smaller towns with comfortable Roman names, for a tribune on a mission for his commander could expect to receive the best hospitality that these outposts had to offer.

When the warriors eventually reached Glevum, they knew that their journey was half-completed, so Maximus allowed them to detour to the fleshpots of Aquae Sulis and its renowned hot waters.

They had luxuriated in the baths and brothels for a few brief days before Maximus ordered them to remount and head southwards again through a new landscape that was strange and unearthly. The long valleys, the tors with towers atop them for signal fires, and the standing stones that seemed to thrum and vibrate under human fingers were eventually forgotten as they discovered new oddities, despite the cold winter that covered the earth with a rime of frost.

'Only Romans would travel with these winds and the scent of snow in the air,' one old smith muttered in the Celtic tongue to his boy as they worked on the shoes of the tribune's horse in one of the small unnamed villages through which the cavalcade passed. The lad was labouring over the bellows and his reddened face was running with sweat.

'You spoke to me, smith?' Maximus demanded from behind his bay. The blacksmith nearly froze with fear as he heard his own language repeated back at him.

'I meant no disrespect, my lord. None at all! But you're travelling the roads at a strange time of year and you're following the lesser-known paths that lead into the south.'

Maximus's face was stony and one hand tapped his scabbard suggestively. The boy had ceased to work the bellows and was trying to decide whether to hide himself from these horrible men with their dark and angry eyes.

'How can I apologise for disrespect, master? I'm sorry for my thoughtless words, but I'm a poor smith, so I spend my days repairing farm implements. I know little of your world.'

'You're a liar! Your words are those of a man who was well educated in the ways of the battlefield. You're only sorry because you've been caught out in stupidity.'

The smith's face became blotchy in shades of grey and red.

'I don't like liars, so reconsider your answers or you'll lie in the mud of the roadway. Perhaps a little pain and reflection on your part might make me listen to your explanations.'

Decius dismounted and his sword was drawn with a threatening hiss. The smith had almost fallen over his feet as he tried to reach the rain-drenched roadway before Decius entered the smithy. He threw himself onto the sodden earth which was liberally spread with dung from the last horse that had been shod, then spread his arms and lowered his face into the foul mud.

Maximus gazed down at the full obeisance usually reserved for emperors or eastern potentates. Reluctant to humiliate the man further, he allowed himself to smile.

'Rise now, smith, and tell me the truth. I'll not punish you further. I want to know where you've served, because I'm curious about you.'

'My name is Alwyn ap Isca. I was a signaller in my youth and I carried the Dracos into battle until I was a man. I served with pride for ten years until I got this wound and was forced to leave the ranks. I needed to eat, so I became a blacksmith.'

Alwyn bared one leg and exposed a long sword cut that ran from his groin to his knee.

'A standard bearer! That would have been a fine role for a young lad. Did you ever let your Dragon fall to the ground?'

Maximus wanted to test the man's response.

'I'm alive, aren't I, master? No standard bearer would want to live if the emblem of their legion was dishonoured. The shame alone . . .'

Even though he was grey and hard-bitten now, this elderly smith, shaking with cold and fearful of this dark Roman with the terrible eyes, couldn't countenance a worse fate than to see his Dragon falling into the dust again.

'There is still some of the legionnaire in you, Smith, although your tongue tends to run away with itself,' the tribune added. 'Get out of the rain now, man, and finish your work on my horse. You can tell your grandchildren that Magnus Maximus let you live.'

His humiliation forgotten, the blacksmith began to shape the new shoe while his apprentice worked the bellows until his face was purple with effort. As always, Maximus found pleasure in watching a smith force the horse to raise its hoof and then smelled the pungency of burning hair as the shoe, still hot, was deftly put into place.

When the smith handed him the reins, Maximus gave the veteran a golden coin. The reward was far too much for such a trivial task. As Alwyn bit into the coin to check on its purity, Maximus laughed and leaped into the saddle, feeling his mount's strength and renewed confidence in its repaired hoof.

'A long life to you, master,' the smith shouted as Maximus kneed his bay and the gelding raced away with a great splatter of mud and water. 'And, if it's fated to be short – then let it be glorious!'

'Remember that man, boy,' Alwyn told his apprentice as the cavalcade disappeared down the makeshift street. 'He'll not make old bones, but he'll surely leave a trail of destruction behind him.'

The rest of the journey to Tintagel passed without incident, except for Maximus's amazement at how much the landscape could change within the space of a few miles. In this strange land even the rivers seemed deceptively shallow and harmless, or sprang from ground that was stained the colour of blood.

Maximus had chosen to ignore a coarse pathway that had been hacked through the thick green sod by the movement of many sharp hooves. Instead, the tribune followed the high ground along the ridges in typical Roman fashion, for he was eager to survey the fortress from above before he committed himself to the plunging downward path. Maximus had scoffed at the notion that these British tribesmen could possibly build an impregnable fortress, given their usual levels of engineering expertise, until he reached the brow of the hill and beheld Tintagel Castell on the cliffs overlooking the Oceanus Atlanticus.

The drop down to the fortress entrance was dizzying. Maximus discovered he was at the same level as the wheeling gulls and birds of prey circling the cliffs in great soaring spirals. Swathes of grass covered the slopes of the peninsula in long, deep waves, carved out by the impossibly strong winds that captured Maximus's red cloak and sent it swooping and diving like a firebird. The path to the castell followed a long curve that wound its way down to a row of flint-stone buildings next to a narrow causeway that shuddered above the raging sea and allowed access to the citadel itself.

Beyond this causeway that was only slightly wider than the width of a mounted horseman, a dangerous lip of a second causeway hung above the boiling waves that dashed against the base of the cliffs. Then, from a guardhouse that was identifiable from the ant-like warriors who seemed to man its negligible margins, a set of carved stone stairs rose up the side of the cliff to give access to the fortress on the clifftops. Those steps rose in a dizzying curve to platforms near the top of the cliffs, where the fortress glowered, surrounded by the huts of the peasant-servants that clung onto sloping rocks overhanging the surging ocean below.

'Hades!' Maximus breathed. 'You could assail that place for a year and get nowhere. Even if an enemy reached the causeway, they'd be picked off from above. I must remind myself never to try to capture Fortress Tintagel.'

Decius stared at the terrifying stairway, uneven and winding, and barely wide enough for one man at a time to stand on each rung.

'I'll be the first to remind you of your decision, master. Those stairs would break a cohort's heart. It'd be bloody murder to try to climb them, especially if the defenders decided you weren't welcome.'

'Now I know why Caradoc is a man to be reckoned with. It's no wonder that Tintagel has never fallen to invaders.'

Maximus felt the hair rise on his forearms and the back of his neck, as if a wight had run its dead fingers over his living flesh.

'This place is intimidating, just as the surrounding landscape is fierce and strange. Look at it! Have you ever seen the like, Decius?'

The horsemen suddenly heard a loud challenge from ahead of them where a group of mounted warriors awaited the approach of Maximus's cavalcade. Immediately a troop of six men rode up the flinty track at a brutal speed on horses that were safely negotiating paths they had known all their lives.

Maximus wheeled his gelding and summoned his men to follow him to meet the Dumnonii warriors on the path. Fortunately his horse splayed its front legs and dug in on its heels, refusing to tackle the incline at other than a sensible speed.

Cursing the common sense of his bay, Maximus dragged his horse to a halt. Better to wait for the guardians of Tintagel to approach him directly than look a total fool by falling off his mount. The six warriors reached the Roman party, who outnumbered them by four to one, but there was no fear evident on their stern and weathered features, only curiosity and expectation.

Though much like other barbarians he had known, these men were subtly different. Their hair was well tended, even with the plaited forelocks that Maximus recognised, but they had decorated the ends of their plaits with bands of gold, plated shells and scraps of red cloth. The look was even more barbaric than he expected. However, they were very clean, and extremely well armoured in tunics of chain mail, while their belts, cloak pins and body jewellery bore the device of a charging boar. They looked at Maximus's standard, the Boar of the Twentieth Legion, and spoke rapidly in their own version of the Celtic language. The tribune doubted that they could speak Latin so he launched into an explanation in the language of northern Cymru as to his identity and why he was visiting the citadel. One of the warriors raised his left hand to halt the flow of words.

'There's no need to struggle with our language, Tribune. Those of us who are close to our king have been trained to speak Latin and are fluent in most of the Celtic dialects. We know who you are, master, and we've been anticipating your arrival for the past ten days. The people of the south-west have a system of signalling which gives us advance warning of movements within the margins of our lands. We expected you to arrive several days ago. We should have realised that you were new to the west and might wish to enjoy your journey and the bountiful wonders that exist in our part of the world. Would you agree that our homeland has a special quality about it?'

One of Maximus's thick eyebrows rose, but he resisted the impulse to comment on the strangeness of the south-western landscape. He preferred not to indicate he was impressed or affected by Britannia in any way. Romans were masters of the world, and even Dumnonii warriors who were conversant in Latin should accept this fact. After all, they were only barbarians.

Decius observed his superior's rigid stance and jutting chin during this discussion. Maximus was still young at twenty-six, despite already having a noble wife and several sons, but his arrogance could place him in harm's way unless he learned to conquer this palpable flaw. 'And you are?' Maximus asked crisply.

'Rowen ap Aidan, sir,' the leader of the Dumnonii guard replied with a lilt in his voice and a half-smile. This warrior was neither affronted nor threatened by the presence of these Romans and Maximus felt his hackles rise higher in response.

'Well, then, Rowen ap Aidan, I presume your task is to present me to your master, so lead on.' The arrogance in the tribune's voice was ignored by the Dumnonii warrior who acted as if their guests were ignorant rather than rude.

Maximus followed the horsemen to the bottom of the steep hill where they dismounted.

'Your horses will be quite safe here,' Rowen said cheerfully. 'Our servants will carry your possessions to the fortress, for you and your men will need both hands for the climb up to the living area of the castell.'

Maximus refused to respond to this patronising repartee. Decius noticed nervously that his commanding officer had clenched his jaw so tightly the muscles were visible.

May Mithras help us, the decurion thought. My master's patience will soon tire from the efforts of these jokesters to provoke a response from him. They obviously have no fear of Roman might. But at the same time Decius acknowledged that the Romans had ridden roughshod over the Britons for centuries; this Dumnonii captain was simply returning the compliment.

The tribesmen and their Roman visitors approached the

causeway in two distinct groups. Decius could almost see the antipathy form a solid wall between them. Instead of taking part in Maximus's sulk, the decurion gazed down at the narrow rocky paths that formed an almost impossible approach to the interior of the fortress.

'Horatius and his two friends would have found this causeway easier to defend than the bridge leading into Rome,' Maximus snapped with a hint of awe.

'I don't understand, master,' Rowen replied as he halted and turned to face the tribune.

'Horatius was a Roman soldier of bygone days who volunteered to be locked out of Rome when it was still a small city. Rome was under attack from an army led by the king of Clusium, part of a large empire which existed to the north. Horatius and his two friends were given the task of defending the narrow bridge over the Tiber against their enemies. The defenders held the bridge and they became heroes.'

Rowen nodded in understanding. 'We've had men fight and die on the very spot where you're standing over many hundreds of years. As you can imagine, this is the only approach to the fortress of Tintagel. The seas around us are treacherous, so no enemy could hope to land a boat in these waters. They'd be smashed to firewood in moments.'

Maximus could immediately see what the Dumnonii meant. The sea was a maelstrom on both sides of the causeway and any persons foolish enough to seek limpets or shells from the boulders below would be dragged into the water, where only the strongest of swimmers would be able to survive.

'I'll remember your Horatius,' Rowen added with another white-toothed grin. 'He must have been a brave man and a great warrior.'

The stones of the causeway were still wet from an unusually high tide, while black, glistening weed had been trapped between the smaller rocks, making the surface slippery. Even Maximus took pains to watch where he placed his feet. Decius heard his commander give a long sigh of relief once they reached the end of the causeway and he was standing on the peninsula itself.

Once the whole party had reached the flat platform that had been carved from the rock, Maximus surveyed his surroundings with interest. The cliffs were sheer at this spot, for the sea and the high tides had hollowed out shallow caves in the living stone. Maximus recognised the remnants of wooden frameworks that had been used to hold up sections of the cliff face repaired after rock-slides, yet the spaces around them were still sufficient that the caverns could be used as makeshift stables for Caradoc's personal beasts when he was in residence. He spotted evidence of a heavy winch that must have been mounted on the cliffs above them, used to bring food and other supplies up to the citadel from the causeway below.

'Come then, Tribune. The stairs are around this corner.' An underlying humour seemed to flicker in Rowen's golden-brown eyes.

They followed their guide around a protruding shelf of stone and quickly found the stairs that lay beyond it. The steps took advantage of the cliff face wherever possible and timber and rope supports had been fashioned to provide handholds for safety.

Every individual step was set at a different height and depth to the ones above and below, so Maximus's thighs and calves began to protest within a few moments of commencing the climb. He began to count the stairs in an effort to defeat the monotony of this endless ascent, but when he had reached a hundred and was still counting without respite, he surrendered and concentrated on each individual step in case he stumbled and fell which, he admitted, was a likely prospect. Again and again, he was forced to clutch the heavy rope handrails in an effort to avoid a dangerous slide on the wet treads. Swearing pungently, Maximus turned his back to the sea wherever possible, until such time as he reached the safety of a small flat forecourt overlooking the causeway far below.

Then, at last, he felt sufficient confidence to examine the glorious view.

Toward the east, the land was darkening as evening began. The earth was a patchwork of light and shadow where colours reflected the brilliance of a late winter afternoon with areas of brilliant orange, pale gold and chocolate brushed with grey where the fields were fallow.

'It's beautiful, I suppose. More importantly, I can see for miles,' Maximus said as he gazed out over the treeless cliffs with a soldier's eye. 'There'd be no sneaking up on Tintagel. It would be almost impossible.'

'Aye! And we keep guard, both summer and winter. A man lives far longer if he keeps his eyes sharp,' Rowen replied with the lazy sense of humour that was starting to drive Maximus crazy with irritation.

Maximus turned in a half circle to face Tintagel.

Tintagel was very old. The tribune's first thoughts were that it resembled a giant beehive which had been built, cell by cell, over a long period of time. The lichen-covered stones had been plugged with moss and heavy clay in the deep external recesses to block inopportune draughts from the inside of the castell. The interior was smoothed with a lime-based mud, reinforced with horsehair, that provided a hard surface and made living conditions quite pleasant. From outside, it seemed as if Tintagel had grown out of the moss-spotted rocks during one solitary evening and, night after night, the fortress had matured into the pleasing structure that Maximus viewed with such surprise.

'I'm amazed, Decius. There's scarcely a single straight line in the whole compound.'

Decius considered the fortresses at Segontium, Segedunum, Deva and Eburacum, which were identical except for their dimensions. Roman fortifications were built to a time-honoured and tested plan, so that they all looked much the same.

But not this place! Tintagel wore its idiosyncrasies like a multi-coloured cloak of woven scraps, brightly hued but not necessarily shabby. A practical fortress, she was obviously snug and warm inside, despite the strong winds that howled out of the west. On a pole atop the highest tower, a pennon flew in the wind and, if Decius squinted, he could just make out the form of Caradoc's emblem that was so like the standard of his own legion, the charging boar.

Tintagel seemed to be a series of towers, gradually grown and built-between, until its longest lines were irregular and bizarre. Reeds had been used to cover the rooftops, and even from this distance Decius could see that they had been pinned into place by stakes of iron, a profligacy of metal that few kings could afford. Yet he noted practically that the roofing was as thick as a man's arm and would last for decades before it would need to be renewed. He would hate to be part of the teams of thatchers who would have to repair these mad turrets that seemed to be suspended in space above the Mare Hibernicus.

Maximus was impatient and cold. The large doors at the entrance to the fortress were firmly shut, although they had swallowed Rowen ap Aidan a short time earlier.

'How long are we expected to freeze our balls off while we await the pleasure of this Caradoc? It may be late in winter, but these winds are damned cold.'

Maximus wrapped his hood and cloak around him and began to pace back and forth as far as the small forecourt would allow. The iron plates on the heels and toes of his boots clattered loudly on the paving which, like everything else in Tintagel, was rough and uneven. Despite this, the tribune noted that the stone had been chosen for its rich veining and subtle colours.

Decius suspected that an explosion from his superior was imminent after their delayed entry to the castell. The decurion bent to stroke the stone under his feet, which was a black, slick local rock, veined with a delicate pattern of white. A trimmed stone next to it appeared to have a softer, grainy surface in which he saw the outline of a strange shell trapped within the slab.

Maximus saw the object of Decius's attention and remembered other samples hawked in the villages to the north to earn a few coins from strangers. 'It appears to be a dead sea creature. I'm told that the villages to the north were once under water in an inland sea, so such remains are fairly common.'

One of the Roman cavalrymen coughed apologetically and Maximus turned sharply to face the opening doors of the fortress. Rowen ap Aidan held the door ajar while an astonishing man, followed by a tall woman and a pair of young lads, moved confidently out into the forecourt. In the darkness of the fortress proper, Maximus was sure that he had seen the light catch on a drawn weapon and his body tensed.

The man who strolled out into the windy courtyard was taller and much broader than Maximus.

Decius watched the two powerful men size each other up like mastiffs as they assessed each other's height, strength and demeanour, in case the relationship should turn sour. It was doubtful that either man had the advantage of the other, a remarkable fact in itself, for Magnus Maximus was acknowledged as one of the finest of the young Romans in the field at this time. Decius winced. The air around the platform overlooking the wild seas was suddenly charged with something other than the usual violence of the weather.

'My lord, allow me to present to you the noble tribune, Magnus Maximus, commander of the garrison of Segontium, and second in command of the Victrix Legions of Deva. His forces destroyed the Hibernian invaders who have carried out raids along the western coast of the British lands,' Rowen said in a portentous tone.

Maximus bowed his head the smallest fraction to indicate his respect for his host.

'Tribune Maximus, I present King Caradoc of the Dumnonii tribe. My king is the Boar of Cornwall, and he wishes to state his pleasure at meeting the Roman commander who has been the subject of so much praise throughout our lands – even here in Tintagel. My lord bids you welcome.'

Caradoc advanced to greet his visitor with his hand outstretched in the age-old offer of friendship that all men of breeding know. His face was wreathed in a wide smile.

If Decius had been a little more superstitious, he might have realised that two great fates had come together with a shudder, and that a new path had been created for these isles, one that would survive beyond the futures of Rome, Gaul, Constantinople, and all their empires.

So easily is fortune changed.

CHAPTER II

THE BOAR AND THE EAGLE

Bella, horrida bella, Et thybrim multo spumantem sanguine cerno.
I see wars, horrible wars, and the Tiber foaming with much blood.

Virgil, *Aeneid*, Book 6

As their hands met, Maximus felt an odd flicker race along his nerve ends, as if his brain recognised this alien flesh as belonging to a kindred spirit or a lost brother. The feeling was so strange and overpowering that the tribune examined the Dumnonii king with far more care and sincerity than he would normally have accorded to a barbarian.

If Caradoc also felt this strange stirring in his being, he made no visible sign.

'Welcome, Tribune. The comforts of Fortress Tintagel are open to you and your body servant. I don't wish to seem untrusting, but I'd be all kinds of a fool if I was to welcome twenty armed men into my home. There are barracks by the causeway on each side of the flood, so all your guard can be comfortably quartered where you can call on them at any appropriate time. They may become a little tired of the stairs, but so it must be.'

Caradoc grinned disarmingly and Maximus wondered if these idiotic grimaces were a strange tribal habit or whether the Dumnonii tribesmen played games with their Roman masters. After all, any manner of resentments could be hidden behind a broad smile. Maximus should have expected that his guard would be forbidden entry to the peninsula. However, in his experience, the most impertinent demands were sometimes rewarded with unexpected success, so he had decided to try his luck with this local king. But his gamble had failed this time, a defeat that left him slightly miffed. At least Caradoc had been honest about his concerns, while common courtesy to a host demanded that Maximus should abide by the king's wishes.

'Of course, sire. I can understand that coping with twenty strange warriors in your citadel might cause some practical difficulties,' Maximus replied smoothly with an implied insult aimed at Caradoc's capacity to be a liberal host. With a small sense of triumph Maximus watched something adamant and icy pass through Caradoc's amber eyes. It glared out at him for a heartbeat, before disappearing as if it had never existed.

Decius sighed in frustration. Why did Maximus always court trouble?

The king of the Dumnonii wasn't particularly tall, but he had at least two inches advantage in height over Maximus. Where the Roman's face and figure were elegant and graceful, Caradoc resembled a bear on its hind legs more than a man, except for the absence of a shaggy coat. His shoulders were huge and his arms were unnaturally long, so Decius decided that Caradoc's swordsmanship would be greatly enhanced by his extra reach. By contrast, his wide and heavily muscled chest gave way to narrow hips and legs that were quite short, as if his upper body was meant to belong to a much taller man.

Maximus had a fine profile of which he was very proud. Unfortunately Caradoc's gods had not been so kind to him in matters of physiognomy, so his face was heavy-set and blunt. The ridge across Caradoc's eyebrow was particularly heavy and jutted well out over a pair of deep, golden-brown eyes that sparkled with intelligence and humour. Shaggy eyebrows completed a suggestion of thuggery in the king's features which a much-broken nose did nothing to dispel. Even the king's jaw was massive, robbing Caradoc's sweetly curved lips of any softness. In all, the king resembled a robber or an outlawed murderer rather than a king – and he knew it.

'My thanks, Tribune,' Caradoc continued urbanely. 'May I call you Maximus? I must say that it's a name that conjures up power, yet it sounds pleasant on the tongue. My name, on the other hand, is a lot like me. It's harsh-sounding, plain and no-nonsense.'

Maximus knew enough of the history of Britannia to recall that another Cymru chieftain called Caradoc had opposed a Roman invasion some two hundred years earlier and had successfully held his enemies at bay for an embarrassing length of time. He realised that this Caradoc was quite aware of the history of his namesake and what that revolt implied.

Maximus murmured something appropriate, although he was a little rattled by the king's candour. He was accustomed to dealing with powerful men but most, if not all, of them avoided any acknowledgement of their own physical defects.

'I hope that you'll excuse Tintagel's deficiencies as far as comfort is concerned. When all is said and done, she's a fortress rather than a palace. At those times when we yearn for relief from the citadel's grimness, we travel south to Isca Dumnoniorum.

It's a sweet spot on the southern coast where the sun always shines, so perhaps you might be prepared to travel with us on one of our jaunts, if you have sufficient time at your disposal?'

Caradoc spread his arms to match his words as the doors of Tintagel opened wide to permit their entry.

Decius paused to order the rest of the men in the company to follow Rowen ap Aidan to their quarters below the citadel, while disciplining any cavalryman who dared to murmur his annoyance that the troop would not be welcome in the fortress proper and would have to face a harrowing descent of the stairs. One soldier expressed his feelings with a muffled oath, so Decius was forced to respond for the sake of discipline among the ranks. He cuffed the man soundly around the ears.

'You'll go down them steps with a smile on your faces and you'll like it, do you hear?' Decius snapped. 'Our hosts will believe you are pussies who are suited only for guarding grandmothers by the fireside, and that you're too fat and too fearful to act like real men.'

Several faces flushed under Decius's scrutiny, but he noticed that the Brigante cavalryman didn't seem afraid of the dangers inherent in the climb or the descent. Sent trotting towards the head of the stairs in Rowen's wake, he accepted his lot without further complaint.

Suddenly, one of the younger warriors froze after descending just two steps. Decius could tell that this lad was rigid with terror, so he refrained from shouting at the trembling man whose eyes were staring blankly downwards as he imagined the fall to the black rocks and turbulent waters below.

Urging the young man's companions to move past, Decius yanked at the man's neck with a claw-like grip that forced him to turn so he would be *facing* the wall during the descent.

'See, boy? If you're facing the wall, you don't have to worry about falling. Just concentrate on taking one step at a time.'

The lad took a couple of tentative steps and a smile suddenly appeared on his face. Within seconds, he was clambering down as if he had been born and bred in the fortress.

Decius sighed and returned to the forecourt of Tintagel. Sometimes a decurion's work was never done, while Maximus would be sour that he'd been kept waiting for far too long. Decius clattered across the forecourt to a narrow rim of light where the glow from an interior lamp was bleeding out into the darkening afternoon.

As he reached the doorway leading into the fortress and skidded in a wet puddle of water, a steely set of fingers straightened him and the decurion looked up into the angry eyes of his master.

'I was beginning to wonder what had become of my body servant,' Maximus said pleasantly, although his grip was bruising Decius's forearm to the bone. 'Hunt up my packs, would you? I have gifts from Theodosius in them that must be presented to Caradoc personally. Hop to it, man! Someone will tell you where to find me once you've located the packages.'

Within the doorway, a series of short corridors led off a small circular space towards the beginnings of Tintagel's maze. Very low doorways led into a dizzying array of tiny, round spaces that appeared to be designed as storage areas.

A servant appeared out of the half-light in front of them, taking up a flare from an ornate iron sconce. He nodded to the king, and then padded off in front of the master and his guest up a narrow staircase barely wide enough to accommodate Caradoc's shoulders. At the top, the small party travelled along a corridor lined with small closed doors until, with eyes dazzled from a sudden flood of light, Maximus followed the king across the threshold of a room that was at least three times the size of all the apartments he had passed so far. This chamber was still far from large, but a whole circle of narrow, shuttered windows ran from waist height to the ceiling, a device that gave an illusion of space. Despite himself, Maximus was impressed and he noted that the stained oak rafters gave purchase to a thatched roof that was blackened from a central iron fireplace, although the air at roof level remained sweet and fresh from the free passage of sea breezes whenever the tight wooden shutters were opened.

'This room is the Eye of Tintagel and it is my window on the world,' Caradoc explained. 'You will see what I mean tomorrow, when you waken and gaze out at your surroundings.'

Servants thrust lamps into sconces to add to the rich golden light of an almost wasteful display of sweet-smelling, burning oil. Maximus was all too familiar with the unmistakable reek of fish-oil lamps, but his nose told him that only the finest oils, sweetened with lavender, had been selected for the comfort of the king's guests, although he doubted that Caradoc would have cared if the air in the Eye of Tintagel stank of rotting fish. Inside the chamber, rough bench seating ran around the circumference of the room, its timbers smoothed over generations into hues of deepest sable. Several stools were positioned slightly off-centre. The seating in the room was backless and incredibly old, to judge by the crude representations of three-faced gods carved into the timber.

Maximus had been told about the British obsession with the triple aspects of their divinities, so he shuddered inwardly as he recalled some of the tales of incredible barbarity attached to the older British religions. Fortunately, many Britons now paid lip service to the new, kinder Roman God and His son, Jesus.

'Sit, my friend, and my servants will bring beer, mead or wine, depending on your preference. I can assure you that I keep a goodly supply of crisp wines that have been traded with our friends from Hispania. I keep them specifically for important visitors to the fortress, as well as personal friends. I seem to recall that you have estates in Hispania and the wines in your lands are highly valued.'

'Aye!' Maximus responded with a slight frown. How had this provincial king learned so much about him? However, with his annoyingly bland smile, Caradoc allowed the subject to lapse and moved on to other matters.

Out of long habit, Caradoc settled onto the oldest and largest of the stools. At the same time, Maximus was grateful that he would be free to sit elsewhere, rather than on one of those squat and threatening forms. Two young servants brought forward a cushion for Maximus while Decius, newly arrived in the room, was left to stand next to the wall with Maximus's saddlebags at his feet.

When the tribune began to speak, Decius was surprised at his master's pleasant manner. Maximus gestured towards his servant who deduced that the gifts stowed in the saddlebags were required.

Fumbling in haste, Decius retrieved the two small packages and presented them to his master, while Caradoc followed the actions of his guests with interested eyes that spoke eloquently of his avid pleasure at the prospect of receiving personal gifts.

'Caradoc, my friend!' The tribune held out the first of the packages. 'Please allow me to present you with a trifling gift for your beautiful wife, a woman whose attributes are famed even beyond these lands. It expresses my personal admiration.'

Caradoc permitted himself a swift, ambiguous smile at his

guest's pomposity. These Romans! They were always so certain that they were the masters of the world by a divine right.

But six months earlier Caradoc had been forced by circumstances to approach the Wise Woman of the Red Wells. The woman had spoken to him at a time when he had need of her healing skills for a sorely wounded servant. At the time, he had been impressed by her surprising demeanour and predictions, so he had listened carefully to her words of advice.

Now, with the Roman watching him so closely, Caradoc decided to reconsider the predictions of the wise woman at a later time, when this charade with his guest was over. Then, he would reassess her words and deduce why the meeting with this particular young Roman was so important to the gods. Smiling with real enjoyment and a feigned cupidity, Caradoc took the gifts like an excited child and carefully began to remove the wrappings.

'For your lady wife,' Maximus repeated, as the nail on Caradoc's forefinger sliced through a thin tie of woollen yarn. The small parcel spilled open and a shimmering river of sea-green, blue and gold silk slithered into Caradoc's lap.

'That's lovely!' Caradoc murmured, his sword-hardened fingers seduced by the smoothness of the fabric. What he held in his palms was a woman's headscarf that had obviously originated in Constantinople, or even further into the east where the yellow men with slanted eyes were said to breed gossamer cloth from the bodies of tiny caterpillars. Both king and tribune found this fable too far-fetched to be believable, but none of these irrelevancies mattered when Caradoc caressed the beautiful silk.

The king thought of his thin-lipped, black-haired wife and the two sons, Cadal and Cadoc, whom she was trying to turn into milksops. His controlled expression slipped momentarily, and his upper lip curled in distaste.

Maximus sensed a hint of dissatisfaction in the king's features, but wisely displayed no curiosity. As Decius had suggested, Tintagel was a strange place. The Dumnonii king, his guards and his fortress seemed so alien that Maximus felt off-balance. Meanwhile, Caradoc had hefted the weight of the second oilskin package with a tentative smile.

'Can this be . . . ?' he began, recognising the shape of the gift that lay under his fingers. As the wrappings fell away, Caradoc seemed as eager as a young child.

'Maximus, this weapon is beyond price!'

The dagger was not excessively long nor was it particularly decorative. The blade was only a little larger than Caradoc's hand and it nestled within a plain oxhide and silver sheath that had been inlaid with the mask of a heavily tusked boar where the leather straps would buckle onto a sword belt. Maximus experienced a moment of pure joy when he realised he had chosen such a wise gift for a warrior king.

Caradoc drew the blade free with a welcoming hiss that could have issued from the maw of a pet dragonlet. The blade was leaf-shaped, sharpened on each side and terminated in a thoroughly wicked point. He tested the blade's edge against the palm of his horny hand and his eyes widened with surprise as he discovered its quality. The decoration on the hilt was unusual, like nothing either the king or those warriors present had seen before. Maximus had puzzled over the linear design for many hours before concluding that it represented two strange, stylised fish that were only recognisable by their bronze scales. Twisted and turned and then twisted again, their forms terminated at the pommel with each trying to clutch at a raw hunk of rock crystal in their toothed mouths.

'This weapon has travelled far,' Caradoc observed quietly while his clever, spatulate fingers made the knife jump and flick from one hand to the other.

'Very far! I purchased the weapon in a market in Tolosa, but the man who sold it to me swore it came from the far side of the Middle Sea. He was uncertain of its origins, but he believed the dark-eyed seamen who once came out of ancient Tyre were its first owners. I cannot tell you if the shopkeeper was telling the truth or boasting . . . but as a warrior, I recognise that this knife is a very good weapon with a noble and ancient lineage.'

With shining eyes, Caradoc thanked him once again and handed the knife to a manservant who whisked it away, along with the queen's scarf. Then the king and his guest settled down to prolonged talk, as they sipped the crisp wines of Maximus's homeland.

Many hours later, after several bowls of a hearty fish stew, the wonderful wines of Hispania and generous amounts of nuts, dried apples, pears and berries that had been produced on the local farmlands, Maximus was shown to a room high in the fortress which had been prepared as his sleeping chamber. Here, a low bed in the Roman style awaited him, with a pallet of lamb's-wool and woven covers that were pure pleasure after many days of travelling on horseback.

Stretching, Maximus luxuriated under the warm covers, oblivious to the wild winds that buffeted the tightly-sealed shutters. For one fleeting moment he wished he'd asked Caradoc for a young woman to warm his bed but, in retrospect, he decided that he'd be far better served by using this warm nest to ascertain what he had learned about his host.

Caradoc might have looked like a brute, but the tribune acknowledged that the king's manners were flawless and his sensitivities were surprising. Maximus was certain that the king's clothing was woven by his own women, but the textures and colours of the fabrics were subtly pleasurable to the eye and to the touch. What jewellery Caradoc wore was spartan and beautifully made, so Maximus had experienced a brief moment of envy at a strangely polished stone in a massy ring on the king's signet finger. The Roman only rarely envied the possessions of any man, Briton or Roman.

'You like my ring, Tribune?' Caradoc had asked while removing the subject of Maximus's attention as if it was a trifle. 'The stone is green amber which is a particularly common bauble along the coasts near Tintagel. Our ambers are mostly of poor quality, but every so often one comes to light that is truly perfect. This is one such stone.'

Maximus had stared intently at the amber, for it was a strange variation on a jewel that was fairly commonplace in Rome. Instead of the golden colour or the whipped-honey creaminess of the good stones that made their way to the lands of the Middle Sea, this gem was pale green with hundreds of small pinprick bubbles of air that had been trapped inside the sticky gum when the tree had relinquished its lifeblood aeons earlier.

Nodding with interest, Maximus returned the ring to his host and their conversation continued.

Later, Maximus's drowsy mind would go over the alarming conversation on political matters that king and tribune had enjoyed at the end of the evening.

The king had revealed a flexible and pragmatic understanding of the situation in Rome within moments of both men turning the conversation to the political realities that existed within the Roman Empire.

'I am aware that our masters in Rome consider the provincial kings of Britain to be little more than crude buffoons. However, I also believe that the vultures of Rome will soon desert the City of the Seven Hills, and the prophecies of the Great Ones tell us that its people will be left to their own devices once this catastrophe occurs. There's no need to protest, Tribune. You're a man of sense, so I understand your position precisely. Both your friends and your enemies know that Rome is slowly falling into ruin. You know it, the tribes in Gaul know it and so do I. Yes, Britannia remains strong and healthy behind Roman defensive walls, so we will continue to accept the protection and culture that comes from our masters. But we are part of a backwater and an island, so the fate of Rome won't have much effect on our way of living. Only our external enemies such as the Saxons, the Hibernians and the Picts can do that. Ultimately, Maximus, we are under no illusions, for we would count for very little if Rome decided to remove the legions and leave us to a future dictated by your goddess, Fortuna.'

Maximus lowered his lids in the hope that he could hide his thoughts from Caradoc's sharp regard. 'I don't believe the legions are likely to leave at any time in the immediate future,' he responded tactfully. 'These lands are rich in tin, lead, iron and the wools that come from your sheep. Rome has enjoyed the bounty of Britannia for centuries, so the emperors of Rome won't easily relinquish such wealth as you give to us.'

Caradoc snorted. 'All true, but the Hibernians, Picts, Saxons, Angles and Jutes come every year to raid the isles with more and more confidence. Rome has built walls to keep out the Picts and the seas protect our shores from attack, but the threat of reprisals from Rome no longer deters our enemies. Fortunately Britannia won't be beaten easily, even if the legions depart from our shores.'

Maximus drained the wine from his mug. To his chagrin, he felt a thin line of sweat running through his close-cropped hair. This barbarian king knew far too much.

Caradoc bit on his thumbnail and frowned. Then he launched into an explanation.

'The British tribes are destined to fall, my friend, but it will take a very long time, perhaps a hundred years or more, before we are destroyed by our enemies. But, as sure as night follows day, we will be defeated much faster if the legions return to their homeland before we have prepared ourselves for that eventuality.'

Maximus nodded noncommittally.

'Why did you invite me here, my lord? I have some small reputation, and my line traces back to the pure veins of Aeneas when he sailed up the Tiber at the will of the gods, but the senators at the forum in Rome continue to treat me like a barbarian, exactly as they would treat anyone from the provinces. I don't wish to insult you, my friend, but to Romans who are born on the banks of the Tiber all other men are lesser mortals who are punished by the gods because they aren't truly Rome's children. You can refer to us as bastards from the Mother City if you will, but I have little influence outside these isles, regardless of what you might believe.'

The slightest trace of resentment convinced Caradoc that Maximus was speaking the truth, but only as the tribune knew it.

'You're a realistic man in many ways, Tribune, despite your rank. I've heard your men in Segontium refer to you as Macsen

Wledig and they believe you are destined for greatness. I agree with that opinion. I will have no hesitation in becoming your friend, for the wise ones have already promised me that I have a similar destiny to you and that our fates are intertwined.'

The two men eyed each other as equals, carefully and with respect.

'Yes, Lord Caradoc, I understand the need for personal alliances. Romans regularly make alliances with loyal friends who protect their backs during times of political upheaval, such as those occasions when an emperor dies or is deposed. A family without powerful allies is similar to a single tree caught in a violent storm. Sooner or later, that tree will snap under the force of high winds. But a grove of trees is a different matter. The closeness of the individual trees in the group gives strength to the whole area of forest. Similarly, alliances influence the direction of events to the advantage of all concerned. Until now, I've met many of the northern tribal kings and found them to be a squabbling clutch of incompetent fools. If you'll excuse my frankness, Caradoc, you're a different prospect from most of the British rulers. I have had trouble understanding your motives, so what I don't comprehend sometimes causes me to have doubts.'

Maximus was speaking with uncharacteristic sincerity, without the usual diplomatic posturing. Fortunately, Caradoc took the tribune's words at face value.

'Well said, Maximus. Your words ring true! My fellow kings are unable to agree on anything. They often remind me of chickens scratching in the dirt, squabbling over a single worm while the farmer is coming after them to cut off their heads.'

Maximus roared with mirth at the vivid word picture, especially as he imagined the pompous, well-fed cheeks and features of the king of the Atrebates tribe, superimposed over the body of a strutting rooster.

'I'll show you tomorrow how my people live and I'll also reveal the inner workings of this ancient fortress. Tintagel has never been taken by stealth and I'm convinced that your legions couldn't smash her defences if we were to seal ourselves within her walls. We have food and water sufficient for two years and the sea can always be harnessed if we need more food. My people must have taken Tintagel from other inhabitants who ruled these lands in long-gone days. We don't know who these earlier inhabitants were, so the origins of our fortress will always be a mystery.'

'I'll look forward to seeing your fortress in the daylight, especially the view from these rooms. Fact is, I can already feel the pull of the sea and the winds that must be rushing through the stones under our feet.'

Caradoc realised that this pragmatic and ambitious Roman was sensitive enough to feel the effects of the Dumnonii lifeblood, and the endless suck and tug of the great ocean as it wore away at the fabric of this long spearpoint of land.

'For all that Tintagel will crumble into the sea one day, we're certain that many generations of tribesmen will live and perish before that day comes.'

Both men sat in a surprisingly companionable silence. Occasionally, the king would crack the shell of a nut in his powerful hands, while Maximus attacked a soft rich cheese that was quite unlike anything the Roman had tasted before.

Eventually, Maximus was caught disguising a yawn with one hand, so the king leaped to his feet, all apologies for keeping his guest from his bed.

And so Magnus Maximus met King Caradoc of the Dumnonii

for the first time and the Roman decided, as he lay in his warm pallet with the freezing rain striking the tower, that this particular Briton was worthy of closer examination. Perhaps there might even be a chance of true friendship.

Tintagel's worn stonework had felt his steps. But they held no fear of him, for even the mightiest of Roman warriors was only a momentary distraction in the long memory of those ancient and enigmatic cliffs.

THE BOAR HUNT AND THE
JOURNEY TO THE RED WELLS

River

Red Wells

Hills

House

Clearing of
Wise Woman

Forests

Killing the
wild boar

Meeting with
old man

CHAPTER III

THE WISE WOMAN OF
THE RED WELLS

All the best days of life slip away from us mere mortals first; illnesses and dreary old age and pain sneak up, and the fierceness of harsh death snatches away.

Virgil, *Georgics*, 3

Six months earlier, when summer had given way to the first falling leaves of autumn, Caradoc had spent a pleasurable week away from Tegan Eurfron, his termagant wife. The queen was beautiful and accomplished, but she was rarely satisfied with her lot in life, although Caradoc couldn't understand what she actually wanted from him. Their marriage had been arranged by Caradoc's father, Llyr, as was the practice in his house; Caradoc had really hoped for much more from the dark-eyed beauty who had been hand-fasted to him more than a decade earlier. He had hungered for a companion with whom he could share his ambitions, fears and dreams. But Tegan Eurfron had no interest in her husband's mind or the rapid thoughts that assailed him with fears for the future. Beyond her sons, her only care was for her complexion and her figure, so Caradoc took every available opportunity to flee from Tintagel whenever the weather permitted.

The joys of camping under the trees and the stars never palled for the Dumnonii king. The nights were mostly clear with only an occasional light drizzle of rain before dawn, moisture that left his world clean-washed. The skies of early autumn were soft grey and the palest blue, while the sun warmed his days as Caradoc enjoyed the comradeship of hunting with his most trusted warriors and servants.

The long days had been spent rousing birds and deer in the deep woods to the east of Tintagel in an area that was almost primordial in its wildness and isolation. Here, the trees grew tall and villages were unknown, although the occasional farmer carved a living out of long-grassed pastures near a knot of streamlets that plunged down out of the hills.

One old crofter approached the hunters on the morning of the second day at a time when the king had only just risen from his sleeping pallet. Caradoc saw the crofter's dog first, a black and white mongrel with a torn ear, a missing eye and evidence of fresh scars on its right side. Then the dog's master hobbled into the clearing, using a tall staff carefully as he negotiated the uneven ground. One leg was roughly bandaged, so Caradoc knew immediately that this old man had need of his king.

'Come to the fire, Grandfather. You needn't fear that any man here will try to harm either you or your dog,' Caradoc said. 'Tell me, how can your king help you?'

The crofter had obviously not realised who this lordling was, despite his urgent need to receive aid from these great ones. Now, the realisation took the old man's breath away and filled his rheumy eyes with tears. He tried to abase himself on the hard ground, but Caradoc pulled him back to his feet and ordered him to sit on a fallen tree stump while he explained his needs.

'I'll give you whatever assistance is within my power, Grandfather,' Caradoc assured him earnestly.

'We have a wild boar tearin' about in the woods, my lord. It's been killin' off all the young cattle . . . and anythin' else that crosses its path. My poor old dog tried to bail up the black devil and almost died for his trouble. You can see what it did to me when I tried to save old Cadwallader here.'

The old man laughed through his tears to see the smile on Caradoc's face, for the crofter had named his dog after one of the great heroes of Cymru.

'I know it be a grand name for a mongrel, but he's got the heart of a hero. He saved me, and I can't say more than that.'

The dog's feathery tail wagged nervously and its bedraggled head swivelled from one face to the other. Caradoc held out a hand, so the dog rose slowly to its feet before shuffling nervously towards him. Then, its one eye glowing with mingled fear and hope, Cadwallader licked Caradoc's hand. The king made up his mind.

'Where did you last see this boar, Grandfather? It seems to be a man-killer, so it'll be good sport to do battle with it. Rowen here will find some food for you and some meat for your fine animal.'

He turned to face his companions. 'What say you, my friends? Do we hunt for boar?'

The huntsmen nodded in agreement, although the king was their master and they would always feel constrained to obey. Caradoc laughed with a light-headed feeling of irresponsibility. Raised to rule, he had obeyed the duties of his birth assiduously for most of his life, but there were many things he despised about the trappings of kingship. He would never have saddled himself with such a selfish and whining wife if his father hadn't arranged a marriage to the daughter of Gwaun pen Mairtin, the romanised ruler of the Atrebates tribe. Compared with enduring his wife's spiteful sullenness, hunting a wild boar was a pleasant prospect, despite the risk.

'Go home in peace after my servants have dressed your leg and treated your dog, Grandfather. Such a brave hound deserves all the care and attention we can offer, just like his namesake. My beaters will start the search for the boar during the afternoon, so you shouldn't hold any fears for your herd or your kin. We'll find the boar, kill it and bring you the tusks as your personal trophy.'

The old man bowed his head and then raised fear-reddened eyes filled with such gratitude that Caradoc felt like a sham. What he saw as a day's sport was a matter of life or death for this old man and his frightened dependants.

Caradoc and his hunters sought traces of the boar throughout that day. But, with all the cunning of a feral animal, the beast managed to elude their best efforts. However, there were plenty of signs of its passage through the wild woods, so Caradoc's hunt master pointed to some scarring along the trunk of a young oak which indicated that it was probably crazed. Not only could that illness kill those men it touched, the space between the tusks indicated that this boar was abnormally large.

Few creatures are more dangerous than a maddened rogue boar, especially one with the dimensions of this creature. As they rested around the campfire that night, Caradoc took particular care with his whetstone when he sharpened his stabbing spear to a razor's edge and honed his long knife so that the blade would pass easily through skin, muscle and bone.

'You seem determined to put yourself at risk, sire. What would we do if you were injured or killed by this beast?'

Trefor, the hunt master, was genuinely alarmed, for he had seen the damage done to the forest trees and bramble bushes through which the beast had ranged. The woodsman knew that only the sparseness of human population in these wild hills had prevented death and injury among the peasantry. As Caradoc's woodsman, Trefor had seen such creatures before, and he knew them to be true demons from Hades. A wild boar was unable to distinguish between a king and a shepherd, so it would attack either at the slightest provocation.

'It's my duty to protect my subjects, so this boar must be killed. Isn't that so?' Caradoc's voice sounded irritable. 'Don't even attempt to argue with me, Trefor, because I've already made my decision. We'll find this beast on the morrow and I'll destroy it.'

The following day gave every indication of being miserable with light autumn rain. The fine, dry weather they had experienced could hardly be expected to last forever.

Meanwhile, the horses were restive in the dank woods, as if they sensed something was watching them from inside the dripping tree line, and this animal was hungering for their blood. Caradoc observed their wild eyes and quivering flanks and knew that the hunting party was on the right track.

He ordered his men to dismount. The horses were already milling and sweating with fear, so the king decided that their usefulness was over. Besides, the hint of a foul stink in the air told him that the hunters must be close to the lair of the beast.

'Be careful,' he hissed to his men as he slid his spear out of the sheath attached to his horse's saddle. Somehow, the huge weapon gave him a feeling of confidence, for family legends described how this weapon had been specifically designed to kill a huge wild boar in distant times. Although Caradoc prided himself on being a practical man, he had complete confidence in the supernatural and primordial power of the hunting spear. In ages past, tribal legends insisted that with this spear the king of that time had killed a gigantic black boar that swam ashore on the wild beaches near Tintagel. The battle was so heroic that all subsequent kings of the Dumnonii tribe had accepted this beast as their family totem.

It was now Caradoc's time to take comfort from its smooth haft and heavy blade as long a man's forearm. Taking his courage into his hands, the king led his huntsmen into a thicket of bracken that stank with the boar's foetid reek.

The undergrowth was almost impenetrable, so Caradoc's hunters were forced to hack their way through. Deep inside this green and thorny otherworld of dripping shrubbery and mud, the king slowly pushed his way ahead with every sense alert to threats that could be sensed in the murk ahead of him. Even though the day had not yet reached noon, the visibility was impaired by rain and thick foliage that turned the lambent light to a sickly green hue.

Caradoc forced his way into a flattened area where cloven hooves had destroyed the tender new growth and left a small circle where the foliage arched overhead to form a cave-like enclosure of dripping leaves. He was forced to crouch, although he had sufficient room to manoeuvre within the vile-smelling space. Scarcely had he taken in the scene than he heard a sharp yell of warning from Rowen. Taking a short, instinctive step to the left, he barely had time to use the spearpoint to deflect the black, rushing shape that passed him. He felt a gust of hot breath and smelled the terrible reek of decay as the beast almost swept him off his feet.

The king spun quickly in the enclosed space as he heard a scream from one of his men who had been knocked off his feet by the boar's charge.

'Don't let it get past! Pen the bastard in!' Caradoc shouted over the melee of struggling men as the boar stood trembling in rage at the entrance to its lair. Retreating as far as he could go to give himself room to move, Caradoc sank into a deep crouch with the end of the spear shaft embedded into the leaf mould and the damp earth in the clearing.

With its snout bloodied, the boar extricated its legs from the thrashing and bleeding body of the wounded hunter. Its small eyes were burning brightly in the half-light, while the coarse black ruff of hair around its neck and down its spine stood on end. As he stared into the feral eyes, Caradoc could read no intelligence, pity or fear in the crazed animal. It would kill them all if it could, and would ignore any wounds it received in the process, if it had the chance to tear its enemies into bloody strips of raw meat. Then, in an instant, the beast charged.

Blinded to anything but the human who had invaded its secret place, the boar scarcely felt the blade that pierced its chest before being deflected by the heavy breastbone. The spear was torn out of Caradoc's fingers and he was forced to throw himself out of the boar's path. Bleeding, the creature shook its head ponderously and turned once more to attack its enemy.

Separated from his spear, Caradoc drew his sword and faced the boar with this wholly inadequate weapon.

'Keep back,' he screamed to his hunters. 'Use your blades to discourage it from making good its escape – and for God's sake pull Huw out of the mud so he can't be injured any further.'

Although his servants were shouting at him, the king blocked out their voices as a distraction. The boar charged again, and Caradoc attempted to hack at it with his sword. But this animal was a twisted hulk of muscle, sinew and bone, so the sword's blade did little damage other than causing it to squeal with pain. Inevitably, Caradoc would have been gored by the boar's tusks had it not been for the treacherous leaf mould under his feet. He slipped, lost his footing and the enraged animal rushed past him.

But years of brutal combat training had made Caradoc strong and agile.

The king turned the slip into a rolling tumble that brought him back to the spear which was half-buried in rotting leaves and crushed brambles. After a brief search, Caradoc snatched it up, wedged the shaft into the earth and braced himself to face the massive boar once again.

The animal hit him like an ocean wave. Only a highly trained, iron-muscled warrior could have kept his grip on the shaft of the spear as the charging boar forced itself down onto the spearhead, determined to impale the enemy on its great, curving tusks. Only a hand's span from the beast, Caradoc was driven inexorably backwards by the power of the boar's legs. Its red eyes glowed with malevolence, and the huge head weaved from side to side as it tried to reach his flesh. And then the boar's eyes clouded over and became blank.

The animal's heavy weight fell to the ground. Nerveless, the head and legs kicked and twitched once or twice – and then the ugly creature was dead.

Heaving and panting from the strain of his exertions, the king rolled away from the dead boar to extricate the spearhead from the body with his knife. He was obliged to place one foot on the carcass for leverage, because the spear had been driven through the breastbone and was firmly wedged inside the heart of the beast.

Caradoc was finally able to yank the spear free with a nasty sucking sound, as if the body was determined to keep the Dumnonii weapon forever. He muttered a low curse of disgust and motioned to one of the hunters to come forward.

'You can cut off the tusks now,' Caradoc instructed Rowen. 'Once you've had them cleaned, you can detail one of the men to present them to the crofter as we promised. As for the beast, you can leave it to rot where it lies. Beasts of this size are full of worms and the meat is so old and sinewy that it's not worth the trouble of butchering it and taking it back to the fortress. Let the bastard rot! I'd prefer to spend the time finding some assistance for Huw.'

Pulling a strip of rag from around his neck, Caradoc began to wipe the blood from the spearhead as he made his way out of the clearing and through the underbrush to where the horses had been left.

'How is Huw?' he added as an afterthought to the nearest hunter. Caradoc wasn't callous by nature or careless of his servant's hurts, but his mind was still engrossed with the terrors and efforts expended in the killing of this boar.

'We need to take him to a healer, if one can be found,' Rowen replied. As the captain of the household guard, he had a good rapport with his king and was free to inform Caradoc of bad news without fear of retribution. One of Caradoc's many good attributes was his preparedness to accept blame, if the situation demanded it.

'Tell me quickly, Rowen,' Caradoc's voice was clipped and his pace through the brambles picked up as they retraced their steps.

'His leg is broken and I've ordered it to be splinted, but he's also been gored in the upper chest where there are two nasty furrows. You know what the tusks of such boars are like. They're filthy, like the animal itself, and Huw's health will deteriorate quickly if we can't get him to a healer.'

'Agreed! But we're a long way from any villages. Where'd the nearest healer be found?'

Caradoc's servants looked back at him with blank eyes. Suddenly, one of the older servants snapped his fingers as a thought came to him.

'The Wise Woman of the Red Wells lives a few miles to the north of here in the direction of the sea, master. I've heard she's knowledgeable on healing matters as well as being a seer.'

'Aye! I've heard of her, but I'm told she never leaves her cottage and she's never made herself known to me. I can't tell you if she'd be willing to help our man. At least she's close!'

As they spoke, Huw groaned and gave signs of returning to consciousness. Even now, so soon after the goring, the wounds were red and bleeding desultorily, while his upper body was covered with darkening bruises.

'Wash the wounds down thoroughly and prepare him for travel to the Red Wells, Rowen,' Caradoc ordered his captain before turning his attention back to the wounded man.

'Can you hear me, Huw?'

'Aye, sire, I hear you. Will I ever walk again, my lord? I don't know how I will get on if my leg becomes useless.' The young man's face was pale under his usual tan at the thought of being crippled, the probable fate of any man who suffered from a broken leg. Huw could see the splints of rough tree branch that had been bound to his lower leg and he groaned between bitten lips at the realisation of a severe breach in the bone.

'I don't know, Huw. As far as I can judge, the break in your leg is clean and simple. We've put a splint on it to keep your leg straight while we take you to the healer who lives at the Red Wells. We could carry you on a stretcher, but I believe it will be best to move you on horseback. But this journey will be uncomfortable, so you can expect to feel a great deal of pain.'

Huw nodded his head courageously as he accepted that there was no other option available to him.

'I think I can ride, but I doubt that I can control a horse very well.'

'Good lad! We'll carry you to the horses and put you on the quietest pack animal we can find. Once we get you settled on its back, we'll find some way of supporting your leg for the journey.'

Carrying the wounded man on a stretcher by foot would make the journey to the Red Wells interminable and Huw would be unlikely to survive the journey if infection set in.

With a general's skill and organisation, Caradoc had arranged for Huw to be tied to the saddle with his broken leg padded with a length of soft wool to spare him from the shocks of his steed's gait. Scarcely pausing to drink a draught of beer, or to cleanse their bodies and sluice their faces with water from the stream, the cavalcade set off on a long and pain-filled trek.

'The horses are well-rested so we'll travel for as long as the light and the terrain permit our continued movement. Huw needs to be with the wise woman as soon as we can safely get him there,' Caradoc said.

As the party mounted, Caradoc noted that flies had already found the carcass of the black boar. The insects were laying their eggs in its glazed eyes and the ragged gashes in its head where the huge tusks had once been rooted.

* * *

The miles were weary and long, while the hunters were forced to rest on several occasions when the light and weather deteriorated. Huw bore the travails of the journey bravely, but he was barely conscious and lolling in the saddle by noon of the next day when Caradoc saw a thin wisp of smoke stir in the still air ahead of them.

Caradoc increased the pace by urging his horse from a walk to a trot, even though the fine animal was weary. The king had already decided that Huw's condition was so urgent that they should continue to the Red Wells without pause, and the men and horses would be permitted to rest once the party had reached the cottage of the wise woman. The wounded man had been untreated for close to twenty hours now, so the wounds on his torso were red and beginning to show signs of the inevitable infection. Huw needed urgent treatment from a healer if he was to survive.

The cottage rested in a fold of land between low hills and the sounds of running water from a stream could be clearly heard by the huntsmen as they drew their horses to a ragged stop outside a low door that had been scrubbed to the brilliance of unmarked, silvered timber. The flint walls caught the gleam of the noon light and reflected intermittent glints of blackness where the walls had been wet earlier in the day. The roof of the cottage was neatly thatched and the building had no openings other than the single door. Smoke from the fire pit was escaping through a hole in the roof, but it was the only sign of habitation that could be seen in the quiet dell.

Caradoc eyed his surroundings with suspicion, for no king rules long if he is not constantly alert to new places and the dangers that can be hidden within them. This croft seemed harmless, with neat beds of vegetables and herbs. Fruit and nut trees were heavy with ripening fruit, while small enclosures held a cow and a calf. Several sheep were cropping grass contentedly; a scattering of hens, ducks and two very unhappy geese flapped their wings at the approach of armed and mounted men.

'Knock at the door, Rowen. You can rouse the wise woman while we find water to cool down Huw's wounds and allow the horses to drink their fill.'

'Someone is coming, my lord,' Rowen replied, his body suddenly rigid and watchful.

Shading his eyes from the light, the king stared towards a coppice of thick trees where a woman, wrapped in a thick cloak of homespun and carrying a heavy basket, was picking her way between tussocks of grass. Two large and shaggy hounds were loping along ahead of her.

When the dogs sighted the group of warriors at the front of the cottage, they stopped dead and growled deep in their throats as their pelts raised in ruffs down their spines. The woman used her free hand to make a motion that clearly told them to remain silent while she walked forward, her skirts swinging with the movement of her womanly hips. The dogs followed obediently, despite their downcast heads and their watchful pale-yellow eyes.

Caradoc recognised the breed immediately. One of their sires had been a wolf, and the intelligence and obedience of these hounds rendered them more dangerous than other kinds. The king's hand itched to finger the sheath of his knife but he refrained from drawing his blade.

Instead, he advanced cautiously and stopped a few feet from her. Spreading his hands wide to show the dogs that he carried nothing that could harm their mistress, he permitted them to sniff at his boots and leather trews.

'I am Caradoc, King of the Dumnonii, and we have come to you because Huw, one of my huntsmen, has been gored by a savage boar that was terrorising the district. We have ridden to you in haste, knowing that such wounds can be fatal. Can you help us?'

The woman lifted the hood of her cloak and revealed a quantity of chestnut hair and a pair of striking blue eyes.

'Yes, sire,' she said in a rich contralto voice that made the hair stand up on the back of the king's neck. 'I've been expecting your visit.'

Caradoc felt as if someone had driven the air from his lungs. 'You say that you've been expecting me . . . ?'

'Yes, King Caradoc. The red waters rarely lie so I have been collecting the simples I will need to treat your servant's wounds. I will comply with your needs, because the gods have deemed that you will satisfy mine. I will inform you at a later time of the payment I will require of you once your huntsman is well again. Do you agree to abide by my terms?'

Caradoc forced himself to look into those alien eyes that seemed like two slivers of strangely opaque glass, so that he was unable to read the mind that lay behind them.

He glanced back at Huw who was almost fainting on his packhorse in his weariness and pain.

'Yes! Your terms are acceptable – because I have no other choice.'

CHAPTER IV

A STRANGE BARGAIN

Something sweet is the whisper of the pine, O goatherd,
that makes her music by yonder springs.

Theocritus, *Idylls*, No 1

As the king ceased to speak, without questions or time for
reflection, the wise woman swept past him to approach the
packhorse with Huw firmly wedged into the saddle.

'Please, my lord, take this brave fellow from his horse and lay
him down on a pallet inside my cottage. You may come with
him and check my quarters yourself, if you desire.'

Caradoc had been considering how to ask this same question,
so he flushed and shivered again at the seeming ability of this
woman to read his mind.

The wise woman's cottage was quite unlike anything that
Caradoc had ever seen. Sweet lavender and herbs were drying
on racks in the rafters just above head height and a huge
blackened pot was releasing the delicious aroma of a mutton
stew. Convenient hooks hung from the ceiling to carry hanks of
wool that were waiting for spindle or loom, all of which lent a

soft haze of muted pastel colours to the roof area. A number of coloured weavings softened a single bed that had been placed by the fireplace, while a pile of worn blankets in large baskets had been arranged for her hounds who leaped into them, then settled down to watch their mistress with adoring eyes.

'Yes! We'll lay your young man down on my own bed until such time as I've examined his wounds and decided what we're going to do with him,' the wise woman told Caradoc as Rowen and Trefor carried Huw into the room on an improvised stretcher.

Caradoc gave Rowen his instructions for the servants and huntsmen. 'You can set up an encampment downstream from the house where you can water the horses and prepare for a stay of several days. I'm not inclined to move Huw again, even if our healer should pronounce him healthy enough to travel. He's exhausted and will be in poor condition for some time, even when his wounds have started to heal. We'll probably send most of the hunting party back to Tintagel and retain only those men needed to aid the wise woman and myself. I'll remain here until Huw is ready to leave.'

Caradoc turned his attention back to the wise woman who was efficiently stripping the clothes away from her patient. Caradoc concealed a smile when she slapped away the boy's hands as he tried to hide his genitals.

'I've seen better often-times, so no foolishness, please.'

When the young man coloured hotly and his head began to lower in shame, the wise woman took pity on him.

'Well, perhaps not better, young man, although I've not measured you precisely. But there'll be no more blither-blather for the moment, my dear.' Her voice was gruff, but it was also kind.

While Rowen and Trefor obeyed their king's instructions, the wise woman began to remove the improvised splint from Huw's leg. She bit her lip in concern at what she saw and then moved to a narrow bench that ran along the back wall of the cottage. With the assistance of a long twig, she lit several lamps and set them into niches in the wall hollows designed for the purpose.

Then she found a jar that had been sealed with wax and a twist of rag. As she poured a small amount of a viscous liquid into a cup, she added a good pinch of chopped and dried herbs from another jar and then filled the cup with water from a kettle that had been boiling in the fire pit.

'Now, young man, you'll oblige old Saraid by drinking this nasty concoction of mine. Once you've drunk it all down, you'll sink into a deep sleep so I can set your leg and help it to grow strong until it allows you to walk again. I'll also be able to treat your chest wounds more easily if you're asleep. I promise not to compromise your virtue while you're in my power.'

Even Huw managed a weak smile.

'You're not that old,' Huw whispered, as he swallowed every drop of the thick mixture. 'Are you called Mistress Saraid, my lady?'

'Of course! Close your eyes now, my boy, and Saraid will make you well again.' Then, to Caradoc's surprise, she kissed Huw on both eyelids as if she was his mother.

Touched, Caradoc watched carefully as Saraid stroked Huw's forehead until he fell into the deepest of deep sleeps. Minutes later, she began to carefully stroke his leg from the knee to the ankle, although Huw stirred fitfully at her touch in the tender spots. Then, after making a few rapid calculations, she instructed Caradoc to take a firm grip on Huw's hip. Finally, she grasped his unfeeling foot and lower leg and pulled downward with surprising strength.

An immediate clicking sound was audible.

'We've got it already, Caradoc. Feel your way along the edges of the break, and you'll be able to tell the bone is back in place.'

Saraid seemed to expect his assistance, so Caradoc ran his hand down Huw's leg and realised that the jagged edges had been perfectly realigned back into position.

He looked at Saraid with renewed respect and wordlessly bowed his head to her.

'That wasn't an over-difficult manipulation, my lord, as long as the trauma hadn't caused major damage to the flesh and the break is in one of the long, straight bones. There wasn't any magic to the treatment at all.' She grinned conspiratorially. 'As you saw, even a woman can do it.'

With the king's hesitant assistance, Saraid bound the leg with lengths of cloth and tied them off tightly enough to restrict movement while still allowing a smooth blood flow to run through the limb. Then she splinted the leg once again, using wooden stakes that had been shaped to fit snugly around a human leg. The device was then bound into position.

Caradoc shivered at the woman's prescience in having splints available that seemed to fit Huw's leg so well. This woman possessed qualities that his logical brain couldn't explain.

Saraid sighed with satisfaction, and then turned her attention to Huw's torso and chest wounds – the most dangerous he had suffered.

Once she started to make her examination of the many bruises and minor contusions on Huw's trunk, Saraid realised that the boar had trampled over the unfortunate young man as well as goring him. These bruises had blackened so that his flesh appeared to be marked like the pelt of a spotted cat. Saraid inspected every rib, his collarbones, and then worked her way down to his hip bones in a fruitless search for further breaks, before she nodded to indicate her satisfaction.

Hunting through her supply of pottery jars, she finally found a small sealed container. Once she removed the stopper, the greasy ointment inside smelled vile. She handed the little pot to Caradoc.

'After we've finished our ministrations, someone must continue to anoint his bruises and wounds to bring the deeper contusions to the surface of the skin so the pain can be relieved. This must take place for some time, even after the patient has begun his return to health. This unguent will help, believe me, but Huw might be embarrassed at the thought of his friends having to massage his naked flesh and dress his wounds. But he can't refuse if his king is the person carrying out the treatment.'

Grunting his understanding, Caradoc tried to decide which of the huntsmen could be given these particular tasks, while Saraid seemed to read his mind and began to giggle like a young girl. Caradoc felt another odd shiver that emanated from the base of his spine on this occasion, and was embarrassed by a sudden partial tumescence in his manhood. He hoped she hadn't noticed as he pushed the container's stopper back into place to lessen its pungent smell.

Saraid's face became serious with a suddenness that quickly cooled Caradoc's ardour.

'You were wise to bring the boy to me so quickly, although I can't guarantee his survival. The tusks of your boar were obviously filthy and I can already feel the heat in the wounds. It will get worse, but we aren't wholly without a cure for the evil infections that lurk in such unclean things.'

'What else can I do, mistress? Huw took the brunt of the charge that was meant for me and I quail to explain to his mother why her only son perished in my service.'

'Such is life, my friend, as you are surely aware. But . . .' She hesitated while her brows knit with concentration. 'We'll try clean water first, after we've carefully cleansed the wounds and trimmed off the torn flesh. Then we'll use drawing salves to remove the poisons from his blood where the tusks have scored him. I'll be using radish paste in the wounds, which will kill any diseases of the blood once we've removed all the filth and corruption. I'll also use pastes that are derived from seaweed to supplement my treatment. You can be assured that I'll do everything in my power to save young Huw, but I'll need your muscle, your brain and your support.'

The Dumnonii king nodded, confused by the list of treatments. As a lad, he had been warned by his father that a king cannot possibly know everything, so he had left healing matters to those who had some expertise. He could see that Saraid was for more experienced than anyone in Tintagel.

'I'm confident that Huw is safe in your hands, Saraid, so what do you want me to do?'

Following her instructions, Caradoc massaged Huw's flaccid body while she slid a waxed sheet of cloth under the boy's body.

'We can't allow the lad to sleep in a wet bed,' she explained. 'He shouldn't wake up in the near future because I've given him a large dose of poppy juice in my herbal tea, but you must be prepared to hold him down if he should stir while I'm working on his wounds.'

Once again, Caradoc gave a terse and nervous nod.

As she poured boiling water from the kettle into a large bowl, Saraid threw selected herbs into the liquid and added seaweed as it came off the boil. Then, as the water began to cool, she used a narrow knife to trim off several flaps of skin so that the furrows on each side of the individual wounds were cleaned and closed in such a manner that scarring could be controlled. 'It's important that we don't seal poisons into the wounds,' she said. 'Any inflammation could kill this fine young man if I wasn't careful.'

She gave Caradoc a small grin that instilled confidence in the king.

'You'll have some interesting sets of scars when this is finished, young Huw,' Saraid informed her unconscious patient, then washed her hands in a bucket of cold water that stood near the fire pit to prevent stray sparks from setting fire to the cottage.

'You could stir my stew to stop it from burning the bottom of the pot, my lord,' she added with another grin that let Caradoc know she was playing games with him.

Caradoc forced himself to swallow a sudden flare of resentment that rose in his throat. Saraid simply smiled and began to wash Huw's torso and clean the remainder of the detritus from the uninjured parts of his body.

Once she was convinced that the injured body had been thoroughly scrubbed and dried, Saraid filled the furrows in Huw's flesh with a radish paste. The two deep scorings were packed tightly and then the flesh around the wounds was thickly covered with another unguent. Finally the whole area was covered with clean cloth and securely wrapped.

'There,' Saraid said with satisfaction. 'We can only wait and see from now on.'

Caradoc straightened his back and stretched luxuriantly.

'Not you, I'm afraid,' Saraid laughed and pointed to the pot of unguent beside Caradoc's hand. 'We still need to take care of Huw's bruises. My radish supply is getting low, so I'm going outside to collect some plants from the garden. You, or one of your men, must continue to massage the lesser bruises on Huw's torso. You'll have some hard work to do, but it must be done gently, as if Huw was a nubile young girl you're trying to seduce. Do you understand?'

With this, the Wise Woman of the Red Wells threw on her cloak and picked up her basket. Then, accompanied by her dogs, she left the cottage behind her. In her wake, she left a memory of her scent, of herbs and roses, and the clean tang of pine sap. Caradoc felt the air itself was lonely without her.

When Saraid returned, Caradoc and Trefor had used the ointment on Huw's bruises and had dressed him in his loincloth while drawing out the waxen cloth from beneath him. Trefor had found a blanket and wrapped the patient thoroughly to keep him warm, while Caradoc had saved the stew from burning by swinging the iron pot away from the fire on its tripod.

'You've saved our evening meal, which is fortuitous,' Saraid said. 'There's more than enough food in the pot to feed all your men, if you'd like to summon them now. Your huntsmen look like they've scarcely rested in the rush to bring Huw to me.'

'Call the men, Trefor, and tell them to bring their plates and spoons.' The wonderful aroma that filled the cramped spaces of the cottage was making Caradoc delirious with hunger. The king was determined that his men should be fed before the offer could be rescinded.

For her part, Saraid laughed as she watched Caradoc lick his lips in anticipation.

'Obey your master, Trefor. I'll bring the stew outside in a moment and ladle it out for all of you. As you can see, I prepared sufficient stew for us all. But I have no beer, only my infusions of herbs or clean, boiled water from the Red Wells. Those waters travel under the earth in a great river and there is no way for poisons to enter the underground streams.'

Once again, both men shivered as they saw the size of the mutton stew strengthened with carrots, turnips, fresh green peas and parsnips that Saraid had prepared in anticipation of their arrival. How could she possibly have known of their approach?

'We have beer aplenty but I'll gladly drink the waters from your wells and would be grateful for the honour. Where are they situated, and why do you describe them as red?' Caradoc managed to maintain a regal stance, although he was seriously rattled by this woman.

Saraid flashed an enigmatic smile at her guest.

Relieved to have escaped from her unsettling gaze, Trefor escaped to rally the men and pass on the king's instructions. In the wake of his servant's departure, Caradoc offered to carry the cauldron outside to a small table that Saraid had set up.

'There's no need to help me, King Caradoc. As you've seen, I'm a very strong woman. I'll show you the Red Wells and explain their history after we've eaten.' She smiled with soft pillowy lips and, once again, Caradoc felt a shiver in the pit of his stomach. 'However, if you're determined to assist me, you can drag that jar outside.' Saraid indicated a large terracotta jug sitting against the wall near the door. 'I must warn you, my king, that it's quite heavy.'

Saraid had already picked up the handle of the cauldron with the assistance of a piece of rag to protect her hands from the heat. She had also found a ladle to serve the stew, so Caradoc lifted the jug and followed the wise woman outside.

While Saraid provided food for her eager guests, Caradoc

took the opportunity to examine his hostess's face and figure with a man's curiosity.

Saraid looked nothing like a wise woman, an eremite or a healer. She was past the first flush of youth, although her hair was still a rich and glossy chestnut, and Caradoc could see there was no trace of grey in the clean, well-brushed mane, which hung free so it brushed the back of her knees when she walked. Caradoc hungered to run his hands through that magnificent fall, and imagined binding her with her own long tresses.

Trefor carefully nudged his king, because Caradoc was staring at the lady like a halfwit, and some of his men were exchanging knowing looks. Trefor had known Caradoc since childhood when they had played on the dangerous paths overhanging the wild seas and cliffs of Tintagel, so his service and friendship encouraged Trefor to bring his king to his senses.

Embarrassed, Caradoc forced himself to concentrate on the excellence of the stew.

Saraid's face was small, pert and attractive. Her nose tilted upwards at the tip and her eyes were merry. Only her eyebrows suggested that she could be other than an attractive matron, because they were dark, almost black, and were slanted upwards at the outer corners. This odd shape gave her eyes a slightly sinister cast and also set men's minds to thinking forbidden thoughts. Caradoc could easily imagine that this woman had strange knowledge and could bring men to heights of passion that they had never previously experienced.

I can't believe this woman lives alone and has no man to share her bed, Caradoc thought. Everything about her screams sexuality and pleasure.

As for her body, Saraid was a little too plump for her height, which was disarmingly short, even when she was standing on tiptoe. She barely reached Caradoc's chest, so she brought out the protectiveness that lives in masculine hearts. Her waist was very small and her hips swayed suggestively whenever she walked.

In a daze, Caradoc finished two plates of stew and drank several cups of crystal-clear water. Eventually, as the sun began its long journey to the horizon, Saraid beckoned to him and he rose to his feet at once. Then, at her invitation, he walked beside her towards a copse of trees where the distant sound of running water originated.

'I have puzzled over you, my lord, and I've played games with you that were neither wise nor kind. But, as I said, the Red Wells speak to me and they send dreams that won't set me free until I pass on some insistent message that they wish you to know. I am simply a conduit in these matters, a bridge that allows information to be passed to you from the unknown. I can't explain how or why these messages come to me. I can only swear that the shadows that live in the Red Wells seem to coalesce into forms and features that I am able to recognise.'

Caradoc kicked idly at a rock that lay on the edge of the path that had been worn through the underbrush by sporadic movements to and from the wells. Judging by the wear and tear along it, Saraid must have walked that path daily. Nor could she have been alone, judging by the depth of the track or the disturbed sod. Pilgrims must have been regular visitors to the Red Wells, but Caradoc had heard little of them.

'Why are the wells so red?' Caradoc asked as his eyes ranged over the landscape.

'The water looks red when it comes to the surface as a stream, and the waters stain the rocks of the watercourse. The wells consist of three stone pipes that go down about twelve feet to an underground river. No, my lord, I don't believe in bleeding rivers that are supernatural in nature, but I do believe there are deposits of iron down there that cause the waters to have a rusty appearance. At any road, the Red Wells are very strange and I, for one, cannot explain why the gods have brought such things into being. You'll probably doubt my sanity, but I rather like to believe that the walls between our world and the otherworld are very thin in this place and so, if the light is right and the gods permit, I'm able to see into the world of chaos, gods and sacred trees. Pilgrims tell me that I'm seeing future events, visions that the fates have decreed will come to pass.'

Caradoc remained silent as they strolled amicably through the trees.

Once Saraid and Caradoc entered the copse, the path began to rise and eventually disappeared into the arid ground of a knoll. A platform was carved out of the slope. There, a huge tree rose up from a cluster of large boulders that were blotched with lichen and mosses, leaving small areas of thick greenery growing like a small miracle, considering the aridity of the exposed hill. The tree was liberally covered with nuts and was surrounded by smaller versions of itself, a mother hazel in a dense carpet of ferns, small orchids and other parasitic plants that turned this flat and protected place on the side of the knoll into a triumph where growing things overcame the ravages of wind and dry stone.

Below the trunk of the tree, a large pond of water surrounded a tangle of tree roots. On the furthest side of the pond, the fresh water had overflowed the banks where it became a small stream that was bounded by verdant life before the waters tumbled down into the forest. On the side closest to the tree, a bowl had been placed on top of a huge boulder that had been hollowed out over aeons by water flowing onto its sandstone surface. Someone had purposely placed this boulder in this position and had planted the hazel beside it to create a sacred shrine into which the nuts from the tree could fall and be collected. Subterranean water was doubly sacred in the tribal religion, for it was live water in which hazel nuts had fallen. The porous stone of the bowl had a red tinge, like the stains of blood from a wound in the earth that had risen to the surface and the sunlight.

The water in this pond came from a fissure in the rocks, so the roots of the tree had knitted together around the riven stone. Closer to the cliff wall was a higher platform, where three holes were sunk into expanses of sandstone, to appear like stepping stones within the mosses and greenery.

Down inside one of the stone pipes, Caradoc could see dark water that seemed to shiver whenever an odd ray of light from the setting sun was reflected onto it. A bucket, attached to a tripod by a long length of rope that allowed water to be drawn to the surface, was lying beside the well.

'Why not capture water from the pond?' Caradoc asked, puzzled by the effort needed to raise a full bucket to the surface, when the pond was only a few body lengths away and was below the level of the knoll.

'That water is holy! Don't you remember the tales told by your mother? I would be cursed if I drew from the pond for my cooking and cleaning, especially as the water is flavoured and nurtured by the hazel.'

Caradoc grunted in response, although stealing water from the primeval darkness seemed just as dangerous as opposing the will of the old gods.

Saraid stared down into the pipe of stone, half-hypnotised by the sounds of water burbling over hidden rocks and ledges as it plunged far below to lightless depths. She began to rock to the beat of the falling water and Caradoc could see that her eyes were glazing.

Suddenly, she began to speak. Her voice had a thready sound totally unlike her normal tone.

'Caradoc, King and Dumnonii Boar, you must remain still when other men rage and leap to judgement. In years to come, a cool head will be needed or disaster will destroy the isles before their time. You must remember what the waters demand of you.'

Caradoc waved a hand before her eyes which now appeared like inhuman pieces of milky glass. Saraid was gone. Only the Wise Woman of the Red Wells remained.

'Your destiny demands that you become the friend of a Roman called Magnus Maximus. His time is coming fast and he is destined to wear the imperial laurel wreaths. Aye! Such a man sees nothing before him but his search for destiny, but you must hold him close because the Dumnonii will need him during the travails to come. Finally, beware of his charms for, like a serpent, he can deceive. Regardless of all temptation, you must remain in your ancestral lands for you must not leave Britannia. If you leave these shores, you will never return.'

'No power on this earth could convince me to turn away from these isles, not now and not ever,' Caradoc swore, but he was sure that Saraid heard nothing of his vow.

'Another man with grey eyes will come to you. You must protect this man, for he will also be important to your house. He will only be a boy when you first meet him, whereas you will be very old. But you must remember these words.'

'Why should I listen to any more of your ravings, Saraid? I don't believe in the Red Wells, and I don't believe in the gods, if the truth be told.' Caradoc's voice was petulant and impatient, but he was unable to walk away, no matter how much he wanted to.

'The message you have just heard is a special gift to you and yours, Caradoc, for your son must learn what has been said – and his son also, for this plan has been long in the making.'

'And what will I gain by agreeing to this one-sided and unfair bargain? It seems that I have nothing to gain and much to lose if I obey you.'

The wise woman seemed to listen carefully to something that only she could hear over the sound of rushing water. Her brow furrowed. 'Your kingdom will be one of the few to survive the upheavals that are to come in the future, and no savages will wrest your acres from the hands of your descendants. In the years to come, your kingdom will remain untouched in a sea of strange tribes. Is that not sufficient justification for you to accept my advice?'

Saraid folded like a dropped length of cloth. He barely had time to reach out for her before she fell down the slope and rolled onto the mossy pebbles of the shrine.

'Remember the Red Dragon, Caradoc, for he shall come out of Tintagel . . . and all the tribes of Britannia will tremble at his birth.' She looked up at him as he stood on the sandstone blocks while she lay on the mosses and ferns below. A cut at her hairline bled sluggishly.

And then, Saraid's eyes flickered and the wise woman was gone.

An hour passed and still Saraid lay as if dead. All Caradoc could do was to make her comfortable . . . and wait.

She groaned.

Caradoc knelt beside her, careless of the mud and crushed ferns. Then her lashes trembled and a pair of tears snaked out from the corners of her eyes to run down her face and into the tangle of her chestnut hair. He wiped those tears away with his blood-stained neck scarf, and raised her torso as she gradually returned to consciousness. The king realised he was sitting on the damp earth with her awakening body across his lap and her head lolling on his breast.

'My head hurts,' she whispered faintly.

'You injured yourself when you fell. Hush now and rest. Whatever took you will let your mind and body go free, so you need to wait quietly. It's time for you to sleep.'

Although the falling darkness dimmed the shapes of wild nature that surrounded them, Caradoc felt at peace. When he looked up, the stars were so bright and close that he almost believed he could pull them out of the velvet skies. Had he been in full control of his senses, he would have been frightened by the clarity and brilliance of this alien night. Unaware of his actions, he stroked Saraid's hair.

Saraid's body stirred against him. She freed her hands and they wandered over the harsh planes of his face with a woman's tenderness, until Caradoc wanted to weep for something that he knew he could never own. She raised herself and kissed him blindly, mouth to mouth and breast to breast, until the king tried to pull away from her importunate lips.

'No!' she whispered fiercely. 'Huw will live and I will have my payment. Here, where the otherworld surrounds us like a dream, there is no time for thinking or for titles, names or symbols of power. What we are and what we do is at the gods' bidding. They will not be gainsaid, master, and neither will I.'

And so, frightened of the urgency of his own body, as if

another power had entered his flesh and guided hands, mouth, loins and bellies so that his will was not his own, Caradoc took Saraid in the garden of the Red Wells.

And he wept for his loveless life in the luxuriant and warm beauty of her arms.

CHAPTER V

THE EAGLE IN THE SUN

But if we are guided by me, we will believe that the soul
is immortal and capable of enduring all extremes of good
and evil.

Plato, *The Republic*, Book 10

Maximus was fascinated by Tintagel. During the first four days in
the citadel, he pored over the lands around the narrow isthmus,
while marvelling at the strange, giant footprint that had been
scoured deep into the stone of the headland that jutted out into
the wild ocean waters. He felt an exhilaration that sent his heart
flying with the hunting birds that soared over the long grasses.

His soldierly eyes assessed the underground granary, where
too was stored an impressive array of dried foods, wines and
beer. A well provided clean water to the fortress and the small
circular cottages of servants that clung like shellfish to the
sloping sides of the isthmus. A network of dizzying paths linked
these tiny cottages. Altogether, Maximus finally came to accept
Caradoc's boast that his fortress could withstand a determined
siege for years.

Every part of the castell was utilised for the benefit of Tintagel's inhabitants. Vegetable gardens flourished on any patch of ground where the soil was deep enough for the plants to take root, although trees weren't able to survive the perpetual sea winds. The citadel itself was amazingly snug. In a sheltered nook near the kitchen, Maximus discovered a beautiful flower garden. The fortress's kitchens had been built in a separate part of the castell where the chance of accidental fire was minimised. Here, he found a number of large pots in which a range of herbs and edible plants flourished. A wild rose climbed over the stone wall from a large trough and its heady perfume sweetened this little sun-trap.

The structure of the citadel seemed haphazard, but Caradoc explained how each generation added to the structure and built on the changes and improvements made by their predecessors. This accounted for the irregular skyline and the number of steps, odd levels and the maze-like quality of the passageways. Some parts of the venerable building were built in timber, others in flint. The various floor levels were unpredictable and were often in perpetual darkness because of the lack of natural lighting. Tintagel was eccentric, but it had a charm that wasn't usually associated with an impregnable fortress.

From Tintagel's Eye, the room that looked out over three sides of the peninsula, Maximus could appreciate what Caradoc had meant during the first night of his visit. From there the king could observe the huge swathe of countryside that lay beyond the approaches to his fortress. More importantly, he could watch the movements of his enemies as they rode down the steep slopes to the foreshore and the first defensive line. Maximus could imagine how a relatively small number of determined warriors could protect the causeway against repeated attacks.

Even if the defenders were to fall, the enemy would then be faced with the dizzying black steps that marched ever upwards to the fortress's heights. No enemy could hope to climb those with arrows, stones and hot oil raining down on them.

To the right and to the left, the land fell away to steep cliffs that would repel climbers, even if they survived the wild seas to reach the peninsula. Yes, this room was Tintagel's Eye and from here a competent commander could hold a legion at bay.

'And there's no timber available to construct ladders or rams. An attacker would have to build their siege equipment miles away in places where the trees are able to grow straight or, alternatively, bring them south from a base such as Segontium.'

'Are you talking to yourself, Maximus?' Caradoc had entered on silent feet. He was leaning against the wall, enjoying Maximus's consternation. 'I was certain that you, for one, would understand the purpose of this room.'

'I'd be blind to miss its positioning, friend Caradoc. Any commander could hold Tintagel against a significant enemy – even our legions, if luck was with them.' The last observation was uttered with some reluctance by the Roman, so Caradoc smiled smugly behind the back of his hand. Maximus had offered sincere praise, grudging but genuine.

'Tintagel has served us well over the centuries, Maximus. Because all the wealth of the Dumnonii tribe is stored here, our citizens have never been threatened in living memory. Not by land – and certainly not by sea.'

'You are fortunate, for the rest of Britannia is an island beset by her enemies,' Maximus replied drily. 'Are your neighbouring rulers as lucky as you are?'

Caradoc laughed. 'Those fools? They're a pack of hounds: some of whom are thin and hungry, while the rest are fat and lazy. But all are dogs who are driven by self-interest. They spend many hours trying to wring concessions out of your master. If that makes them fortunate, then they're Fortuna's sycophants.'

'You're a hard man, Caradoc.' Maximus hastily recalled everything he'd ever heard of Caradoc's neighbours. Several descriptions came to mind immediately, ranging from greedy to idle, brutal and two-faced.

'You can make your own assessment of my neighbours if you have a few more weeks that can be spent away from your command,' Caradoc responded. 'I've only just received an invitation from Gwaun pen Mairtin, the king of the Atrebates tribe in Venta Belgarum. The fool likes to think of himself as a second-hand Roman, an attitude that nauseates all good Britons as much as it irritates true Romans. He's a kinsman of mine through marriage, so I've been forced into his company more often than I want.'

'Hmmmmf!' Maximus grunted. 'What does the invitation entail? I take it from your attitude that you're not overfond of this Gwaun pen Mairtin.'

'Not much,' Caradoc replied bluntly. 'But Venta Belgarum has been tarted up by the Atrebates so it looks like an expensive whore. It certainly has pleasures superior to anything I can provide, so perhaps you'd be amused to see all the local kings pretending to be sophisticates and jostling for your favour.'

Maximus almost laughed. Since their first meeting, he had been impressed by Caradoc, who was proving to be a man with a steely core under his amiable façade. Unlike so many of his peers, Caradoc had no desire to ask for any favours from his Roman guest and offered the familiar, homely pleasures of riding, hunting, and dining on wholesome produce. Caradoc's wines were excellent and his women were gracious, despite the sullen queen. Maximus had taken pains to court the lady who had unfurled like a flower under his flattery, while Caradoc watched with dry amusement. Much to his own surprise, the Roman realised that he actually liked the Dumnonii king.

'Who'll be at Venta Belgarum, Caradoc? I'm interested in making such a journey, especially if we were to meet with Britons who might be of use to Rome's interests in this part of the Empire.'

Caradoc grinned like a lazy predator.

'Let me see,' he began. 'The Dobunni king will certainly attend. He's called Adwen, which means fiery in our language, but don't expect any exuberance or passion out of that one. He's erected his hall in the style of a Roman villa and he pretends to have Roman blood inherited from the daughter of a tribune who came to these lands with the original expeditionary force led by Caesar.' Caradoc snorted derisively. 'If such a woman ever existed, she would have been a camp follower, so you may take his pretensions with a grain of salt. For comfort's sake, he has built a bathhouse and a hypocaust, so he's clean – if nothing else! Yes, Roman, you may laugh! In the lives of the kings of Britannia, cleanliness is an unimportant consideration. I might add that Adwen also sports a purple-edged toga.'

'Ye gods! I'm so tired of second-hand Romans aping their betters. Is he the only one, apart from Gwaun, who thinks of himself as a citizen of Rome?'

Caradoc considered the affectations of Gwaun and Adwen were laughable, but he couldn't help bridling a little. The Roman's contempt still stung.

'Aye! But Gwaun and Adwen are easier to mix with than some of the others, all of whom are less than fragrant.'

'Lovely,' Maximus muttered, and found his nose was wrinkling in dislike.

'Bleise ap Bladud takes pride in living much the same way as his ancestors in the days before the Romans occupied our lands. To Bleise, tradition is far more important than good relationships with Rome. He's the king of a small but very wealthy tribe, the Belgae, who are positioned along one of my borders. Bleise's land is very rich and very ancient, so we've always accepted that the Belgae people are peculiar.' Caradoc snorted deprecatingly as Maximus muffled a hoot of laughter.

'I know! You're suggesting that the Dumnonii shouldn't throw around insults like I've done, because all Britons are a little strange. But the lands in which we live dictate the way we view the world. Do you agree? Our land is bounded by water. The sea has become our master, but it is the source of our wealth.

'By comparison, the Belgae lands were once covered by water, but those inland seas have all but gone now. The tors, the standing stones and the remnants of strange religious worship are signs of a landscape that remains mysterious.

'Bleise is a neighbour of mine. I know him well, but I have no faith in him. His acres might be few, but they bear prodigious quantities of produce. He's a very devious man, so I'd avoid placing any trust in him, even if you can get close to him without gagging.'

'Now that you've convinced me to lock myself away in Tintagel, is there anyone that might be worth my attention? You've described a thoroughly unlovely group.' Caradoc was almost certain that the Roman wasn't joking.

'At the risk of frightening you off entirely, Fiachna ap Tormud of the Durotriges is a violent and brutal man with an uncontrollable lust towards rape. He is a loathsome man on all counts and is so venal that his taxes have stripped his tribe bare of any wealth, so that he can glory in his hoard of gold. His lasciviousness is second only to his miserable parsimony – he'll keep loaves of bread for the sake of having them, even if they rot while his family and servants are chewing on dry crusts.'

'You're fast convincing me to avoid this feast,' Maximus warned.

'The last of my neighbours with whom you will meet, however, is probably the most dangerous of all. Fortunately, his lands are regularly attacked by Saxons and Angles who appear every spring to prey on his kingdom and his subjects. This king is clever, violent and ruthless, so he would happily wage war against his friends if he had no outland enemies. He is Sorcha ap Sion and he will try to wrest men and weapons from you to protect his people in the Regni lands.'

Maximus scratched his chin. His brown eyes were acute and hooded under the long eyelids that gave his face a sly look from some angles. Then, as if he had come to a difficult decision, he began to chuckle. As his laughter began to fade, he slapped his knees, rose to his feet and opened a shutter in the Eye so he could see the mainland spread below him like a vivid green carpet.

'I've a notion that I may regret this decision, but forewarned is forearmed. Any intelligence I can provide for my commander will be of incalculable worth to Theodosius. After your intriguing descriptions, how could I not be anxious to meet such a cadre of interesting men, if only to discover whether they are truly as objectionable as your descriptions suggest. It's always useful to know the natures of the local aristocracy.'

'Rome always tries to look ahead,' Caradoc said with no emotion in his voice.

'True! My masters rarely gamble, and they never take risks on the characters of minor kings. I will attend your feast, Caradoc, but I'll be depending on you to warn me of any bear-traps that have been set to mutilate or humiliate me.'

With a gasp of surprise, Caradoc accepted that this Roman was unaccustomed to sarcasm.

A useful detail to remember, the king thought with pleasure. The man's a fool! He believes that Rome, and all things Roman, are superior in every way.

So, with a promise to travel to Venta Belgarum with his friend, Maximus sent word to his guard to ready themselves for travel within the coming week.

Decius swore vigorously. 'Why in hell are we riding to Venta Belgarum? So the master can meet some mucky-muck minor kings who have no bearing on the security of this damned country? He's up to something, but I'll be damned if I can work out what it is. In the past, the tribune would never have given a cracked pisspot for the opinions of the tribal kings.'

Grumbling, he warmed his body before a fire that had been allowed to burn brightly inside the barracks at Tintagel, while a circle of horse guards gaped at their officer, puzzled. They were accustomed to his cursing, but Decius was usually very respectful of Maximus and his edicts.

One of the enlisted men polishing his greaves looked up from his task and grimaced at Decius's show of temper. This soldier, Lorn, was distinguished by his shock of sun-streaked tow-coloured hair, a rare colouring for a Roman or even a Briton. Nothing marked his outlander birth more clearly than his pale blue eyes.

'For Christ's sake, Decius, we have to obey all orders given by the tribune, so why are you complaining and bitching like a woman over decisions that aren't yours to make?'

Decius moved from the fire pit to stand threateningly over Lorn, so the younger man was forced to put his greaves to one side and stand so he could face his superior officer.

'You've no cause to question me, Lorn. You're no Roman, and nor have you ever seen the back of these isles. I've been told that you were born in the far north beyond the Vallum Antonini and Bodotria Aest, where the Picts and outlawed tribesmen live in perpetual misery.'

Lorn's equanimity was shaken and his clean-shaven jaw jutted forward obstinately.

'Are you accusing me of being a traitor, sir? How many men in this room have ever seen the River Tiber or walked the pavements of the Palatine? No one here can sneer at our comrades' lack of pedigree. We're not mongrel dogs, sir, and I object to being treated like one, just because I commented on your bad temper. We've obeyed all orders from our master, regardless. Why would we complain about this latest one, when we can't do anything about it? Why bitch at me?'

Decius fumed. His face and neck became a fiery red and his dark brows furrowed, while his tense jaw jutted forward even more aggressively than Lorn's had done.

'If you were Roman, and if we were under the command of a born aristocrat from the City of the Seven Hills, then you'd be flogged to death for your comments. Fortunately for you, I'm a generous man who grew to manhood in Sicily, so I don't hold with mindless violence to enforce discipline. But don't push your luck, Lorn! Let's see how you enjoy riding halfway across this benighted land in the rain, just to attend a feast of local kings in Venta Belgarum. These Britons have no call to love us and any hand extended in friendship does so for a reason. Check your fingers, your toes, your prick and especially your purse, if any Britons should smile towards you. I'd not wish to be inside Venta Belgarum's walls, unless our number was significantly larger than it is now. I don't trust these bastards as far as I can kick them.'

'They'll hardly dare to offer violence to our tribune,' Lorn replied, his face as white as Decius's was red. 'Our numbers may be reduced across the isles of Britannia, but we can still smash any British force with half their number.'

'You, Lorn, are still thinking like a Pict!'

Lorn's fists tightened. 'Picts expect chicanery, oath-breaking and treason from Romans and Britons. And I'm not a Pict!'

'No? You're not thinking clearly about numbers! Use your brain! A hundred men wouldn't help us. Good men have often died by stealth in these lands. Poison or disease have ended the lives of more cautious men than Maximus. One thing is for certain, the legions wouldn't march on Venta Belgarum because our tribune died from the shits, would they? I think not! And British herb masters could kill all of us, and never be caught for the crime.'

'But most herb masters are women,' Lorn gasped. 'Would they poison our tribune?'

'Really? Do you understand these women and their motives? I don't! But I respect their knowledge enough that I won't underestimate these old grand-dams with their harmless potions and busy hands. Good murderers are never caught,' Decius added in a sarcastic voice.

Lorn shrugged. 'Then we'll need to be very, very careful, won't we?' His eyes had darkened with the passion expended in defending his viewpoint.

'Exactly as I've been saying, Lorn,' Decius responded. 'I believe that our master should not take unnecessary risks with his person.' He grinned in triumph and those men who had followed the conversation began to guffaw with approval.

Out-manoeuvred, Lorn's parchment-coloured face reflected his fury.

Before the disagreement became even more serious, Lorn opted to back away from the edge of disrespect towards a senior officer. The decurion could have ordered him flogged, but old Decius was far too wise for such an extreme course of action.

'We'll need to be on our guard, boys,' he told the group. 'We'll have to avoid carousing with our hosts, for drunken men can easily be manipulated and overcome. Our task will be to protect our tribune from all threats, no matter how trivial they seem. Is that understood? So get some sleep, boys, while you can.'

'Can we trust the Dumnonii warriors? They seem like good fellows,' one grizzled veteran asked from his position beside the fire where his toes were toasting.

'We can trust them as far as one can trust any of our allies – which is no distance at all! We are King Caradoc's guests, so we are under his protection while we are in his fortress. He is sworn to protect us, so I believe he will do his best to keep us breathing. His duties as a host are one thing, but a smart man tries to help Fortuna along. Organise your kit, boys, and be ready to ride at short notice. Meantimes, use your whetstones carefully if you want to survive this shit.'

The guardsmen returned to a gloomy consideration of their weapons and several of them took out their whetstones and began to hone their spears, swords and knives into even more razor sharpness than usual.

Lorn hefted the sword in his hand. 'I think I'll keep you for a little longer, old friend,' he whispered, before allowing the perfectly balanced blade to tilt towards the stone floor.

'You'll have no joy with that weapon, if you allow the point to blunt,' Decius reminded him. 'She's not a pretty lady, is she? But she'll kill cleanly for you if you always keep her razor-sharp.'

Lorn nodded as Decius wandered away, whistling between his teeth. His bad temper was completely forgotten as he considered the small tasks that a good decurion must perform if his tribune's orders were to be effectively obeyed.

CHAPTER VI

A NASTY JOURNEY

Nemo Bonus Britto est. No good man is a Briton.

Decius Magnus Ausonius, *Epigrams*, 1:19

The road to Venta Belgarum was circuitous and dreary as an early winter gave warning of freezing days ahead. The combined cavalcade of Dumnonii and Roman cavalry was leaving the more moderate climate of the far west for the harsher weather of southern Britannia.

The grasses in the fields were sere and brown; even hardy brambles snapped when the mounted guardsmen brushed against them. The ploughed fields seemed empty except for the occasional bird still hopeful of finding exposed grubs or worms disturbed by the ploughshares. The skies were leaden and Decius could smell snow in the air.

Maximus might have chosen to ride at a moment's notice, but Caradoc was a far more methodical traveller. The men in his guard were carefully chosen so that the fifty-strong guardsmen were warriors of nobility, young and old, who owned fine horses and splendid equipment. With many protests, Rowen had been left behind to protect the heir and Caradoc's family, in case someone with avaricious eyes tried to take advantage of the king's absence. With cloaks of the check woven by the Dumnonii women to indicate their status, the guard was an impressive and dignified sight as they assembled five abreast beyond the causeway leading out of Tintagel.

Not to be outdone, Decius led his troop to form a phalanx of horseflesh in front of the Dumnonii guard. His men had outdone themselves in their preparations. The metal of their mailed shirts, their breastplates and their shoulder guards glinted in the sunlight; their red cloaks stirred in the wind; their helmets gleamed and their horses had been brushed and curried briskly until they glowed. Decius felt a moment of intense pride in his men, in the standard and in the legion. His back straightened, his shoulders squared and his tanned and wrinkled face radiated his pleasure.

When Caradoc and Maximus rode over the causeway, they also experienced the same feelings. Above them, a weak sun attempted to banish the gloom of a winter morning.

Roman roads hadn't penetrated into the Dumnonii lands on the western coast, so the route to the closest large centre, Isca Dumnoniorum, was along tracks used by farmers to take their produce to market. Because the cavalcade was on horseback and was accompanied by a single supply wagon, the Dumnonii trip should have made good time, but the land here was steep and occasionally difficult and heavily wooded in the remote areas.

Now and then strange and ancient stones reared out of the green sward in odd groups, so Maximus was reminded of other circles and long columns of local rock that could be found throughout Cymru and deep into the south.

Caradoc viewed one group of stones with casual familiarity,

but Maximus discovered that the hairs were rising on his neck and arms. Here, three squat stones, liberally blotched with lichen and moss, had been covered with another large flat stone to create an open chamber.

'What could be the purpose of that structure? It must have taken an inordinate effort for farmers to complete such a task, but I'm damned if I can see what it could have been used for,' Maximus muttered. He crossed himself surreptitiously, causing Caradoc to smile at this unlikely display of superstition.

'Legend tells us that the little people erected those stone chambers as tombs. According to the tales told by the common folk, earth was packed around the chamber once the corpse of a great man had been placed inside it and grassy sod laid on top. Whenever I see a small hill now, I always wonder whether some old king or magician has been buried there.'

He stared at the mute old stones for a moment. Then he laughed raucously, causing a pair of crows in a nearby elm tree to rise into the air with a loud flapping of wings and shrill, indignant screams.

'You mustn't fear them, my friend. The people who laboured to raise those stones are long dead and have left nothing behind them, other than the mystery sealed in these formations. Tintagel was supposed to have been built by those self-same people, but I can't swear to that. What I can swear to is that the stones don't have the power to touch living and breathing flesh. We must marvel how people who left no records behind them, not even a single carved word, could have cut those stones without the use of metal. They must have been highly skilled in the use of flint.'

'It seems your island is full of mysteries, Caradoc. Not far from Segontium, a small stone circle sits at the top of a slope that leads down to the straits and Mona Island.' Maximus crossed himself and even Caradoc, who was a pagan at heart, paled a little under his tan. 'The druids died there in their hundreds, but rumour has it that those stones are far older than the time of those fanatics.'

'You'd have to think of them so, Maximus, because they resisted Rome. Even the destruction of their sacred groves didn't deter them, so your masters were forced to spend many months herding them onto Mona Island where they could be killed. Despite being unarmed!'

Maximus raised one of his brows. 'Do I detect a trace of criticism in your voice, Caradoc? The generals must maintain order and the druids persisted in fomenting rebellion.'

'Aye! On those ancient wrongs, we will have to disagree, my friend.' Caradoc's blunt statement left Maximus on the verge of losing his temper, but fortunately Caradoc recognised the signs of a man stretched to his limits, so offered the Roman an olive branch of sorts.

'But the murder of the druids is long past and cannot be remedied, Maximus. Only a fool would blame the sins of the father on the sons. I'd prefer not to be at odds with you, certainly not because of decisions made before any of us were born. We're both Christians now, but I can understand the demands of securing an island like Britannia and the need to remove the religious leaders of any resistance.'

Caradoc's capitulation mollified Maximus a little, but the gulf between them remained wide because the Roman resented any criticism of decisions made by his forebears.

In a spirit of conciliation, Caradoc offered his hand to Maximus, who stared at it for a brief moment before moving his horse closer and offering his own hand in return. Although Maximus still smarted at the uncomfortable exchange, he was man enough to admit that Caradoc had sound reasons for complaint. He said as much to the Dumnonii.

So, with a certain degree of amity, the troop rode away from the standing stones, and headed towards the sea.

The great southern Roman road terminated at Isca Dumnoniorum, a pleasant town situated on a river that emptied directly into the sea known as the Litus Saxonicum, although Saxons rarely journeyed so far into the west of Britannia. In a fertile river valley, Isca Dumnoniorum enjoyed a mild climate, even in winter.

Maximus looked down at the river valley and noted with pleasure the neat farms and plump livestock. As they rode down from the hills, the size of the imposing cavalcade attracted considerable attention, especially as the Dumnonii standards proudly proclaimed the presence of the king. Farmers, their wives and children hurried out of the cottages with work-worn hands that were filled with homely gifts.

The Romans in the cavalcade noted the obvious signs of health in these peasants. Maximus, who was overfamiliar with the effects of war, knew that starvation and disease struck the poor first and that the cumulative effects of hunger were brutal. Here he was seeing the physical signs of happy people who lived in a peaceful land, so realised that Caradoc's wise rule was probably the main reason for their well-being.

As one elderly woman pressed a circlet of daisies into his hand, Maximus was impressed by the respect and love being showered on Caradoc by his people; they reached out to touch the edge of his cloak or pat the flanks of his horse.

Although the frequent halts to greet his subjects slowed the troop's advance, Caradoc insisted on dismounting and greeting his subjects personally. He made sure that he treated all his subjects with the same courtesy, especially when he kissed the hands of raw-boned, wide-rumped women. Similarly, he won the hearts of awe-struck children by ruffling their hair as they gazed wide-eyed at the troops. The king would cajole, joke, pull faces or compliment the children until he saw tremulous smiles appear. Then, with the best wishes of subjects who often kneeled to demonstrate their respect, Caradoc remounted his gelding and the journey continued.

'Do you ever tire of these bucolics, friend Caradoc?' Maximus asked one night as they ate some excellent bread with butter, a gift from one of the peasant farmers.

'I'd be a fool if I did. I'm forced to call on these men and their sons to fight for me in times of war. The loss of a good foot soldier is a nuisance to us, but to these peasants, the death of a son is the loss of grandchildren and their future. I've found that the men in my tribe go into battle willingly out of love; better that than being forced to fight by some distant and uncaring ruler. After all, what does pleasantry cost me? Nothing! And, in return, I am given gifts like this excellent bread.'

But constant interruptions slowed the pace of their journey, so Maximus was glad when the cavalcade approached the low walls of Isca Dumnoniorum and, behind it, the grey of the sea.

Two days were spent in the township, while Maximus chafed with impatience at the constant demands on Caradoc's time. However, there were compensations. Maximus used his time to reconnoitre the town and evaluate Caradoc's summer palace, if such a word could be used to describe a rambling compound consisting of a large hall and minimal facilities suitable for short official visits. Nearby, a simple rectangular house on Roman lines offered clean facilities for a number of visitors to Isca Dumnoniorum, while a barracks for troops and the usual stables had also been constructed.

Caradoc spent some of his time in the city dispensing justice between citizens and farmers, or in earnest meetings with the town's dignitaries. By the time they were ready to leave, Caradoc had given a promise to the city fathers that the guard would return to hunt down a small cadre of outlaws who had been carrying out vicious crimes against lonely farmsteads in the surrounding district. He had an aversion to murder, rape and robbery within his kingdom; he promised Maximus some sport by bringing these miscreants to justice, once they had completed their business with the British kings in Venta Belgarum.

The Roman road leading towards the east was broad and well maintained, and the combined guard of Dumnonii and Roman horsemen made good progress. Maximus was uncharacteristically silent during the first leg of the journey to Durnovaria, the town of the Durotriges, so Caradoc watched his guest unobtrusively as Maximus's eyes surveyed the countryside with the practised eye of an intelligent and observant military commander.

What can he be thinking? Caradoc wondered on the eve of their arrival in Durnovaria. Unlike the rest of the Romans, Maximus had been prowling around the campsite and, when challenged by Caradoc, made the excuse that he had been unable to sleep.

Then, when he settled himself in his light travelling tent, Maximus tossed and turned restlessly. From his small shelter on the other side of the dying fire, Caradoc watched his guest and wondered if this clever and charming tribune could ever be totally trusted, before he decided that such pointless thinking was a waste of good sleeping time and sank into a soldier's sleep.

Durnovaria may have possessed a Roman name as a sop to its conquerors, but nothing Roman seemed to exist within this fortified town when the troop approached the first shabby buildings at noon on the following day. As he recalled Caradoc's description of its king, Fiachna ap Tormud, Maximus sat up straighter in the saddle and ensured that his right arm was free and close to his scabbard. Signs of poor leadership were in evidence wherever he looked. Durnovaria was filthy, although its outlook and site were spectacularly beautiful.

Situated a few miles from the shore, the town had the dispirited look of an abused slave. The familiar hovels and crude traders of anything marketable, including girls and boys, were even grubbier and more verminous than the usual detritus that formed a scum around any outland township. As their horses approached the gates to the town proper, Caradoc hawked and spat on the roadway. It was a true measure of his contempt, because the king rarely acted in an uncouth manner.

'You can believe it or not, but Durnovaria was a pretty place in the days when Tormud was king.' Caradoc pointed to the rubbish that had been piled in a section of lower ground to the right of the gates. 'Only barbarians would site the public midden so close to their living quarters.'

Although winter gripped the town and a thin layer of dirty snow was conspiring to hide the worst of the filth, only a blind man without any sense of smell could miss the heaped piles of rotting garbage that oozed with corruption. Immediately adjacent to this space of stinking vileness, three sturdy sets of gallows had been erected. To Maximus's disgust, two were occupied. One corpse was relatively fresh, although the birds had torn away the eyes, the protruding tongue and some of the soft, appetising parts of the dead man's face. More sickeningly, a swollen greenish-yellow carcass hung grotesquely from the other set of gallows and looked as if it had been there for some time. The face had been reduced to a shredded, oozing lump, but the rags of a skirt cutting tightly into the swollen abdomen indicated that this victim had been female.

It was Maximus's turn to hawk and spit now, to remove the taste of decay from his mouth and nose.

'Jesus!' Maximus blasphemed when he saw that three small children, shivering in rags, were scrambling through the filth of the midden in search of stray scraps of food. Anything they found would have to be protected from several wary and starving dogs so hungry that they were prepared to risk stones or sharp weapons to ease the pangs in the hollows of their bellies.

On the battlements above, two warriors looked over at the grisly scene, laughing uproariously at the impromptu and deadly conflict below, while making wagers on who would eventually claim the prizes to be found among the garbage. One of the men threw a crust of coarse bread down onto the snow and laughed as two children tore at each other to win it. As they fought, one of the mongrels stole the tasty morsel, leaving the children to weep and recommence their hunt for sustenance.

Sickened at this callous display, Caradoc kicked his horse into a gallop; relieved to put this ugly scene behind him, Maximus followed in close pursuit.

No one challenged the troop at the gate.

'Fiachna must have been expecting us. I suppose he's had scouts out on the roads to warn him of our impending arrival,' Caradoc said. 'Faugh! This place smells as bad as that midden, if that's possible.'

'I see what you mean,' Maximus replied. He was happier now that his hand was resting openly on his sword hilt. A sensitive spot between his shoulder blades was itching with anxiety, because he could feel hidden eyes following his every move.

The buildings within the walls of Durnovaria were no different from the businesses and houses of Isca Dumnoniorum. The contrast lay in the narrowness of the streets which wound aimlessly between blank-faced structures that lacked any whitewash or colour, but sported bars and boarded windows as if neighbour protected himself against neighbour. The hour had yet to reach noon, but these crooked lanes were mostly empty and the citizens who were abroad were clothed in drab cloaks, while their mouths were covered with ragged mufflers, only their eyes visible. Near the gates, the waiting prostitutes were unwashed and verminous, and they were desperate enough to arm themselves for protection from their peers.

Maximus nodded towards one hard-eyed harridan who was wrapped in a faded and torn blue cloak so bedaubed with mud that its colour was almost indistinguishable from the plaster of the building against which she was lounging. The heavy lines on her face and her scrawny neck indicated that she must have been at least forty years of age. Then, as she called out an invitation, Maximus saw that she had lost most of her teeth.

'I'd have to be crazed to let that grand-dam near me,' he muttered, disgusted. 'I wouldn't touch her, even if she paid *me*. She must be diseased!'

'You tight-arsed bastard!' the harridan shrieked as she made a coarse hand gesture towards the cavalrymen. Her hennaed nails indicated that she must have had some custom if she was able to afford such a luxury, but the reddish-brown talons tipping the skeletal fingers reminded Maximus of dry blood.

A quick glance behind him assured the tribune that his men were maintaining discipline with frozen faces, despite the curses that the whore hurled at them. But then she was joined by several other prostitutes. Made brave by the presence of her peers, the woman picked up a stone from the roadway and threw it.

The missile struck a horse that screamed, reared and had to be forced down by the strong arms of Lorn who was unfortunate enough to be in the line of fire. Several other objects were hurled from both sides of the narrow street and a large clod of mud struck Maximus on the chest.

The Roman drew his sword without further hesitation.

In an instant, Caradoc had wheeled his horse and charged at the drab, who tripped over her own skirts as she tried to run. She sprawled into the slushy mud, exposing her naked buttocks and pudenda, wailing in terror as she tried to cover herself.

Caradoc's horse skidded to a halt above her sprawled form.

'I could kill you for your insults, bitch, but I'll leave your punishment to your lord and master. King Fiachna lacks basic courtesy towards his guests, but he'll not wish to go to war for direct insults against a Roman tribune.'

'Forgive me, master. I lost me temper and me last man to a Roman layabout in Venta Belgarum. Please, master!' As the shrivelled, painted mouth quivered in terror, she was suddenly just a pathetic old woman.

'Leave her be, Caradoc. The insult isn't of such importance that you should sully your blade on her,' Maximus said in a contemptuous voice.

'Listen well, woman! If your king should bother to ask, you may tell him that King Caradoc of the Dumnonii has allowed you to remain alive at the request of Magnus Maximus, second in command of Roman Britannia. Now, get out of my sight . . . all of you!'

Then Caradoc wheeled his horse again, careless of the woman as she scrambled to escape. In disciplined ranks, the Roman and Dumnonii troops trotted towards the heart of Durnovaria and Fiachna's hall.

* * *

By nightfall, any desire to linger in this benighted town had fled for even the most exhausted and indiscriminate guardsman. Caradoc had been informed that King Fiachna had already departed for Venta Belgarum with a troop of his personal guard in attendance. Meanwhile, the fare and beds offered by his steward were so inadequate that Maximus would rather have slept on the roadway.

The face of the king's steward was dominated by lean and hungry features, but was marred by a ferocious squint. Caradoc understood the reasoning of men such as Fiachna, so he decided immediately that this steward must be a kindred spirit to his king, for a steward who couldn't see straight would be of little use. This unprepossessing man must have other talents and the ones that came to Caradoc's mind were not very pleasant.

The steward was almost unbearably arrogant.

'I don't know what my master will say if I have to feed eighty hungry mouths.' He wrinkled his nose as if he could smell something putrid. 'I daresay your clod-hoppers will want to eat us out of house and home.'

Both Caradoc and Maximus stood taller at the implied insult and their eyes hardened.

But this steward was impervious. 'I suppose your men could bed themselves down in the stables. I'd not be prepared to put them into the barracks. Our men have left their personal bits and pieces behind, and I'd have to answer to my king if anything went missing.'

'You're calling us thieves?' Maximus's voice held a clear warning that the steward ignored as he continued to make inadequate provisions for his uninvited guests.

'It's possible that I can find some stew from the barracks.

Failing that, I can ask some of the women to make some bread. We also have cheese and beer, so that will do at a pinch.'

'I am a Roman officer!' Maximus snarled with a deadly glint in his flat, raptor eyes.

Caradoc saw the disaster that was opening at his feet like a crevasse, so he launched into rapid speech in the local language, hoping that Maximus couldn't follow the discussion.

'Listen, you fool. When I inform Fiachna about your stupidity, he'll want your head – if not your balls! He's gone to Venta Belgarum to meet with this particular Roman, not to insult him by referring to his personal guard as thieves. Are you quite mad? The Roman is also known as Macsen Wledig. I'll forgive the insults you've directed towards me, the king of your nearest neighbour, but I will refer your appalling behaviour to your master. I do not soil my hands by using my sword on dangerous idiots. But if Fiachna wished to receive any favours from Magnus Maximus, then he'll probably be out of luck.'

The awful truth began to dawn on the steward, so he paled visibly.

'I . . . I . . . Why didn't he say who he was? I didn't know he was Macsen Wledig. How can I be expected to know every Roman in Britannia if I'm not told anything?'

The steward continued to bluster and apologise by turn.

'My master frowns on any hospitality to travellers who come to our halls,' he wailed. 'He's often refused shelter to noble visitors when they arrive uninvited. It's not my fault, for the master has given me my instructions in these matters.'

The unfortunate man began to gibber in terror. 'The master will probably kill me if his plans in Venta Belgarum fail to reach fruition.' He was weeping now and Caradoc began to feel sorry for the fool.

'I don't care what this Fiachna does to you,' Maximus snapped and, unlike the Dumnonii king, the Roman's eyes held no pity. 'I'll be surprised if he lets you live, so I'd suggest that you take to your heels and run like the mongrel you are. If I were you, I'd depart as soon as possible.'

'Did you understand what we said in that discussion?' Caradoc asked Maximus as he turned to face him.

'I'm very good at languages, my friend. A man must think ahead if he's to succeed in the Roman legions, so I'd be a fool to depend on translations from other men. I try to learn a little of every language in the lands where I serve.'

'Hmmmm!' Caradoc eyed his travelling companion with humorous respect. 'No wonder you've earned the name of Macsen Wledig throughout Cymru.'

Maximus grinned, displaying his long sharp teeth. This man will devour the world if the gods smile on him, Caradoc thought with an uncharacteristic feeling of fear.

Then he remembered the words of Saraid, and her prophecies on Maximus's future.

'Are you still here?' Maximus demanded of the steward. 'You'd be wise to make haste to the kitchens and find me a decent meal.' The steward scampered towards the door.

'With any luck, we can be gone by first light,' Maximus told Caradoc in his controlled Roman voice. 'I have a sudden desire to meet this Fiachna, son of Tormud, and I don't expect we'll remain friends for very long.'

Caradoc almost laughed, but then he realised that Maximus wasn't speaking in jest. He bellowed for his servants as a long and uncomfortable night began.

THE OUTLAW AMBUSH
AT VINDO CLADIA

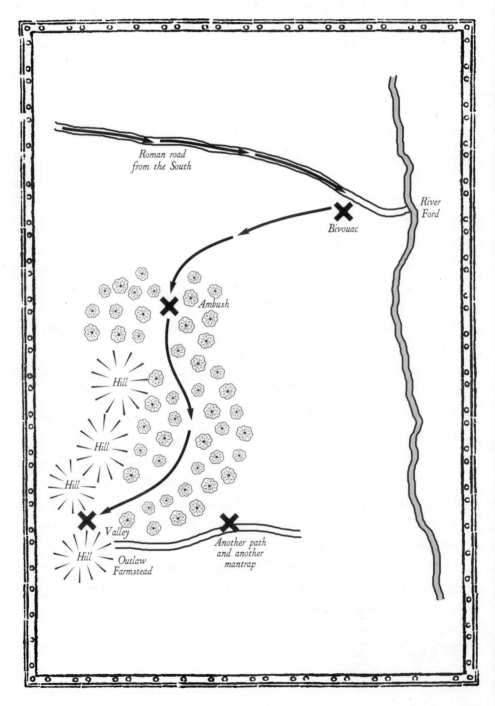

Roman road
from the South

River
Ford

Bivouac

Ambush

Hill

Hill

Hill

Hill

Valley

Outlaw
Farmstead

Another path
and another
mantrap

CHAPTER VII

AMBUSH

He who sees what is now has seen all things.

Marcus Aurelius, *Meditation*, Book 6

As a parting gift for the rudeness of Fiachna's steward, Caradoc ordered his men to confiscate a supply of portable viands before the cavalcade left Durnovaria on the next leg of their journey. They also appropriated one of Fiachna's supply wagons, for their own wagon had already proved inadequate for the demands of their journey.

A number of chickens, still alive and squawking indignantly, were carried upside down by several of the more provident Dumnonii warriors, while the remainder of the guardsmen foraged for sufficient provisions to cater for their next three days on the road. Like termites, they burrowed into the separate kitchens behind the king's hall and eventually the cavalcade left the filthy town with several wheels of cheese, numerous loaves of bread, several cured sides of bacon, and some apples and vegetables. These treasures were supplemented by several flasks of a vile but potent plum brandy. In the belief that they had repaid their absent host for the lice with which they had been infected in the stables, the Roman cavalrymen and British warriors left the Durotriges town without hesitation or regret.

'We'll inform Fiachna that we've helped ourselves to selected items from his winter stores,' Caradoc said with a boyish grin. 'And I'll pay him for the use of his wagon.'

'Certainly!' Maximus agreed.

Both men eyed the ramshackle, much-repaired vehicle that should have been torn apart for its materials some years earlier. Like everything in this town, the cart was ancient.

'If that heap of shite arrives at our destination, we'll recompense him for it. However, I'm still toying with thoughts of demanding reparation for the accusations of thievery.'

Caradoc spent some little time describing the inland route that would have to be followed once the Roman road turned away from the sea. To the north, the poorly maintained roadway led them through a wooded area between two rivers until they reached Vindo Cladia, one of Fiachna's smaller towns. The state of this major road was a clear indication that Fiachna's parsimony extended to maintenance of the vital arteries that kept his trade routes open. Caradoc clicked his tongue with disapproval.

Maximus groaned aloud at the thought of another night with Fiachna's minions as their hosts. 'I swear that I'd rather sleep on bare earth under our tents,' he stated without hesitation, the grotesque memory of that painful night spent under the roof of Fiachna's hall still fresh in his mind.

Tactfully, Caradoc changed the subject to elaborate on what could be expected from the next stage of the journey. They were about to enter Belgae territory and pass through the towns and hamlets that swore allegiance to Bleise ap Bladud.

'I seem to remember that he's the king who tries to turn back time,' Maximus muttered in irritation. 'More dirt, I suppose.'

Caradoc chose not to be insulted. 'Bleise is certainly in need of a good scrub, Maximus, but my people were almost as barbaric in the time of my grandfather's father. We were fortunate in that we had iron and our smithing was the equal of anything that the Romans produced. In fact, Dumnonii lead has been mined and sent to Rome for years beyond counting, so we had close contact with Roman culture long before most of the other tribes. But I can promise you comfort in Bleise's towns, at the very least. The hospitality of townsfolk in this area will be warm, for courtesy is inbred into their ways.'

'I'm relieved,' Maximus retorted, but the irony in his voice was obvious to the king.

'Besides, my friend, I'm well known in the Belgae lands, so we can expect decent treatment,' Caradoc added and watched as the Roman's face cleared a little. Then he recalled the monument known as the Giant's Dance. His face lit up in a brilliant smile.

'Sorviodunum is close to the Giant's Dance, or Carol, so it's a place with a strange history. For reasons that can only be appreciated when you see it for yourself, these long plains attract many soothsayers, itinerant magicians and lore masters. They aren't druids, mind, but they *are* men and women who are eager to take advantage of superstitious and uneducated fools. You should warn your cavalrymen to avoid these charlatans, not to buy charms and to avoid speaking with fortune tellers. They should also avoid all offers to purchase relics from the past. In fact, they should avoid anything that might separate them from their coin.'

Maximus nodded. The tribune knew that scoundrels always flocked around the legions, and were always eager to part young men from their money. But, above all else, he was surprised to find that Fortuna was sending him to the site of the one oddity that he had long desired to see. 'I've heard of the Giant's Dance, but I didn't realise we were so near to it.'

'We'll pay it a visit,' Caradoc decided happily. 'We're so late now that it scarcely matters if we take an extra week to arrive at Venta Belgarum. The kings can hardly imprison us for tardiness, or punish us for viewing the scenery along the path of our journey, can they?'

Both men laughed at the thought of a Roman tribune being punished by anyone, least of all a king such as Fiachna ap Tormud.

'From Sorviodunum, our route takes us to Venta Belgarum via another Roman road. This last thoroughfare is direct and fast. Then, friend Maximus, our diplomatic difficulties will begin.'

'At least I've had an opportunity to evaluate the worth of some of your kings as we've passed through their territories. It's been very educational.'

A quiet voice whispered to Caradoc that the Roman tribune was learning altogether too much about the Britons, while ensuring that very little was revealed about himself – or his motives. He recalled Saraid's ambiguous warnings about Roman intelligence.

As Caradoc explained to his guest, the road headed north once Durnovaria was behind them. The warriors in the cavalcade were fortunate that Roman engineers had built sturdy stone and timber bridges across the many rivers and smaller streams that ran towards the sea, else their journey would have been protracted by an interminable search for suitable fords.

The journey to Vindo Cladia was blessedly incident-free. The land was exceptionally rich and the crude cottages were poorly maintained, perhaps copying the laziness of their master, Fiachna.

Yet here nature had conspired to bless the farmers with her greatest gifts. Their farmsteads were surrounded by chocolate-coloured soil that produced all manner of growing things, including excellent feed, so the ever-present cows could munch contentedly on the last grasses of autumn, regardless of the thin snow. Soon, they would have to move their beasts into the barns for the long, cold months of winter but, unlike the lands around Segontium, the early winter was mild and free from killing frosts. Rivers still tumbled noisily through this fecund land, not slowed by the cold weather.

The surly attitude of the people who enjoyed this bounty was the only thing that had not changed. Forewarned, the horsemen in the cavalcade opted to eat dry rations from their stores and sleep under their travelling tents rather than cohabit with the local population.

Vindo Cladia's name was impressive, but the town was little more than a hamlet in a pretty landscape. Its narrow streets and a general lack of cleanliness blurred the sharp outlines of a number of well-built Roman structures. How these buildings came to be sited in this tiny Durotriges town was a mystery to everyone, including the Durotriges, although chickens seemed to enjoy rooting for food or roosting in the exposed rafters. Now a common alehouse, the largest of the buildings offered shared rooms to weary travellers, but no one was interested in finding space for eighty hard-faced warriors. After several more hours of tedious travel, the cavalcade moved to fields beside the next river, a pleasant spot where the commanders selected a site for their overnight bivouac.

The landscape here was soft and generous, but surprisingly little of it was actually under cultivation, although the flat expanse where the troop made camp showed evidence of the plough at some time in the past. A chain of low hills separated this section of the border lands from Belgae territory. Maximus noted heavy forests at the feet of the hills and their primordial density told him that passage through these barriers would be extremely difficult.

The terrain here was comforting for Maximus, because there was little opportunity for enemy warriors to mount a surprise attack on this bivouac. There was no obvious danger associated with the camp, but thoughts of security had leaped unbidden into his mind.

In obedience to Maximus's orders, Decius sent most of his cavalrymen out in scouting parties. Their ostensible task was to forage for food, although Decius was convinced that their pickings would be slim in this deserted countryside. But Maximus's real reason was a prickling on his forearms and across his backbone, a presentiment of approaching trouble that he didn't quite understand. Something had triggered a feeling of threat, something observed, but so trivial that his conscious mind didn't grasp it. Perhaps his scouts could find an answer.

He would soon discover why the fertile land supported such a small population.

Lorn had ridden out with one of his fellow Romans and a Briton in what had been a fruitless search for a farmstead, or even a source of larger game that might fill the cooking pots in the camp.

Later, when the afternoon was well advanced and the skies were darkening, Lorn thundered back into the camp. He was alone. His helmet was missing and his horse had been wounded by a shallow slice across the chest from which blood was still oozing slowly with every movement of the steed's powerful heart.

Before he could be assisted, the warrior threw himself out of the saddle with a hurried instruction to his friends to care for the animal, before limping painfully towards Caradoc's tent, where Maximus's standard had been planted. The warrior's thigh was leaking blood from a puncture wound at every step, but the weapon used must have missed the vital arteries or nerves, because Lorn was still able to walk, despite his obvious pain.

Although fear and anger spurred his feet, Lorn could only shuffle at a very slow pace. His face was pale from shock and loss of blood, but his eyes were downcast as if he was carrying a shameful secret.

Even with the horror of what he'd seen, Lorn's sense of duty drove him to ensure that his master was made aware of the ambush into which his small patrol had blundered.

'What the hell?' Maximus swore, as Caradoc drew his attention to the approach of the Roman warrior. 'He's bleeding. We'd best call the warriors back to the bivouac until we know what's happened.'

Now Maximus's fears had been made tangible through Lorn's wounding. Now he had an enemy of flesh and blood that he could confront.

One of the younger cavalrymen had started to pull a brass horn from his pack, but Caradoc dashed the lad's hand away before he could raise the instrument to his lips.

'No! No horns! If we're under attack, we'd be wise to remain as quiet as possible.'

Caradoc sent one of his men to alert those warriors who were still in the vicinity of the camp, while Maximus instructed Lorn to rest on a folding camp stool.

'Catch your breath, Lorn. No, my young fire-eater! Don't try to explain yourself until we can make sense of what you're trying to say.'

Panting, Lorn obeyed and accepted a measure of spirits from Maximus's personal flask. The raw plum brandy burned Lorn's throat and its potency took his breath away, but a little colour appeared on his face and he began to tell his commanders of the unprovoked attack that had almost cost him his life.

'We were ambushed on the slopes of that line of hills over there. Six outlaws attacked us initially, by stretching a rope across a path that leads into the woods on the far side of the largest hill. The bastards had dug a large pit just beyond the rope that was built to trap anyone who blundered into it. I think they're part of a large band, so they employed a series of mantraps to protect themselves from outside interference. It worked well – for them! We rode straight into the ambush.'

'Shite, Decius! That hurts!' Lorn yelped as Decius yanked his bloody trews away from the wound where the blood had dried on its edges. Once again, the nasty puncture wound began to flow copiously with fresh blood.

'Don't cry like a babe! Your wound is little more than a flea-bite, so it's not likely to kill you. It's a bit torn inside, so I'll need some of your brandy, my lord.' Decius turned to face Maximus with an enigmatic smile on his weathered face.

The tribune immediately pulled out his flask and removed the stopper.

Decius made no sound, but Lorn's eyes grew very round as he felt himself gripped from behind by several of his comrades. Before he had time to protest, Decius poured the spirits directly into the wound, where it frothed and bubbled wickedly.

Lorn screamed over and over again, while his body writhed and bucked from the sudden assault of extreme pain.

Then, once the liquor had served its purpose and Lorn had caught his breath, Decius applied one of his soothing agents directly onto the reddening flesh.

The slice in Lorn's thigh had been very deep and might still be a source of deadly infection.

'What did they use on you?' he asked the scout as he continued to peer into the puncture wound which appeared to be triangular in shape.

'One of them had a pike, but instead of the normal spearpoint, it had been furnished with a different sort of head from any I've ever seen. It was barbed, so it would have been very difficult to remove from my body if it had penetrated the muscle of my thigh. I was lagging a little behind the others when we reached the mantrap, so I missed seeing the rope ahead of us. Then, by sheer chance, my stallion pulled up before I reached the concealed ditch that swallowed my companions. One of the outlaws came at me with the pike. I was lucky enough to stop the set of barbs from sinking deeply into my thigh muscles, or I would have been dragged from my horse. But it still hurt like the devil. It was a fiendish weapon, Decius, and I think it was one of the smaller barbs that tore at my leg.'

Caradoc thought briefly. 'I think it's a type of stabbing spear with small barbs at the point, as well as a series of larger ones that make the spearhead difficult to remove. My servants use similar weapons to catch large fish. The whole weapon must be pushed through the flesh to remove it. A warrior can be dragged off his horse, or he can be pulled out of the line in a battle if such a spear is used. You have to use it at close quarters and a strong victim can drag the man wielding the weapon off his feet. If this happens, the attacker's advantage is lost. But why would outlaws possess such arcane weapons in these remote parts?'

M. K. HUME

Caradoc turned his attention to Maximus. 'As for an ambush aimed at Dumnonii warriors and Roman cavalrymen, such actions and weaponry are hardly normal for outlaws at any time. Why would a six-man patrol take such a huge risk?'

'Did you see what happened to your two companions?' Decius asked. The decurion was applying some vile-smelling ointment to the wound before binding the sides together. 'Don't fuss, lad, for the evil humours are flushed out when a wound bleeds copiously. That salve has saved my life more times than I've had women, so you'll survive your aches and pains. It's time to speak to the tribune now, so he can make those buggers suffer for their attack on our men.'

'Well, they'd dug the pit and disguised it with branches and tree litter, so I suppose we must have been close to their camp. The pit was right across the path, from side to side. It must have been there for some time, because it was quite large and it would have taken a long time to excavate. I couldn't understand why it's there, except for protection. Such a narrow and disused path wouldn't be of any use, if its purpose was to trap itinerant traders or wealthy travellers who were journeying to the Durotriges or Belgae tribal areas. No, it must have been designed to protect the main base which the outlaws call home. By the gods! How many of the bastards are holed up in there? And why haven't we heard of them?'

'Describe the attack to me, Lorn,' Maximus demanded. 'You can be as detailed as you like. The more you can give me, the better I'll like it.'

'Ercol and Cessus were riding together and they were making jokes. I was a little behind them. The rope caught Cessus when it was pulled taut. By a miracle, he managed to keep his seat, but one of the outlaws was dragged out into the open. Then, before either of my comrades could stop their horses and turn, they fell into the bottom of the pit. They had no chance to evade the trap and tumbled in together. It was a hell of a mess with screaming horses that couldn't climb out of the ditch. I thought Ercol would have been trampled almost immediately, but the outlaws fired arrows into the melee. I heard Cessus scream . . . Hell, I don't know, master, for it was all so confusing. I had time to pull my shield down so their arrows failed to touch me. But before I could do anything else, that bastard caught me with the barbed pike. I remember dropping my shield and I grabbed at the spearhead with my hand. I stopped the weapon from ramming home, but my flesh was torn when the small barbs were pulled back after my horse reared. I tried to extricate my sword with my other hand, but my stallion pulled away.

'That's what saved me. That and my natural caution! I'd be dead now if I'd been joking with Cessus and Ercol. Instead, I was concentrating on the woods on either side of the path, because I was hoping to see a deer or a rabbit, anything that could be tossed into the cooking pots. Perhaps I sensed danger in the woods around us. I just don't know.' Lorn sobbed, deep in his chest.

'What happened to the outlaws? Did you manage to strike a blow?' Caradoc asked.

Decius looked at him curiously, although Maximus understood the question.

'A wounded man bleeds,' Caradoc went on so that all were aware of his reasoning. 'We might have been able to follow blood trails with the arrival of daylight.'

He turned back to the wounded Roman. 'Did you have a chance to revenge yourself on your attacker?'

'I caught the bugger with a sword swipe across the face, and I hope the bastard lost his nose,' Lorn responded with a snarl of triumph. 'My companions had no chance to strike a blow. They didn't even have time to draw a weapon. That pit must have been a hellhole for them and the outlaws still fired arrows down into the trap like the cowards they are. Ambush is a coward's way to fight a battle.'

Lorn had lapsed into painful silence, but he squealed as soon as Decius began to tie the final length of bandage with a tight knot.

'Are you trying to kill me, Decius?' he yelped, then blushed in embarrassment as redly as the blood that stained his scarlet cloak. 'I'm sorry, sir. I wasn't thinking.'

Decius cuffed the young man affectionately, but still contrived to use some force.

Better that Lorn should hurt from a superficial blow from a friend than he should be permitted to blame himself for the abandonment of his fellows. Decius knew that guilt killed more soldiers than his masters would have believed, for the battlefield was an ideal place to commit suicide. But none of the decurion's men would suffer such a fate if he could help it.

'Now you have something to whine about,' the decurion muttered with a slight softening in his eyes. Let the boy hate his decurion, but not himself.

'Did you have an opportunity to learn the fate of your companions before you made good your escape?' Maximus asked. Decius could have kicked his commander for his choice of words.

'My horse took off and I was occupied trying to regain control over it – and myself! I'd have gone back, master, I swear, but those horses in the pit were wild with pain and they would have trampled my companions for sure. The poor beasts must have had broken legs and, in their madness, they would have been more dangerous to their riders than the outlaws. I also wanted to make sure you were warned of the danger we were in.'

'Very well, boy. Stay with the wagon now. No! Don't protest, Lorn, for a man with a wounded leg is no use to me in the field.'

The tribune faced Decius. 'Inform the men what we learned, and order them to mount up. I don't intend to ride away from these outlaws – we'll let them to learn what happens when the foolhardy attack the might of Rome.'

Decius began barking rapid-fire orders, with one eye fixed on Lorn who was still sitting on the camp stool with his head sunk in despair.

The Dumnonii king trotted away to deliver his orders to those Britons who had already returned to the camp. When he turned to discover what Maximus was doing, Caradoc saw that the Roman had stalked off to collect his helmet and weaponry, while Decius was still speaking with some urgency to the young lad who'd revealed the details of the ambush. As the intense conversation between them continued, Lorn was shaking his head and seemed to be protesting, but the decurion slapped him lightly across the face. Although he was very busy organising his own men, Caradoc began to wonder what Decius was about.

Some sixty men were ready to ride now, so Maximus ordered Lorn to take charge of the bivouac during their absence. The young man shook himself and squared his shoulders. Those stragglers who returned after the departure of the main body were ordered to remain in the camp to guard the supply wagon.

Meanwhile, Caradoc offered Maximus the services of a lean, dark man called Raibeart, whom he described as the best hunter in the Dumnonii lands. 'He has eyes like a fox and is well used to hunting by night.'

'Good,' Maximus replied grimly. 'I also have a tracker, Eugenius, who has eyes in the back of his head. His centurion once described him as a ghost who could track a soul over the River Styx into Hades and then return to his masters with coins stolen from the Ferryman. I'll get these bastards! And when I do, they'll learn the error of their ways.'

'Melodramatic,' Caradoc whispered cynically to Trefor, but some of the other cavalrymen were in earshot, so his criticism was noted.

The hastily assembled party set off along the route followed by Lorn during his return to the bivouac area. The tracks of his horse were clear in the sod, even in the half-light.

'You're very quiet, Caradoc,' the tribune observed to the Dumnonii king as they headed towards the low hills and the circlet of forest that grew around the flanks of the nearest one.

'I don't make threats, Maximus. My men know my expectations and my intentions.'

Then the king spurred his horse forward to follow the dark shapes of Eugenius and Raibeart who were still on horseback as they followed the general direction of Lorn's retreat.

The ride seemed interminable, so Caradoc sighed deeply once the tree line was reached. Eugenius and Raibeart dismounted and ran like hounds, their heads close to the ground as they searched for tracks by moonlight. Fortuna must have been smiling down on the troop, for the night was cloudless with scarcely a breath of wind. The troop slowed to a crawl as the trackers sniffed at the earth to find the track that led into the forest.

One of the two trackers made the sound of a hunting owl as both men swung back into their saddles. Although the trees cut out much of the light, the barer tree branches permitted enough to illuminate a narrow track that was just wide enough for two men to ride abreast.

Decius now realised why Lorn had survived. The young scout had been riding behind his comrades because there wasn't room on the path for all three men.

Maximus raised his hand and the troop stopped. 'If you're prepared to follow the track on the left side, I'll enter the woods on the right side,' he whispered. 'If you come across the enemy first, use the owl call and we'll come to your aid. You can do the same, if we find our quarry before you do.'

'You'll hear us because we'll be killing them,' Caradoc retorted. He should have been insulted by Maximus's automatic assumption of the leadership for this attack, but kept his thoughts to himself. Any attempt to find an outlaws' camp in the middle of the night was foolish enough, without the leaders of this debacle fighting over who held the ultimate responsibility.

As it turned out, the Britons handled the woods with more skill than the Romans, men who were unused to fighting in the darkness. Without any further reference to Maximus, Caradoc ordered his men to dismount. Then, leaving two of his men to guard their horses, he led the rest of his command, near to forty in total, into what little light existed among the trees.

Trefor, the hunt master, appeared at Caradoc's elbow like a drift of smoke. The Briton's superior skills shone, even among this group of superb warriors, so his feet made no sound on the sludge of dried-leaf mould and rotten branches that littered the forest floor.

'The Romans are noisy, lord. They're ahead of us, but they can be heard far too easily.' Trefor hissed his warning so that his king was the only man who heard him. 'The ambush site must be very close now. I checked the path and I could see the prints of three horses moving south, with another set retreating northward, in some haste. The latest spoor was driven deeply into the loose earth, because the rider had little control of his animal. There are also signs of fresh blood that has only recently dried. The leaves haven't wilted on the broken underbrush and the sap hasn't dried where some of the smaller branches have been broken on the edges of the forest. Any damage is recent. The disguised ditch is damned close, my lord, so we must avoid blundering into it in the darkness.'

'I agree, my friend. The Romans seem to have ceased ploughing through the darkness, so they might have found something. Head off after them and see what they've got. We'll follow behind you, but I'll ensure our movements are slowed until you let us know what's happening.'

Trefor slid away. Somehow, even with the moon shining cleanly through the web of tree branches, the huntsman had the capacity to evaporate like mist in a strong breeze.

Caradoc gathered his men, who then wormed their way back to the winding path. By keeping to the verge of the tree line, the Dumnonii warriors edged their way towards the noise of stamping horses and a small cone of light.

Raibeart appeared in front of his king with disconcerting abruptness. 'We've found the trap, my lord, although the outlaws took the time to disguise the ditch with branches before they left the scene. I could be wrong, my lord, but I believe they expect us to come after them.'

'What of the two missing warriors? Are they dead?' Caradoc tried to keep his voice calm as they approached a bend in the track where the light exposed some thin shrubbery along the verge.

'They're dead. They were left to rot in the hole, along with their horses. The bodies have been stripped of all their valuables and the horses have been butchered for the meat on their haunches.'

Caradoc spat with disgust, not because he wouldn't eat horsemeat if his need was great, but because the outlaws had taken the time to select the best cuts, yet left fellow humans to rot under the bodies of the beasts.

Judging by the expression on his face and the deep creases between his eyes, Raibeart remained concerned.

'What's wrong, Raibeart?' Caradoc asked.

'Our Roman friends are far too noisy, both on foot and on horseback, so it's almost certain we'll be ambushed if we keep moving. It's craziness to blunder into a trap out of anger or our lack of familiarity with the terrain. We're announcing our intentions with every step.'

Caradoc nodded. His warrior was only voicing aloud what had become painfully obvious to all the Dumnonii cavalrymen.

The track seemed to have widened a little. Someone had lit a makeshift torch and the darkness was driven back to the verges by the feeble light. Caradoc led his men towards the mellow glow.

He stopped before the lip of the trench where Maximus was standing with his arms akimbo. The horses were stamping and whinnying, so Caradoc was certain that any advantage of surprise they might have won had vanished, because the twenty Roman horsemen had travelled so fast and so hard. Fortunately for their safety, any ambush sites prepared by the outlaws would probably be closer to the enemy camp.

'Raibeart! Trefor! Scout ahead! We need to know where the enemy camp is, and whether they have set up an ambush to kill us,' Caradoc instructed the scouts in a deceptively calm voice. He resisted the urge to stare into the ditch before issuing his orders, because he was familiar with this scene in all its ugliness.

As the two huntsmen vanished into the darkness, Caradoc finally stepped to the lip of a trench that was twice the depth of a standing man, and at least twice as wide and twice as long. Its sides had been reinforced with roughly shaped timber to prevent a collapse during the months of the thaw. He immediately concluded that this mantrap was a permanent defensive strategy, for no one would dig such a huge hole on the off-chance that a few British or Roman warriors *might* blunder into it. Almost certainly, other mantraps would have been placed between here and the site of the outlaw's camp, since these outlaws had proved to be so cautious.

The bodies of the two horses almost filled the narrow space. They had been slashed across their exposed throats as they struggled to escape, but their contorted bodies showed that they had died in agony. The bottom of the hole, where it could be seen, was a bloody and churned mess.

Inside the trap, the two warriors had been smashed between the thrashing hooves of the horses and the deadly weight of their dying bodies. From the gashes, the arrow-wounds and their agonised faces, these two men had died hard. Their mouths gaped in silent screams and their bones had been fractured by the weight of the struggling and kicking horses so that their limbs had been twisted into unnatural angles. Steeled by years of ghastly carnage, Caradoc didn't flinch. In fact, he burned the horror of the two bodies into his brain so he could recollect it later when he had the time to reflect on the evil enacted in these dark woodlands.

He could see that a number of boots had churned the lip of

the trench at the point where the outlaws had watched the hapless warriors struggling for life below them.

Perhaps this fact, written in the damp sod and mud, was the main cause of Caradoc's disturbed state. At least six of the outlaws had watched the dying warriors who must have pleaded for assistance. But they had been rebuffed. Perhaps the outlaws had joked as they fired arrows into the ditch, but the arrow wounds didn't appear to have killed the suffering warriors and seemed almost to have been fired at random. Eventually the outlaws had cut the throats of the horses so they could harvest the juiciest cuts of meat, and they could have offered the blessing of death to the dying men as they did so. But the renegades had rejected all pleas for clemency. Caradoc would not forget what the footprints in the mute earth were telling him with such eloquence.

'Fill the trench in as it stands,' Maximus ordered in a rough voice, although Caradoc supposed that this Roman would have seen more graphic sights at any number of battles. With a fixity of purpose that Caradoc knew would be immovable, the Roman tribune was staring down into the trench with a face as stern as any granite statue.

'The perpetrators of this ambush will pay for shedding the blood of this Roman. The outlaws who killed my soldier were aware of his status. These bastards have stolen his helmet and legionnaire regalia as trophies, so I'll crucify every man who dared to sully the corpse. Don't attempt to dissuade me from revenging myself on these killers, Caradoc. With you, or without you, I intend to have their bodies and what passes for their souls.'

Caradoc expelled the air from his lungs in one long exhalation. How dare this Roman threaten him?

'Can't you count, my lord? A Briton also lies there,' Caradoc stated firmly. 'He's been stripped of all he owns, just as your man was defiled. More importantly to me and to my warriors, this man was a Dumnonii. I've known him from childhood. His wife will go on through life without her husband, and his children will cry for their cold hearth. You may commence your search for these murdering bastards, if so you choose, but I intend to track them down in the light of day, rather than make a hare-brained dash into a further ambush, fuelled by blind arrogance and insult. My forty men will stay here, and I will use the time to remove our dead comrades from this mantrap. I plan to cremate them at a time when we have some leisure, for the Dumnonii leave no warriors behind when they die on alien soil. You may go on if you must, Tribune Maximus, but I thought you were a sensible commander.'

Angry and frustrated, Caradoc stalked away from the torchlight, issuing orders as he went. He sent for the horses and ordered his warriors to form a defensive perimeter that encircled the area of the path and the verge of the trees. Then six brawny young men were lowered into the pit to release both bodies so they could be raised to the surface.

Meanwhile, warriors were told to secrete themselves among the tall tree trunks to act as warning piquets, while Caradoc selected an oak tree for himself that boasted a forked branch just above head height. Nimble as any boy, the king swung up into the tree to settle his length along a limb and wait for the first light of a new day.

CHAPTER VIII

DEATH IN THE MORNING

Even a god cannot change the past.

Agathon, *Nicomachaean Ethics*, Book 6

'Caradoc?' The peremptory voice cut through the king's dreamy thoughts like an axe-blow. 'Where the hell are you? Stop sulking and talk to me!'

The tone alone was insulting, so Maximus's words snapped the king into full consciousness.

Refusing to hurry on principle, Caradoc stretched his cramped muscles and the slight rustle of a branch under his left foot alerted the Roman to his presence. Peering into the gloom, the Roman looked upwards until he saw a flicker of movement as Caradoc bared his cowled head.

'Would you please come down and discuss our problems sensibly, man to man? I'll get a crick in my neck if I have to talk up to you.' Frustrated, the Roman scuffed and tore at the earth at the base of the tree with his booted foot.

'Please! I'll apologise if that's what it takes to assuage my supposed insults to your honour. We were both angry at the fate that had befallen our men.'

'Supposed? Sulking? You make me sound so unreasonable, Tribune.'

Maximus had seemed curt and petulant rather than apologetic, so Caradoc responded in kind. But he understood that this attempt to placate him by the Roman was probably the best penance he could expect.

Caradoc swung down from his branch and landed nimbly in the leaf mould. The cold air caused him to shiver, although his woollen gloves were still in place and he was wearing a knitted cap under his cowl.

'Well then,' Caradoc replied as he rose to his full height and stretched before wrapping himself in his cloak. 'How much time do we have?'

'It's no more than three hours past moonrise, so sunrise is still some hours away.' Maximus stamped his cold feet and blew on his fingers to warm them. His breath was steaming in the chill and the amber of the guttering fire was reflected in his feral eyes.

'Your scouts have returned, but they will only report directly to you,' the tribune snarled.

Caradoc could tell that Maximus was irked by this state of affairs and he swore audibly. 'They could have reported to you, for God's sake.' Caradoc knew he would obviously have to start mending bridges. 'Where are they?'

The Roman whistled softly to summon the scouts and Trefor and Raibeart appeared within seconds, sauntering along the pathway with the easy grace of athletes. When they reached the two commanders, they bowed low to both men, marks of respect that immediately mollified Maximus's mercurial nature. Caradoc sighed with relief.

'We did exactly as you asked, Lord Caradoc. We moved parallel to the pathway and there was no sign of activity for some distance,' Trefor reported. 'Then, in a small valley between two hills, we almost fell over two of their sentries. They were concealed in a hide of branches and leaves on the left side of the path, but they were fast asleep.'

'Did they see you?' Maximus asked crisply.

Raibeart picked up the thread of the report.

'No, my lord. We were careful and we gave them a wide berth. We crept downwards toward the head of the valley where we could see a light and smell woodsmoke on the wind.'

'A farmhouse?' Caradoc asked, and Raibeart nodded.

'We reached a low rise above the encampment, so it was easy to observe the outlaws as they carried out their various tasks,' Raibeart continued. 'An old farmer's cottage and a large barn seemed to be at the heart of their hiding place. We thought that most of the outlaws were probably asleep, but we counted at least fifteen men who were awake and preparing for their departure. There were three fully loaded wagons. They didn't have horses in the traces and the farm eventually became silent. Again, Trefor is sure that they're loading everything they own to get away at first light. I don't think they expect you to make an attack so soon after our scouts blundered into their ambush.'

'We took the opportunity to find two other sentries, but we let them be in case other men are sent to relieve them during the night. If that had happened, the outlaws would have been warned that we'd found their camp,' Trefor added. 'I hope that decision meets with your approval, my lords?'

'Yes! Excellent, thank you,' Caradoc replied as his mind worked furiously.

Their report given, the scouts bowed their heads and waited

for orders. Although they had spent the whole day in the saddle and half the night tracking their prey, their bright eyes and obvious enthusiasm spoke powerfully of their eagerness to see their task come to a satisfactory conclusion with a red death for the outlaws.

'You'll need rest,' Caradoc advised them. 'If you wish, you can stay here with the corpses of our dead while we deal with their killers. You've done more than enough in this pursuit.'

The two huntsmen blushed with pleasure at Caradoc's praise, but they refused the offer to stay behind and catch up on their sleep. Trefor was appalled. What Briton of any mettle would sleep while his companions went into battle and risked their lives?

Caradoc had no choice other than to agree, so he ordered them to find food for themselves, water their horses and then rest until camp was broken. The two warriors obeyed without question and departed.

The night had reached that hour when dying men succumb to their fate and demons steal around cottages to bring dread to the belly and horror to the mind. Moment by moment, the mostly invisible moon was sinking lower into the sky behind the cloudy winter skies. The air was freezing and Caradoc could smell fresh snow on the breeze. He had hoped to reach Venta Belgarum before the weather turned for the worse, but the rising wind warned him that they were too late.

'We should leave now, if those animals are planning to take to their heels,' Maximus insisted, now that Trefor and his friend had departed to find some rations. 'The bastards might slip away unless we attack them at first light.'

'I agree! But any movement must be silent. I'll leave two of my men to mount a guard on our dead, although they won't be happy at the thought of being left behind.'

Maximus agreed, and went into action with typical Roman efficiency. Within a short period of time, the troops had wrapped their feet and their horses' hooves in cloth to muffle some of the sounds of movement. Then the riders moved noiselessly along the narrow path like wraiths. The three scouts ranged ahead to silence all the sentries.

The moon was almost down by the time the troop reached a low rise that overlooked the outlaws' enclave, so the cavalrymen, on foot now and leading their horses, fanned out quickly to ensure that none of the renegades could escape. Maximus and Caradoc dismounted and assessed the farmhouse and barn with cool, analytical eyes.

'Those wagons are fully laden and they're very close to the ground. I can almost hear the axles groaning from here,' Caradoc hissed. 'I don't know what's in those chests, but it's heavy.'

'I imagine these outlaws have been preying on the border towns for years. The farm is well defended and the men have dug themselves into the landscape like cattle ticks,' Maximus whispered, as his eyes continued to range over the landscape below them.

A low stone wall had been erected across the margins of the field, close to the farmhouse, that would provide a simple line of protection for any defence of the property. Although the wall could cover archers during a skirmish, it was below waist height, so horses could jump over it with ease. Caradoc was certain that any obvious defence by the outlaws could be easily countered. He had no hesitation in sharing his thoughts with Maximus.

'Your precious kings haven't taken any action against these bastards, so they've become bold. They are so confident that they are prepared to attack a large cavalcade under Roman protection,' Maximus replied. 'Their arrogance has grown and grown,

117

because they've been allowed to live comfortably in this remote valley for a long time.'

Maximus had a point. The defensive wall, the farmhouse and even the mantraps indicated that these outlaws had occupied this valley for years. The local kings had obviously done nothing to track down, contain or destroy these outlaws who were a clear threat to travellers and the local population.

'Aye!' Caradoc sighed. 'I suspect that some of our kings have paid a tribute to these renegades to leave the farmers and traders alone and unmolested. If my suspicions are correct, those wagons will be filled with gold and treasure that's been taken from the poor and the vulnerable, or bribes given to the outlaws by kings who should have cared for their subjects. In which case, neither the kings nor the outlaws can be trusted.'

'We should wait until they're ready to depart, and then fall on them from two sides. I'll lead my men to the cottage while you attack the barn, Caradoc. Trefor believes the bulk of the outlaws will be asleep in its straw but we can change targets if you wish. It's all the same to me!'

Caradoc was affronted. He wondered if Maximus doubted the ability of his men to mount an attack against such a large force.

'No! My Dumnonii warriors will welcome the opportunity to burn that rats' nest to the ground, with or without the lice that breed in it.'

Without any further chatter, the two commanders moved to join their troops. The orders were quickly passed down through the ranks so, experienced in the ways of war, the cavalrymen rested beside their horses and waited for the signal to begin the attack. Meanwhile, the wind began to rise with sleet in its teeth.

Just then, a light bloomed within the cottage as a fire pit was lit. Several raised voices carried to the watchers on the hill, but the sense of the words was lost in the distance. Again, some activity became obvious inside the doors of the barn and a solitary figure ventured out, moved to the side of the outer wall and stood reflectively.

'What's he doing?' Maximus asked.

'He's taking a piss. The others will join him soon. Faugh! Only the dumbest of beasts shit and piss near the place where they eat and drink.' Caradoc was contemptuous of such foolish behaviour.

The area around the buildings began to boil with the shapes of busy men, all of whom were loading wagons, moving horses into traces or setting fire to the barn and cottage. The flames rose quickly, throwing the bodies of the outlaws into sharp relief, as those among them who were mounted on horses were forced to control terrified animals who wanted to shy away from the fire growing in intensity behind them.

'It's time, I believe,' Maximus said formally as Caradoc nodded in agreement. 'Mount up,' he shouted. The time for subterfuge was over.

The Roman and British warriors threw themselves into their saddles with joy, for the night had been long, cold and frustrating. Finally they could see an enemy ranged before them and it was probable that the three wagons at the farmstead contained riches that all could share. Like hounds quivering with excitement as they waited for their master's order to pursue game, the Britons and Romans held their horses in check. Their eyes were fixed on the outlaws below them who were still ignorant of their presence.

'Form up,' Maximus bellowed, careless of the noise. 'Show these bastards what *cataphractarii* can do, even if we are few in number. Ride them down!'

Before Caradoc could issue his own orders, the tribune had

led his small troop of horsemen thundering down the slope.

'Quickly! Form into line abreast,' Caradoc roared. 'Let's teach the Romans that it's not the first to arrive on the field who go on to win the day. Kill everyone! No quarter!'

The Britons seemed to hang suspended for a moment before they followed their king down the hill, galloping directly towards the press of bodies around the wagons. The outlaws attempted to manoeuvre their heavy wagons into a defensive formation, but the horses in the traces were terrified by the proximity of the flames, the radiating heat and the noise that battered at them from all sides. They fought against the outlaws, struck at them with their hooves and tried to drag the wagons away into the pre-dawn darkness.

Into this chaos, the disciplined Roman troops descended on the outlaws like the sweep of a peasant's scythe. Outnumbered, but with the precision that becomes second nature after years of training, each Roman picked out an outlaw as a target and struck him down. Then each man wheeled his horse before renewing his attack on another target. As those outlaws who weren't mounted tried to gut the Roman's horses from below, the *cataphractarii* forced their horses to act as deadly weapons during the hand-to-hand encounter. The horses had been trained to strike out with their hooves and use their great weight to pound their enemy into a red paste. Meanwhile, the Britons had encircled the surviving outlaws, forcing the renegades to keep their backs to the murderous fire in the stables while facing a line of inexorable, highly trained warriors.

One large and shaggy outlaw threw down his spear in surrender, but Caradoc merely laughed, drove his horse at the press of bodies and beheaded the man before retreating beyond the reach of defensive spears and swords. His actions were so fast and precise that Maximus, who saw the manoeuvre from the corner of his eye, was forced to grin in admiration.

'Better to have him as a friend than an enemy,' he muttered, before charging at a filthy, red-bearded villain who was fighting two-handed with a sword and an axe.

For effect, Caradoc continued to roar out his commands in the local tongue. He wanted these outlaws to anticipate the ugly inevitability of their fates.

'No prisoners! This battle is for our dead at the mantrap. Kill them all!'

And so, as dim light heralded the beginning of a new day through a haze of freezing rain that set the fires to guttering, the cavalrymen obeyed their masters with a fierce joy.

'They were worse than fools,' Caradoc decided as he sat on the lip of the wagon and wished fervently that the outlaws had left some shelter that could protect his men from the biting sleet.

Maximus tore his gaze away from his blood-soaked mittens. His hands were damp and sticky, so he removed the gloves and cast them into the remains of the fire where they began to smoulder.

'Well! I'm amazed! They set fire to their buildings before they were ready to leave. That was sheer stupidity! They could have held us off for some time if they'd kept the barn as a defensive fortification. As it stood, there was nowhere to run and several were cut down with their backs to the flames. The rain put out the flames, but it was far too late to save the outlaws.'

'These men weren't professional warriors,' Maximus agreed. 'Their leader surrendered soon enough when he realised they had no chance of fighting their way out of the trap they were in. I'm sorry I disregarded your orders, Caradoc, but I wanted to come to grips with our enemy. I wanted to stare into the eyes of the bastard who had the gall to attack and kill my man.'

Caradoc had the distinct feeling that the outlaw chief would rue the day he surrendered to the Romans.

'Did he tell you who trapped Ercol and Cessus and killed them?' Caradoc also nursed a desire for revenge, although he had been raised to crush such time-wasting personal urges.

'Of course! We have two men awaiting retribution once we've dealt with this place.'

'Then God save their souls, my friend, because I know you won't be merciful.'

The two commanders sat in relative companionship after purloining several wizened apples from a basket in what proved to be a supply wagon. Hungry now, they munched their way through what would be the only food to break their fast during a busy morning.

'Have you carried out an inventory on the other wagons yet? I told Decius to give Trefor whatever assistance he needs,' Maximus asked. In fact, wealth meant little to him unless it could further his influence. He took far more pleasure from the contents of the supply wagon which freed them from foraging or dependence on the charity of farmers and townsfolk.

'Decius and Trefor are both working on the lists as we speak. I trust both men implicitly,' Caradoc added, in case Maximus held any doubts about their honesty.

Maximus shrugged idly to indicate his lack of concern. 'That wagon is sitting quite low and its wheels have been driven down into the mud by the weight it's carrying. Only gold or silver, other than lead, will have that kind of mass and I don't believe outlaws would try to carry lead away with them.'

'That lot wouldn't be interested in lead. Not them!' Caradoc laughed at the mental image of thieves trying to protect ingots of that base metal with their lives.

Around them, British and Roman cavalrymen were busy. Destruction of the detritus of battle was an important consideration after a battle like this one. The threat of disease from rotting corpses was minimised by interring the enemy dead in mass graves while cavalrymen were detailed to collect valuable weapons and equipment that could be reused in the future.

The dead outlaws were stripped of all items of value and their corpses were cast onto a pitiful pile in the very place where they had been relieving themselves an hour or so earlier. Forlorn wails or weak screams of pain indicated places where the victors found a wounded man who was still alive. Without healers, and far from any form of medical treatment, wounded men would die horribly, so the cavalrymen had no hesitation in putting them out of their misery.

As for their own casualties, such a violent conflict left few who were wounded with survivable injuries. Like their enemies, the severely wounded cavalrymen received the quick release from pain that each warrior understood. Those with survivable wounds were treated by their comrades with some assistance from Decius and his healer's kit.

'It's poppy juice,' Maximus explained succinctly when Caradoc saw Decius making a concoction. 'Pain kills, so poppy must be kept for those who can be saved. Decius knows what he's doing.'

Caradoc watched as the two officers completed their rough catalogue of the wagon's contents on a scrap of hide, using a stick of charcoal as a makeshift writing implement. Then, before they approached their commanders, Decius ordered three badly wounded cavalrymen to be placed onto the tray of the wagon. Their dead would be tied over the backs of their horses for the return journey to the main camp, where Caradoc and Maximus would preside over their cremation. The commanders had decided that urns would be easier to transport than corpses, and the remains wouldn't be a source of decay and disease.

Once they were satisfied with the arrangements for the return journey, Decius and Trefor approached their masters with their folded strip of hide.

The two officers bowed low.

'How go our prizes, Decius?' Maximus asked.

'Those incompetents were far better thieves than warriors, my lord,' Decius began to explain. 'Trefor has the accounting, but they've obviously collected tributes from a variety of sources, as well as the proceeds of their thievery. There are ear-jewels in a box in the wagon with dried blood on the pins that screwed into the earlobes of wealthy women, and there are a number of necklaces, bracelets and rings that have been stained with blood. Some rings are still on the fingers that were cut off, while other valuable gems were simply torn off dead bodies.'

'I've itemised some of the smaller objects, including most of the silver amulets and rings that would have been worn by farmers and traders. I counted one hundred and forty-six items in just one of the boxes,' Trefor added. 'But there are another four boxes in the wagon that have to be assessed. They are even larger than the first box. There's a huge mountain of jewellery.

'We've also counted a number of silver and gold bars, all of which were minted and marked with the legion insignia. The gods alone know what hands these ingots have passed through, but the outlaws have obviously been given them by a wealthy patron. I doubt this vermin had the ability to take them off a Roman paymaster in normal combat.'

'Can you make a guess at who would have paid the tribute?'

Maximus asked sharply. 'I'd like to know some of the details before I reach Venta Belgarum, if that's at all possible.'

'I'm sorry, my lord,' Trefor replied as he handed over the long list of their spoils. 'Except for the markings of the Ninth Legion, there is nothing to indicate the source of the treasure.'

'Eburacum? That gold has travelled far.' Maximus furrowed his brows. 'I'm certain the outlaw chief will tell us, so summon the men, Decius . . . Trefor! I'd prefer we made examples of these bastards in public.'

Both cavalry troops were assembled as the two surviving prisoners were brought before the commanders for interrogation. Although the light was watery and the sleety rain had stuttered to a halt, the clouds marching in from the direction of the sea gave a promise of more rain later in the day. With his nose bright red and beginning to drip from a head cold, Caradoc prayed fervently that their dead comrades could be sent to the fire and their ashes collected before the weather finally broke. They had been extremely fortunate to lose so few warriors, mainly because their cavalry had such a significant advantage over foot soldiers in such an engagement. On the other hand, they had four severely wounded men. These men would not be able to ride.

The same pessimistic thoughts about the weather had occurred to Maximus, so he ordered three of his men to collect suitable lumber from the partly burned barn. This material would be used to construct a cross for use once the interrogation of the captured outlaws had been completed. At the same time, the ruins of the cottage would be packed with the corpses of the dead outlaws and set on fire.

While the living outlaws stood in a cleared space in front of the barn with ropes around their necks and their arms bound behind them, several of the cavalrymen began the task of setting the ruined cottage alight. A container of oil suitable for burning had been found in one of the wagons; the still-damp timber took a little time to catch, but even wet thatch will smoulder and then burn eventually. The reek of roasting flesh was soon making breathing unpleasant.

'The beasts of the forests and the air will clean up anything that the fire rejects,' Maximus explained. 'But we will have done our best to minimise any threats of disease.'

Caradoc merely grunted and covered his nose and mouth with his scarf until the wind changed direction and blew the reeking smoke away from the massed cavalrymen.

Once the problems of dealing with their dead were resolved, Maximus gave orders for the two outlaws to be dragged away from what was left of the half-burned barn. Both men were bruised, bleeding and covered in filth, although little of their private thoughts could be read on their faces. They wore their hair long and their faces were covered with bushy and untended beards. Not only were there no warrior plaits on their heads, but their hair was tangled and matted. The drab-coloured locks were too dirty for any real colour to be discerned and Caradoc found himself scratching. Even from several spear-lengths, the Dumnonii king could see lice crawling along the receding hairline of the outlaw chieftain.

The second outlaw, who admitted to being at the site of the mantrap ambush, was a sorry specimen of a human being. Short in stature, the man possessed a fearsome squint and a nasty sword cut had almost sliced away the lower cartilage of his nose. Caradoc noted that the wound had been covered by thick salve and a makeshift bandage had been tied around his head; it had slipped to expose part of the wound which was oozing anew.

The chieftain was an unusually large man, at least twice as

heavy as his fellow prisoner. Had that excess flesh been muscle, he would have been a formidable warrior but, unfortunately, rolls of fat larded his belly and shrouded his arms, thighs, chest and neck in quivering layers. Even so, the man's meaty lips and piggish eyes spoke eloquently of a blustering character who threw his considerable weight around.

The smaller man was terrified of his master, mainly because his chieftain glared at him every time the unfortunate minion snivelled with fear. He was caught between the monster he knew so well and this strange Roman with the deadly eyes.

'You!' Maximus began, while pointing his dagger negligently at the smaller man. 'What's your name, villain. I like to know the names of those men I'm about to crucify.'

'But I never killed anyone,' the man wailed, aghast. 'I nearly lost me own head when I tried to stop one of them devils.' The man jerked his head towards Trefor, who responded by spitting at the feet of the outlaw, and then glaring balefully at him.

'I want your name! I won't ask again, unless you'd prefer that I assist your memory with my knife.' Maximus spoke softly, but Caradoc and the outlaws knew that this meant he was probably at his most dangerous.

'My name is Robat . . . Robat!' he shrieked, before subsiding into a limp whimper.

'Can you give me any reason why I shouldn't crucify you on what's left of the barn doors? Your master didn't give you permission to kill one of my men in such a filthy and cowardly fashion as those you killed in the mantrap. I now have the souls of two of my dead cavalrymen who are screaming to me from Hades. They are demanding justice because you denied them an honourable death.'

If possible, Robat paled even further under the ingrained dirt of his face. 'I was only on scout duty, my lord, and I damn near pissed meself when these two men rode their horses into the trap. I dropped me pike and I only picked it up in time to strike at the third rider who tried his damnedest to take off me head with his sword. By the time I picked meself up, me friends had done the business on the two men in the pit. You can kill me if you must, master, but please kill me quick. I didn't kill yer men. I can swear it on me mother's life.'

'Your mother's a whore and you're a filthy liar,' the outlaw chieftain yelled, spittle spraying. 'Where's your balls, you useless pile of shite?'

Trefor elbowed the fat man in the face and enjoyed the crunching sound as some of the villain's few remaining teeth broke from the force of the blow.

'Your own answer will decide your fate, so don't whine. I can't stand cowards,' Maximus answered in the same tones he used when he was bored. Robat almost fainted with terror when the Roman's basilisk stare bored right through him.

Now that one outlaw had confessed, Maximus turned back to face the chieftain, a man who was far less likely to be frightened into submission.

'You! Whatever your name is! I'm led to believe you have gold from the legions of Eburacum among the treasure in your wagons. How did you come by Roman property? And how is it that you possess such a large quantity of that precious metal?'

The outlaw chieftain spat at Maximus who stepped aside deftly to allow the globule of phlegm to miss his face. Trefor hit the fat man at the very centre of his diaphragm, so that the chieftain doubled over. He was forced to gasp for air and his chins wobbled grotesquely.

'I expect honest answers from you, or I'll be forced to

encourage you to speak,' Maximus repeated in his usual calm monotone, but Caradoc could feel the repressed violence that underlay it.

The outlaw chieftain shook his head vigorously. Maximus was certain that this man was filled with unspoken hatreds and intended to take his secrets into the shades with him.

'For the sake of all that's holy, Elphin, tell 'em what they want to know or we'll both suffer,' Robat shrieked, his voice as thin and as high as a young girl's.

'Shut your face, you arsehole!' Elphin snapped as he spat a tooth onto the muddy earth.

'You'll tell us what we want to know, either just before, or just after I start working on your balls,' Maximus continued. 'Who or what are you protecting? Would they provide the same protection for you?'

'No! Those bastards wouldn't, but I'm not going to tell you anything either,' the outlaw chieftain snarled, his hirsute face puckered with resentment and hatred. 'Get it over with, you Roman bastard. You know you're going to kill me anyway, regardless of what I say. You can get one of your underlings to do your dirty work for you, if you haven't the balls to do the job yourself.'

'The local kings paid it,' Robat interrupted. 'It were Fiachna and Bleise that paid it.'

'Shut up! Shut up!' Elphin was struggling in his bonds like a mad thing.

'Why?' Caradoc asked, confused by Elphin's refusal to give what he considered was relatively minor information. The outlaw looked up at the Dumnonii king with eyes that leaked tears and blood in equal measure.

"Cause we give nothing, nothing at all, to them that think

they rule us,' Elphin explained as if he was speaking to a child. Caradoc flinched away from the loathing in the outlaw's expression.

But Maximus remained unmoved. 'Kill this one,' the Roman said, pointing at Robat. 'He's earned a quick death.'

He turned back to the outlaw chieftain.

'But my friend Elphin and his moral scruples are a totally different matter. We're going to allow him to live, but he'll be pinned onto a cross that will be nailed to the barn doors.'

According to Trefor, Robat died quickly and silently. Decius beheaded him from behind in such a fashion that the small outlaw had no time to feel the thrill of fear.

Caradoc watched with a sick disgust as Elphin was nailed to the door through both wrists and ankles. His abhorrence was such that he almost missed Decius's actions when the decurion climbed a rickety ladder he had found in the ruined stables. His head was close to Elphin's and he whispered something into the agonised man's ear. Then he held a small flask to the blue lips of the slowly choking man whose own excessive weight was causing his chest muscles to contract in such a way that breathing was almost impossible.

With some difficulty, Elphin swallowed the dark-brown liquid, despite losing a small amount that escaped to drip down his chin.

Decius climbed down the ladder and cast it away. His face was quite expressionless as he gathered up his kit and headed towards his waiting horse. Speechless and confused, Caradoc watched him as he rode off.

The three wagons were already on the move, piled high with valuable trophies, the spoils from the outlaws' supplies and possessions, and the four wounded cavalrymen. The execution had taken some time, but Maximus had no intention of waiting until Elphin died or lost consciousness before leading his command back to the safety of their bivouac.

'Let the crows feast on him while he's still alive,' the Roman ordered.

Their departure had been delayed until the early afternoon because of the time needed to burn the farmer's cottage and prepare the convoy for the short journey to the bivouac site at the river. Eventually, with a blazing fire roaring through the ruins in which the corpses had been unceremoniously dumped, Maximus decided that he'd achieved everything possible to cleanse the site of the battle.

As the whole convoy began to trundle away, Caradoc watched the strained breathing of the doomed man who was trying to drag in just one more breath into his straining airways, and could see that the outlaw's eyelids were beginning to flutter.

What had Decius given him? What had the decurion whispered to the outlaw before he offered him the flask of dubious brown liquid?

Elphin's head drooped and his bitten and bleeding lips sagged open loosely. But then, above the outlaw, a large, very black crow fluttered through the open roof to sit on an exposed rafter. Without the slightest trace of fear, the carrion bird gazed down at the earthly king with glittering eyes that seemed ageless, malignant and wise beyond measure.

More crows and ravens flapped onto other beams and waited for Caradoc to depart. Suddenly, the king's confusion was blown away. He remembered the jar of poppy juice and considered how easy it must have been to add the soporific to Fiachna's brandy. Elphin would lapse into unconsciousness, and then he would die. Ultimately, he would cheat Maximus of his revenge and the birds would feed on a dead man rather than on living flesh. Maximus would never know, but perfect justice had still been done.

But why had the loyal Decius cheated Maximus of his victory?

Caradoc rejoined his men and his horse joyed in the short canter that the king permitted. Ahead of him, Maximus rode carelessly at the head of the column, his squared shoulders demonstrating his triumph and satisfaction.

But Decius snatched an occasional glance over his shoulder at the wagons until he noticed that the puzzled Caradoc was staring directly at him.

CHAPTER IX

VENTA BELGARUM

There is one safeguard known generally to the wise, which is an advantage and security to all, but especially to democracies against despots – suspicion.

Demosthenes, *Philippic*

'There it is,' Caradoc shouted, his tired face wreathed in smiles. One hand pointed over the long swathe of agricultural land that ran on each side of the wide, cobbled Roman road. Although snow blurred the ploughed furrows with several inches of pristine whiteness, the deep brown soil was obviously prime farming loam. Off to one side, Caradoc recognised two more arrow-straight roads heading towards a cluster of towers in the distance. Like the spokes of an enormous wheel, all roads, great and small, led to Venta Belgarum, the lovely city of the south. At last, Caradoc and Maximus could feel the relief and satisfaction that comes with reaching a far-off destination.

The crisp winter air stung the eyes and its sweetness made the heart beat a little faster in Caradoc's chest. But the air, its smell and the transparent light were familiar to him. He hadn't seen Venta Belgarum since he was a boy, when Llyr, his father, in company with Caradoc's grandfather, had brought him to this clean and ancient place to see the true face of Constans, Emperor of Rome, who was the son of Constantine, the emperor who built Constantinople, the golden city of God. Caradoc had scarcely known whom he was meeting, but he was struck by the realisation that Constans was so young as to be little more than a boy.

Even after so long, Caradoc could remember that gilded, magical day more than twenty years earlier. The regal visit had taken place in winter which, with the wisdom of hindsight, now seemed an odd time for an emperor to travel. White snow and marble had covered everything with a mantle of crystalline purity so that Caradoc, with his wild hair and square body, had seemed a poor thing in comparison with the boy emperor. Constans had been dressed in a snow-white toga liberally edged with purple, and some minion had wrapped him warmly in a thick cloak of wool in that same opulent colour.

His grandfather and namesake had pointed out the tall, slender figure of Constans as the young ruler entered the hall.

'See that cloak, boy? A hundred men died to make the purple and another hundred perished in agony for the toga and the fur-lined boots he wears so easily. The Roman rulers act as if they are gods, so the lives of other mortals don't matter. Remember this lesson, Caradoc, because all you'll ever be to Rome is a source of military fodder or frightened slaves that will provide him with his purple dye.'

'I don't understand, Grandfather,' the boy had stated, for he had been raised to ask questions. 'It's a pretty colour, but it's not worth so many lives.'

His grandfather had been a gifted storyteller, so Caradoc

could see the bearded shellfish, black and plump, as they were shovelled into the great vats where the dye was extracted. That process released a deadly poison, so the slaves who worked with the dye vats sickened quickly. Without exception, they deteriorated into blindness and died from raving lunacy. 'Such a high cost for vanity,' Caradoc Major had said with a sad sigh.

The boy Caradoc had never forgotten the tall, unearthly figure, and the nervousness that threatened to overcome him when he was ushered forward to be presented to the emperor by both his grandfather and his father. The emperor had the beardless face of a boy and his arms and legs, under the golden cuffs of his office, were smooth, hairless and feminine. His eyes were wide and innocent, although Llyr had whispered that Constans had seen sights of such depravity that the eyes of lesser men would have shrivelled in their heads.

Eight years later, that same golden boy perished, dragged from a temple in the Pyrenees and murdered out of hand by Roman cavalrymen. In the political void that followed, many men would claim the crown of empire and die to hold it, but Caradoc would always remember one golden youth in a marble hall at Venta Belgarum. He could still taste the flavour of his first Falernian wine.

The last leg of the journey to Venta Belgarum had been cold, but uneventful. Once the troops had returned to their bivouac outside the hamlet of Vindo Cladia, they were forced to spend a day collecting firewood to burn the corpses of their six dead, for one of the wounded had perished on the journey. The cremated remains, packed in wooden boxes, travelled now with the outlaw's hoard of treasure, until such time as they could be relinquished into the safe hands of their families.

Sorviodunum rested gracefully in bare plainlands, although an extensive area of forest needed to be traversed to reach those windswept expanses. The town appeared like a small jewel from a distance, and was constructed from plastered stone, thatch and painted timber. The influence of Roman culture was obvious; tall-peaked roofs, topped with rushes, stood cheek-by-jowl with lower ones of red terracotta tiles, pinned together in an unlikely collaboration that should have been ugly, but somehow worked. When the cavalcade rested on a low rise outside Sorviodunum, Maximus was struck by the freshness of the air, for the winds soughed over the long plains, to blow away the woodsmoke from local industry and the fires of the township. The skies seemed very high and wide, unlike the close clouds and low fogs of other towns in the south.

The Roman road passed through land that reeked of age and strangeness. Maximus had commented on this oddity, so Caradoc tried to explain one of the most bizarre places in all Britannia. Covered by sheets of snow, a number of large stones could be seen in the distance.

'Come and ride with me, Maximus, and I'll tell you a tale.' He smiled. 'We are only an hour from some of Britannia's true wonders, if you're prepared to see them. You've seen Rome and all its architectural marvels, but I'll wager a golden coin that you've seen nothing to rival this place. Are you bold enough to accept a wager, my friend? Our troops can rest here, before we find a suitable site to bivouac for the night.'

Caradoc's easy manner challenged Maximus's competitive nature. Their relationship had suffered a little during the outlaw attack, but although Caradoc had not forgotten the Roman's thrusting need to be in control, matched with his cruel application of justice, he was mature enough to remain cheerful and friendly. On the other hand, the self-absorbed Maximus scarcely noticed animus on Caradoc's part.

Any residual irritation that Maximus felt was because of the king's obvious physical prowess and the devotion of his warriors, talents which annoyed the Roman for reasons that he admitted were spurious. Each day, Caradoc's skills forced Maximus to face the unpalatable truth that this British king was as able and as beloved as he himself was.

Caradoc's challenge goaded the tribune. Within a short span of time both men were ready to ride, although Decius and Trefor insisted on accompanying them, while the remainder of the troop rested in the weak sunshine. A pleasant river bank was adjacent to the spot where they had halted, so Decius issued instructions to Celsus, his assistant, that the guardsmen should water the horses and permit the placid carthorses to rest after many days of hard labour in the traces.

Maximus recalled his earlier curiosity concerning the Giant's Carol, so he was eager to see this wonder. Even more pressing was his determination to win Caradoc's wager.

After several days of thick forests, leafless under their mantle of snow, these windswept plains had a spare beauty all their own. Maximus felt as if he could see forever, for few trees blurred the long lines of the horizon and the plain had obviously been a site of human pilgrimage for generations, demonstrated by the multitude of paths worn through the sod to reach the chalk beds below. How many thousands of bare feet had so worn these paths that, centuries later, their tracks were still evident in this empty place?

'You must speak to your men, Decius.' Caradoc reinforced his earlier warnings about charlatans and frauds who preyed on innocent travellers visiting the carol.

Caradoc's earnestness convinced the dour decurion that the warning was kindly meant. For his part, Decius decided to make a concerted attempt to be more forthcoming, for he sensed that Caradoc was a man of exceptional depth. Sooner or later, Decius knew, he would be forced to have a private conversation with the king, for secrets between them had been kept sacrosanct. Yet, for all that, he knew that an explanation was owed.

They rode on in silence over fields of dry grass dotted with with patches of thick snow. The Giant's Carol appeared suddenly in a low fold in the ground. It wasn't very large by Roman yardsticks, so Maximus was a little disappointed, but the odd structure was awe-inspiring, once the onlookers had time to consider the tales that these rough-hewn stones could tell of ancient times and long-dead people.

'What is it?' Maximus asked after dismounting and climbing to the top of a circular mound that hemmed in the monument.

Caradoc shrugged. 'We don't know. Charlatans will tell you it's a temple and the large, flat stone in the centre is an altar. They've convinced the credulous that men and women were sacrificed here for thousands of years. But they don't know the truth, and neither do I.'

But, sunk in thought, Caradoc gazed at the huge mound and ditch that ran around the perimeter of the whole precinct. For some reason, he believed that Decius could understand the wonder of the carol.

'The ditch that your master is standing on must have taken many, many generations to build. Curious treasure seekers have dug into the mound, but all they found were some of the picks used to dig into the hard soil. What do you think they were made of?'

Decius's curiosity was piqued. 'Iron?' he hazarded. 'Perhaps even bronze?'

'No! The ancients had no metal at all, so they were forced to use what tools were available to them. They used deer horn! Yes, this huge ditch was dug and piled up using picks made from deer horn. Can you imagine how many picks broke and how difficult they were to replace? Consider the decades that this one task must have taken – the centuries – and this is the smallest part of the carol. Then try to convince me that Rome could match the wonders of the task that was set before the original builders.'

This last challenge was aimed at Maximus, who was examining the circle of huge stones in the centre of the monument, but Caradoc knew his words had been heard.

Decius dismounted and allowed his reins to dangle, so his horse wandered away in search of dried thistles at the base of the mound. Excitement sped the decurion's stride as he hurried towards a large, single stone that was rearing out of the soil at an angle. From its top, Decius could see along a straight avenue of stones that ran directly to the largest part of the open structure, a horseshoe of massive trilithons that consisted of two uprights and one crosspiece, the altar stone lying in the centre of this strange focus point.

'Did it ever have a roof?' Maximus asked as he scratched at an irritating fuzz of black beard. 'Shite, but I'll be glad when I get an opportunity to remove this hair from my face.'

Caradoc's short beard only required an occasional trim, so he considered the Roman predilection for clean-shaven faces and hairless bodies to be a time-wasting eccentricity.

'I don't see how the structure could have been roofed,' the king answered. 'Besides, look closely and you'll see a series of circles that have been cut down to the chalk layers. These purposeless holes run around the whole monument. They are inside the ditch and the mound.'

'There's also a smaller circle of single stones that are of a strange blue colour,' Decius added from atop the single monolith where he was balancing on his haunches.

'Aye! The legends insist that a giant carried the stones across the Oceanus Hibernicus from the north of Hibernia and planted them here.'

Maximus snorted derisively. 'Do you expect us to believe that giants built this . . . this thing?' The Roman failed to notice a dull, red flush that was climbing up the Dumnonii king's face from his throat. Decius realised that Caradoc temper was fuelled by his master's thoughtless insult.

Yet, when he spoke, Caradoc's voice was as calm and as even as ever.

'The old tales say that the stones come from far away. But I can assure you that many men have searched for similar stones and have found nothing like them in the lands of the Britons. None of them exist in the south-west, at any rate. So how did these mystery stones reach here? We'll agree that they didn't fly. Although the blue stones are smaller than the monoliths of the full circle and the central horseshoe, they're near as tall as a man. How would you like to be the one who volunteered to move them?'

'I have no doubt that my Roman engineers could do it,' Maximus boasted.

'I'm sure they would make a valiant attempt, but could they show us how the large stones that straddle each pair of the larger monoliths were raised into place? And how do they remain in such an unstable position?' The Roman strode across to the large, irregular stones of the inner circle. The distance between them was such that Caradoc had to shout to be heard, so he began to walk towards his friend.

'While I'm on the subject, your Roman engineers couldn't have used the tools used by the original builders,' Caradoc added once he had reached Maximus. 'There'd have been no ropes or metal tools, and there'd have been no fulcrums. All they had were flakes of flint, some fire and the use of stone, hand-held hammers to shape the rock. Perhaps they could have used plaited leather, but I've been forced to wonder how any part of this monument could have been built.'

Staring up at these imposing groups of rough-cut and split trilithons, Maximus was soon scratching at his whiskered jaw again. The stones seemed to be bonded exactly, although they had apparently been cut without the use of iron or bronze. Nor was mud used to bind stone to stone, or the concrete used by the Romans. But Maximus still refused to believe that those old architects shaped such huge stones with simple flint blades and hammers.

This isn't possible, he told himself. If Roman engineers couldn't design and build a monument like this, it can't be done. Yet he acknowledged an uncomfortable possibility. Could another culture have surpassed Roman skills and practical applications?

Meanwhile, Decius had followed his horse around the horseshoe of trilithons at the centre of the monument. Some years earlier, the decurion had seen the wonders of Rome, the Colosseum, the Baths of Caracalla and Trajan's Memorial column when he had been stationed in Italia with the legion. This small cluster of undressed stone could fit into most Roman buildings many times over, but Decius knew that size alone was not the mark of greatness. This structure was a mystery that had obviously taken centuries to erect and he, for one, was puzzled and amazed by its every aspect.

He remembered the eye-popping awe he had experienced when he was first confronted with the wonders that human beings could create but, on this occasion, Decius felt removed from these unfathomable stones and their purpose, so he was repulsed by them. Somehow, their great age and the patience needed to erect them sparked no understanding or compassion in his heart.

However, this revulsion had its uses. Peering upward, while trying to recognise something in the construction that was either familiar or recognisable, Decius finally saw why the giant crosspiece, the lintel of the trilithon, had not fallen from its precarious perch where it was balanced at a height of at least two men above the ground.

'Look, sir!' Decius shouted, his hand pointing to the right edge of the lintel. 'Do you see? The stone has been carved to create a peg in the bottom of the crosspiece.'

Decius trotted to the other end of the lintel and peered upward to see if another peg was holding it in place at the far end.

No! The carving skills of the ancients couldn't be exact with the primitive equipment that was available to them. The edge of a circular hole showed a narrow, dark rim shaped like a half-crescent, but the purpose of this hole was a mystery to Decius.

'A peg on the lintel at one end fits into a hole on the top edge of the left monolith that stands upright,' the Dumnonii king explained. 'I believe that the fit would stop the stone lintel from slipping out of place. Would you agree with that?'

Caradoc grinned at Maximus, for he held a genuine admiration for the cleverness of those ancient builders of ancient times.

'Can you see the other end of the lintel? It has a hole in it. I'll bet my balls that there's a peg carved into the top of the upright on the right-hand side. It's just a really simple concept.'

Light began to dawn on Maximus's face. 'Aye! You're right! When the ancient builders used a hole and peg construction, the stones were locked together and only a blow from our largest catapult could bring the three stones down. Ingenious! But the whole building still has no purpose. There's a circle of stones with a horseshoe inside the circle, and an altar within all of that. What's the purpose? There's not even a roof to keep the rain off it. You've presented me with a pointless mystery, no matter how enticing the puzzle might be.'

Then Maximus mounted his horse and rode off laughing. By the time Caradoc joined him, the Roman was hiccupping with belly laughs.

'So? What's so funny?' Caradoc demanded, as the monument of the Giants' Carol became smaller and smaller in the landscape behind them.

'You'd have to be Roman to appreciate the irony, Caradoc.' Maximus tried to explain. 'You lot are such humourless, grim people. If we believed you, Britannia is the centre of the world, the one place that the gods protect above all others.'

'So?' Caradoc snapped.

'See? You're doing it too, my friend. I thought you had more sense.'

Caradoc spurred his horse so his stallion leaped away from the other three men. Decius's face showed embarrassment and Trefor was sullen with affront, for they had heard Maximus's comments as clearly as Caradoc had been insulted by them.

'The priests tell us that the shadow of the stone you were

standing on runs along the avenue when the sun rises on the morning of the solstice. On one day of the year, and that day only, a shaft of light from the sun reaches the altar and bathes it in light. What say you, clever Roman? Why would barbarians use the earth and these stones to find one day alone, of all the days in the year? You speak to us as if we are backward, but which of your great buildings can do such a wondrous thing?'

Even Maximus had finally realised that Caradoc was seriously offended, and moderated his tone.

'Don't be concerned, Caradoc. Don't you see? Britannia has mysteries aplenty but, as with your system of tribal leadership, the Giant's Dance is perplexing, indescribable, pointless. If I were to flatten the monuments and destroy them, nothing would be lost, just as your precious cabal serves little purpose.'

'You insult me, Roman. I am the king of the Dumnonii tribe and I don't see myself as pointless.'

'You're piqued over a few mysterious stones. Shite! Romans never feel a need to pander to the local savages. How many of us have bothered to visit Tintagel, invited or not? Five? No! Two? No! One? Only me! I'm the first Roman to visit the impregnable fortress of Tintagel, and I'm at a loss to understand why I was asked to meet with you.'

Maximus was serious now. Caradoc knew the Roman was practising some subterfuge for some unstated purpose, but he had no idea what the tribune's plan could entail. Still smarting from Maximus's ridicule, the Dumnonii king's manner remained stiff and his responses were curt.

'We are different, we two,' Caradoc said at last. 'Although we state that we each want some of the same things.'

'And how are our differences such a bad thing?' Maximus challenged him, as he was forced to kick his stallion in the ribs to keep up. 'As long as we each take pains to avoid insulting the other, or his people, I've found that we rub together surprisingly well. We defeated the outlaw band by working together as one, didn't we?'

It was Caradoc's turn to chortle. 'Those outlaws were hardly a match for *cataphractarii* or trained British cavalry. Shite, Maximus, they were fortunate to possess decent weapons, despite lacking any real fighting ability or tactical skills.' The Roman felt his lips twitch with irritation again.

'At any rate, you've now seen the Giant's Dance and, strange as it seems to my eyes, our British people didn't build it. It's far older than we are in the long-gone history of these islands. One day, I'll show you another monument that would be of interest to you. It consists of a representation of a giant horse carved into the sod along the side of a hill, so huge it can only be seen from a distance. The horse is depicted by the chalk that lies just below the topsoil. Again, we know nothing of its history, but our people accept that area is a plain where the gods once walked.

'Gods or no gods, all I want from life at this moment is to see the walls of Venta Belgarum. You've promised me a bath in that city and I'll insist that you keep your oath.' Maximus scratched at his armpit below his armour and recoiled from the reek of his own flesh.

Caradoc laughed at his fastidiousness. What would Maximus make of the always-filthy kings of southern Britannia?

In the days that followed, they passed through Sorviodunum and headed south along wide, well-kept Roman roads. Even so, both commanders decided to stop short of Venta Belgarum in order to prepare for the difficult diplomacy that lay ahead of them.

Their bivouac, an hour's ride away, was a collection of leather tents grouped around the five wagons that carried the outlaw's hoard of treasure, their wounded warriors and their supplies. But the grey afternoon clouds smelled of snow.

So far, heavy snow had fallen behind them, but Fortuna had been kind and the worst weather, while snapping at their heels, had failed to slow their journey.

None of the men cared to spend another night in the open.

Caradoc realised that any Roman goodwill towards the British kings in Venta Belgarum would be eaten up by the promise of another night under leather tents surrounded by snow and freezing cold. Still, provision must be made to ensure the security of their treasure.

They would also need accommodation for their men and a secure storeroom where they could mount a guard over their valuables for the entire duration of their visit in Venta Belgarum. Caradoc considered that the comfort and happiness of their men was paramount after their long and trying journey.

He called Trefor to him and instructed him to take a long and rather tart message to Gwaun ap Mairtin, with a request that King Caradoc and Magnus Maximus should be welcomed and housed in a manner in which their respective ranks entitled them.

Trefor recited the message back to his master twice, but his brows twisted with an unasked question.

'To Gwaun ap Mairtin, King of the Atrebates tribe and Master of Venta Belgarum, greetings from Caradoc ap Ynyr, King of the Dumnonii tribe.

'I trust that you are well and have not been worried at our late arrival. We have been delayed until late in the season and await your pleasure an hour's ride from your city.

'Tribune Magnus Maximus, a close kinsman of the great lord, Theodosius, Overlord of Britannia, accompanies me with his personal guard. He has been wearied by our journey and would appreciate a warm welcome indoors where he is out of the inclement weather.

'I trust that accommodation of a suitable nature can be quickly found for our guest and his men so they don't have to endure another night under their leather tents. I would also welcome your hospitality, as we have been in the saddle for two months on what should have been a relatively simple journey. We are in need of a secure room urgently, where we can place items of some importance and value under close guard.

'There are eighty-two of us and five wagons, plus a slightly larger number of horses.

'May the lord be with you.'

After reciting the message with all its pauses, emphases and expressions that Caradoc desired, Trefor's face was as bleak as a thunderstorm. Caradoc noted his huntsman's distress and finally succumbed to curiosity.

'Why are you so glum, Trefor? Surely, you'd like to have a decent bed if Gwaun were to offer us accommodation as early as tonight?'

Trefor coloured hotly. 'I'm sorry, my lord. I never meant to upset you through my confusion.'

'Well! Spit it out, Trefor.'

The huntsman wrung his hands with nervousness. The king would discover his servant's reservations and might be offended. Gulping audibly, Trefor surged into speech.

'Why must I recite your words like a slave? Surely, we would petition Lord Gawain ap Mairtin more appropriately if I were to carry a scroll to him? This way, we both appear to be ignorant barbarians and our Roman friends will scoff at our awkwardness.'

'I wish this message *could* be delivered by virtue of a scroll, Trefor. I'd certainly express myself more bluntly if I wasn't fearful of Gwaun's reaction towards you when you delivered my message. But I can't send a scroll because the kings can't read! They have priests who manage their writing for them, but I'm not prepared to share information with one of Gwaun's creatures. Would you want me to depend on some third person to explain my messages to the other kings?'

Surprised and appalled, Trefor's expression changed. As King Llyr had insisted that the clever sons of prominent men within his court were to be educated, along with his sons, Trefor had always been grateful for the education he had received from the old Dumnonii king.

'No, my lord, I wouldn't! If they truly cannot read, you would be most unwise to trust a priest to explain your wishes accurately to any of these kings. You're wise, my lord, as always. And I have been a little foolish.'

Touched, Caradoc embraced Trefor, who swore he would petition Gwaun for palatial quarters for them as soon as possible.

'Perhaps we'll ask for the best quarters for the Romans, Trefor. But I'll be happy just to be warm, because this journey has been one of the coldest for many years.'

Trefor rode away into the deepening snow. Before Caradoc had time to return to his tent, Maximus approached him, curious about the huntsman's task.

Knowing only that the truth was appropriate, Caradoc explained his message to the Atrebates king and why it had been sent by hand. Maximus snorted with amusement.

* * *

Two hours later, a small party of visitors arrived at the bivouac site.

A shivering young nobleman with a fur-lined cloak, an elegant tunic that reached to his knees and beautifully made fur-lined boots eased his way out of the saddle with the assistance of one of his two guardsmen. Every movement and gesture was exaggerated and he minced over the ground to meet the visitors. Caradoc realised that this beautiful young man wore high heels on his boots to give him an illusion of extra inches. Moreover the exquisite youth had cultivated both a lisp and a careless drawl.

'May I welcome you to Venta Belgarum, Your Highness? My master, King Gwaun, is so pleased that you have finally arrived. He was very worried that you might have been attacked on the roads, but now that I see your warriors, I cannot imagine what fools would dare to attack such strapping young men.'

This speech was accompanied by much eye-rolling and fluttering of stiblum-darkened eyelashes, such that Caradoc had to control an urge to box the young man's ears.

'Your name, sir?' Caradoc inquired with only the slightest movement of his traitorous right eyebrow. 'You'll have some wine, I'm sure? We can offer you a reasonable Falernian. Oh, I've forgotten my manners! You may make your bow to Magnus Maximus, of whose importance to Roman Britannia you must have been made aware.'

The exquisite appeared to be unconcerned although both men were presented with the exaggerated display of a preening peacock.

'Silly me! You are the king. I must have left my head back in Venta Belgarum. My name is Drustan ap Drust and my father is the lord of Portus Adurni. I'm thrilled to make your acquaintance,

Lord Tribune. My father will be so proud that I've made the acquaintance of one of Britannia's noble protectors.'

Then, to the embarrassment of all present, he offered his soft white hand to the Roman.

Gods! I hope Maximus behaves himself, Caradoc thought. He watched the tribune smile like a hungry wolf who has spied an especially plump lamb.

Maximus gripped the soft wrist directly over an ostentatious wristband and squeezed.

The edge of the band immediately bit into the gilded youth's flesh and he blanched, even as his own limp grip tried to clutch at the tribune's wrist-guards. Well schooled, the youth made no complaint, although his mobile face revealed his pain and chagrin.

Trefor looked at Caradoc and the two Dumnonii men shared a moment of contempt, before Caradoc placed his own right hand over the entwined brown and white fingers, appearing to endorse the friendship expressed, but warning Maximus that he must release the poor fool.

'I'm truly honoured to meet a nobleman from the aristocracy, especially one whose ancestral lands include the trade town of Portus Adurni. Your birthplace plays a crucial part in the passage of vital trade and this excellent wine probably passed through your family's cellars.'

The Roman is amusing himself at the boy's expense, Caradoc thought furiously. I hope I don't have to pry his hands off the boy's throat.'

Just when Caradoc decided he would have to intervene in earnest, Maximus released Drustan's hand, offered the boy a brimming horn of Falernian wine and threw his arm over the boy's quivering shoulders.

'Drink up, lad, and then you can tell us what Gwaun has planned for us. I hope that he hasn't suggested another night in the snow, for I'd be very upset.'

Maximus laughed loudly to show he was only jesting, while Drustan opted to gulp at his wine. His eyes darted from king to tribune like a frightened rabbit.

'Yes! ... Yes! Silly old me! King Gwaun is rushing to find suitable quarters for your guard, even as I speak. King Caradoc and your good self will be quartered in luxury in Gwaun's new hall. You may each have two body servants, who will use quarters adjacent to yours. Whenever you are ready to leave for the hall, my lord will be eager to meet with you and express his pleasure at your arrival. Oh, and a large strongroom attached to your accommodations has been provided, exactly as you requested.'

'Well, then! I suggest we strike camp immediately. What say you, Caradoc? Yes, I thought you'd be eager to meet with your fellow kings. We'll be right behind you, Master Drustan ap Drust. Perhaps we can speak about trade and the movement of trade goods through your fine home in Portus Adurni, once we are ensconced in the city.'

Caradoc noticed that the lad looked appalled at the thought of answering detailed questions about such a crass subject as trade.

The bivouac was struck with alacrity. Although they were tired, stiff and hungry, no warriors made complaints at the order to pack their gear, mount up and head for Venta Belgarum. In Gwaun's city lay warm beds, four walls, women, hot food and hot baths for the Romans. What more could a soldier demand of life?

'Is that extremely pretty idiot playing a role as a catamite? Or is he really as useless as he seems?' Maximus hissed his questions at his Dumnonii comrade as he mounted his gelding. The weary horse bridled and refused to answer to the reins until Maximus struck it across the buttocks with the flat of his gladius.

'The young man's an exquisite, and that's the truth, although I'd say he's really as he presents himself. Be honest, Maximus. Such a display in a land of overtly masculine warriors takes courage. But it says more about Gwaun's court than it does of Drustan's character. I fear you will be constantly irritated.'

Caradoc, though grinning, was seriously alarmed. He might despise the natures of his neighbours, but he was appalled at the prospect of the tribune causing an open breach between the tribes. A friendless tribe in Britannia could find existence difficult.

'Gods, Caradoc! I've got nothing against bedding a sweet, plump boy. I had a short-lived passion for a fellow student when I was a young man and was sent to Athens by my father to gain some polish. I assure you, Caradoc, that the love of a man for his fellow man is damned near compulsory there. However, such a friendship as mine was quite different to that of those mincing fops who possess so much power in the Western Empire in Rome. They make my teeth ache.'

And with that curt message, Caradoc was forced to be satisfied.

As it was his first visit to Venta Belgarum as a grown man, Caradoc was relieved to see that this southern city was still beautiful, especially under its cloak of snow. It was also very clean. The small houses that clustered around the northern gates of the city were far less odorous and grimy than those they encountered in Durnovaria and Vindo Cladia. Any executions were obviously conducted out of sight and the city midden was also, mercifully, sited where visitors to the city would never see it – or smell its odours. Because the cavalcade had arrived during the evening, few of the circular huts or storefronts were lit and few owners were in evidence to watch the guard of armed men pass by their homes.

At the city gates, the guardsmen waited while Drustan issued instructions to the gatekeeper through a small door that had been cut into the huge main gate to allow for easy access. Caradoc noted that Drustan stamped his feet and squawked his anger at the length of time it took the snaggle-toothed door-keeper to unbar the twin gates from the inside. As he waited, Maximus examined the vast iron hinges and the mechanisms of the portal and was impressed at their strength.

Inside the city, the streets were dark and some laneways were just as narrow as those in Durnovaria, but Maximus's experienced eyes noted that the main thoroughfares were wide and cobbled in the Roman fashion. The streets were noticeably bare of domestic rubbish and, while the air carried smells of excrement, cooking fires, meat and cabbage, the combination was not unpleasant.

The buildings in Venta Belgarum were much like those in the public faces of Durnovaria. Shop fronts lined the main thorough-fare, where a succession of wine shops and inns, designed for travellers, were in evidence. Whores stood negligently near lit doorways, but these women were wrapped in colourful cloaks and the glint of cheap jewellery showed at their wrists, ankles and throats. Decius cautioned his men against any fraternisation with the *working girls*.

'You'd be surprised at the diseases you can catch from these night kittens, boys. I suggest you find a maid or a bored wife if you need a woman, but don't risk your balls on these lovelies.'

As the horses jostled down the main thoroughfare, a single

horseman emerged from the gloom ahead of them. Drustan squealed with pleasure and relief, for he was obviously keen to rid himself of these brutal visitors.

'Oh, Hellyn, I'm ever so glad to see you,' Drustan trilled. 'Has Master Gwaun allocated the accommodation for our guests?'

Hellyn was another slender boy-man, but this lad was very tall and wore a mane of reddish-brown hair with elan. Although his face was clean-shaven and cadaverous, his hair hung almost to his waist in a mass of ringlets that any woman would have envied.

'You can lead the guard to the hall of warriors where room has been allocated for their use, Drustan. You can leave the nobles to those of us who have more experience, so run along now. I'm sure you'll do very well with these nice young lads.'

An experienced pair of hazel eyes ran over the column of troops. Trefor felt himself blushing at Hellyn's overt invitation, although he had loved men in his teens and was not usually offended by such things.

'Sirs, my master has instructed me to take you to your quarters,' Hellyn told Maximus in a warm, convivial voice. 'Can I assume that these men are your servants? Excellent! We have already arranged for an adjoining room to be used as your strongroom.'

Hellyn's gaze enveloped Trefor and Lorn, who both coloured under his aggressive gaze.

Meanwhile, Caradoc asked the two scouts to speak privately with him on an urgent matter. 'Mount a four-man guard over the treasure-wagons as soon as we arrive at our accommodation. Once we've settled into our rooms, ensure that all our men are detailed to transfer the valuable items into the strongroom. Then a four-man guard must be mounted over the room until such time as we depart Venta Belgarum for the journey home.

The guards will be on duty for six hours at a time, with no slacking in their behaviour while they carry out guard duty. There'll be no unfortunate incidents while we're here. Is that understood?'

Caradoc now nodded towards Hellyn to show that the party was ready for the short walk to their accommodation.

'Follow me, good sirs. Your servants will be sharing an apartment beside yours. As we have so many guests this week, my master apologises for the fact that you must share, but we have a series of rooms for your use, including a small triclinium if you wish to entertain other guests as well as yourselves.'

Hellyn fluttered his lashes beguilingly.

'We are so excited by your visit, Lord Maximus. We've never had a military man as a guest who stands so high in the protection of our isles, so we're agog to hear what exciting tales you can tell us.' Hellyn spoke without a trace of sarcasm, but no one was fooled.

Compared with Drustan, this gilded young man was another matter altogether. Somehow, the lad inserted himself and his horse between Caradoc and Maximus so their ride into the heart of Venta Belgarum was decidedly awkward. Both the king and the Roman became interested in the buildings on either side of the wide roadway, so Hellyn was kept busy describing the new structures raised by Gwaun during his reign, including a large public bathhouse.

'The common people are gradually being brought around to enjoy an occasional soak in the hot waters but, unfortunately, they are accustomed only to washing their whole bodies at birth and at death – so what can one do?'

'What indeed?' Caradoc responded urbanely. Somehow, he managed to quell a bubble of laughter.

'I can see their point,' Maximus stated. 'The weather is hot in Rome so Romans need to bathe because the heat causes so much sweat and disease. Conversely, Britannia has a very cold climate, especially in the winter months.'

Finally, atop a low rise, the small group of horsemen reached a large, flat forecourt that was surrounded by two-storeyed buildings that seemed to lean inward towards the earth, as if bowing in homage. Across the forecourt, a huge hybrid building constructed from timber and stone rose up in two storeys.

'You are looking at Lord Gwaun's magnificent new palace,' Hellyn said proudly, one hand pointing out items of interest. 'My lord designed the building himself, so he spared no expense.'

The guests had only a few moments to dismount, retrieve their saddlebags and hurry to join Hellyn on the broad stone steps that led to the palace.

The building squatted rather than soared. It boasted huge doors twice the size of the tallest man, carved in the tribal design called interlace, which provided a continuing, decorative line that defied the viewer to find the beginning or the end. Two sinuous dragons spat poison and malice out at any newcomer who wished harm to the owner of the hall.

The heavy timber seemed to soar upwards as if it was ready to take wing. Even Maximus was impressed.

'Behold the dragon,' the tribune said with a flourish of his hand.

'The dragon of your legion was never so lean and hungry,' Caradoc pointed out. 'That's a northern dragon if ever I've seen one.'

Once the doors swung outward, the next few minutes were confusing and disorienting as the small party followed a group of four soft-footed servants carrying trays of food and drink, soft towels and the commander's saddlebags. The route taken as the honoured guests were led through the dark building was long and circuitous. Eventually, they reached a set of doors that seemed to indicate they had reached their destination.

With a flourish, Hellyn opened the door that led into a large room divided into two sections. The front part of the room possessed several comfortable stools and eating couches arranged around a low table. He showed Trefor and Lorn to a small side room, but rough as it appeared to be, the pallets on the beds were stuffed with fresh, clean wool and Trefor's heart sang.

Back in the corridor, Hellyn unlocked a large storage area that had the virtue of being windowless. As there was only one entrance, both the tribune and the king decided that this strongroom would suffice. Maximus, sniffing, noticed a faint aroma of apples.

Hellyn saw the Roman's flaring nostrils and apologised immediately. 'In the past, lord, we've used this room for food storage, especially in winter. I'm tolerably certain that there hasn't been an infestation of vermin in this new palace but . . . the old building! Well! I've never seen so many rats in my life. And when the king ordered the building to be burned, I swear there were hundreds of the little buggers . . . all scaly tails and sharp teeth!'

'Thank you, Hellyn. I'm sure we can manage now, since you've been so efficient. I'll just take the key for safe-keeping,' Caradoc said smoothly, trying to draw Hellyn's attention away from the tribune who was looking very green around the mouth.

The door had no sooner closed behind the young sophisticate than Maximus was cursing vigorously. Eventually, he had to draw breath.

'I hate rats, especially their tails and the noises their claws make when they're running on the floor,' he snapped. He was shivering with distaste.

Caradoc quickly sent Trefor and Lorn to organise the unloading of the treasure and its transfer to the strongroom. Several trips might be necessary because some of the men would need to carry out guard duties at various points along the route.

There was no time like the present to carry out this task, for there was little domestic activity in the palace during the hours of darkness, and few servants or guests in the passageways to be curious about what was happening.

Finally, Lorn and Decius were told to liaise with each other and arrange an effective guard roster that would protect the strongroom at all times.

'What do we do if someone in authority objects to the presence of common warriors and legionnaires traipsing through the palace? What do we say?' Lorn asked plaintively, his gaze switching from Caradoc to Maximus.

'The truth is our best defence,' Caradoc decided. 'If someone of quality should ask, you are carrying an integral part of a very special dowry that must be kept under constant guard. If they wish to argue the point, send them to me.'

'Or me!' Maximus exclaimed and faced his legionnaire. Caradoc was pleased to see that the tribune's face was clear of any panic or nausea.

The servants departed. Once Lorn had been entrusted with the massive key to the strongroom, the Roman tribune and the Dumnonii king returned to examine their quarters and partake of the light meal that had been left for them. Both men were suddenly ravenous with hunger.

In the main chamber, the back part of the room was divided between two luxurious beds, each more than large enough for several sleepers. The shuttered window was snugly fitted so that not even a breath of cold air could steal into the chamber.

Maximus sat on one of the couches, sniffed at the flagons of wine and began to pour the rich, ruby liquid into a goblet of real glass. Caradoc inspected an olive with suspicion and then placed it gingerly into his mouth.

'Well! Well! Would you say that this place might be a gilded trap, friend Caradoc? I wonder what Gwaun ap Mairtin is up to, because everyone here has been very polite and friendly.' Then he shuddered. 'Except for Hellyn's reference to the presence of rats.'

'For God's sake! Don't let Hellyn know you're fearful of rats or he'll mention them in every conversation. I think I prefer the company of Drustan ap Drust.

'I'll pulverise the arrogant bastard if he annoys me,' Maximus retorted. 'As Mithras rules in the battlefield, I swear that I'll cut out his tongue if he causes me any discomfort.'

'Oh, you of little trust!' Caradoc responded. 'I agree with you. Gwaun didn't come to greet us, we are taken to our rooms by the most difficult route possible and the whole palace seems deserted. We haven't met a soul who could be questioned, except for the graceful young gentlemen who have been our guides since we arrived. They seem to have been chosen deliberately to confuse or embarrass us. I believe we are meant to be on edge.'

'In which case, Gwaun has succeeded in whatever he tried to achieve. Let's eat this excellent meal, drink some of this superb wine and sleep on the beds provided for us. Where the hell are Trefor and Lorn? They're probably lost, which I'm sure was his intention. We're supposed to be too overawed to stir out of our rooms until Gwaun gives us permission. Since we are such honoured guests, I intend to show my pleasure by taking a bath. I suggest we act like guests and become high-handed. As soon as the men return, I'm going to send Lorn to find the bathhouse.'

Maximus fired a grin in Caradoc's direction. 'Did you notice that Hellyn didn't even bother to give us directions on how to get to the latrines?'

And, with these thoughts paramount in their minds, the two men ate and drank their fill and discovered that the food was tasty and well cooked. As they ate, a constant stream of Dumnonii and Roman warriors carried heavy box after heavy box into the confines of the strongroom and stacked them as far as possible from the door. Then, while Maximus prowled around the apartment like a caged big cat, Trefor and Lorn slipped away to reconnoitre the palace under the guise of hygiene.

Caradoc sat quietly with a glass of wine and stared at the key that Lorn had returned to him. It was attached to a large ring so that it could be worn around the wrist and contained a complex series of teeth designed to trip notches and releases in a locking mechanism. The design was obviously Roman, but Caradoc had never seen anything like it before.

Meanwhile the torches were beginning to splutter, reminding the tribune how completely he had been entrapped. He joined the Dumnonii king as they waited upon chance, or the orders of their absent host. The best news of all would be the return of their scouts with detailed information about the complexities of this palace.

CHAPTER X

A FEAST OF VULTURES

[He] who the gods love dies young.

Menander, *Reliquiae Selectae*

Caradoc and Maximus ambled along the narrow corridor in the direction of the main hall where they expected to find their host. Behind them, Lorn and Trefor strode out in an arrogant manner, even going so far as to provide guidance to their masters if they were in danger of taking the wrong turns. During the night, the two scouts had made the palace their own as they roamed through the building's hidden passages in accordance with their masters' orders.

'I'm starving! Being really clean after a long soak always sharpens my appetite,' Maximus exclaimed.

'That might account for your snoring,' Caradoc retorted.

'I don't snore! And if I did, I wouldn't give a shite on a beautiful morning like this.'

'I enjoyed my first truly Roman bath,' the king added, while smoothing his clean hair with one strong, square hand.

'Do you suppose we were expected to find the bathhouse for

ourselves, Caradoc? Or were we meant to ask our catamite friend to give us directions to the facilities in the palace?'

'I believe Gwaun wants us to feel on edge and even insulted. I think he wants us to be separated from our guards and unable to find essential basic facilities such as latrines, baths or water for shaving. We're meant to be at a disadvantage.'

'It's a good thing that neither of us is prepared to stand on ceremony.' Maximus replied while stroking his cheeks that Lorn had shaved to the smoothness of a baby's flesh. Then the tribune grinned widely.

'Gods, our host would have watched in amusement as we hunted for somewhere to take a morning piss if Trefor hadn't found the latrines for us. Gwaun will be very disappointed at that little miscalculation. It would have served him right if we'd pissed in the corners of his passageway like puppies.'

Both men had bathed late at night when no servants were abroad to observe their secretive foray. The water wasn't quite as hot as Maximus liked, but the pleasure of cleanliness far out-weighed the tepid temperatures inside the pools.

A container of fine oil had been left on a shelf near the calidarium, so the king and the tribune helped themselves to a liberal amount. Later, with their pores wide open and cleansed, both men and their servants lay in the steaming waters like pale dolphins, occasionally swimming languidly to loosen their tight muscles.

'You swim very well, Caradoc. I'm surprised, because very few people bother to learn how to protect themselves in open waters,' Maximus observed. 'I've always hated the thought of choking or drowning, so I was determined to learn the art of swimming as soon as I realised that most of the units in the legions travel by sea. It's nice to know that I could survive at sea if the need should arise.'

'We lived on the ocean's edge, so we played in boats from childhood. Every child in Tintagel would have drowned during our formative years if we hadn't learned to swim,' Caradoc explained, while Trefor spouted a jet of water at Lorn, who couldn't swim, from his mouth. Lorn sat on the steps and only ventured into water that was less than waist-deep.

Shaved, polished and tidied, the masters were taken to a clean and perfumed under-cover latrine outside the rear door of the palace, where several guards watched them narrowly. These superior latrines were obviously provided for the exclusive use of Gwaun and his guests, so the guards made no complaint.

When Trefor and Lorn had reconnoitred the palace on their masters' orders, they had discovered the apartments where the other kings had been domiciled, if the sleeping guards outside each door were any indication. Maximus grunted with contempt at the lazy and undisciplined behaviour of the servants and warriors in Gwaun's palace, an observation that might prove useful if they struck any trouble with their host in the future.

Their beds were excellent, so both men slept well and woke refreshed.

When morning came, Maximus and Caradoc dressed with care for their first meeting with King Gwaun. As King Caradoc and Magnus Maximus were discovering, they were involved in a type of bloodless war where the winners reacted with sangfroid to whatever the other group threw at them.

Over their fine woollen tunics, leather trews and polished mailed shirts, their breastplates gleamed with gold, silver and cabochon gemstones. The two men looked magnificent. Maximus wore a cloak of vivid scarlet, while Caradoc donned the check of the Dumnonii with a rich lining and a huge white fur hood made from the winter pelts of wolves. The effect of this contrasting raiment was arresting.

'Around about now, Gwaun will be thinking of sending for us, believing that we've been cooling our heels and waiting for his call. He'll be surprised,' Caradoc stated.

'Let's hope he chokes on his disappointment,' Maximus countered.

'The grand hall is at the end of this corridor,' Trefor informed Caradoc. 'There are guards outside the entrance doors.'

The guards looked down the passageway in surprise when they heard the sharp, military click of hard leather heels on the stone floor, drawing their swords part way out of their scabbards as a warning to the interlopers.

'Fools!' Lorn snapped, with his own gladius partly drawn. 'Haven't you been told about the presence of Tribune Magnus Maximus and King Caradoc of the Dumnonii tribe? These special guests are here at your master's personal invitation.'

The two guards paled, and then flushed, obviously unsure of what to do. They had been informed that it would be some time before the new arrivals would be escorted to the hall. Yet here they were, strong and arrogant, and in total command of the situation.

'Well? Are you going to leave us to cool our heels out here? Or are you going to announce our presence to your master? I take it he's within the hall.' Caradoc's voice was scathing.

The tallest of the guards, a middle-aged man, stumbled into hasty speech. 'Er . . . master . . . our lord is with his guests and they are breaking their fast. He ordered us to bar all entry to any other visitors. Please forgive me, my lord, for I don't mean to be disobliging.'

'But you are being disobliging, you fool!' Maximus responded, curling his lip in a way his troops and his enemies had learned was dangerous for those who offended him.

Caradoc threw the embarrassed and shaken man a sliver of hope. 'Good! Good! We are both starving. We are, of course, important guests of Lord Gwaun, so I'm certain he'd never intend us to be barred from entering his hall.'

Caradoc matched his request with an artless smile and walked towards the closed door with a nonchalance he didn't feel. Maximus followed hard on the king's heels, so the guard had no choice other than to retreat.

Caradoc used the flat of his sword and his callused hand to open the low door at the front of the hall, and they entered. It was lit by two rows of tall windows, two storeys higher than ground level that allowed a little of the early morning light to enter. But today's ambient light had been dimmed by the approaching snow clouds, so Gwaun had instructed his servants to close the shutters and light a row of wall sconces and a fire pit in the centre of the room to ensure that his guests were entertained in a warm and homely atmosphere.

Five pairs of eyes rose from their silver platters with various expressions of surprise, dismay and annoyance at the entrance of these interlopers. Five pairs of hands clenched, formed fists or jerked in guilt as Caradoc, Maximus and their guards swept into the hall with expressions of friendly greeting on their faces and the physical confidence of men who owned the world.

'So we've finally found you,' Caradoc began, spreading his arms wide to encompass all the men sitting around a table laden with food from which delicious smells wafted upwards to tantalise the guests. 'I assured the tribune you'd be breaking your fast alone in the belief that we'd be exhausted after many weeks on the road. But we're rather tough, aren't we, Maximus?'

'And hungry,' Maximus added wolfishly.

Then Caradoc struck his forehead with one dramatic hand. 'I'm sorry! I'm forgetting my manners, gentlemen. For those of you who don't know me, I'm King Caradoc ap Llyr of the Dumnonii tribe, and I have been invited to join your gathering by King Gwaun of the Atrebates tribe. May I present my friend, Tribune Magnus Maximus to you? He's a close kinsman of Theodosius, Lord Commander of Britannia. Maximus accompanies me at the behest of Theodosius who wishes to cement friendships with the noble kings of southern Britannia. Some of us are strangers to each other, a regrettable situation that should be rectified as soon as possible, but I'm aware of the nobility and reputations of each of you.'

Maximus enjoyed seeing the sight of his friend playing games with a host who had treated him with such casual arrogance. Caradoc was able to dissemble as Maximus never could, so he contrived to hide his true nature under a mask of naïve innocence. Several men at the table were already trying to hide smirks of satisfaction behind their hands.

'King Gwaun ap Mairtin, king of the great Atrebates tribe and Master of Venta Belgarum, may I present Tribune Maximus and commend him to you.'

A plump, soft-skinned man of middle height rose to his feet and smoothed down a long robe of pale blue wool so fine that Maximus could tell at a glance it had been woven in far-off Constantinople. The man wore a series of golden chains around his corpulent neck; their quality and weight screamed wealth. With a small shudder of disgust, Maximus noted an earring of large pearls and gold hanging almost to the large man's collarbone. Every pudgy finger wore at least one ring and a number of armlets pressed into the soft forearms. Out of devilry, Maximus considered offering his hand in greeting, but Caradoc anticipated this provocative action and fired off a warning glance at his friend.

Superficially, Gwaun appeared to be an effete, superficial and idle man more concerned with pleasure than his duties of rule. Yet Gwaun would never have survived as a king unless he had a ruthless streak. His land was far too rich and much too important to the trading needs of southern Britannia to be held by a fool. It seemed that Gwaun ap Mairtin could play games as deftly as Caradoc. The difference between them lay in the Dumnonii king's recognition of the flaws in Gwaun's character, while Gwaun's snide smile revealed that he was ignorant of Caradoc's potential for guile.

Recovering from his surprise, the Atrebates king bowed neatly. But he performed this polite task as if he was conferring a gift on the two men standing at his table.

'Allow me to introduce Fiachna ap Tormud, king of the Durotriges tribe.' Caradoc and Maximus nodded in the direction of the man who rose and bowed perfunctorily at them.

Fiachna was neatly dressed in drab wools but any superficial respectability fled when Caradoc spied the dark crescents of filth under Fiachna's nails and a line of scum staining the wattles of the man's neck. His long hair was greasy, his clothing was stiff with accumulated grime and the material was stained with sweat. To top off a careless toilette, Fiachna hadn't shaved for several days.

Bleise ap Bladud was an elderly man with iron-grey hair bound into the familiar plaits of a warrior. Although he wore wool like his fellow kings, the material was coarsely spun and woven, while the vegetable dye used had been inexpertly applied. Maximus recalled that Bleise insisted on living in the traditional

British style, a way of life that rejected trade goods and luxury items. To his credit, however, King Bleise had shrewd and intelligent eyes that observed the newcomers with care and sincerity and the smile he gave them was warm and pleasant.

The last two kings were enigmas. Although Adwen ap Rhys was a near neighbour of Caradoc's, they had never met and the man was a complete stranger to him.

Adwen, like Gwaun, was dressed in a Roman tunic covered by a toga with a narrow border of purple dye. For his part, Adwen was overtly Roman in his clothing, the cut of his hair, his jewellery and even the use of Latin terms that he continually inserted into his conversations. At first, Maximus doubted that Adwen was serious in his slavish aping of Roman mannerisms but, as he watched the king eating so casually and rudely in front of the visitors, he concluded that Adwen believed himself to be descended from Roman ancestors.

What an arrogant prig, Maximus thought. Such affectations should only be the preserve of a supreme ruler.

The other man, Sorcha ap Sion, was the king of the Regni tribe that ruled over the rich countryside to the east of Venta Belgarum. His lands were suffering from regular incursions from Saxon invasions that had spread after landings on the shores of the Litus Saxonicum.

Sorcha was comfortably dressed. A short, athletic man, with ridges of hard muscle that bulged out from his clothing, his nervousness could be clearly seen through callused hands that were constantly catching at threads on his robe. Caradoc and Maximus immediately recognised one of their own kind, a warrior and a man of action who had been forced to petition these men for assistance.

But Sorcha's muddy eyes and sour expression repelled and

annoyed them both. He had a reputation for violence and thuggish behaviour, which was shown by the coarse grunt he gave to them and his refusal to stand as a mark of respect. Sorcha accorded nothing to strangers who had little to offer him and were, as far as he was concerned, unproven as men of ability and worth.

Maximus filed Sorcha away as someone who needed a lesson in manners.

'May we be seated?' Caradoc asked artlessly into a dead silence. Maximus was certain that they had been the chief topic of conversation before their entry. But the room was thick now with unspoken duplicitous words.

'Of course you may, Caradoc. Please sit and refresh yourself,' Gwaun responded with a commendable effort at bonhomie. 'Please? My servant will bring you plates of whatever reheated food you might desire.'

'I've been looking forward to breaking my fast,' Maximus said, trying hard to emulate Caradoc's bland innocence. 'The exigencies of the road have meant that we often ate dried rations. I'm a soldier, so I'm accustomed to existing like that for months at a time, but every man who makes his living by the sword dreams of food while he's doing his duty.'

The assembled kings nodded with various degrees of understanding, but Sorcha's were the only eyes that showed any real comprehension of life in the saddle. Both Caradoc and Maximus grinned and thanked the soft-footed servant women who approached them with bowls of porridge sweetened with new honey, hot and cold meats, platters of boiled eggs and parcels of fish. A male servant filled glass mugs with mild beer. Maximus licked his lips with anticipation and took out his eating knife.

Gwaun took the opportunity to watch the Roman's table manners. 'Are knives such as yours used regularly in Rome?' he asked, his curiosity evident on his face. 'We've seen such knives in the south of Britannia before, as well as personal spoons, but they've invariably been in the hands of northern kings who have more experience of our Roman overlords than we do.'

'You wouldn't want to use your fingers to eat messy foods, would you?' Maximus asked with as much diplomacy as he could muster. He was aware that Fiachna's fingers were still greasy from the bones that he had thrown to the floor for Gwaun's servants to retrieve.

'I've seen many Britons who use eating knives during my travels,' Maximus added. 'Caradoc for one!'

Caradoc obliged by pulling out his own well-used knife with the shape of a fish embedded into its handle. 'My father presented me with this knife when I was still a lad, so its use has been a long habit for me. All the men in my family learned to use knives and spoons as soon as they could hold onto the handles.'

Gwaun stared tellingly at the other kings as if he had won a minor argument concerning table manners. Ignoring any undercurrents, Caradoc and Maximus began to slake their hunger.

The two men ate their meal with obvious gusto and washed it down with deep draughts of the excellent beer. When they had finished, both of them sat back, sighed luxuriantly and the tribune went so far as to belch loudly.

'An excellent meal, Gwaun,' Caradoc congratulated his host. 'Truly excellent! I was so hungry that I would have cheerfully demolished anything and everything that was placed in front of me. Your choices of fare and the quality of its preparation were magnificent.'

Blushing at the fulsome praise, Gwaun steered the conversation onto politics.

'What news is there from the north, Lord Tribune?' Gwaun asked on behalf of the assembled kings. 'We've heard that the Picts, Hibernians and Saxons have attacked both coasts simultaneously and have been putting many of our tribesmen to the sword.'

'Our enemies have been beaten and the remnants of their forces have been sent home to their mothers and sweethearts,' Maximus told him. 'Those men that were still breathing were forced to leave our shores. The northern warriors were no match for the legions and our allies in the north of Britannia, although the raiders drove deeply into your lands with their first attacks in the south. Unfortunately, I believe they will come again, once they've regrouped.'

'How long will the peace last?' Bleise ap Bladud ventured. The man seemed far from kingly, so Caradoc wondered how such a frightened little man could hope to hold the ambitious lords within his tribe in some sort of check.

'How long does it take to grow from a babe to a man?' Maximus replied curtly. 'Our enemies suffered great losses, especially the Picts and the Hibernians. The Saxons are another matter, for they are capable of multiplying like ticks on a blanket. In fact, our northern allies refer to the regularity of the Saxon attacks as *Saxon Summers*.'

'But what about your troops in Londinium?' Sorcha ap Sion growled. 'Your troops there have been as useless as tits on bulls when it comes to protecting the Regni lands from them Saxons. And where are your galleys?'

'Yes?' Maximus inquired silkily as Sorcha picked up a cold chicken wing with his dirty fingers and began to crunch the small bones.

'They're total failures if they're supposed to protect the tribes on the Litus Saxonicum. In summer the Saxons come without hindrance! We drive 'em off, but then the buggers come straight back again. Where are the legions when we need 'em down here?'

'God helps those who help themselves, Sorcha,' Caradoc said. 'You should have called for help when you needed it. I would have answered your call and I'm the furthest away from your lands. I'm also the least likely to be attacked by those savages who plunder the homes of your peasants. You, and all of your peers, should be discussing a joint response to the Saxon menace. We'll never get rid of these bastards if they gain a permanent foothold in your lands. If they establish themselves near Londinium, they will eventually become our overlords.'

Maximus nodded in agreement as he continued to devour food from the platters that surrounded his silver plate in a crescent. Idly, he wondered at such ostentation, for silverware tarnished so readily. Gwaun must have demanded hard work from his servants, because it was spotlessly clean.

'We were considering some kind of temporary alliance during the summer months when you joined us,' Gwaun explained brightly, but Maximus could see that the king's fingers were restive. 'We'd mostly been discussing the cost.'

So! These incompetents intend to keep the Dumnonii out of their cosy little alliance, Maximus thought sourly. Is he too talented? Or would he be too inflexible to be involved in activities that offended his sense of justice? Perhaps he's too clever for the other rulers? Maximus was certain that they did not want any Roman involvement.

'Surely a wise king would ensure that all domestic threats to the peace were removed from his lands *before* any alliances against distant enemies were decided,' Caradoc said.

Gwaun raised his eyebrows in surprise. 'That conclusion would seem to be obvious, but are you speaking of any particular threats?'

'Certainly, Gwaun! I must inform you that we were delayed for well over a week after we had a serious confrontation with a band of outlaws on the roads between Vindo Cladia and Sorviodunum. This particular band had ensconced themselves in a farmstead in a remote valley, so they had obviously been preying on the local population for many years.'

Fiachna's face coloured to an ugly plum shade that extended all the way to his thinning hairline. On the other hand, Gwaun looked even more perplexed, so Maximus acquitted him of any knowledge of Elphin and his murderous bunch of malcontents.

'Outlaws? So many, and so close? Did you know about this cadre, Bleise? Your borders must be close to this farmstead.' Gwaun's face was curious and grave by turn.

'Um! . . . I may have heard talk of such a band of outlaws in the woods,' Bleise responded with feigned nonchalance.

'From what the outlaw chieftain said to us before he lost all power of speech, I believe that you knew of this band as well, Fiachna. In fact, the treasure that they'd amassed was quite remarkable. I imagine that someone was paying them a large tribute in gold,' Caradoc's eyes were bland, although his mouth was set in a thin line.

'Treasure? What treasure?' Sorcha asked. 'You were just crying poor to us, pleading that you had no coin to add to the fund for mercenaries and weapons.'

The two kings implicated in the extortion, Fiachna and Bleise, had obviously been unaware of the funds paid to Elphin's band by the other, a coup that had been adroitly played by the dead outlaw chieftain. He had proved to be a dab hand at manipulation and, for one short moment, Caradoc regretted that they had executed the villain so quickly. What information Elphin possessed had died with him.

'Perhaps you should explain, Fiachna,' Maximus added with a twist of his lips that set the Durotriges king on edge with nervousness. Meanwhile, Adwen's feet began to scrape back and forth on the coarsely paved floor.

'There has been a large outlaw band attacking traders and small, undefended villages for several years now,' Fiachna said in a conciliatory voice. 'During that time, I've sent troops out to confront them on a number of occasions. But, after striking at my warriors from well-disguised ambushes, they always managed to elude us. I was suffering severe losses of men, equipment and coin. On each occasion, the bastards would attack my warriors, and then disappear into the forests like the mist. This happened over and over again. Ultimately, I was left with no choice other than to pay them to go away and leave us in relative peace.'

Fiachna wrung his hands nervously and glanced at Sorcha and Gwaun, who were staring at their fellow king with distinct displeasure. Bleise was silent, but looked like a guilty schoolboy. Adwen was so cowed that he refused to meet anyone's eyes.

'In the end, it was far easier to pay the bastards off,' Fiachna continued in a muffled voice. 'We ceded them a small payment in coin for every trading party that passed through the forest. It was expensive, because they continued to attack the travellers anyway.'

'Is there no honour among thieves?' Caradoc asked blandly.

'And you?' Maximus demanded, turning his chair to face Bleise.

'I can see no reason to answer to a Roman,' Bleise blustered, but the squeak in his voice betrayed his feeble attempt at belligerence for what it was, the last gamble of a guilty man.

'I'd warn you that Maximus is a senior officer in the Roman occupation of your lands, and a man who never accepts insults with equanimity. Maximus and I were attacked by *your* outlaws. We were forced to do battle with villains who believed they were protected and untouchable. The Roman and I have both lost men. We demand an explanation for ourselves and for everyone in this room.'

Caradoc's bluntness wrung an unwilling grunt of agreement from Sorcha, who was inclined to distrust anyone who rode with a Roman. The other kings looked down at their hands and left Bleise to fidget and tremble, while his rheumy eyes began to fill with self-pitying tears.

'I never knew the name of the ruffian, but pilgrims who came to visit the Giant's Carol were robbed, tortured and murdered by the outlaw band. Eventually, the town's prominent citizens insisted that I do something. They even provided most of the coin that was paid on a yearly basis. That was the price of doing business!'

'Why didn't you unite with Fiachna to defeat them? The outlaw band couldn't have resisted the combined forces of two kings.'

'I didn't know that Fiachna was also paying them,' Bleise complained. 'Our Durotriges friend spends most of his time complaining that he has no gold to spare, despite the fertility of his lands.'

'I don't have a steady stream of pilgrims that come to see the Giant's Dance, do I?' Fiachna countered, his face mottled with anger.

'Gentlemen! Gentlemen! Remember your stations, my friends!

This is perfect proof that communication between the kings is vital if any of you hope to survive the travails that will begin to confront us in the years to come,' Caradoc urged.

Then Maximus called Lorn forward. He had been standing with Trefor in the shadows at the back of the room, and now he moved forward with a small bag in his hands.

Maximus took the bag with a flourish, drawing out a small bar of gold impressed with the stamp of the legion and a Roman numeral.

'And which of you gentlemen gave legion gold to common outlaws, eh?' Maximus's voice was hard. As he waited, the apprehension in the room was palpable, broken only when Maximus slammed the gold bar down onto the tabletop with a loud thud. The tableware shook from the force of the blow.

Fiachna's eyes were round with shock, but his greed overcame him. He reached out with a dirty finger to touch the bar, but instantly withdrew his hand when Maximus's eating knife was suddenly buried in the tabletop beside the ingot. Caradoc immediately acquitted Fiachna of any guilt. This man would never, ever, part with gold.

Likewise, Bleise looked thoroughly puzzled. 'I don't understand!' He read the embossed Roman numerals upside down and his mouth formed a little moue of surprise.

'Eburacum . . . the legion from Eburacum,' he muttered. 'How did that ingot get here?'

'Precisely!' the tribune snapped. 'More to the point, I have to ask how this bar, and another two hundred and nineteen similar bars, could find their way into the cache of a common criminal near the town of Vindo Cladia.' Maximus focused on the other three tribal chieftains.

'Two hunded and nineteen bars of gold?' Gwaun bleated.

'Two hundred and twenty,' Caradoc corrected him gently.

'Don't look at me! If I had two hundred and twenty bars of gold, I wouldn't be trying to convince my neighbours to form an alliance that would protect my lands,' Sorcha said grimly, his eyes threatening trouble to whoever had been holding out on him.

All eyes settled on the toga-clad Adwen ap Rhys of the Dobunni tribe. His natural good looks were spoiled by a tendency to store fat around his thickening belly that was quivering with nervousness as he breathed under the hard scrutiny of his peers.

Caradoc watched the play of emotions on Adwen's broad and increasingly florid face as his silence dragged on. To speak? Or to keep silent?

Finally, Caradoc watched as the Dobunni king flinched, and then closed his eyes. Adwen had arrived at a decision.

He's going to confess, the Dumnonii king thought triumphantly. He aimed a quick glance at Maximus who winked back at him.

Adwen stared at his entwined fingers. 'My family held this gold legally for over half a century after a payment from Emperor Constantine to my grandfather's father. The empire was in turmoil at the time. Emperor Constantius had perished at Eburacum and his son ruled for a brief year before chaos tore the whole fabric of the empire to bloody shreds. Then, the great Constantine took the throne. I don't know the half of the deal made with the emperor's men in those bygone years, but my ancestor was asked to shore up the south of Britannia against a slew of aspiring claimants who rose up like poisonous mushrooms to grasp at the crown. My grandfather claimed that other tribal kings had also been paid to provide services to the empire because these rulers were sympathetic to Constantine's strong right arm. As far as I know, the whole agreement was made through proxies, but my family fulfilled our part of the agreement.'

The other kings at the table sat gape-mouthed at Adwen's confession because, in their ignorance, they had no understanding of the storms that raged within the seats of power in Rome, and further afield in the vast empire. Of those present, only Maximus could truly understand Constantine's odd bargain with a group of influential kings. For their part, the Dobunni had kept trade with the empire hale and strong, so their support had been worth the two hundred and twenty ingots of gold offered some sixty years earlier. As it turned out, Constantine had ruled for many years and had stabilised the world that Maximus knew.

Adwen took heart from the understanding he could see in the tribune's eyes, so he drew a deep breath and carried on with his tale.

'I knew of the Eburacum gold, of course, for I had been charged by my father to keep it safe from harm. Before he died, my father told me where it was hidden, but he cautioned me against using the treasure because it would be a potent weapon if kept intact. To be truthful, I never felt an inclination to look at it. Unfortunately, I have never discovered how other men came to know of it. Perhaps my father told a bed-partner or his general might have told another man when he was in his cups. But persistent gossip about a treasure trove of Roman gold, held in Dobunni hands, was rife among our neighbours. I lied to my first wife when she confronted me with this rumour, for women are notoriously quick to boast and talk. I will probably never know how treason nearly separated my head from my body, but it almost did.'

His audience was rapt. As Adwen gained in confidence his

gestures grew more expansive and his language became more colourful.

'My eldest son by my first wife had no desire to wait for me to die a natural death. I won't speak his name, because I still feel pain when I think of him. I married young, so he was twenty-five when he started along the path to treason and patricide, after convincing himself that I'd treated his mother poorly and had brought about her death. My beautiful son fell very far and very fast.' Adwen sighed with regret.

'In truth, my first wife loved wine more than the children she bore, so she eventually set herself afire during one of her drunken moments, along with a large section of my hall. My son blamed me for the accident. He hated my second wife and her children, because he was resentful of the affection I felt for them. At any rate, he fomented rebellion within the tribe by making promises to distribute the Roman gold held by the family.'

'I knew you had executed your son, but I never heard the details,' Sorcha observed. His dark brows were furrowed with resentment, although Caradoc had no idea why the Regni king should feel this way. Adwen's personal tragedy had won Caradoc's sympathy. 'That was near to five years ago, but I still can't see how the gold became part of an outlaw hoard.'

'The Dobunni tribe was at war with itself for five years. At first, my son played on the ambitions of the younger warriors in the tribe. I was forced to flee from my own hall as I tried to save my wife and children. Yes, you must know that I lost all but one boy, Llew, who is now my heir. My hatred for my eldest son was hot and ugly, and didn't abate until I drove him into the forest and killed him. But you can't kill his kind of betrayal. It still lies in my heart like a heavy stone weight.

'When I finally took back my hall in Corinium, I was surprised to find that the Roman gold had been removed from the place where it had been hidden. No one knew anything of the theft, so what could I do? The entire cache had been taken! Until you told me of its continued existence, I'd heard nothing of it for five years.'

Adwen tried manfully to pull himself together, for his tears had begun to fall as he came to the end of this tragic story of loss and betrayal.

'You may think of me as a fool, if it serves your purposes. I probably am, but that cursed gold has cost me my family and has given me too much pain. I will refuse to make any claim on it, for all that I remain committed to our part in the old bargain. In all truth, I'd prefer that it was returned to the emperor's war chests in Eburacum so that it can be used in the interests of all of Britannia's people.'

Adwen gave Maximus a brief smile. 'The gold should be owned by Rome. You may return it, if you so wish. It's no odds to me.'

He asked one final question. 'Incidentally, did you gain any information regarding the source of the gold? The hoard has followed a strange path, so I am curious about the identity of the man who led your band of outlaws.'

Caradoc gathered his scrambled wits. He had never expected to feel any sympathy for Adwen, a man he had always considered something of a fool. Like all the southern kings, he had heard of the internal troubles that killed so many of his neighbours, but Adwen had asked for nothing from the Dumnonii. Caradoc had minded his own business, seeing tribal civil wars as a means of maintaining the status quo in southern Britannia. Besides, the Dobunni had always been too rich and too strong for his liking.

He decided to tell Adwen and the kings what he knew of the outlaw band. If Maximus didn't like his description, then Maximus would have to put up with it.

'The outlaw chieftain told us his name was Elphin, but we never heard his father's name or his tribe. He was clever and frightened of nothing, for all that he was a scabrous, foul-mouthed savage. One thing I can swear to is that Elphin was a genuine leader. His band had been successful for a very long time and he died without any appeals for clemency. I wouldn't be surprised to discover that he'd once been a warrior of sorts.'

'That's strange,' Gwaun remarked.

'How so?' Maximus demanded.

'That name! The name means *white* in the Latin language. But in our tongue it refers to someone who has been so unfortunate as to have had his birthright unfairly stolen from him. His life history would have been enlightening.'

'We'll never know who he was, except that he was an excellent thief and a superior rogue, one who had a huge cache of Roman gold in his possession. I'm tired of old ghosts, so I'd be happy to let the dead bury the dead,' Adwen said, suddenly looking like a cadaverous old man. The king who had seemed barely middle-aged earlier in the conversation had been replaced by a grandfather who was as dried up as winter grasses, blown out of the earth by freezing winds.

According to Gwaun, who rarely let an opportunity for carousing pass him by, it was time for the feasting to commence.

A hunt gave no one very much pleasure, except for the peasants who were paid a measure of the meat that was slaughtered under the guise of amusement. None of the kings mentioned the Roman gold or Adwen's personal tragedies, but

Caradoc maintained a close watch on the Dobunni king when the man's strength returned and he began to immerse himself in a vain pursuit of superficial pleasures.

In the long evenings, Maximus proved his power to charm his peers by siding with Sorcha. Without any hesitation, he leaped at the opportunity to champion an argument in favour of an alliance between the six kings that would be formed to oppose the Saxon raiders.

'What will happen if Sorcha should lose a coastal port to the Saxons?' the Roman demanded of Fiachna. 'I know you insist that his problems have nothing to do with you, but what will inevitably follow such an inroad into the Regni lands?'

'They'll spread out! That's what will happen! As sure as night follows day, the Saxons will be threatening me if Sorcha allows them to get a toehold,' Gwaun complained. Strangely, the Atrebates king could see the emergency with the same clarity as Sorcha, but it was only when Maximus drew a graphic description of the consequences on the tabletop with a piece of charcoal that Fiachna and Bleise began to understand the dangerous situation they were in.

'This platter is your land, Gwaun, and this, Fiachna, is yours.' Maximus deftly moved a number of table implements to approximate the tribal boundaries. 'Now! If you imagine that the Regni platter has been taken over by the Saxons, where would the surviving Regni refugees go? Would they all flock to Gwaun's lands?'

'Not if they're sensible,' Caradoc said. He was entering the conversation as an interested party and, much as he hated to consider the possibility, Maximus was explaining the probable future of the British tribes with far more expertise than Caradoc could ever have mustered. Suddenly, the miles between Tintagel and Venta Belgarum were not as vast as he had previously believed.

'The refugees will take to their heels and head as far as possible from any likely threat to themselves or their families. They'll head towards the Durotriges tribe, the Dobunni or the Belgae,' Adwen decided. His narrowed eyes were alive with the intelligence he had just gleaned. 'They will head away from the coast, for the Saxons will be attacking from that direction.'

'I won't be feeding any refugees,' Fiachna snapped.

'Don't be an idiot, Fiachna! If the Saxons really attacked, you wouldn't have much choice in what would happen, so stop your whining,' Sorcha put in. He had little sympathy for the grimy Durotriges king.

Maximus drew black arrows on the tabletop . . . towards Portus Adurni, along the coast towards Durnovaria and then inland towards Sorviodunum.

'Consider the Roman roads,' Maximus said. 'The cleverest of the Saxon thanes won't bother with Venta Belgarum because it will be too heavily defended. It would be far easier to inveigle their way into your most powerful city by stealth – in fact, it will come through trade. This Saxon triumph won't happen in a month, or a year, or even a decade. These disasters will occur in your grandchildren's time or even later, but whenever you repel the Saxons, you are setting back the terrible times that will come. Meanwhile, it's better for the Saxons that they attack weaker sites around the prized cities, places that are only lightly guarded because their rulers believe no sensible Saxon would bother with them. Places like Calleva Atrebatum, Durnovaria, Clausentum or Sorviodunum are real prizes. A network would be built, piece by piece, that will lead inexorably to their capture. Your lands, gentlemen, will be taken from your heirs before the enemy steals Venta Belgarum. I would plan to defeat Gwaun in just this fashion, if I were a Saxon.'

Fiachna and Bleise stared at the platters and the charcoal marks on the tabletop. Both men were beginning to understand that, ultimately, an attack on one tribe would be a threat to all.

'In the north, the Picts harry the Otadini and the people who inhabit the borders,' Caradoc continued. 'At the same time, Hibernians attack the Brigante, the Ordovice and the Deceangli, while the Saxons pose a constant threat to the whole eastern coast and the lands of the south. What if our tribune and his friends were recalled to the continent, taking with them the manpower, equipment and fighting skills of the legions? Could we survive?'

During the time that Maximus had been speaking, the Dumnonii king had accepted the fragile nature of Britannia's peace and how swiftly it could be swept away. He felt like a man who had awakened from a beautiful dream to discover that reality was cruel and dangerous.

'You'll be sitting pretty whatever happens,' Fiachna sniped. 'Who'd want your windswept coasts?'

'Time alone will tell,' Caradoc retorted. 'So! It's time to announce our intentions. Who is in favour of a united opposition to the threat posed by the Saxons? Or, for that matter, any attack by outsiders?'

Hands rose, slowly but firmly, because the tribal kings were finally aware that they must fight the coming battles as one single entity. Predictably, Fiachna was the last ruler to capitulate.

The first tentative alliance in Britannia had been formed. All that remained were discussions on the minutiae that would be needed to give full effect to their treaty. Then, only time would decide if the loose confederation of tribes would have any lasting value.

Two days later, a small troop of Roman cavalry arrived at Venta Belgarum and craved the attention of Magnus Maximus. Within hours, Maximus had left with a wagon piled high with several heavy boxes of treasure that represented Caradoc's share of the outlaw hoard.

'I've been recalled to Segontium because my master, Theodosius, is about to be appointed to the post of Magister Equitum for pacifying Britannia. The scroll he sent to me explains that we are bound for Gaul and service with our master, Gratian.'

Although neither Maximus nor Caradoc was truly comfortable with the other on matters of politics, they trusted each other as men in a strange companionship that Caradoc would miss. He said as much to Maximus and prepared to complete the formalities by thanking King Gwaun for his hospitality and making good his departure.

On a whim, Caradoc tore his cloak pin out of its usual position on his left shoulder. A green enamelled fish had been curved in a large circle so it bit at its own tail. In its gaping mouth, the fish bore a pearl of unusual size and beauty.

'Don't forget us, Maximus, or the time we spent on the road together. We've had our disagreements, but there's no man I'd rather ride with when the journey is hard and dangerous.'

Maximus took the brooch and stroked it with his callused thumbs. When he spoke, his voice was rusty.

'I have no such personal gift of equal worth to give to you, my friend, but I'd like you to take my eating knife. It's very old and my mother swore it had once belonged to a Roman general during the time of the Republic. I value this reminder of my happy youth, so I'd like you to have it. It will happily transition from my house to yours.'

Both men had little further to say.

'If I should return, I will surely come to Tintagel to visit you. This I swear, my friend,' Maximus vowed as he and his men prepared to depart from Venta Belgarum. With a lump in his throat, Caradoc could only nod his response.

The troop was no more than a line of dark mist on the road when Caradoc suddenly remembered that he hadn't discovered why Decius had given a merciful death to Elphin, the outlaw chieftain.

With a sad shrug, Caradoc turned away from the city gates, telling himself that he would never again see Tribune Magnus Maximus. Some mysteries are best buried by time.

CHAPTER XI

A CUCKOO COME TO NEST

The Roman state survives by its ancient customs and its manhood.

Ennius, *Annals*, Book 5

Time passed by. The stars wheeled through the night sky, while the sun continued to rise and set in the endless cycle of the seasons, and changes came to Tintagel in ways that Caradoc could never have expected.

In the summer following Maximus's return to the Eagles, a messenger walked down the long roadway leading to the barracks at Tintagel. Shaggy and unarmed, he was dressed like a pilgrim in a torn and faded blue cloak. The visitor's eyebrows were unnaturally long and they grew together over his nose, so that a long hairy caterpillar appeared to march across his face.

With his bushy and straggling beard, rope belt and necklace sporting a piece of flint carved to resemble a leaping fish, this pilgrim could have belonged to any place and any time, and could have worshipped any god, including the Old Ones, or those nameless deities whose presence was maintained at the Giant's Carol.

Caradoc tried to assess the man's intentions. Was he a hermit? Did he think he was a Druid, returned to warn the people that ugly times were coming? Or was he a lunatic, searching for a hot meal?

Once the man had been searched by the guards and helped up the steps to the citadel, Caradoc was waiting for him in the forecourt. Huw was standing watchfully behind him with bared hands. Out of the corner of his eye, Caradoc could see Rowen, the captain of the guard, with a bow in his hands, nocked and ready to fire.

Well, I'm not likely to be assassinated by stealth, Caradoc decided as he moved forward to speak to his visitor, one hand extended in greeting

'Welcome, traveller. You have a message for me?'

The man's hand was cool and dry, and unexpectedly clean for a man who had tramped for many miles in sunshine and in rain. Perhaps he was a Christian priest.

'If you be Caradoc, King of the Dumnonii, then I bear a message from Saraid of the Red Wells. I be Hergest of Llanio, come on a pilgrimage from Holyhead to take the sacrament in the Church of the Blessed Joseph at Glastonbury.'

'You're a priest?' Caradoc asked, pleased that his guess had been correct.

'I be Brother Jude in my church-name, King Caradoc. I begged for permission to make a pilgrimage to that holy soil where Our Saviour is said to have trod in his youth. I was fortunate to see the church that the holy trader built with his own hands, after he forsook Jerusalem to travel far from home.'

Caradoc had heard of these legends, but he doubted that any

Jew, even one baptised by Christ's own hands, would willingly sail across the Middle Sea and through a wild ocean to settle so far from his homeland.

'Whether you are Brother Jude or Hergest of Llanio, you are welcome here.'

'I seldom hear my birth-name. You may call me Hergest if you be content with that.'

'Very well, Hergest. But what does Lady Saraid ask of me? She saved the life of my warrior, Huw, who stands here with us. We are both indebted to her.' Caradoc was still careful in the presence of this road-weary traveller, but courtesy cost little. Besides, Lady Saraid's wonderful hair rose in his memory, night-dark, but rich with chestnut streaks and a hint of red.

'Lady Saraid requests that you attend on her as soon as is practicable. She asks that you remember the debt that you owe her and, although you have kept your side of the bargain, she says that fortune has changed her circumstances and she has need of your help.'

As if Caradoc could forget. 'How did you come to meet with Lady Saraid? The Red Wells lie to the south of Glastonbury and aren't well known by any means.' Caradoc accepted that only a matter of great urgency could have forced her to request assistance from any man, even him.

'The Bleeding Pool at Glastonbury is a sacred gift from Almighty God. When I prayed at its mouth, I was told by one of the priests about the Red Wells and how they have been sacred to the Old Ones for time beyond counting. I'm afraid that I'm a curious man. It be my besetting sin, so I set forth along the roads and pathways to see this marvel for myself.

'As for Lady Saraid, she be well but I cannot say why she calls for your assistance. I swore to be silent and refrain from speaking of her to any person but you. I have already stretched my oath by speaking of her in front of a third party.' Hergest nodded in Huw's direction.

'Lady Saraid saved Huw's life after he was wounded by a boar's tusk. She would never resent words spoken in front of him, and nor would Huw speak thoughtlessly of anything he heard of her,' Caradoc assured the older man.

'Still, I'll say no more of the lady. She can explain her needs when you see her.'

And, from this position, Hergest refused to budge. When he was certain that the brother would reveal nothing further, Caradoc gave him a bed for the night with the citadel guard and offered him a silver coin for his troubles.

'I cannot accept payment for what was a God-given duty. I thank you for the offer of a place to rest my head, which I'll happily accept, But that is all.'

Accompanied only by Huw, who refused to be left behind, Caradoc took horse for the Red Wells and the woman who waited there to receive him. In those times when his queen had been particularly difficult in Tintagel, Caradoc's mind would recall the soft lichens and lacy ferns of the Red Wells and memories of love would fill his heart with longing for a way of life that he could never have. On those occasions when the king gazed at the tall form of his son, a stranger amid the circumstances of an arranged marriage, he felt a tearing in his gut that made him very angry.

'It's the tradition of the aristocracy, Huw. We are mated like good horses or cattle to strengthen the bloodlines and secure more wealth. Often-times, we pay for our casual attitudes to love. But we must have what we desire, or we suffer for its loss.'

'Aye, my lord,' Huw replied, although he hadn't the slightest idea of Caradoc's meaning. The lords of the land frequently acted in ways that seemed quite crazed to more humble men. Of course, sons must marry to improve the family wealth and blood. Every farmer's son or servant's daughter knew that. Only the great ones could hope for the freedom to follow their hearts, yet his king had still been trapped inside his own marriage.

They left at dawn and rode for several hours, heading away from the coast and the smell of salt air on the winds. So great was the distance to the Red Wells that Caradoc and Huw were forced to sleep under leather that night and could expect at least one more day of hard riding before they arrived at their destination.

The familiar cottage hove into view as the sun was setting on the afternoon of the second day. A thread of smoke rose from the vents on the roof and the door was ajar to catch every ray of sunlight. The two large mastiffs raised their heads and bayed a warning from a nearby field filled with wildflowers, and then bounded back to the entrance of the cottage where they stood on guard, their hackles raised.

'Stay with the horses, Huw,' Caradoc ordered, his eyes fixed on the quivering dogs. 'Hoi! Lady Saraid! Call off your hounds so I can speak to you.'

His voice rose over the pleasant sounds of evening birdsong, and, from somewhere out of sight, he could hear the lowing of a cow for her calf. From inside the cottage, Caradoc could hear the sound of a crying infant. He felt his heart lurch and his mind struggled with a sudden unexpected possibility.

'Sian! Siarl! Down!' At the familiar contralto voice the two mastiffs sank back on their haunches. 'Come in, Lord Caradoc. I swear that my guardians won't hurt you.'

Caradoc stepped out manfully, ignoring the low, rumbling growls. He pushed his way into the cottage.

The large room had changed little in the many months of his absence. Caradoc focused on the only appreciable change – a cradle suspended from the rafters in a position where an infant could be warmed by the fire pit, yet lulled to sleep by even the slightest of breezes.

Lady Saraid was standing by the cauldron over the fire pit, her amazing hair shining with shades of copper in the firelight.

'My lord,' she whispered and bowed gently from the waist. Her body bent like a lily in a river breeze and Caradoc was entranced by her anew.

'Lady Saraid,' he began, clearing his throat awkwardly. 'I have come in response to your call. I hope I find you well.'

'I'm very well, thank you, Caradoc.' As she gazed up into his face, she seemed even smaller than he remembered. The soft roundness of her flesh was at odds with her cool, appraising eyes. 'Will you sit and share a hot infusion with me?'

Caradoc nodded and sat on the stool closest to the fire pit while Lady Saraid drew up a larger chair from the corner of the room. The king would have helped her, but she stopped him with a careless wave of one hand. 'You should remember, my lord, that I am really quite strong. Rest yourself while I prepare our tisane.'

Finally, once he held a cup of steaming liquid, she consented to seat herself with a graceful sweep of her skirts. The aroma of strawberries and mint filled the cottage.

'You must have wondered why I have sent for you, my lord. I never expected to trouble you again, but circumstances change, so I've been forced to call for your assistance. I've prayed for your arrival, for my need is great.'

Caradoc realised that his fingers were shaking. He tightened his grip on the cup.

'I'll always come whenever you call. I feel as if there's a link between us, like a ribbon of flesh, especially when I'm close to you. I can't deny you, Saraid.'

He paused, and then asked the question that had been on the tip of his tongue from the moment he entered the room.

'I see that you have a cradle hanging from the ceiling. Whose child is it?' The question came out more abruptly than he had intended, but he already knew the answer.

Lady Saraid lowered her eyes momentarily as if she had been dreading this moment. Then she raised her face and stared at the king from across the rim of her cup.

'The impossible happened to this old witch. No! Don't say anything, my lord! Just listen and you'll soon understand why I need your assistance so badly.'

Caradoc knew that his mouth was opening and closing like a newly caught fish's.

One of her hands reached out to fleetingly touch his mouth. 'You're not too old,' he protested, just as he had when he first met her.

'Oh, Caradoc, I surely am. I'm far too old to allow myself to fall pregnant like a giddy girl. But I did, although I couldn't believe it for many months. It was only when I felt the life move within me that I knew for sure. She Who Must Not Be Named had sent me a gift for reasons that only She could know and understand. I could have physicked the child away and scoured my womb clean, but somehow such an action seemed sinful.'

Suddenly, Caradoc felt his face redden. Why he should suppose that the child came from his loins was pure vanity, yet he was certain that the infant in the cradle was his.

'So I chose to bear the child. I mastered my fear of the confinement and found a local widow with a tight mouth who agreed to live with me in the last weeks of my pregnancy. I was wise to accept the woman's help, because my travail was long and very painful. I'm convinced that it was only the plans of the goddess that, eventually, permitted my child to be born alive and well. You have a daughter, Lord Caradoc, as you have probably guessed.'

'I . . .' Caradoc began.

'She's in the cradle, if you wish to meet her. I've called her Endellion.'

Slowly and fearfully, Caradoc approached the hanging cradle and peered over the side. The child who lay within was large, slender and at least five months old. Although Caradoc was accustomed to the appearance of children, he was stunned to see how mature this one was. Instead of a cap of thin baby fuzz, this infant had thick black hair that was already long enough to sport a topknot bound by a small brass clip. Caradoc felt himself smile at this proof of Saraid's maternal love.

The child's eyes were a clear grass-green that spoke of lacy ferns and forest glades. Caradoc caught himself blushing as he thought of that fern-lined shelf where the Red Well came closest to the surface.

When Endellion looked up at her father her small face puckered with alarm and she wailed at the sight of a large, masculine face looming over her.

Without stopping to think, Caradoc picked up the howling child to draw her close to his breast. Out of long habit, he began to bounce on the balls of his feet, clucking his tongue at her and playing the game of *horsies* which his own sons had loved on those few occasions when he had been permitted to play with them by his possessive wife.

Within minutes, the babe began to smile and gurgle with pleasure. Caradoc felt his weary heart begin to melt as he whispered to her in the sweet sing-song language that babies love. Glancing at Saraid, he saw that the wise woman's eyes had filled with tears. Gently, he returned Endellion to her basket and then rocked it until the little girl closed her eyes to sleep.

As he turned away from the cradle, the king discovered that Saraid had refilled their empty mugs with some potent spirit made from apples and plums.

'She's a lovely girl and likely to grow into the promise of her name, Saraid. She'll have intelligence, character and courage, as well as beauty.'

Saraid sipped at the fiery spirits and her face regained a little colour. During his game with his daughter Saraid had become increasingly pale, which suggested that the woman was either terrified or deeply unhappy. For the life of him, Caradoc was unable to understand why. Did Saraid suspect that he might deny his child?

'What's wrong, Saraid? You're very quiet and something's obviously worrying you.'

Saraid had been holding her breath to stop her sobs, so she suddenly began to hiccup with distress. The strong and vibrant woman who had seemed impervious to fear had vanished.

'You've done nothing wrong, my lord. It's me, I'm afraid. In the last days of my pregnancy, I worried that Endellion would be wanting in her wits, or afflicted physically in some way, for such tragedies often afflict the children of older mothers. But, as anyone can see, Endellion is perfectly formed.'

Saraid's voice was frantic, so Caradoc put down his mug and put his arms around her for comfort. She tried to push him away at first, but then she appeared to relax and leaned her heavy head against the king's breast. They stood there for a moment in the cone of light created by the fire, while the only sounds in the cottage were Endellion's soft breathing and the crackle and snapping of burning wood. Then Saraid pushed him away.

'I apologise, Caradoc. I'm feeling sorry for myself, instead of explaining my problems to you in a brave and direct manner.'

'I'll just make myself comfortable and wait for as long as you need, my dear.' Caradoc smoothed her frown lines, as if she was no older than Endellion.

Under his ministrations, Saraid visibly gathered her thoughts together.

'I've decided that you must take Endellion and raise her to adulthood, as she deserves. I have been the receptacle that brought her into this weary world, but you are the parent who will smooth her path in life. I'm afraid I cannot do it.'

'Why not?' Caradoc demanded. 'A child should stay with her mother, especially a girl-child. What do I know about raising infants? And what would I tell my wife? She'd not welcome an infant into Tintagel who is not her own. Any bastard child of mine would have much to bear.'

Caradoc was aghast at the enormity of Saraid's request. He was truly horrified at the thought of raising any child, least of all a female whom the world would judge as having no worth. Such a fate was a terrible burden for anyone.

'Why can't you raise your own child?' he insisted. 'I don't understand.'

'You must care for Endellion because I can't do what is best for her, Caradoc. I know my limitations, and I understand the demands that she places on my life's work.'

'Your life's work? I really don't understand.' The concept that a mother might not want to care for a child was totally foreign to him. Even Tegan Eurfron never cavilled at the raising of her sons.

'I fell into a trance at the Red Wells two days ago, that totally incapacitated me. I remembered nothing until late in the night. Endellion was alone in her basket for the entire time I was in the trance. I have set her cradle above the ground in case wild animals should try to reach her during my absences, but I can't delude myself any longer. Once she can walk, my situation will be even worse. Without my constant attendance, she could easily fall into the fire pit or wander away and drown in the stream. I dream every night that she has died in each of a thousand different ways.'

Saraid wiped her face once more to clear the tears from her face.

'Oh, Caradoc, what else can I do but give her up to you? I love her as I had never thought to love anything in this world, but I cannot protect her from harm. I will never understand why the Mother gave her to me.'

'Do you have other kinfolk who can assist you?' Caradoc asked, his mind scrambling for a way out of this difficult problem.

'No. Both of my parents died when I was still a girl and neither my mother nor my father had siblings. I am alone in this world, and so is Endellion. You are the only person who can protect her.'

The king rose and walked to the door, for he'd remembered that Huw was waiting stoically with their horses and pack animals.

'Set up camp, Huw, and picket the horses down for the night,' Caradoc instructed. 'We'll be staying at the Red Wells for a little longer than I expected. I believe our hostess can be prevailed upon to feed us tonight, but a few rabbit traps set during the dark hours might provide the mistress with some additional meat once we've gone on our way.'

Huw flashed a grin as he unsaddled the horses and piled their possessions onto a campsite close to the nearby streamlet.

His duty done, Caradoc returned to the cottage and the serious matter of his daughter's fate. In his absence, Saraid hadn't moved. Her face was sunk into her hands.

'If there is no other choice, Saraid, I can take Endellion and raise her as you would wish. In fact, she's so young that she won't miss your presence after a short length of time. However, she will ask after you as she grows older. I'd not have her believe that you didn't love her, so I'll think on this particular problem until I discover a feasible answer.'

'Why not tell my girl the truth? She's likely to be clever enough to understand the situation I found I was in after her birth,' Saraid suggested softly, her eyes filled with a new hope.

'But she'll resent you, Saraid, for she will know she has been deserted, even if I tell her that she was rejected out of love. Children rarely see the world through the same eyes as adults.'

'Whatever is meant to happen will happen! The Mother will decide!' Caradoc realised that she had already considered this dark possibility.

'But what of you? I've seen women sicken when their children are taken from them, even if they have agreed to the separation.'

'My whole life has been dedicated to the goddess and to the Red Wells from the time that I was nine years of age. Don't feel sorry for me, my lord, for an indigent, orphaned girl-child is often dedicated to a god or goddess against their will. The Christian Church also takes such children who become nuns, brothers or priests when they reach adulthood. I wasn't born for motherhood: and neither was I destined for the pleasures of family life. The goddess ensured that my babe would be a girl and, therefore, no threat to the sanctity of the Dumnonii succession. But your queen will be very unhappy, as you say. I have thought carefully about this; I asked the goddess for her advice on what should be done.'

Caradoc gave a sardonic smile. If the Old Ones existed, then they had been powerless to protect their own people from the Roman invasion, just as the Christian Church had been unable to save its nuns and priests from the Saxons who killed them so indiscriminately. Caradoc preferred to rely on his strong right arm and the courage of his warriors to ensure the safety of his realm. If he favoured any god, then it was the Jesus who embraced all people, regardless of their race or their power.

'The goddess answered me at the Red Wells. She told me that you will raise Endellion with love, but she will be very difficult to marry to any man other than the one she eventually chooses, for few potential husbands will live up to the image of her father. If she finds love, do not quibble or reject her choice out of hand, for she may not find another.'

In the face of such faith, there was nothing Caradoc could say to change her mind.

'She Who Must Not Be Named has promised me that Endellion will marry a man with great courage. She will bear sons aplenty, but a girl from her womb, child or grandchild, will become the most beautiful woman in the world and this child will return to bring glory to your house.'

Time seemed to fold and bend like a piece of parchment. Every moment in the small cottage seemed charged with power.

'We're only men and women, Saraid, and we're flesh rather than metal. Promises are not enough to provide for a child's welfare. Endellion will be hated by some influential people at court and she can only be protected as long as I'm alive. She might become alone and friendless in an alien world.'

Saraid shook her head and the firelight caught the chestnut tones in her hair so that she seemed to be wearing a crown. Caradoc blinked and the image vanished.

'I don't have the gift of prophecy, Saraid, so I can't have your certainty about the future. I can only fumble my way through each day as it comes. But Endellion is innocent of the faults and sins that brought her into existence. Yes, I'll take her into my care. But I demand a proviso in our agreement that she'll be given the chance to come to you when she's old enough to understand all that has happened in her life. Then, if she decides to return to your care, I'll consider my duty has been done. You must welcome her then, for all your fears will be over and she'll come to no harm.'

Saraid sighed with satisfaction, so Caradoc realised that she had feared he might reject his own daughter.

'You've wronged me, Saraid. I could never deny Endellion. Never! But nor will I endorse your selfish desire to give her up. You have chosen to retain your freedom rather than abide by your responsibilities to your child. You like the adoration of pilgrims and you enjoy your reputation for healing and sooth-saying. Yes, Saraid, you even do some good. But your desires are just as you described them: selfish reasons at best.'

'You're a harsh man, Caradoc,' she countered. Her eyes were beginning to show signs of anger.

'Perhaps! But I can only judge matters as I find them. You have chosen your road, Saraid, so it's to be hoped that you've made the right choice. In the years to come, I hope you remember that that I half loved you, but my love was for yourself rather than for a seer. I have never cared for prophecies or power, for I've always known that hubris waits to trap us all. Be safe, Saraid.'

Caradoc stood and drained his forgotten cup of potent spirits in one long draught.

'Can I impose on your hospitality further, and ask for some of your stew for myself and my man-servant? We will stay for one day, and then leave once the horses are fully recovered from their labours. You will have ample time to say your farewells to your daughter.'

'Thank you, Caradoc. You have always been a fair and noble man. If you wish to share my bed, I wouldn't try to dissuade you.'

'I would rather avoid the risk of siring another unwanted child. The goddess might need a boy this time, to fulfil some long-held destiny.'

'You wrong me, Caradoc. I've become honour-bound to relinquish little Endellion.'

'You must stop fooling yourself, woman. You don't love the child enough to keep her in your life, so perhaps she is better off at Tintagel. I'll give you my thanks now and bid you a good evening.'

Before the king turned to leave, he paused beside the baby's basket and peered at the sleeping girl. In repose, the child's face revealed traces of his own father's features under her baby fat and Caradoc realised that she would become a beautiful and bewitching creature.

Poor little thing, he thought. You never asked to be born and all you need is love. I'll give you love enough for two, little one, so that you'll never regret leaving this place.

He stroked her cheek with one finger and Endellion raised one plump hand in her sleep and grabbed at his forefinger with a tight grip. Then she stirred restlessly and Caradoc was able to slide his forefinger away, after which he walked to the open door without a backward glance.

The air smelled cleaner and fresher once he was out of the cottage. What had seemed so enchanting was ragged and poorly lit now, for it was stripped of the glamour that had trapped his heart for a year. Free at last, he marched off to help Huw with the horses.

Of necessity, the journey back to Tintagel was very slow. Saraid had prepared several small flasks of breast milk and cold porridge which she promised would more than satisfy Endellion until such time as they found a friendly crofter who would replenish the flasks with cow's milk. In her basket, and tied firmly into place, Endellion travelled in front of Caradoc. Quite quickly, she made her feelings known about this mode of transport. She wanted to watch the unscrolling road, the birds in the hedgerows and the animals in the fields. Prone in her basket, she had been unable to see the richness of the landscape around her.

Consequently, on the first night of their journey home, the king fashioned a sling to hang around his neck that would allow the infant girl to see what he saw, yet still feel the comfort of his strong torso at her back. Endellion quietened immediately and began to gurgle and wave her little arms at anything that took her fancy. She rarely cried now, unless her loincloths were wet; her nature was so sunny and curious that only the hardest-hearted person could resist her charm. Certainly, the farmers and their wives along the route were entranced by her and refused any payment for milk or food. But all idylls must come to an end, so the peninsula on which Tintagel rested eventually came into view.

Caradoc had rehearsed his excuses for foisting an infant onto his household but, eventually, decided that the truth would best. As soon as he arrived at the fortress, he sent for the mistress of the citadel's kitchens and ordered her to find a suitable wet nurse and several maids to care for his daughter. He allocated three rooms in one of the towers next to his own quarters and consulted his steward to ensure that these rooms were prepared for Endellion's comfort. Then he called for the master of the guard to join the steward and await his call.

'Is this your daughter, master?' his steward asked, his face incredulous as he watched the amazing sight of his king carrying a little girl in a sling around his neck.

'Aye! Endellion is five months old and is the daughter of the Wise Woman of the Red Wells. She is under my care now and will remain so until such time as she is wed. In the meantime, I expect you and your fellow servants to treat her with the same respect and devotion that you have always given to me. Your task is to inform the other servants and guardsmen that they must obey my wishes in this matter at all times.'

'We always abide by your instructions, my lord. Does the mistress know yet of the young lady's presence?' Even as he spoke, Morien realised that he'd made a serious error of judgement.

Caradoc frowned in anger that any servant would dare to demand information from their king.

'Communications that take place between the queen and the king are none of your business,' he snapped, so Morien hastily apologised.

'You may leave now, Morien, and go about your duties. You have much to do if you are to ensure that the needs of Lady Endellion are carried out to my satisfaction.'

Morien ran to obey his master's bidding.

When Rowen ap Aidan arrived, he halted inside the doorway, his face impassive.

'Ah, Rowen! I want no gossip about the matter in hand, and certainly not from my servants or my guardsmen. I expect you to protect my daughter, even at the cost of your own life. Is that understood?'

'Of course, my lord!' Rowen's face relaxed and he grinned at Endellion, making one eyebrow dance up and down. The babe was entranced and reached out towards the warrior.

Caradoc cleared his throat noisily and Rowen immediately became serious.

'I'm sorry, my lord. Do you wish me to assign a warrior to guard her room at night?'

'I don't think a guard is necessary, Rowen. I doubt that Tintagel hides an assassin who intends to harm Endellion.'

Caradoc's son and heir, Cadal, was the first to challenge his father's decision.

The boy was an attractive youth of sixteen years. He had commenced his arms' training when he was six and had since been educated under the care of several priests who acted as his tutors. Although he was Caradoc's heir, the queen had done little to ensure that her son had a full appreciation of his father's position in life.

In appearance, Cadal was a refined version of his father, although his legs were considerably longer. His hair was also black, but it curled a little, which gave his face a certain distinction. His mouth turned up at the corners so that even in repose, it seemed to be curled in a sincere smile.

Cadal entered his father's apartment with the same force as a gathering storm, barging into the room without preamble and setting the babe to crying when he slammed the door closed.

'What do you think you're doing by foisting your little bastard onto my mother? You've shamed her by passing off your by-blow as quality. I'll not have that creature in Tintagel.'

'What did you say?' Caradoc's eyes were chips of black ice. 'How dare you presume to lecture me, your king, over my behaviour. I am the master in this castell, and if I wish to fill Tintagel with bastards, as you chose to refer to your sister, then I will do so. Are you listening . . . boy?'

Cadal's father had always been a distant figure and his mother had always implied that Caradoc was a weakling who was more interested in running away on pointless hunts or minor skirmishes than facing up to his duties at home. Cadal had become used to the idea that if his mother could upbraid the king with impunity, then so could he.

His mother had raged when word of the child reached her, so Cadal had borne the brunt of her fury. Full of righteous indignation when he entered the king's chamber, he had been pulled up by the shocking realisation that perhaps his father was dangerous.

Suddenly, Cadal's mouth was as dry as the dust of a desert. He drew himself up to his full height and tried to stare his father down.

'What you do holds Mother up to ridicule and the vulgar gossip of our people. She will be humiliated by your actions.'

'Aaagh! I can hear your mother speaking through your voice, Cadal. My queen is the only person I know who would be distraught over damage to her reputation by the arrival of an innocent babe. Only your mother would use such words as *bastard* and *by-blow* to describe a harmless child. If you ever plan to become king, you'll need more than your mother's spite or her skewed vision of the world to keep the Dumnonii tribe safe from the ring of enemies who surround our walls.'

Cadal blushed hotly, revealing his own doubts about his mother's motives.

'Whatever you say, Father. But it isn't right to thrust your child upon Mother without warning her in advance.'

'I also had no warning. I've been in Tintagel for an hour, boy, with no time to discuss anything with your mother, or with anyone else. But don't allow yourself to be misled. Endellion is my child and I have decided that she will be raised as my daughter. I'd be less than a man if I allowed her to perish to save my family from a little embarrassment.'

Cadal was torn. He understood that his father was telling him that a true man stands up, admits his mistakes and then takes responsibility for them. Yet he experienced a pang of disloyalty when he acknowledged that his father's actions might have had some justification. He had been his mother's son for too many years to cast off her influence so swiftly.

Sensing a weakening in the boy's resolve, Caradoc picked Endellion up from her basket and thrust her into the boy's arms. The child's eyes were huge and her face was wet with tears. Loud noises and raised voices were new experiences, and they frightened her.

Cadal held the child awkwardly at first, until she began to protest. When he lifted her so she could see Caradoc, she settled immediately and began to play with a large brooch on the young man's shoulder that was shaped like a leaping hound. Seeing the sweetness of her slow smile, Cadal felt his animosity begin to melt.

'She's a beautiful little girl,' he admitted.

'I agree! Fortunately for Endellion, she doesn't take after her father. But she has no means of threatening your succession in the family line. In time, she'll be married to a suitable husband and will bring more land and wealth to our house. She's harmless, Cadal, and she will be looking to you for protection.'

Cadal handed the child back to his father, but he flashed his sire a distinctly wicked grin.

'Unfortunately, my new role doesn't include having to change her loincloths. She's just wet herself and . . .' Cadal sniffed delicately at his sister. 'I believe she might have soiled herself as well.'

'Aye! I believe you're right.' Caradoc began to laugh as he placed the babe back into her basket.

Endellion watched the two most important men in her life with cool, green eyes; Cadal wondered what childish thoughts were making this infant so enchanting and so enigmatic.

Unfortunately, there was to be no charming of Tegan Eurfron, Queen of the Dumnonii and Golden Breast in the annals of Caradoc's people. Her name suggested compassion and love, but these emotions had no place in her world.

The queen was tall and broad-shouldered, with jet-black hair and strongly arched brows that gave her face a permanently quizzical appearance. Her skin had a golden hue although she avoided any direct exposure to sunshine; her black eyes snapped with sudden rages and reinforced a whispered rumour that Queen Tegan had Pict ancestry. She should have been a beautiful creature, but the rigidity of her small mouth warned those men who knew her well that she was a woman of passionate emotions and inflexible will.

Caradoc approached Tegan's rooms with mixed emotions. When the king entered her apartments, she was sitting on a stool beside an open window. Surrounded by her women, she was weaving at her large loom. The pleasant sound of the shuttle was almost soporific and the women seemed to be drowsing over their mending, embroidery and muted conversation. In the rear of the small room, a young woman played a mournful melody on a stringed musical instrument.

'May we speak, my dear Tegan?' Caradoc was surprised to discover that his voice was conciliatory, given his reasons for venturing into her world. He immediately felt a moment of shame that a mere woman could so easily strip away his defences.

'Anything you need to say to me can be shared with my attendants.' The queen refused to look at him as she concentrated on threading a new coloured skein through the loom. Her voice was as stiff as the set of her shoulders.

'I'll be the judge of that, madam.' He turned slightly to face the servant women.

'Ladies, you shall leave this room immediately, and you'll stay outside until such time as I give you permission to return.'

The ladies responded like frightened birds as they stirred, swept their skirts out of his way, fluttered their hands and rose to their feet. Several of them looked back with concerned expressions, although the queen showed no fear. She merely nodded, dismissing them. Once they had vanished through the doorway, Caradoc closed the door firmly and seated himself opposite his wife.

'I've already spoken to Cadal, so I know you're aware of the commitments I have made towards the welfare of little Endellion. I want us to have no misunderstandings about my decision, Tegan, so you now have your chance to make your objections. Out with them!'

'Very well, husband, if such is your desire!'

Caradoc sighed. Tegan appeared to be sucking on something bitter, and its taste had aged her otherwise smooth face.

'How dare you insult me by bringing your by-blow into my house?'

'As ruler, I do believe Tintagel to be my house, Tegan.'

'Very well! Your house! You may use whatever terms you select, but the insult to me remains the same,' she snapped.

'I am the king, Tegan, so I have every right. If I want to fill this castell with my bastards, I can. As I've already explained to my son and heir, I will do exactly as I choose. Endellion can be no risk to our sons, so her presence in Tintagel will have little impact on you. In fact, you only need to see her on those occasions when you wish to do so.'

'And what do you think the nobility will say? I will be the butt of their scorn and their laughter, and I'd sooner die than tolerate such disrespect.' Tegan was glaring resentfully at him now.

'The aristocracy will neither laugh nor gossip, unless you give them a good reason to discuss your affairs. They'll soon forget that little Endellion hasn't been here forever if you are prepared to act like a true queen and ignore her presence.'

Caradoc thought for a moment. 'Look at me, Tegan. I'll speak the truth. I never planned to foist my child on you. In fact, I wasn't aware of her existence until her mother told me. Nor did I truly betray you. A moment's foolishness brought this infant into the world, but any further liaison with her mother would be unacceptable. The White Witch of the Red Wells belongs to no one but the goddess, which is why I have been forced to accept Endellion. What else could I do? Would you expect me to leave this child to starve?'

To this last plea, Tegan turned a bland, unforgiving face and Caradoc was revolted by her gloating. He was amazed that he had shared a bed with this creature.

'So the child is flawed as well! I suppose we can expect her to fall into fits and tell the fortunes of all and sundry. How vulgar will life become?' She shuddered artistically, while her husband clenched his fists and imagined how her delicate nose would split, bleed and swell if he was to strike her down.

'Don't be so crass, woman. Endellion is a pretty and precocious little baby who will soon have no memory of her mother. Were you a more caring and understanding woman, she would attach herself to you without hesitation ... but I can see from your manner that I've expected too much of you. However, even if you should hate her, I am insisting that you will treat her decently. This includes a requirement that you will refrain from referring to her as a freak or a bastard. When she is old enough, I intend to marry her off to a suitable husband and we will all profit from the process. Men will be glad to marry into the House of Caradoc and become a part of the Dumnonii tribe. All you are required to do is to tolerate her.'

'And if I don't?' Tegan snapped.

Caradoc rose slowly and, with ponderous calm, he approached the seated queen and pushed the loom away from her. It skidded across the floor.

'Then you will face the full force of my displeasure. The boys are old enough to survive without you, so perhaps your sensibilities would mend if you entered a nunnery. The nuns would pray for Christian mercy and love to grow in your shrivelled heart but, best of all, I wouldn't have to gaze at your sanctimonious face or listen to endless, unedifying complaints.'

For once, Caradoc had found a threat that silenced the queen. As it happened, an isolated nunnery flourished within a day's ride of Tintagel, and Tegan was aware that this particular punishment had been used by other rulers to remove embarrassing women whom they weren't able to execute. For the very first time, the queen was fearful of her husband's power.

The prospect of violence hung heavily around the king and the queen like a chill dark fog. The king gripped her pointed chin firmly with his fingers.

'Do you understand your position, Lady Tegan?'

'You have made my lack of choice very clear, my lord,' she replied. Her eyes were still defiant, but he could sense the anxiety swimming in their depths.

'And my hand will fall heavily on your sons if you use them to punish this girl-child. I hope you understand my meaning, woman, because I'll not repeat myself.'

Tegan knew she had been defeated. Her bile and anger boiled behind her pupils so he could see his wife in all her inner ugliness. Perhaps men and women were fated to be forever at war with each other.

'I understand your meaning and I will obey your commands, husband. The least said about this shameful incident, the better. May I return now to my weaving?'

'Of course! That wasn't so difficult, was it? I knew I could trust to your common sense.'

Angry that she had forced him into making such unmanly threats, Caradoc strode from the queen's apartments, pausing only to send her women back to her rooms. Behind him, the queen sat like a painted doll, with all emotion leached out of her eyes and face. The light from the open window was absorbed in her midnight hair and dark, invincible eyes.

'God help any man who trusts to the loving natures of women,' Caradoc murmured aloud, as he stalked quickly down the corridor. He was anxious to leave her icy presence behind him.

But he couldn't escape the freezing chill which seemed to have settled into his bones.

THE WAY TO ANDERIDA

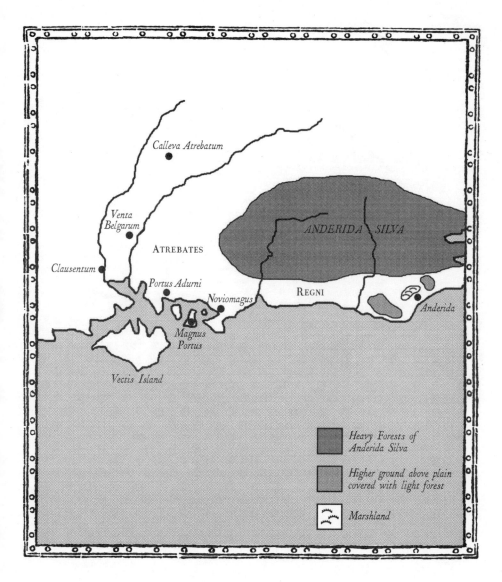

THE BATTLE OF ANDERIDA

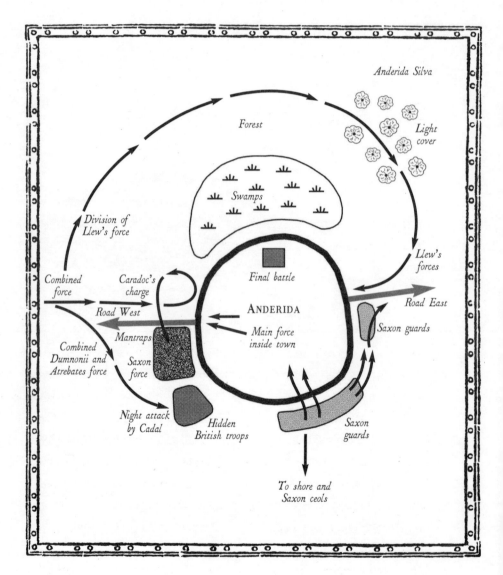

Anderida Silva

Forest

Light cover

Division of
Llew's force

Swamps

Llew's
forces

Combined
force

Caradoc's
charge

Final battle

ANDERIDA

Road East

Road West

Mantraps

Main force
inside town

Saxon guards

Combined
Dumnonii and
Atrebates force

Saxon
force

Night attack
by Cadal

Hidden
British troops

Saxon
guards

To shore and
Saxon ceols

CHAPTER XII

A SAXON SUMMER

It is never right to do wrong or to requite wrong with
wrong, or when we suffer evil to defend ourselves by doing
evil in return.

Socrates, *Plato Crito*

The years passed, as did the troubles and joys that afflict all
human beings, while Caradoc held his kingdom together in his
firm hands. His hair became liberally sprinkled with grey and
Cadal took on more of the duties of ruling. The king's younger
son, Cadoc, married one of Gwaun ap Mairtin's younger
daughters, Guenor, who came to Tintagel to brighten the life of
Caradoc. Cadoc's mother had opposed the wedding, for Tegan
Eurfron could never look with love on a girl who might one day
become mistress of Tintagel. Consumed with vanity, the queen
was determined not to relinquish her youth, so the thought of
grandchildren filled her heart with horror.

Guenor was russet-haired, brown-eyed and tiny. Cadoc loved
her passionately and pressed his brother to join him in wedlock,
but Cadal watched as Guenor suffered under Tegan Eurfron's

constant demands that continued until the poor girl was little more than a slave.

As the household settled into new and unfamiliar patterns, Caradoc watched the child's suffering and knew instinctively that any partisanship on his part would rain even more hell down on her head. Tegan Eurfron had not forgotten her defeat at her husband's hands, so any affection that the king showered on the young girl must be lavished on her when the queen was absent. The king's household tiptoed nervously under the queen's unreasonable desire to remain forever young and beautiful.

'Something must be done to solve this family dilemma, my boy,' Caradoc decided. 'I, for one, am tired of constant ructions in this household. It's time you were sacrificed, Cadal, so perhaps it's time to marry you off. You've been footloose and fancy-free for far too long. I think we'll present your mother with a fait accompli.'

'What?' Cadal yelped. Whenever his father made a decision like this, someone in the family would be required to experience a measure of inconvenience to fit in with Caradoc's carefully formulated plans. Was he to be the latest hapless victim?

'I don't want to marry, Father, so I won't have some poor cow foisted on me. You claim you aren't happy. I know that Cadoc isn't happy, and neither is Guenor. Everyone in Tintagel suffers except Mother. Why should I be miserable too?'

Cadal's pugnacious chin, so like Caradoc's own, was thrust forward in defiance of his king.

'Don't worry, Cadal. I wouldn't force a girl on you that you couldn't come to like. I hope to find someone suitable while we're on our next little jaunt, if the fates are kind to you.'

'Little jaunt? God help me!' Cadal mumbled plaintively.

Once Caradoc had made up his mind on a course of action, stopping him was like trying to hold back the sea. Eventually, Cadal agreed to travel through the towns of their northern neighbours in search of a suitable wife, a prospect that filled the young prince with horror. Had he realised how torn his father really was, he might have faced the journey with more patience.

Caradoc had vowed to spare his children from arranged marriages, and was determined that Tegan Eurfron would not be allowed to dig her claws into the throat of Cadal's future wife. With this in mind, the true reason for father and son to journey into the north must be kept secret.

With Cadal in tow, the small party set off with the complaints of his queen ringing in their ears and a promise from Cadoc that his father's throne would remain secure during his absence. Caradoc had no doubts, for Cadoc was a stolid young man who ignored his mother's tantrums; he often wished his eldest son had been imbued with the same calm and steadfast nature.

Despite his wife's disapproval, Caradoc decided to take Endellion with him, thereby adding considerably to the size his cavalcade and slowing the progress of the journey. Endellion was young for such a long trek, but she was more mature than most girls of her age and had an endearing nature that was certain to charm Caradoc's neighbours when she was presented to them. As usual, Caradoc was playing a deep game.

'Are you mad, Caradoc?' his wife sniped. 'You'd rather risk the child than be without her company for a few weeks? She's far too young!'

'Do be quiet, Tegan! It's time Endellion saw something of the world around her.'

Endellion was only six years old but, other than one notable instance, she had rarely been ill. The journey was a wonder for her, although her nurse and the maids slowed the speed of their journey with their constant demands for rest. Cadal risked his father's ire by querying his purpose.

'Think, Cadal,' Caradoc explained patiently. 'I don't want to enter my neighbour's lands with just you and my personal guard in tow. Endellion's presence suggests that our visit is peaceful.'

Still, regardless of the plethora of suitable young ladies who were paraded before his mulish son like prize livestock, none had caught Cadal's interest or fancy. Girl after girl was introduced to him: all vied for the coup of capturing the heart of the Dumnonii heir. Cadal passed through the feasts, the hunts and the private visits with a vague smile plastered on his face, as he ignored the eager young butterflies who fluttered about him. Careless of their feelings, he remained disengaged and distant.

By the time the party reached the town of Venta Silurum, Caradoc had begun to believe that Cadal was deliberately being obstinate. Father and son were almost at outs by the time they entered the ancient, misty land of Cymru with its soaring mountains, deep forests and swift rivers. In such a romantic landscape, Venta Silurum nestled like a small, clean jewel.

Once the travellers arrived in the Silures capital, Caradoc realised that this idyllic town was ruled by a friendly, jovial king and a generous queen. But he had given up hope of gaining a betrothal, so he decided to treat this sojourn as a last holiday before returning to Tintagel.

Caradoc was surprised anew at the strange laws of physical attraction. To his surprise, his stubborn son gave his heart to the eldest daughter of the House of the Silures without any encouragement or hesitation. In Caradoc's opinion, the cheerful, red-haired Ardunn had no special beauty or exceptional talent to win the heart of the prince. But Cadal was lost, as was Ardunn, in a sweet idyll. With a surge of hope, Caradoc realised that Ardunn was a grand girl, more than capable of deflecting with Tegan Eurfron's mercurial temper. And then Cadal surprised his father once again by insisting that their betrothal should be speedily drawn up so he could wed his lady before they returned to Tintagel as man and wife.

Aelheran ap Einion and his queen, Aoifi, would normally have been required by custom to travel down the coast to Tintagel, where their daughter would be delivered into the hands of her future husband and family. With rare understanding and tactful diplomacy, Cadal suggested holding the wedding in Venta Silurum so that the bride's parents and friends could host her wedding feast.

In retrospect, Caradoc decided that the happy young couple had acted with wisdom. After only a week or two in her company, Caradoc knew that Tegan Eurfron would dislike this spirited girl. But his difficult wife would be forced to accept the marriage with as much good grace as she could muster.

After a month of celebration, the party returned to Tintagel, with Cadal and Ardunn married and bedded, to face the fury of Tegan Eurfron. Rage she did, but Ardunn merely smiled infuriatingly and took no notice. Under her tutelage, the timid Guenor also learned to refuse the queen's more excessive demands, although she shivered like a frightened rabbit whenever she defied her mother-in-law's selfish edicts.

Through it all, Caradoc congratulated himself on his brilliant scheme and began to enjoy the fruits of a happy family, at long last.

Years passed, until Caradoc had almost forgotten that Maximus had ever come to Tintagel's halls. While age spotted Caradoc's hands and weakened his sword arm, he retained the strength and longevity of his ancestors. He fully expected to see his four grandsons grown and married off before the shades came to sweep him into the darkness.

As for little Endellion, she grew like a weed, as beautiful as any girl who ever graced the tribe. Caradoc doted upon her and dreaded the day when custom would demand that she be married. Her love kept him youthful, and he held it close to his aging bones like a warm blanket.

Like a slender, brightly coloured bird, Endellion sang and danced through the seasons and brought love to places where there had only been indifference. The guardsmen and the servants at Tintagel were enamoured of the child, so she could easily have been spoiled. But the outpourings of affection and interest showered on her were balanced by the queen's unending criticism and her father's common sense, so Endellion remained free from any character flaws.

Only one major incident marred this period of joy in Caradoc's life. One night, the child had awoken, screaming, after experiencing a night horror. She was scrubbing her hands wildly, and seemed hysterical, so her terrified maids scattered until Caradoc arrived to manage the disturbance. What the king heard and saw caused him some concern as several old fears returned to haunt him.

As he straightened her bed and gathered her into his arms. Endellion gradually quietened and he asked the seven-year-old what had so thoroughly frightened her.

'Father? Are dreams true?' she asked desperately, as her eyes flooded again with tears.

'No, sweetheart. The gods have been known to send messages to a rare few, but dreams are usually stories that come to us when we are sleeping. These stories often involve matters that have been worrying us when we are awake. Dreams aren't real! They're just shadows of life.'

'But I'm sure that my dream was very real. I could hear and smell everything as if I was there,' Endellion wailed.

'Were you a part of the dream, poppet?' Caradoc asked kindly, stroking her hair.

'No, Father. I was watching, but I don't think I was there. No one seemed to see me.'

'Oh?' Caradoc's stomach tightened, because Saraid had described her visions as if she was an invisible watcher who hovered above the crowd. He hoped his instincts were wrong, for the curse of foreknowledge could prove to be fatal.

'I saw an old man, Father. He was dressed in a red cloak and he had many big pins on his chest. I think he was a soldier like the ones we saw at Venta Silurum when we went to find Ardunn. You know, Da,' she said softly, the endearment used by the citadel's servant children falling naturally off her tongue.

'What was there about the old man that you really noticed, Endellion?'

'They tore away his brooches and badges, Father, and then they broke his sword. It was horrible, because the old man just stood at attention and let them do it. I saw then that he was weeping. Why would anyone want to make an old man feel so bad?'

'I don't know, my darling, but some people are simply cruel. Did you learn who *they* were?' Caradoc was hoping to discover something that gave him a clue to the identity of that old man.

'No. The person in charge was wearing a crown of golden leaves. The crown looked strange because it was tilted on his head and was ready to fall off. Everybody bowed to him.'

'Oh . . . I think I understand.' Caradoc struggled to keep his voice steady and natural.

'It was awful, Father.' The tears returned as Endellion began to remember the details of the dream. 'A man in a mask walked up to the old man and stood beside him. The old man gave him several coins, and then promised to forgive him. After that, the man in the mask put a thin cord around the old man's neck and choked him. The old man's eyes bulged out and his tongue was hanging out of his mouth. I didn't want to watch, but I couldn't close my eyes. Was it real, Da? It looked real.' Then Endellion began to cry in earnest until Caradoc fed her some warm milk with a dollop of strong spirits to assist her to sleep. She grimaced at the taste but swallowed it all at her father's coaxing.

Caradoc released her hand after Endellion succumbed to sleep. Even then, the child stirred restlessly until she was covered with her favourite blanket. Caradoc was forced to brush silent tears away from her eyes. He was prepared to protect her with his life, but how could he save her from afflictions that lay within her own mind?

As the king rose and left the room, his mind was awhirl with dire possibilities.

No one spoke of Endellion's bad dream. The servants presumed that the child had been overexcited, while Caradoc feared to raise the spectre of the White Witch of the Red Wells. But the dream of a Roman execution was so unexpected and so alien to Endellion's life experiences that Caradoc's mind was distracted by futile guesses at the identity of the victim. He never doubted the veracity of Endellion's dream and believed his daughter had viewed a real incident that occurred in some far-off place in the Roman world.

The child could not have known anything of such matters for

she had been protected from all such ugliness. Yet his daughter had known so many of the small details associated with the execution of an aristocratic Roman.

Maximus had told the king that executioners placed coins in the mouth of a victim once the garrotte had served its purpose. In this way, the Ferryman on the River Styx would be paid to ensure that the soul of an executed Roman could continue its journey into the Underworld.

No, Endellion could not have known anything of this. As for an emperor with a crown slipping from his head? Caradoc preferred not to consider the meaning of *that* evocative image.

Eventually, Caradoc might have forgotten this vivid dream, for his daughter reverted to her usual sunny nature and no graphic visions returned to trouble her in the coming year. But news filtered slowly into Britannia from the continent. Gossip from Rome eventually reached Tintagel, via Gwaun ap Mairtin, that Theodosius the Elder was dead, so Caradoc remembered Endellion's night of horror with a fearful pang. After a series of battles in northern Britannia and Africa, Theodosius fell out of favour with the new emperor, Valentinian. Despite his many years of faithful service to the empire, he had been strangled by the imperial executioner. Caradoc's mind turned back to Maximus, and he wondered if his friend had met a similar fate.

Unfortunately, little of interest had been heard of Maximus, except that he had been promoted to the post of Dux Moesiae Secundae for his successful campaigns against the Goths.

Caradoc shook his greying head with admiration. Once again, Maximus's luck had held, so Macsen Wledig had survived to live and thrive for a little longer.

Spring followed winter and was replaced in turn by summer and autumn. Still nothing changed, except for the frigid, disdainful face of Tegan Eurfron when she succumbed to the passage of time. Fine lines began to net her eyes until her reflection in the mirror filled her vain heart with fury.

Into this world of peace and plenty, the same barbarian hordes that had looked towards Britannia with lustful eyes in the past resumed their raids on vulnerable places along the British coastline. The Hibernians, Picts and Saxons all made uncoordinated attacks during a pleasant spring when the seas were quiet and the snows had retreated back into the frozen north.

Endellion was eleven, almost twelve, when Caradoc and Cadal rode off to honour their treaty obligations with the Atrebates and the Regni tribes after a large force of Saxons gained a foothold at Anderida, from where they threatened the safety of the entire southern coast. Cadoc protested when he was told that he must remain behind to act as regent in his father's stead, but he understood that someone must stay at Tintagel to rule the tribe. Predictably, the queen raged about uncaring husbands who were prepared to abandon their wives during perilous times, while Endellion knew she would be at the queen's mercy during her father's absence.

Ardunn remained brave, for she had been raised in a royal family and understood the duties that were required from heirs to the throne. However, despite this advantage, talk of Cadal's absence frightened the children, who had been alarmed by Tegan Eurfron's constant warnings that their father would never return. Ardunn asked the queen to refrain from her warnings of destruction, but here pleas had no appreciable effect.

'Please, Mother. My children look to you for comfort, but you're frightening them by insisting that their father will die in the coming battles.'

'How dare you attempt to censure me,' the queen had hissed back. 'Somebody in this house must be realistic! The barbarians are only a few weeks away from us. So who will protect Tintagel in his absence? Cadoc will try, but he's never been to war. Meanwhile, my husband intends to play at a war that is none of his business. What will become of us?'

Ardunn listened to all of Tegan Eurfron's complaints and kept her tongue firmly between her teeth. No reasoned argument would ever work with this queen.

Regardless of Caradoc's soothing promises that he and Cadal would take extra efforts to ensure each other's safety during the campaign, Endellion knew exactly what her fate would be during his absence, which would invite Tegan Eurfron to take some of her anxiety out on the unprotected child.

The girl understood that Caradoc was now an old man, but she had never faced the possibility of his mortality. Each day seemed to bring new fears.

Meanwhile, Caradoc tried to coax his daughter out of her terrors.

'Nothing will happen to me, child. You're fussing and weeping for no worthwhile reason. I must lead my men. I know – I'm bent in the back and my hands are losing their strength. But I'm only fifty! There's still fight in me, and my warriors would be disheartened if I were to skulk at home like a rabbit. A king must lead from the front, or he's not worth following.

'As for you, my darling girl, the queen may try to throw your birth in your teeth, but you must always remember that your birth-mother, Saraid, is a woman of true power in her own right. She is famed among our people for her healing, so you must never be ashamed of her.' Caradoc bit his thumb and considered his daughter's position.

'You may speak your mind, Endellion, if the queen attacks you. You don't have to be discourteous or disrespectful, but you may say what should be said, if she makes cruel remarks to you. No one in Tintagel will think the worse of you.'

This long speech was unlike Caradoc. He was determined to die, if need be, to hold the treaty in place, understanding instinctively that the unity of the kings was vital to the survival of the southern Britons. He also knew that where he led, the other kings would follow. The Romans were fully occupied in the north as they fought ongoing battles with their old enemies, the Picts and the Hibernians, so the tribes in the south and south-west could expect no help from their masters.

'But why is Cadal going with you? What if you are both killed?' Endellion wailed this last complaint, for she dearly loved her half-brother, who was second only to Caradoc in her fulsome heart. She couldn't imagine a world without these two men, despite the love she also held for Cadal's brother, Cadoc.

'Poor Cadoc! I suppose he can be sacrificed, as long as Cadal and I are safe.' Caradoc laughed at his daughter's suddenly horrified face, before he pulled her into his arms. 'There! I understand! But you must allow me to go about my duties with a smile on your pretty face.'

'Oh, Da, I could never wish harm to Cadoc. How could you think such a thing? I don't want any of you to go riding off and leave me behind. Can't I go as well? I swear that I'd not get in your way.'

'We men are paltry things, my dear, and our characters are weak and frail. But we fight because we must. It's our God-given duty to save our families from terror or the need to hide themselves from vicious, murderous oppressors who would put them to the sword. I don't want to hear any more talk of travelling with me. I'll be much safer on the battlefield if I don't have to worry about you and my other darlings.'

He smiled into Endellion's eyes and all teasing fled from his expression.

'I want you to promise me that you will help Ardunn and Guenor to protect their boys. I love my grandsons, but they're not old enough to save themselves if Tintagel should come under attack. I'm trusting in you to help me, petal. Will you carry out this important task for me?'

Endellion swore with her hand on her heart that she would accede to his wishes. Her eyes glowed with the ardour of her promise, so Caradoc was content.

Summer came; and so did the hot breath of death. The Saxon raiders ranged across Anderida Silva at will as they burned villages, killed and raped indiscriminately and stripped the countryside of every item of value. Every church was razed to the ground, including many where the priests and nuns were still at the altars when the buildings were gutted.

At the same time, driving rain came to the land to release the baking earth from the heat. The ever-present dust was replaced with mud, but the Saxons still roamed where they chose, while the predators and scavengers of the air followed their trail.

Eventually, the combined Dumnonii and Dobunni army drove the Saxons back towards a collection of mud huts that bordered the swamplands in a bitter series of attacks that brought them ever closer to the sea. Three months had passed in debilitating heat as the oppressive humidity and unnatural storms whipped the skies into cauldrons of turgid clouds. In bivouac, the warriors endured the misery of regular rainstorms, strong winds and the oppressive heat that heralded each period of bad weather.

Three men were in command of this force. The young Dobunni king, Llew, was still unblooded in warfare. However, he was under the tutelage of old Caradoc, as wily a strategist as any of the kings in Britannia. The third in the triumvirate was Cadal, Caradoc's son and the heir to the Dumnonii throne. The prince was also a tyro on the battlefield. Inexorably, after numerous ambushes and desperate spells of vicious fighting, the British army had pursued the Saxons raiders as the northerners made a series of strategic withdrawals towards the safety of their base at Anderida. Here, in the balmy waters of the south coast, lay the ceols that would carry the Saxons and their plunder back to their homes in Saxony.

Llew ap Adwen was slender like his dead father, but Caradoc was pleased to discover that this young man was a strong and determined leader. Time had passed and many of the kings who made their mark on that first treaty were dead now. Unsurprisingly, Fiachna had succumbed to an infection in his leg that poisoned his body. Maximus would have laughed himself sick at this news, for the original injury had been caused by a bite from a bedbug.

'It's a pity that Maximus isn't here. He'd have made mincemeat of these Saxons,' Caradoc mused, forgetting that Cadal was riding close enough to hear. Cadal was keeping a close eye on his father as the troop neared the margins of the woods, for they would need to cover a patch of exposed ground at some speed. He suspected that the troop could be riding directly into the path of Saxon arrows fired from ambush.

'Who, Father?' Cadal asked, as he tried to dry his sweat-drenched hair with a strip of cloth. His muddy helmet was hooked onto his saddle and the younger man promised himself that he would polish its dulled surfaces if these miserable lands would stay dry for even a few hours.

'Magnus Maximus! Don't you remember? He was some sort of kinsman to Theodosius the Elder. Theodosius the Younger, the old man's son, has become the ruler in Constantinople. Can you imagine that, boy? Theodosius is Caesar, yet his father was executed by Emperor Valentinian for treason! As it happened, Valentinian was also sent to the shades in much the same way as Theodosius.'

'Oh! . . . You're talking about your Roman friend,' Cadal replied dismissively. 'I don't think I'd like to be an emperor in Rome. They scarcely seem to last longer than a few years before they're killed off. Worse still, they're usually slain by their own guardsmen – or their kinsmen.'

'Gwaun is adamant that the Roman Empire is in decline,' Caradoc said. 'If he's right, it will be our people who'll suffer if the legions should return to the continent.'

Cadal's eyes swept the sea of long grass and the rutted track leading to an impoverished town that lay between the salt marshes and the sand dunes. The scene seemed disarmingly quiet and empty, so Caradoc was on his guard.

'Yes, lads, the northerners are out there,' Caradoc explained to his two deputies as the three leaders stood on a low rise overlooking the terrain that must be crossed if the Britons were to reach the gates of the small town. 'They've probably got some of their number dug into the fringes of the swamp, while more of the bastards will be in the long grasses beside the road and more again embedded among the walls around the perimeter of the town. This Saxon commander is trying to suck us into a trap.'

'He seems to be more astute than most of his fellow northerners,' Llew observed.

'So? What are we going to do?' Cadal asked.

These two young men were alike in many ways, despite the differences in their thought processes. Cadal preferred to deal with factual essentials, while Llew tended to mull over the reasoning behind the strategies adopted by the enemy commander. Both men were impatient, but Caradoc was confident that he could harness their differing talents.

'More to the point, what do you young bucks think we should do?' Caradoc challenged, his dark eyes twinkling. 'I'd like to hear your thoughts, gentlemen.'

Llew realised he'd been dismissed for the moment, so he turned and cantered down to his cavalry and the baggage train. His mind was already searching for a sensible strategy that would crack Anderida open like a particularly sweet nut.

Caradoc watched Llew go, before turning back to Cadal with a face that seemed to have been chipped out of granite. 'There's one final aspect that you should consider about my Roman friend. He will do well for himself now that his kinsman is the ruler of the Eastern Empire. But, if he should return to Britannia, his friendship will be a boon to those Britons that he holds in high regard. This group would include those who will eventually rule the Dumnonii tribe.'

'Thanks be to the gods,' Cadal muttered under his breath with acidic sarcasm.

'I heard that, Cadal,' the older man faced his son directly. Cadal was surprised to discover that his father was very angry.

'Will you never learn, boy? I had hoped you had stopped listening to your mother.'

His heir bridled and his face coloured in a hot flush. 'I'm

thirty, Father, so I'm no boy. And Mother is occasionally right in what she says.'

'How long do you think Britannia would survive if Rome and her legions should leave us to fight our own battles? We'd manage for a generation or two, because we're strong and we can exercise self-discipline if the threat to our people is sufficiently pressing. But we couldn't last against truly implacable enemies. We'll continue to crush the Saxons for some time, but they'll keep coming back, again and again. We're surrounded by enemies who won't give up.'

Cadal thrust his helmet onto his head and turned his horse to join Llew, where he hoped to find a more sympathetic and receptive listener.

But he was disappointed. Cold, reasoned and dispassionate in manner, the Dobunni king deferred to Caradoc's experience and approved of the Dumnonii king's *Roman* attitudes to the impending attack on their Saxon enemies.

Then, as they were speaking, one of Llew's scouts approached his commander after completing a two-hour reconnaissance within the Saxon lines.

The news that this woodsman passed to the Dobunni king was so important that Llew insisted on informing Caradoc immediately.

'Sir,' Llew began respectfully. 'I've just received some intelligence from my scouts that will be vital to any plans you make for our attack on Anderida. I apologise for disturbing your meal, but the information couldn't wait.'

'What have you discovered, Llew? Caradoc asked, his mouth half-filled with food.

'One of my scouts has just informed me that two nests of Saxons are dug in and waiting for us. One long trench is just over there!' The Dobunni pointed towards a dead tree to the left of the dilapidated town gate. 'If you look very closely, you'll see a faint line in the tussocks some forty feet in front of the tree. That line of camouflage runs across the track, so it's about twenty paces long. According to your own scout, Trefor, that's the place where a nasty series of trenches and mantraps have been filled with sharpened stakes that are just waiting for a cavalry charge.'

Caradoc squinted and his eyes found the tree, but locating the trench was too much for his failing vision. 'Where are the rest of the Saxons located?'

'They're dug in, so they must be level with that dead tree. They've burrowed into the sandy soil to create a hide, so it's an excellent place for them to attack us from behind if we were able to evade the mantraps. Can you see a long line of shrubbery that's growing in an almost straight line? Yes? Well, that's a ruse! Those branches are different from the others around them, because they were cut down from this forest.'

The landscape in the vicinity of Anderida's western gate was unremarkable. A wet spring and a dry summer had nourished the swathes of long grass, so the heavy heads provided an ideal environment where the defenders of the small town could secrete themselves in their shallow trenches. Moreover the land undulated in waves, as if sculpted by the forces of wind and water.

But the landscape also provided cover that could be used by the Britons, who could also use the long grass, loosely piled boulders and occasional hollows to hide their warriors away from Saxon eyes.

Even as he spoke to his two deputy commanders, Caradoc's gaze continued to range over the strip of land between the forest and the walls of the town, while he searched for weaknesses that could be exploited during the coming battle. Finally, his plan became clear.

'When did the Saxons become so damned clever?' Cadal wondered. 'You had me convinced that they favour headlong charges where they can cover themselves in glory. Fighting as part of an organised whole wouldn't normally be to their liking.'

Caradoc looked at his son with affectionate scorn.

'The Saxon bands reflect the abilities of their commanders, and this thane has demonstrated his strategic brilliance on many occasions. Huw caught one of their stragglers a few nights ago and his warriors worked hard to loosen his tongue. He refused to reveal any usable information despite their best attempts at torture. Such loyalty is difficult to overcome.'

Caradoc smiled at his two deputies who gaped at the king's admission.

'Don't frown, Cadal! We're at war with these Saxons, so it's necessary to gain intelligence in any way we can. Perhaps torture isn't the most honourable method of interrogation, but the scout we captured had no intention of speaking to any of us. I tried to reason with him myself, but I wasted my breath.'

'Why didn't you inform us that Huw had caught a spy?' Cadal demanded. 'Didn't you trust us to assist you in the interrogation?'

'You're both inexperienced, so you lack the stomach for some of the dirty tactics that must be used if we're to crush these Saxons. I intend to win this battle, Cadal, and I'll use every means to achieve that end.'

'Did the prisoner divulge anything at all?' Llew asked slowly but respectfully.

'The Saxon thane is a landless man from the mouth of the Albis River. Our prisoner referred to him as Harald Ironfoot. The name is something of a jest because as a boy he killed his first man with a well-placed kick to the back of the neck and the name stuck. Now he's gathered a large band of followers around him who are eager to pillage the coasts of Gaul and Britannia. He has six ceols of his own, and more are made available to him whenever he needs them. Our enemy always seems to win, so he's admired by his warriors. Damn him!'

Both younger men looked puzzled, so Caradoc explained. 'Ironfoot is an experienced commander and he wins his battles. Consider the resistance that we've struck from these Saxons since we made our first contact with their main force. He ravages the forests, villages and small towns of the Regni tribe, and then disappears like a wisp of smoke. He keeps his men moving. His strategy is always to retire in good order and his warriors make forced marches that lead them back to their base in Anderida. He gathers anything of value as he goes, and he always remains at least one step ahead of us. His ceols await his return, which indicates that he has no intention of staying in Britannia, at least not on this particular raid. For the moment, his plan is to make good his escape with his captured slaves and his stolen gold.'

'Harald Ironfoot has cost us dearly at every step of this campaign. The Saxon have hit us a couple of times with short, sharp ambushes, but we haven't been able to get them to face us in a direct battle,' Llew complained.

'Exactly! Ironfoot knows what he's about. He strikes with stealth and speed, and then retreats. He's very flexible and, to be honest, he caught me off guard.'

Caradoc bit at his thumb, a sure sign that he was worrying away at a problem

'Ironfoot has already won one major battle when he caught a troop of Sorcha's Regni in the ambush that killed Sorcha's heir. The man will be hard to beat, especially as he wants us to take the initiative. We got very little out of our prisoner except the name of his master and a few unimportant details. In fact, the bastard laughed when I boasted that we'd crush his Saxon friends when they finally stopped running, so we're treading on dangerous ground. I gathered that Ironfoot already has a plan to counter any attack we might mount on his defences in Anderida.'

'I suppose you killed the poor bastard,' Cadal retorted.

'You must learn as much as you can about your enemy, Cadal. I didn't have to kill the man – because he swallowed his own tongue and choked. Could you imagine how much hate and determination would be needed to do that?'

Both younger men looked appalled.

'Saxons don't betray their thanes, even when they are under torture. He decided to kill himself when he realised he might be forced to reveal important information. Every man will crack when the agony eventually becomes unendurable.'

'Well, how can we defeat such determined men?' Llew asked bluntly. 'Like you, I believe we have to win a decisive victory here, if only to stop this commander from returning next spring with a new band of followers.'

'We go back to the basics,' Caradoc replied promptly, pleased that his explanation had brought both of these young pups to heel. He was always prepared to spend a little time passing on his experience.

'Where else could the Saxons be entrenched?' he asked. 'A leader as sharp as Ironfoot would never settle for a single defensive response to an impending attack.'

Llew cleared his throat. 'Trefor said as much when our scouts found the mantraps, so he went out last night to look at Anderida from the east. He located another set of traps on the southern side of the town and also saw several Saxons in the town proper where the spaces between the buildings are very narrow. He is certain that they'll use the town as their last line of defence if their perimeter starts to shrink back into the town. The houses are walled so they are defensible, especially if the Saxon mantraps should weaken us. We'll be forced to fight, street by street, and building by building.'

'So what do we do, Father? My instincts tell me that we should ride down on them, take our losses and then plough over the top of the bastards,' Cadal said, looking sombre. 'But I have a feeling we'd need twice the number of warriors that are at our disposal if we want to take such direct action. Are those open gates meant to lure us into making a charge?'

'That's exactly what they want, so we definitely won't do that. We're going to divide into two forces, but we'll be waiting till tomorrow afternoon to mount our attack. We'll let them rot in their holes for a day or so, and let their nerves stretch from the tension.'

He paused.

'Besides, Llew, you'll need a fair length of time to carry out the orders I'm about to give you. You are to mount an attack on the eastern side of Anderida. You'll take your force through the forest to the north of the town before positioning yourself in light woodland that lies to the east. It's a long journey, but any attempt to cross the swamps would be impossible in the time available to us. The Saxons will have their scouts out and about, but we'll send our own men into the forest to unsettle them. Ironfoot intends to abandon Anderida soon, so his scouts won't range far into the forest. You'll probably have to ride throughout the night and make a concerted attack from the south-east in the late afternoon. Could you accomplish this task?'

'What about the beachhead?' Llew's voice broke nervously.

'Do we need to destroy the ceols to prevent a Saxon escape?'

'Why would we attack troops who are alert and waiting for us? Ironfoot's strategy is to protect his ceols, because he doesn't want to be trapped in that piss-poor little town. Your task is to attack the town gates on the eastern side and scythe down anything that moves. But I believe the Saxons guarding the ceols will attempt to reinforce the eastern gate and set up ambush positions inside the town proper. You'll have to fight hand-to-hand and hut-by-hut, but the Saxons will be at a disadvantage with many of their number embedded in the defences on the beach side of the town.'

'When do I begin my charge?' Caradoc was pleased to note that the young man was concentrating on the important elements of his task.

'I'll arrange for a signal fire to be lit on a hillock on this side of Anderida. Its smoke will be your attack signal. While you push on with your attack on the town, our forces will be mounting a charge on our side. If Fortuna is with us, we should meet up with you in the town centre.'

'Aren't we doing exactly what they want us to do? We'll be charging down at their concealed men,' Cadal asked. 'Could we divert some of their attention away from what we're doing?'

'Agreed! We can't attack Ironfoot's Saxons without being seen and they're expecting a cavalry charge tomorrow. But we'll do something that isn't expected. Could you lead one hundred men to that cluster of rocks below us tonight if you were crawling on your bellies? You'll have to spend the best part of tomorrow's daylight hidden away in absolute silence, so we'll be asking a lot from your warriors.'

Cadal stared off into the distance. To the right of the dead tree, and slightly behind it, rose an area of rocky scree topped with a cluster of boulders on land that was more sand than soil. 'It will take most of the night, but we can do it.'

'Good! Your men will need to burrow into the landscape in two groups under the command of their own officers. You'll be in overall command of both groups.'

If Caradoc was experiencing any fears for his first-born son, he was showing no sign of nervousness. Cadal recognised Caradoc's manner for what it really was and knew his own features bore the same calculated detachment. Leadership in combat demanded a chill and clear brain, else the battle could well be lost.

'What do we do once we have successfully positioned ourselves behind the Saxon lines?'

'You dig in! Once you've settled into your attack positions, you have to wait for the sentinel fire to give off its trail of smoke. The waiting will be the hard part. If you are to catch your victims unawares, you must mount your attack against the Saxon rear the instant they rise to their feet to attack my cavalry. Is that understood? Come over here, lads, and I'll make a drawing that will show you exactly how our plan must work.'

Caradoc rose creakily and began to draw lines in the soft soil.

'I'll be leading our cavalry along the road at a trot. When I raise my hand, the signal fires will be lit and Llew will attack on the eastern side of the town. They will charge out of their positions in the woods and wheel at the last moment to capture as much of Anderida as they can before we eventually meet up with them. We expect a Saxon counterattack on the southern beaches, but they'll have to hunt for you among the houses and the narrow streets of Anderida. It will take some time for these Saxons to organise. Use your bowmen as much as you can once you're inside the town – they must take as many arrows as they can carry. Meanwhile, your prime objective is to draw as many Saxons into the town as you can – and then kill the bastards. God speed, my boy! Now get on with it!'

'Aye! Thank you, my lord.' Llew looked grim and determined under the shadow of his helmet.

Caradoc turned to face his son. 'You, Cadal, will be dug in and will have been waiting all day for the signal to move off. The Saxons will be expecting my cavalry to fall into their mantraps, but I'll wheel my men off the road before I reach them. Then I'll charge directly at them. I'll make one good run at them to break up their ranks, and then I'll withdraw and make another advance again, in an attempt to ensure we have their full attention. By that time you should be formed up behind them, Cadal, and we can manoeuvre them into the jaws of a pincer movement.'

Caradoc's facial expression was fierce and wolfish; his eyes seemed yellow in the afternoon light. He ground his hands together as if he was crushing a walnut.

'We'll have them! I've sworn to Endellion that we'll survive this battle and I intend to keep my promise.

'We'll make camp for the rest of the day and sleep for as long as we dare. Eat now, Cadal, and ensure that your warriors have eaten and carry enough rations to last through tomorrow. Huw and Trefor will act as your forward scouts while you're crawling across the open ground. You can trust them to locate any Saxon lookouts and deal with them. For your part, be ready to move as soon as night falls.

'One further task must be carried out, Llew. Five of your less-able warriors and one of the elderly officers must be entrusted to build a cairn of timber that will become the sentinel fire. These men will be responsible for lighting the fire when I give the command. When you've delegated this task, get yourself some sleep until such time as I wake you.'

Caradoc was looking younger by the moment, as his eyes danced with excitement and steely determination.

'One final matter, boys! Tell your men why we're fighting tomorrow. Remind them of the burned-out villages and the corpses of the children bloating in the summer heat. We're the only protection that our peasants have, so we must make Ironfoot pay for his murderous rampages and ensure that he never comes back to Anderida.'

'Aye!' Both young men replied in chorus, their faces vivid with anticipation of the challenges ahead.

The sun slanted through the trees and spread its dappled light over the faces of the young warriors who were resting on their saddles. While the junior officers began to recite the orders, the men prepared for the coming combat with relatively good humour. All were aware that a soldier must eat, drink and sleep whenever he had the slightest opportunity, for who knew when the last great sleep would come? In good order, the cavalry under the commands of Llew and Cadal settled down and attempted to gain some rest.

CHAPTER XIII

THE RETURN OF
THE ROMAN

Oderint, dum metuant.
Let them hate, as long as they fear.

Accius, *Atreus*

The harsh spikes of grass irritated Cadal's skin through his woollen cloak. The sun bored down on the back of his head so that sweat trickled through his hair and soaked the strip of rag around his neck. Sand grated between his armour and his skin, irritated his gritty eyes and clogged the back of his throat every time the wind blew and lifted sugar-white granules into the air.

Cadal manoeuvred his shoulder so he could slowly raise his head an inch or two to scan the landscape from behind a convenient shrub. Peering around him, he was amazed at how thoroughly his men had camouflaged themselves into the rolling grassland so that the occasional flash of suspicious eyes was the only sign of their presence.

Several times during that endless day, he had wished that he'd dug his hole a little deeper and wider than the shallow trench that was barely sufficient to cover the mounds of shoulders and hips. At least twenty of his men had been able to use the rocks and scree as concealment and he could have used his rank to ensure a more comfortable perch, but the troops were heartened when he was the first to dig a hide. If the heir to the Dumnonii throne could last through the interminable morning and the heat of noontime, then so could they.

'Take on the hardest part of this task for yourself,' Caradoc had hissed one last piece of advice to his son before the long crawl towards the enemy trenches. Belatedly, Cadal admitted to himself that his father's words were wise.

He scanned the irregular undulations in the earth crowned with lines of drooping shrubbery or clumps of dried grasses. Damn! He suddenly realised that the foliage that had hidden his warriors was dying at a rapid rate from the heat of an unnaturally warm summer.

Perhaps the Saxons won't realise it, he thought. After all, they're doing the same thing.

And they were. When Cadal looked to the left at a line of limp dusty branches, he recognised that these clumps marked poorly disguised mantraps.

Looking closer, he estimated that these were probably about the depth of a horse's leg. He tried to picture the chaos that would result if he and others rode into such a snare, and imagined the sensation of the earth suddenly opening beneath him, followed by the tearing and piercing of his horse's entrails and the chilling screams from agonised beasts as they twisted and struggled on the terrible wooden spikes. A second row of riders might try to swerve and avoid the mass of struggling bodies, but they too would surely be impaled. Perhaps the third row of riders might survive, if they were lucky.

The young man forced his attention back to the place where his enemy waited for him.

'The Saxon warriors must be as tired of waiting as we are,' he told himself, stretching his leg muscles below his buried cloak. All the men would need a minute or two to regain full feeling in their cramped limbs, regardless of any precious time lost.

Once again, Cadal cautiously turned his head to the left so he could rest facing towards the looming forest from where he expected to see the smoke from the signal fire. The angle of the sun told him that the afternoon was more than half gone, so Caradoc would soon give the command and unleash his forces. But not until the right moment, when the enemy was weary and on the very edge of sleep.

But there was still no sign of movement from his father.

Cadal's mind began to churn. Had the old man sickened? He was hearty and buoyed up with excitement when Cadal left the bivouac, so sudden illness seemed unlikely. Had they been attacked from behind when the enemy, this Ironfoot, outman-oeuvred them all and outflanked the force that was sheltering in the forest? Would his men have heard the sounds of combat if a disturbance had taken place in the trees behind them?

Had Llew's detachment been intercepted and ambushed during his roundabout trek through Anderida Silva to his position on the eastern margins of the small town? Harald Ironfoot would have made detailed plans to ensure that his troops and the ceols were protected. The boats were essential if they were to escape back to Saxony and his winter encampment on the Albis River. Could the Britons defeat Ironfoot without the hundred men in Llew's command? The odds were already in favour of the Saxons, but there was nothing that Cadal could do.

He must wait and pray that the signal fire would soon be lit.

Still the sky remained depressingly clear of smoke from the signal fire. At least it was clear of rain, although dark clouds had been massing over the seaward side of the town.

Cadal was drooping from nervous exhaustion in the heat and humidity and he wondered what he should do once night fell.

Retreat? Unthinkable!

Attack? Impossible!

And then a stone fell, almost on the tip of his nose.

Startled, Cadal raised his head a little and saw Huw's sharp eyes and the edge of a plait only a few feet to his left. The scout had burrowed himself deeply into the surrounding earth.

'Look, Lord Cadal! The signal fire has been lit. It's almost time to rise.'

He rubbed his eyes with numb fingers. There, above the crown of the forest, a plume of thick black smoke was rising into the pale sky. A vague hint of scarlet could be seen between the thick tree trunks and some blurred movement was obvious where the rough track emerged out of the thinning line of trees along the verge.

'Wait!' Cadal called as softly as he could. 'Pass the word along the line. We wait until the Saxons come out of their holes and are committed to the battle.'

A long column of horses suddenly erupted from the trees. Sitting tall in their saddles, the imposing figures of massed cavalrymen in their colourful cloaks were trotting down the track that led towards the town. In the leading rank of the column, the pennons of the various tribes were flapping in an invisible breeze with a representation of the Boar of Cornwall in front, charging out of a green background with its thick, ribbed muscles and exaggerated, curving tusks.

A little in front of the tree, the soil, bushes and long grasses appeared to boil as if a giant, invisible spoon had stirred the pot of the earth. Cadal could make out the helms of concealed men when they climbed out of their trenches and stretched their numbed limbs.

Then, at a signal from Caradoc, the cavalry's speed increased. The air and the earth seemed to still as the newly exposed Saxons and the Britons in their trenches waited expectantly for the first screams of men and horses as they fell into the mantraps. With his breath catching in his throat, the Dumnonii prince watched his father as he rode, upright and fearless, like a man half his age. The horsemen drew closer and closer to the mantraps as Cadal signalled to his own men that they should kneel behind their sparse cover.

Although he was too far from the column to see his father's face, he imagined that Caradoc was grinning with a gap-toothed smile of pure enjoyment.

Still, the Saxons hadn't realised that Cadal's force of foot soldiers was behind them.

The British cavalry increased its pace, although Cadal knew his father would save the best of his speed for the charge towards the Saxon forces. As he watched the horse-soldiers riding gloriously towards a determined foe that held a significant advantage, he swore that he would not let his father down during this time of need.

At the last moment, the rows of horsemen wheeled to their left at full stride and turned away from the mantraps that were only barely visible in the glare of sunlight, avoiding disaster by the barest of margins. Cadal felt the remnants of the sandy soil as it cascaded down his back when he began to rise to his feet. He saw the cavalry wheel again.

'There's so many of the bastards!' Cadal whispered aloud as he watched the huge, hulking northerners move out of their trenches and turn to face Caradoc's approaching cavalry. The ground seemed to boil near their trenches and still more men began to appear, bolstered by another group of warriors who came running through the town gates from their places of concealment among the shabby huts. The Saxon's original plan was now brutally clear. If Caradoc had charged into the mantraps, the riders who survived would have been caught in a pincer movement.

'Up!' Cadal ordered crisply, and Huw and his men rose stiffly from the depressions in which they had hidden for so many hours.

Wonder of wonders, none of the Saxons seemed to have sensed the British warriors who were forming at their rear. Within moments, Cadal's force began to move towards the dead tree and the Saxons whose attention was totally focused on Caradoc's cavalry as it wheeled away from the mantraps. Cadal's heart swelled with pride at the neat tactical movements that had been achieved at speed.

Caradoc swung his sword and caught the sunlight with a flash of scarlet silk. In ranks of ten riding abreast, the horsemen waited for the order to charge at their enemy. The king's upraised sword dropped, and in a sea of hard flesh, iron, bone and muscle, the charge began.

'Form ranks!' Cadal yelled. 'At the double! Run like the devil and we'll re-form on the other side of the Saxon ratholes. Move!'

The waiting British infantry ran with a sense of mingled fear, excitement and purpose. The British force would have lost nothing if the Saxons saw them now, because the trap had already been sprung.

In an arrowhead formation, Caradoc charged his cavalry directly towards the heart of the Saxon line. The discipline that had forced the Saxon foot soldiers to lie in wait as a single unit was breaking down, so their normal lust for personal glory came to the fore. Similarly, the realisation that Cadal's force was approaching their rear made no difference to them as they continued to charge towards the cavalry with their axes, swords and circular shields at the ready. Battle cries rose from hundreds of throats, roars that chased the birds of the forest onto the wing, before they settled again to wait for the inevitable feast.

'For Britannia!' Cadal roared, as he skirted one large hole in the landscape that had sheltered a number of the Saxons during the past two days. 'For Britannia,' he bellowed again.

The corresponding chorus from a hundred British throats resounded behind him.

Then Caradoc's cavalry hit the Saxons with the force of a hammer-blow. Cadal could feel its power through the trembling of the dry earth.

The cavalrymen carved through the Saxons like a dagger slitting an unprotected throat. Blood stained upraised swords as the Saxons died in untidy rows when they were singled out and smashed under iron-clad hooves. And then the cavalry was through the Saxon lines and were forced to slide into sharp turns to both left and right to avoid Cadal's foot soldiers. Then they turned, circled and began to isolate small groups of Saxons and cut them to pieces.

'Advance!' Cadal screamed as his warriors charged into the rear of the Saxon force. 'Hit them hard and push the bastards towards the cavalry. For Britannia!'

The rest of the engagement was a dim blur for Cadal. Men appeared in front of him, fierce and bear-like in their fur-edged cloaks, screaming curses and battle cries. Sword play became a simple exercise in hacking and slashing at any exposed flesh. Blades shivered and shattered, while straining men fought with stolen and scavenged weapons snatched up from dead or dying hands. For those warriors who couldn't find replacement weapons, teeth and nails were acceptable substitutes to rake at eyes or tear throats open. There were no rules, just an individual need to stay alive in a melee of thrashing bodies and jostling shields.

Over all hung the stink of death. Men in extremity voided their bowels and bladders; similarly, blood tainted the air with the unmistakable reek of hot metal accompanying the sharp smell of vomit, pierced entrails and sweat.

Even the earth on which they stood had been transmogrified by the fierce blood-letting. Gore lay in pools around the growing pile of corpses, soaked into the earth and created ghastly pink slurries to stain the feet and legs of the living. Men looked like scarecrows that had been bathed in red paint; dried or fresh, blood obscured the men's eyes and dripped from their gauntlets until Cadal was sickened by its stench.

Somehow, the prince managed to blot out all sound, except for the guttural curses of those Saxons who were running directly at him. Suddenly, a horn shrieked brazen orders and the enemy began to melt away like smoke.

'Hold! Hold!' Cadal screamed. The Saxons were retreating towards the township, except for a small rearguard of fanatical combatants who refused to obey their orders.

'After them, lad! The cavalry will clear the way, and I'll see you in the town square. Burn down any buildings that can't be cleared of Saxons,' Caradoc shouted down at his son from the saddle.

The old man's arms were bloodied to the elbows but his eyes were twinkling from the success of his tactics. Every muscle in his face seemed to be glowing with a fierce joy.

'Collect any of the riderless horses that can be caught and join me. And, while you're at it, order Huw to kill off those stragglers,' the king snarled, pointing towards a small cluster of Saxons that continued to frustrate the Britons.

'The rest of you can follow me at a trot,' Cadal yelled to his men. 'You heard the king – it's time now to kill off the rest of these bastards. These will be for Britannia, and for our dead.' Some sixty of his original one hundred warriors arranged themselves behind him. His losses had been heavy.

A riderless horse ran directly towards him, the reins dangling and its eyes maddened with fear and pain from a shallow cut that extended beyond its breast armour to leak blood down one leg. Except for that slight wound, the beast seemed unhurt, so Cadal grabbed at one of the trailing reins and dragged himself into the saddle. The horse calmed immediately with the presence of a human on its back, so it sidestepped a small pile of bodies fastidiously before Cadal turned it towards the township. Beyond him, other Britons were either running at his side or catching the remaining half-dozen riderless steeds.

In the chaos of the continuing conflict, Cadal somehow found himself on the outskirts of Anderida. He led the way along the straggling track leading into the town before it divided itself into two clear halves, opting to begin his assigned task by clearing out one of the narrow laneways between two rows of shabby huts. The rubbish dumped outside the buildings indicated that these buildings had been in regular use, but the silence in the town was eerie and the stillness total.

'Light some torches,' the prince ordered two of the men who

were trotting at his side. Then, with an angry hum, an arrow whizzed past his ear to bury itself into a sod wall across the narrow pathway. 'Quick! Set fire to those two buildings and we'll burn the bastards out.'

He indicated the shack from which the arrow had been loosed. 'You! And you! Burn that bastard out for me!'

As one warrior used his already-torn cloak to create a makeshift torch by attaching the wool to a broken spear shaft, another opened his tinder box and used his flint to strike the sparks that would light a small fire. Several other warriors used their shields to protect both men from arrows as they coaxed the torch into life. In the meantime, arrows continued to whizz through the air, forcing the remainder of Cadal's men to find shelter wherever they could.

Cadal was paranoid about bowmen, for no armour can be so finely wrought that a man could be completely safe under a hail of arrows. The only thing he feared more than barbs from an archer was the prospect of an oil fire. The prospect of cooking within his armour caused even the most fearless of warriors to bleach white with horror.

House by house, Cadal led his men towards the heart of Anderida in a door-to-door search for Saxons, burning the town around him as he went. The reed roofs flamed up as fire devoured the dry thatch and burned the rafters down to charcoal. Inside the buildings, the enemy warriors were either incinerated or suffocated. Alternatively, if they refused to accept the searing heat, they made their way out of the guttering huts to be cut down by the waiting Britons.

Finally, his troop reached a large open square to discover that their side of Anderida had fallen. Total destruction prevailed over the northern side of the town.

* * *

Before death came to visit Anderida, Llew's contingent of Dobunni cavalry had waited in a position where a thick copse of trees offered some protection beside the dirt road that took travellers into the east. Remote from the action, Llew had felt cut off and of little use in the struggle to regain control of the town. But a cursory glance from the brow of his hilltop vantage point changed his opinion.

The bay sparkled with sunlight reflecting off the white caps. Some of the Saxon ceols had been pulled up onto the sandy beach where they were being carefully loaded with boxes and barrels.

'This'll be the treasure that's been pillaged from Anderida Silva,' Llew said to a dour, black-haired warrior called Mabon. 'You can see how they're stowing those boxes evenly throughout the middle of the ceol to keep the vessel balanced.'

'Bastards!' Mabon muttered. Unusually soft-hearted, this warrior had been outraged at the sight of dead women and children when the Britons pursued their quarry among the farmsteads, crofts and villages of Anderida Silva. 'They'd steal the eye out of a needle.'

'Or a rattle from a babe,' Llew added with feeling. 'With luck, we'll take this wealth back and return it to its owners.'

'What will become of it if the owners are dead?' Mabon snapped. Llew had no idea who the man's anger was aimed at, but he found himself bridling with affront at his subordinate's argumentative tone.

'There'll be widows enough and there'll be scores of orphaned children by the time we've sorted out this band of Saxons. Every child who dies through neglect because their parents have been slaughtered should become a blot on those of us who should have protected them. The booty must be shared out in such a way that all of the indigent receive a portion.' At twenty-five, Llew was still an idealist.

'The Regni and the Atrebates kings will all demand a share of the proceeds, so there'll be little left for those who can't fight for themselves,' Mabon retorted, his dark eyes staring at the sun as it slid lower in the afternoon skies.

'It'd be best that you check on the men, Mabon, and ensure they're ready to mount and ride as soon as we see the signal fire. They understand their orders.' Llew continued to scan the landscape. The town was too empty, and it was too still.

'Aye, my lord. They'll be ready to do their duty for the glory of the tribe.'

'Then see to it, Mabon, because the waiting is almost over.'

Beyond those ships that had been beached for loading, further ceols were awaiting their turn in the shallows. A large number of ships had arrived from Saxony to reinforce Ironfoot's expedition during the spring, so he could capitalise on his successful forays into the south of Britannia.

Llew could understand now why the Britons had suffered so harshly at the hands of their enemy. The army had killed and killed, but for all the casualties that had been suffered by the Saxons, they seemed to breed overnight. In fact, shiploads of reinforcements had been arriving regularly. Then, in turn, these same ceols would return to Saxony with the spoils.

The burn of anger at the sight of these vessels came slowly to Llew, but once his rage had been triggered, it grew and grew until such time as it was slaked. Such anger was foreign to his fellow Britons who were creatures of sudden, violent fury that dissipated almost as quickly as it began. Llew's cold fury would last until his enemies were crushed.

The town lazed in the summer sun like a dirty, disreputable dog. Yet no animals stirred in the streets. Badly maintained and shabby, Anderida seemed to be empty of townsfolk, as if the population had decided to leave the Saxons behind as the sole inhabitants of this small fishing town. Llew however knew that the Saxons would never leave enemies alive to sit at their unprotected backs; the citizens of Anderida and the farmers from the surrounding district had probably been dead for months. A clever commander like Harald Ironfoot would know better than to leave the dead to breed disease, so they must be buried somewhere close, unshriven and without prayers to speed their way to Paradise.

No chickens picked away at the sod and there were no farm animals in the small pens attached to the small houses. The vegetable patches were baked hard in the gardens and all green plants had been stripped away. Anderida had been picked clean by a ruthless enemy.

Llew raised his eyes to look above the town. With surprising clarity, considering the dust and smoke in the air, he could see the forest to the west of the township where the signal fire smoke would eventually begin to rise. Every muscle in his body was stiff and cramping with tension.

Like Cadal, Llew chafed under the tension of waiting while the afternoon wore away. The sun was obscured by cloud for a short period and Llew prayed for some cooling rain to break the hot grip of summer that caused him to sweat within his armour and turned his helmet into a burning circlet around his aching forehead.

When the smoke from the signal fire finally plumed into the sky, Llew's concentration on the plans for each step of the attack on Anderida was so deep that he almost missed it. Caradoc had ordered the Dobunni king to select suitable terrain inside the town where his twenty bowmen could dominate the positions of the defending Saxons, a task that Llew dreaded. In front of the Dumnonii king and his tyro son, Llew had lacked the nerve to ask any deep and exacting questions, and now he would be forced to make important decisions.

What if he chose positions that could be easily crushed by his enemies? What if he had underestimated the strength of the enemy and never made it into the town?

From his vantage point, he could see the scars on the landscape where the Saxons had dug themselves into the sand dunes, but what if there were more defenders and defences than Caradoc had thought? What if the Saxons hadn't left half of their number to protect their boats sheltering near the beach?

'Sir! Sir! The signal fire! It's been lit!' Mabon shouted urgently from behind his master. 'See? The smoke is rising over the tree line.'

Llew felt his stomach lurch: the time for action was at hand.

'It's time to move, Mabon. I'm glad you noticed it, because I was miles away.'

As Mabon issued orders to the cavalry, the archers climbed onto their calm and compliant farm horses. The nonexistent fighting skills of the bowmen were well known, so these peasants would bring up the rear where they could be protected by the cavalry. Thinking furiously about the tasks that lay before him, Llew swung into the saddle and turned his horse to face the Saxons embedded in the town.

'At the trot, move out,' he ordered and took satisfaction from the firmness of his commands. He could only pray that he had prepared himself for the test that confronted him, for the lives of his men would depend on the clarity of his thinking.

The troop had initially formed into pairs but the riders were starting to fan out, now that they were picking up speed and moving towards the walls on the eastern side of the town. Llew could see the boiling movement in the concealed trenches that overlooked the sea as soon as he permitted his steed to pick up speed.

'Ready?' he yelled in a strong, clear voice. 'Into Anderida! At the gallop! Charge!'

The horsemen wheeled their steeds and took up their allotted positions as soon as they felt the hard road beneath the hooves of their horses. Forming into rows of four, as many as could be accommodated when they passed through the open town, Llew's troop moved smoothly into a gallop and the horses were soon at full stretch.

Saxons appeared in front of them with their pikes raised to take horses in the chest. But the defenders were too slow to mount a defensive line, just as those Saxons who were running from concealed positions along the foreshore could never play a part in the initial stages of the battle that was about to be joined. The first rows of horsemen hit the gates' defenders and Llew felt his horse shudder from the force of the contact. A trained war-horse, this steed was more accustomed to battle than its rider, so it lashed out with its iron-tipped shoes and one of the Saxons reeled away with his chest crushed. From the corner of his eye, Llew saw Mabon fall, but the commander was already through the gate and had entered the town. Disorganised, the defenders were already on the run. Everything was happening so fast.

'Hunt the bastards down,' Llew screamed, and was surprised that his voice remained so firm. 'No quarter! No quarter!'

Meanwhile, some of Llew's horsemen were peeling off from their ordered ranks to attack small groups of Saxons who had formed into small circles where two streets intersected. Llew barely paused to think.

'Bring up the archers to kill these bastards. They don't deserve good deaths, so don't waste good Dobunni blood on them. Kill them with arrows,' he shouted.

Several of the archers immediately appeared from out of the confusion behind the cavalry and a hail of arrows began to scythe down the Saxon defenders.

'Get the archers onto the roofs! Up there! And collect as many arrows as you can.' Llew pointed towards a two-storey structure that overlooked the intersection. 'Six of you! Up there! You can control the whole street from that position.'

Even as he continued to force his way down the narrow street with some fifty cavalrymen stretched out behind him, Llew could hear the whizz of arrows as they drove deeply into the defences of armed and desperate Saxons.

Resistance remained stiff, but Llew recognised panic in the ad hoc nature of the defence. He was also aware that British casualties were less than he expected. The advantage of surprise gained during his initial attack and his stolid use of his cavalry was clearly evident, for the northern raiders had no answer to warriors who remained beyond the reach of the Saxon's weapons. Roman-trained, the British cavalrymen used their horses as fighting weapons, while the beasts' armour had protected their riders from the gutting blows from axes or long knives.

In the midst of nasty hit-and-run raids against the Britons by small groups of Saxons, Llew set archers onto the roofs of three of the tallest buildings in the town. One, a Christian church, had a simple wooden tower with a small bell used to call the faithful to prayer. It offered cover and the height that would permit the archers to see the broad sweep of most engagements within the town. Driving hard and slicing through all resistance, Llew moved ever deeper into the maze of the town until an open space loomed ahead of him.

'It's the market square, my lord. The headman's hall is over there,' one of Llew's cavalrymen said when he noticed his commander's raised eyebrows. The man pointed to a shabby, circular structure.

'Secure all the lanes and buildings on our side of the town,' Llew ordered as he scanned the empty, muddy space around the archaic building. 'Let's hope that Caradoc arrives here before the Saxons are reinforced by the warriors who are manning the boats,' he added under his breath.

He sent out sorties to assault those streets that hadn't yet been cleared, until he noticed that signs of fire and smoke were obvious now in the north-western sector of the town. His hopes soared, for this conflagration could only be an indication of Cadal's advance from the western side of the town. They had almost caught up with each other, flame to flame.

Belatedly, Llew ordered his men to begin burning those buildings that might harbour small groups of Saxons, cursing himself for having forgotten the deterrent of uncontrolled fire.

Then, as the first thick plumes of smoke rose into the air near where the eastern gate had once been, Llew racked his brains for anything else that he might have forgotten.

He swore vilely as he remembered the Saxons would need an open approach to the beach if they were going to gain access to their ceols. He must send a small group of warriors back into the areas where fierce fighting had already taken place. After selecting one of the more experienced of his junior officers, he briefed the man and selected a small squad of warriors to carry out the mission.

'Set all the houses alight on the seaward edge of the town. I realise I'm sending you into danger, but the tribe requires this effort from you. We can't allow them to man their boats and make good their escape, so any Saxons you meet must be forced to flee from the flames in our direction. We'll be able to neutralise them once they enter our loving arms.' He grinned encouragingly.

The hard-faced men selected for the mission laughed and nodded their understanding, while the Dobunni king tried to forget that he was sending these men to almost certain death. Fortunately, some of the archers were still in place on the edges of the more dangerous streets in the south-eastern sector.

'Wherever you can, use your archers to keep the Saxons pinned down. Take five bowmen with you from one of the buildings close to the headman's house. The square can be defended without them!'

Once again, his hand-picked veterans nodded; they understood that taking these archers with them would give them a chance of survival.

Then, from out of the drifting smoke, Cadal rode into the town square on a wounded horse with half his original warriors loping along behind him. All carried swords dripping with blood, and many brandished makeshift torches. Their faces were black with soot and a memory of fire and violence flamed in sooty eyes framed by networks of white wrinkles.

'Where's Caradoc?' Cadal shouted over the melee of conflict and the roar of flames. 'I thought he was ahead of me.'

'You're the first to arrive,' Llew answered, happy that the horror of decision-making was now shared.

'If the old man has gone and got himself killed, then I'll . . . I'll be forced to follow him into Hades to drag him back again. My sister will kill me if anything happens to the old bugger.'

Llew grinned, despite the seriousness of the situation.

'From my observations, your father seems to be a very difficult man to kill.'

'Humpph! That's as may be, but I swear the old devil is off in a corner somewhere, and he'll be adapting the plan to keep himself amused.' Cadal slammed his fist into the palm of his left hand in frustration. 'He's always doing things like that to me. He's quite happy to ignore his own rules when he fancies.'

So, as Anderida burned and the Saxons were driven closer and closer to the town square, Cadal and Llew were kept busy ambushing the enemy who were prepared to die rather than run. Fire had served the Britons well. Those Saxons to the south of the square had been driven into the waiting clutches of the Britons. Those to the north had nowhere to go, except for the mud and quicksand of a huge swamp beyond the town.

This war of attrition could have continued for hours, for Anderida was burning on three sides now. But news of Caradoc came with a triumphant courier who rode into the square just as the sun was setting. The man threw himself from the saddle, and Cadal realised the rider was Trefor, who had caught a loose horse on the field outside Anderida and ridden like the wind in pursuit of his master.

'What of the king, Trefor? Is my father well? Has he engaged the enemy?' Cadal asked in rapid-fire.

'King Caradoc was well when I left the line to the north of the town, my lord. He is forming a new perimeter along the northern side of Anderida adjacent to the sucking swamps. He has blocked off the enemy's options to the east and the west, so they have nowhere to run. The enemy has almost reached our line on three occasions and they formed themselves into a shield wall to repel our troop when we went on the attack, but we have repelled them each time. When he knows that he has bottled up as many of the Saxons as his perimeter can hold, he will mount a serious attack on them with our remaining cavalry and foot soldiers. He intends to kill them, down to the last man.'

'Has my father issued new orders?' Cadal asked. 'His strategies seem to be working well on all counts, but the Saxons seem to be massing between the square and the swamp. Huw? What have you seen so far?'

Huw edged his horse into the circle of powerful men grouped together in the middle of the square. The British troops had formed a line around the square that faced the streets on all four sides, routes that led to freedom away from the narrow, burning streets.

'The bowmen have kept many of the Saxons pinned down, but whole groups of them have made their way towards the laneways in the north of the town, choosing to risk their lives in some form of concerted action, rather than be picked off piece-meal by our archers.'

'Send two troops of twenty men to guard the eastern and western gates. Let no one escape,' Llew ordered crisply. 'The rest of us will add our forces to those of King Caradoc. He's decided on his battleground, so that's enough to convince me.'

'It might be worth our while to keep the bowmen in a ring around the town square to pick off those stragglers who try to rejoin their thane,' Cadal added. Llew concurred.

As they spoke, a small group of five blackened scarecrows returned after completing their mission along the southern extremity of Anderida. They were the only survivors of the small patrol sent out by Llew to torch the buildings along the southern wall. Surprisingly, there were more survivors than Llew expected.

'Most of the Saxons along the southern side of the city have been killed, my lord, as you ordered. Any who are still hiding down there can be picked off by our archers if they try to escape. There are still four archers holed up just outside the southern wall and they are prepared to remain in their present position.'

Llew thumped each of the five men on the shoulder.

'There will be time to laud your courage and write songs in praise of your dead at a later time. But, for now, what say you to cleaning out the last of this rats' nest? If you're weary, I'll not be critical if you have a need to rest and regain your strength.'

The five remaining warriors looked scandalised at missing out on the last battle of Anderida. Their leader, a hard-bitten veteran with only one ear, spoke for all the men.

'It's a good day to die, King Llew, and I'd hate to miss the very end of this battle. We intend to fight while a single Saxon remains alive.'

Trefor added one further order from their commander. 'King Caradoc wishes you to begin a lane-by-lane, hut-by-hut, drive towards the northern outskirts of the town. If the gods are with us, we'll make contact with the Saxons somewhere in the middle and we can crush them, once and for all.'

'So, why are we waiting? Gather together all the men who'll be going with us,' Cadal ordered. 'Night is here but Anderida's burning makes the town as bright as the sun. I agree with your brave warriors, Llew. Whether by sunlight or moonshine, it's a good day to die.'

Llew and Cadal issued the necessary orders before riding off with the cavalry and the remnants of Cadal's foot soldiers at their backs.

Eyes that were irritated by smoke and heat from the fires stopped watering, while the last traces of twilight allowed for relatively safe movement. Both of the young commanders were concerned that the series of battles had consumed too much time and the Saxons might reap the benefit of a night where they could sleep in the filthy alleyways of this wight-haunted township. But there would be little rest for the Britons, forced to mop up the remaining Saxon warriors if they were to achieve a complete victory.

Night finally fell to the sounds of barking foxes and hunting owls. The thick darkness was full of strange sounds as Anderida turned to ash behind them, while Cadal cursed and sent out men to form a large semi-circular perimeter that would keep the remaining Saxons confined within an area of British choosing.

But no one would sleep tonight while the Britons were sweeping the Saxons before them. Those northerners who tried to fight were trapped and slaughtered. Above the burning cinders, the white moon seemed so close they could touch it with their outstretched hands.

The Britons' progress during the night was frustratingly slow. Whenever a nest of Saxons was found, they must be dealt with before the British troop could move on. The soft darkness hid desperate struggles and the evidence of swift and violent death.

Long after midnight and with the moon sliding down the sky towards morning, Cadal and Llew realised that their men were tired out. At one of the more important crossroads, Trefor set up a roster of sentries and ordered the unassigned warriors to sleep for several hours at times when they could be spared. Exhausted warriors would be of no use to Caradoc on the morrow, and many of these men had been awake for almost two days. They had fought themselves to a standstill.

Yet, although they were so weary that they could barely think, both Cadal and Llew found sleep was elusive. Finally, they managed to drift off into a light doze that allowed their bodies to enjoy a short rest, even if their minds remained watchful.

Light came fast. A slice of sun appeared on the eastern horizon with the brilliance of spilled blood. Yellow and white light edged dirty thatch and exposed the bared rafters of burned buildings. But there was no trace of the Saxons.

Cadal and Llew pushed forward with their men. An arrow whizzed past Cadal's ear and embedded itself in the thatch of a house across the laneway. All the warriors ducked in reaction and Llew roared out a warning to several foot soldiers as he pointed towards a small church. The small building was little more than a hut surrounded by a dilapidated and weed-choked graveyard, enclosed by a stone wall, where only humps and hollows indicated that Christians had been buried inside these hallowed grounds. There were no gravestones, no sarcophagi and not even a large stone cross to mark the earth's holy nature.

The stillness raised the hair on Cadal's neck. Such a threatening quiet was unnatural, so he halted his column and signalled that his troops remain alert.

The eerie silence, devoid of birdsong, dragged on.

Then a horn sounded to the north beyond the graveyard, an unfamiliar clarion call. What was this new threat? Somehow, Cadal's sword appeared in his hand as he pulled his shield away from the thongs that attached it to the saddle. Nerves tightened as the horn sounded again, brazen and close. Too close.

Suddenly, the door of the church swung wide and a huge, bow-legged man in a cloak made of fox pelts in their winter white stepped out into the field. Other men materialised from the shadows under yew trees, from behind and within the church, and from hollows in the ground between the grave plots. The Saxons had chosen this site for their last stand and had prepared to ambush Cadal and Llew as they rode to join Caradoc, but the sound of the horn had driven them out.

The bow-legged Saxon, who was obviously one of their thanes, roared out a challenge, while his warriors thumped on their breast armour with swords and axes and howled out their responses. Cadal strained to make some sense from what the thane was bellowing.

'Do we hide like rats in burrows like Britons who are waiting to die?'

The words were shockingly clear and Cadal realised how foolish he had been to allow his force to get so close to Harald Ironfoot's position in the cemetery. He was also aware that the Saxon's first challenge had been in his native tongue, but his next insults were roared out in the British tongue.

The Saxons warriors shouted their responses, forgetting in the heat of the moment that they, too, had skulked in holes in the ground to ambush Caradoc's men during the previous day of mayhem and sudden death.

'Do we Saxons use fire to kill our enemies? No! Not even on cowardly British scum?'

'No!' The response was accompanied by the thud of near to a hundred stamping feet.

'Do we Saxons depend on the Romans to do our dirty work for us?'

'No!' This final shout sent dozens of birds flapping and clattering through the yew trees and upwards towards the lightening sky. Llew realised that the trees were full of carrion birds waiting to feed.

'What Romans?' Llew asked.

'Those, perhaps,' Huw hissed. Suddenly, from beyond the

wall, a contingent of some fifty Roman cavalrymen appeared as if they had suddenly materialised from Rome itself. At their head, a man on a white horse sat at his ease beyond the stone wall. His scarlet cloak, his gold-embossed helmet and his highly polished armour marked him as an officer of some rank.

Then, wonder of wonders, Caradoc joined the mounted Roman with a wild whoop of exhilaration. With the sunlight shining along his blade, Caradoc swung his sword over his head. 'For Britannia!' he shouted in a powerful voice.

'Attack! No quarter!' The Dumnonii king roared out the battle cry as his cavalry poured around the ranks of the Romans, cleared the low wall on their chargers and struck at the Saxon shield wall with a cruel, resounding clang of metal against metal and flesh against flesh.

Shaking his head, Cadal gave the same order to send his own men into the fray from the southern side of the graveyard. Even as he fought, the prince's eyes sought out the tall figure on the white horse who was waiting with his men to dispose of stragglers that strayed in their direction. He had met this man, many years earlier, when he was little more than a boy. And then he remembered.

'Magnus Maximus,' he exclaimed as he stabbed at a tall Saxon who had unwittingly exposed one side of his body when he struck out at the prince's horse with his axe. The warrior screamed shrilly when Cadal's sword slid into his side and then ripped upwards to make the killing stroke.

My father's friend, the Roman, has come again, he thought. The tribune has returned.

CHAPTER XIV

AN ODD REQUEST

Just as the sweet-apple reddens on the high branch, high on the highest, and the apple-pickers missed it, or rather did not miss it out, but could not reach it.

Sappho, *Rossetti*

'You're always around when the spoils are divided,' Caradoc joked, his whole face alive with excitement. The arrival of Maximus from out of nowhere had powerfully affected the Dumnonii king, who felt the years roll away, for he had last seen his friend when his arms, his back and his eyes were still sharp and strong. Invigorated and energetic, Caradoc could barely sit still, continually leaping to his feet and waving his horn mug of pillaged wine so violently that the sweet nectar within was spraying over his son. Cadal barely noticed his impromptu bath as he grinned at the sudden exuberance of his father's victory dance.

'Perhaps that's because I'm following you,' Maximus retorted lazily as he lounged on a makeshift pallet of saddles in the sparsely cobbled square. He raised his personal wine cup that he'd fished out of his saddlebag and began to sip on the sweet, heavy wine with the Hispanic sun trapped inside its body.

'I have to hand it to Harald Ironfoot, may his soul rot in the Underworld until the end of time.' Caradoc raised his mug in an impromptu toast. 'He knew a good wine when he stole it.'

'Your assistance was late, but nonetheless appreciated,' Caradoc added. 'When your troop rode in from the east, I thought my old eyes were playing tricks on me.'

Cadal nibbled on a purloined slice of salted meat that had been sliced directly from the bone. The Saxons had been very busy. Prior to the battle, they had begun loading their booty for shipping home to Saxony. Loading stores was a time-consuming task, so Cadal had been surprised to find that one of the larger ceols had been filled to the gunnels with preserved meat, dried fruits and wines of all kinds. Confused by his first battle, and exhausted after thirty-six hours without sleep, he listened to the two older men's repartee and tried to keep his gritty eyes open.

The day had seemed impossibly long. Although the last Saxons had been outnumbered, if the Roman guardsmen were included, the northern warriors were proud and vicious fighters who were extremely dangerous when they were backed into corners. The sun was scarcely up when the combined British forces charged at them, again and again, and were forced to shed some of their own blood for every Saxon life taken. In this brutal war of attrition, Caradoc's success had been won at a huge cost. Over half of the force that had entered the forests to take Anderida would not return to their homes. On the other hand, only death would release the Saxons from the ugly trap in which they found themselves. The best that Harald Ironfoot could hope for was to die gloriously and to take many of his enemies with him when he entered the shadows of death. And so he would win his entry to Valhalla, the hall of the heroes and the gods.

The strongest warrior weakens when he is forced to fight under the summer sun, even under the mild suns of Britannia. Cadal's head began to ache dully and his eyes were unable to focus. His stomach heaved as if he had overeaten and his arms soon became too heavy to lift. But Saxons appeared in front of him, determined to kill him with axe blows that few men could withstand. His youth and dexterity saved him from a fatal blow on several occasions, but by noon, when the Saxons were down to their last twenty men, the Dumnonii heir had received a shallow wound across his ribs when he was too slow to avoid a swinging axe. A more serious wound to his shield arm rendered his whole hand effectively useless, although he could still move his fingers independently.

With the dull realisation that he was completely exhausted, he stared at his wounded hand and the fingers barely opened and closed. Perhaps he would have perished there, staring at nothing in particular and too tired for thought, but Rowen ap Aidan, Caradoc's captain, saw his distress and dragged him bodily out of the front line. With some violence, the guardsman shook his master until he eventually broke through the haze of weariness and blood loss.

'Retire to the rear, Master Cadal. Someone will see to your wounds when you get there. Do you hear me, Cadal? Retire! Now!'

And so Cadal was able to watch the hideous finale to that terrible Saxon summer from a place of relative safety beyond the stone wall.

As so often happened in protracted conflicts, both sides

paused, as if the protagonists had fought themselves to a standstill. As the tribal warriors retreated back to their line and the Saxons hastily repaired what was left of the shield wall, Caradoc moved into the open. Although he was an easy target for any Saxon archer who remained alive, the Dumnonii king had the measure of Harald Ironfoot. The enemy had made their final stand on the uneven ground of the graveyard, a place where horses proved to be dangerous. Caradoc had ordered his remaining cavalrymen to dismount after the first charge, when the sunken earth of old graves and the elevated mounds of fresher interments felled some of the horses and injured their riders. Now, knowing that Ironfoot desired a good death before all other earthly boons, Caradoc was confident that a cowardly bowshot would be rejected by the thane as an unmanly act.

'Do you still live, Harald Ironfoot?' he called out into the suddenly quiet field where only the groans of wounded men and the cawing of scavenger birds broke the unnatural stillness. The noontime shimmered in the heat haze and visibility was further reduced by smoke and dust. When the single line of Saxons shivered and opened, Ironfoot stepped out of their ranks. His features were red-tinged, bloody, and sweat-stained, but his weary eyes were undimmed by the reality of his defeat.

'Aye! No Briton has yet hefted the blade that can kill me,' his stentorian voice boomed out as the tight press of Saxons behind him raised their battered shields in defiance.

'Come forth, Harald Ironfoot, so we can talk like men. No one here will loosen arrows or spears to kill you by foul means. I swear this on my daughter's life.' Caradoc made the sign of the cross over his breast and Cadal, leaning on the far side of the wall in a haze of pain, was surprised at the gesture. Caradoc was technically a Christian, but the king had a personal preference for the soldier's god, Mithras, whose altars had been deserted in favour of the Jewish messiah.

Harald Ironfoot stepped away from the locked ranks of Saxon shields and his huge, bear-like figure shouldered his way to the front to stand within reach of Caradoc's sword. Ironfoot's own weapon remained in its scabbard, so Caradoc felt no fear. Ironfoot might be a barbarian, but he remained true to his own code of honour.

'Your Romans were a surprise, Briton, but they haven't spoiled our little game. What is your name? We have never met in battle before and I would like to know the name of the man who thwarted my return to my homeland. I would like to watch you from the abode of heroes, although I'll warn you that I don't intend to die easily.'

The Saxon's voice was very deep as befitted the wide chest and bowed legs that were as thick as young trees. His great height, at least a hand taller than the tallest Briton, made him very difficult to kill, but he was carrying several minor wounds which, despite having bled on his armour, seemed mere gnat's bites on the body of a behemoth.

'You are honoured, Ironfoot, for our visitor from Rome is Magnus Maximus, also known as Macsen Wledig, the hero of hundreds of battles across the world. He has assured me that he will take no part in our conflict, for you have wronged my people – not his.'

Ironfoot darted a quick glance at Maximus and inclined his head.

'As for your second question, I am Caradoc ap Llyr, King of the Dumnonii tribe who live along the wild coast to the west of Britannia. No boats, be they Saxon, Roman or Middle Sea, will venture willingly into my waters for fear of their total destruction.'

'So you have no argument with me and mine,' Ironfoot retorted.

'A blow at my allies, my brothers, is a blow at me.' Caradoc shrugged deprecatingly, but Ironfoot could tell that the word of this king was as strong and as razor-sharp as his sword.

'I believe you are an honourable man, Caradoc, so I would ask a boon of you. If I should win a good death, I ask that you don't demean me by displaying my head on the end of a spear. I have sons and, although they will never see my humiliation, they might hear word of it.'

Caradoc thought for a moment. Yes, he acknowledged to himself, Ironfoot's head would normally be displayed on a spearhead and passed through the villages and towns of the Regni and Atrebates lands so the population could hurl abuse, dung and rocks at those hated features. But would he face the same fate with equanimity if their roles were reversed?

'If I have anything to say on this matter, your body will be burned with the corpses of the rest of your men. That is my practice and I see no reason to change it.'

Harald Ironfoot knew that Caradoc could lie to him. He understood, too, that the old king could perish in the last throes of the battle, rendering promises worthless. Still, the thane was heartened by Caradoc's assurance. He acknowledged his fate. He would soon be with the Valkyrie, flying high and fast in the arms of the warrior women towards the abode of the blessed. The only matter in doubt was the manner of his death.

'I bid you farewell, King Caradoc. Perhaps we will meet in the fields of the gods where warriors go after death to drink and carouse with the gods until Ragnarök. I pray that will be so, for what use is life and its struggles if there is no judgement waiting for us in the afterlife? I wish you and your daughter well.'

'I wish the same to you, Thane Harald. If any religion rules the shades, then I have no doubt that the Blessed Jesus will know if you have lived your life honestly and you have acted with valour. Let both our hearts be judged by what we did in this world, given what has been meted out to us.'

'Do your friends believe as you do? Your black-crow priests promised us the fires of your Hades, even as we killed them.'

'Then it's to be hoped that neither of us will be judged by such a narrow yardstick. Take my respect with you as you travel to the land of heroes. I will remember you, Harald Ironfoot.'

'And I, you! Farewell, Caradoc of the Dumnonii.'

Harald Ironfoot bowed once, before turning to rejoin his men.

And so, with the knowledge that his troops had gained a little rest during this impromptu truce, the Saxon strode back to his command and the line opened up to swallow him.

Caradoc scorned to act the coward, so he turned his back on his enemy and swaggered back to the British lines.

Inevitably, the final battle began as the sun began its long slide towards the horizon.

Cadal jerked awake as a callused hand shook his shoulder.

'Hades! What's happening?'

'Sorry, son, but your snoring is making it difficult for us elderly dodderers to hear our own voices.' Caradoc patted his son's knee. 'Get off to your pallet, lad, and leave the night to us old men who'll know the darkness all too soon.'

'Speak for yourself, Caradoc, for I'm still in the prime of life,' Maximus retorted from across the open fire.

From over the sea, isolated sheets of lightning were flashing and dull clusters of thunder could be heard in the distance. The smell of ozone was making the hot air crackle with unleashed energy, so Caradoc hoped that a storm might finally arrive to dampen the oppressive atmosphere.

Awakened by the sound of thunder, Cadal stretched luxuriantly and vigorously ruffled his hair like a waking hound.

'I'm awake now. Do we have anything worth drinking?'

His father pulled out a leather flask of beer and poured a draught into his son's mug. Cadal hazarded a sip and discovered, much to his surprise, that Saxon beer was very good.

Meanwhile Maximus returned to the conversation.

'I have been elevated to the position of Comes Britanniarum and I'm charged with the task of destroying the Picts, Hibernians and the northern Saxons who persist in challenging the Roman legions as soon as they recover from their last bout of defeats. They never seem to learn.'

Caradoc offered his congratulations.

'I hadn't realised quite how important you've become, Maximus. Well done, my friend. I was sorry to hear the news of your kinsman's fall from grace some years ago, but it seems that his son now sits on the throne of Constantinople and rules the Eastern Empire. For all that, I have a distinct feeling that you still had to come to the emperor's attention by feat of arms.'

Caradoc grinned mischievously and waved his hands at his friend. 'Aye! I'm a busybody, near as bad as any of the old dames who gossip in the villages. Some things are certain. You've risen high and, if your dead uncle is any guide in this matter, your promotion wasn't given to you because of your bloodline.'

Maximus snorted and his mobile mouth twisted. 'Definitely not! The new Theodosius is a man of intelligence and subtlety. I can assure you that I had to work like a dockyard whore to gain my preferment. Shite, I worked my arse off when Theodosius minor was Magister Militum per Illyricum. The Goths and Visigoths make your Saxons seem pleasant and peace-loving, so I found myself fighting in Samatia, Thrace and Zagoria.'

Caradoc had no idea where these exotic-sounding places were, so nodded expansively to cover his ignorance.

'I boiled in my armour during their summers, and froze solid in their winters. You can believe me, Caradoc, when I say that the wind in the mountains of Thrace and Dacia is hideous and the howl that comes from its play through the pipes and caverns of the mountains will give the shudders to any sensible man. Gods, I can still hear it . . . no sane man would choose to go to those parts of the world. And the local tribes fight like maniacs.'

'Where else have you served?' Caradoc hazarded, hoping he might recognise some place that his friend described. Oh, to travel to such places; to smell the different earths and to be warmed by a different sun.

Maximus scratched his chin in a familiar gesture that Caradoc remembered well.

'Africa . . . Egypt. And even the borders of Germania in the distant north. Only the Lord knows how the locals survive in some of those places. Germania is a wilderness of vast forests, cold rivers and very dirty and savage barbarians who live to the north of the Rhenus River in perpetual winter. I didn't have a bath for six months. Your Saxons come from that part of the world, and the landscape showed me why the bastards are so bad-tempered and so eager to find a better place to live and raise their families.'

Caradoc understood that Maximus wasn't a fop, although his conversation sometimes suggested as much. As the Roman had once explained, a little dissembling sometimes revealed deeper motives or prejudices in the listeners. Maximus discovered much about people by throwing out contentious comments just to elicit a response. However, his observations of the Saxons, while offered in a jocular fashion, were also a warning to the Dumnonii king. Britannia was a prize, a rich and generous land when it was compared with more northern lands that endured long, harsh winters.

'Egypt is one of the truly strange lands, Caradoc. I thought of your Giant's Dance when I first saw the Egyptian pyramids. They also sit on the landscape as if they've always been there. You'd probably laugh at my foolishness, old friend, but your small and very-ancient monument had a stronger pull on my superstitions. I remember how I was dismissive of the Giant's Dance before I actually saw it, because I was still a relatively young and immature man in those days. But times change us, don't they?'

'Tell me about the pyramids, Maximus. What were they built for?' Caradoc asked, curious.

'Imagine a four-sided structure rising up to a point on all four sides, like sloping triangles that are joined together at the top. So high, Caradoc! It was as high as forty men standing on each other's shoulders. I can't imagine how it could have been built. When we saw it for the first time, surrounded by its smaller fellows in the desert, it was like casting our gaze onto a man-made mountain. The giant stones used in its construction had been fitted together so perfectly that I couldn't insert my knife into the seam. There are no doors to gain entrance and no easy way of climbing its smooth, steep sides.'

Caradoc opened and closed his mouth several times like a netted fish. 'But why was it erected? Such a structure would have taken generations to build.'

'No one seems to know, my friend. I was told that the pyramids were built to house the tombs of great Egyptian kings from bygone days.'

'Tombs? I can't believe it!'

Maximus nodded. 'I had difficulty accepting such a bizarre notion, but I was assured that the words of their scribes rang true. Even more amazing, one of the Greek scholars with whom I spoke insisted that the pyramids were at least three thousand years old.'

Caradoc shook his head in disbelief and wonder. 'I haven't the ability to imagine such wonderful constructions, but my father often told me that our world is full of marvels that can't be understood by mere mortals.'

Both men sat quietly for a moment or two as they pondered the many things they had seen that were beyond rational explanation. The fire crackled loudly and a soft breeze stirred the air with a cooling touch.

'You've explained where you've been and why you've returned to Britannia. But what brought you out of the early morning darkness to visit my campsite when I never thought to see you again? Truly, Maximus, I felt the touch of something greater than both of us when your horse loomed out of the shadows.'

Caradoc settled himself a little closer to the fire so he could warm his tired bones.

'And Decius is still with you – older, greyer and as difficult as ever. He's proved to be a difficult man to kill over the years.'

Caradoc held onto a memory of a dying outlaw crucified on a stable door. Hovering on a ladder beside him, Maximus's decurion had offered the outlaw some liquid from a flask. The Dumnonii king pushed the image aside firmly; the last thing he wanted was Maximus's sharp eyes burrowing out an old secret and bringing it into the light of day. Decius and the Dumnonii king were bound by their secret, although Caradoc remained ignorant about Decius's reasons for hastening the outlaw's death. I intend to find out the truth of that incident, Caradoc thought. But I will need to be careful.

'Decius? Yes! My friend was too old to serve on the line, so I offered him a snug little farm in Italia and an honourable retirement. But he'd have none of it. I've made him my personal servant, so he can still be part of the legions and assist me when the opportunity arises. He's the one person in the legions I can truly trust with my life.'

But would this noble Roman still trust Decius if he knew what his decurion had done with the crucified outlaw?

Thoughts of the proud Decius, a Roman soldier to the core of his being, now employed in the role of a menial servant, shocked Caradoc. Decius's pride must have been sorely hurt by the demotion that advancing age had brought on him.

'But age catches up with all of us,' Caradoc muttered under his breath without realising he had spoken aloud.

The Roman gave no indication that he had heard, but he recognised Caradoc's unspoken criticisms and tried to explain the situation in which he had found himself.

'Decius insisted on undertaking this servile position, although I argued with him over his decision to accept it. He could have stayed in Britannia with a tribal wife and several sons, but he'd have none of it. When Decius realised that his swollen joints had become so debilitating that he couldn't carry out his duties, he came to me in tears with a proposition that would keep him in my service. What else could I do, Caradoc? To deny him would be to throw him out of the legion and cast him adrift in the stews of Africa.'

'No! I can see the difficulties of your position. I don't know what I'd have done in your place, so how can I judge you? I'll be pleased to speak once more with Decius, at any rate. I admire him for his grit, his honesty and his talent for clear thinking. I look forward to seeing more of him.'

A shadow passed across Caradoc's face. That unfinished business continued to hang between the king and the ex-decurion, especially the direct stare that had been exchanged over the crucified body of Elphin. The questions came flooding back.

'The decision to come here and meet with you was quite deliberate, my British friend. When I heard that there had been a Saxon invasion in the south, I wondered if the alliance between the southern kingdoms was still holding together. Did you know that your motley group of kings are the first rulers in Britannia to band together for mutual protection? I was curious. A few days of detour would be of little consequence to my campaign because, as you know, I can travel at speed if I must.'

Maximus was so self-assured that Caradoc wondered at how much his Roman friend might have changed during the years of his absence.

'I plan to travel to Deva initially for discussions with the local commanders in that district. From there, I'll proceed into the north to finalise my administrative tasks and set my plans in order. There will also be a number of staffing matters to resolve, involving some necessary promotions and demotions. Then, once my problems have been solved to my satisfaction, I'll mount an aggressive campaign in the north. The Picts have been raging throughout the north in recent years, but I believe the main reason for this sorry state of affairs can be nailed at the doors of our Roman commanders in the field. There are too many pale-arsed, flabby and talentless Romans who have come to Britannia after receiving unearned gifts from the rulers of the Western

Empire. Gratian was a fool to entrust his borders to some of the most useless administrators who ever left the City of the Seven Hills, men who couldn't find their backsides with both hands. I've returned to Britannia to crush the Picts once and for all, so I intend to re-establish order from the mess that prevails in the northern border regions.'

'I'm pleased you thought to see me first, and I'd be a liar if I said that your fifty men hadn't frightened the Saxons during that short moment when you were standing and watching over our clean-up of the northern invaders. They were aware that if they managed to defeat us, there was a possibility that they might have to face a full-strength Roman legion.' Caradoc drank deeply from his leather flask and passed it on to his guest.

Maximus raised the flask in a silent toast, and then drank sparingly.

'You were doing well with your own resources, so you didn't really need me. Fire-eaters such as Llew and Cadal bode well for your Britons in the future.' Maximus's lips twitched. 'Besides, my friend, you seemed to be enjoying yourself.'

The two older men continued to speak in companionable voices but, try as he might, Cadal realised that his eyelids were drooping. He was about to nod off to sleep when a sudden exclamation from the Roman officer roused him out of his torpor.

'Damn it all! We've been talking for an hour or two, but I've still not told you the reason for stopping off to see you. Tell me, Caradoc, do I strike you as an over-imaginative man?'

'Not you, Maximus! You're not likely to be impressed by anything that you haven't actually seen.'

'Aye! And so I thought of myself. Do you believe in the truth of dreams?'

Of all the fears and irrational concerns he might have expected from his friend, Caradoc's list would never have held this one. At the same time, his thoughts winged away to his daughter, Endellion, who had asked a similar question.

'I've had the same dream for five years. Sometimes it afflicts me night after night without cessation. Sometimes, I won't experience it for a month or two, but it then returns again and again. I dread sleep, because I know that my dreams will take me back to this place as surely as night follows day.'

For the first time in his experience, Caradoc noted the sheen of sweat on the Roman's broad forehead and the restless fingers that pleated and re-pleated the edge of the material that lined his red tunic. Caradoc decided that Maximus's affliction might be a message from some form of spiritual power. Concerned, he explained the nature of the dreams suffered by Saraid and Endellion and watched as the Roman's complexion paled in the light from the dwindling camp fire.

'You're not an imaginative man, Maximus, so I'd advise you to take your dream seriously. It might be best if you were to consult a priest.'

'What could they do?'

'You've got nothing to lose by sharing your concerns with a priest, and you might learn something useful.'

Maximus reached over and squeezed the older man's shoulder. 'Thank you for not laughing at me, Caradoc. God knows, most of my Roman colleagues would be amused by thoughts of the mighty Maximus being brought low by night horrors. I'm happy to tell you the substance of my dream, friend, because I know you won't laugh at my discomfort.'

Cadal listened surreptitiously with his eyes closed and his breathing consciously slowed. Satisfied that he couldn't be overheard, Maximus stumbled into awkward speech.

'The dream starts quietly. I'm standing in an open field and thick snow is falling. Although I can't see what's ahead of me, the snowflakes appear to be magnified so they grow bigger and bigger, and then float down to the earth in long wavy sheets. One strikes me on the shoulder and I expect to be knocked off my feet by its size, but the huge, delicate thing simply explodes on my body with a gentle, soundless kiss. I raise my hand to shade my eyes and start to stamp through the freezing landscape. Every step I take mars the perfect snow.

'My feet are cold but I cannot stop, although I passionately want to sit and rest. There is a castell in the distance, a tall fortification that seems as much Roman in style as anything else. I can hear the sea booming behind me, so I'm immediately sure that I'm somewhere in Britannia. But, to be honest, I could be anywhere. I feel a sense of anticipation and recognition that is so strong that I want to run and discover for myself the reason for this strange place.'

Apologetically, Caradoc interrupted. 'Are you aware of a castell near the sea that fits your description, Maximus? Surely, you must have some instinct for the existence of this place if it recurs in your dreams with such regularity.'

'No . . . there are several places in Rome where castells are built on elevated expanses of land to protect their owners, and these fortifications are often found close to the sea. There are also similar strategic locations near the Rhenus River in Germania. But I truly believe my castell is somewhere along the remote western coasts of Britannia. I swore to myself that I would return to your lands and carry out a search for my Roman fortifications. I know it is here! I know it!'

He sighed before continuing with his tale.

'At any rate, I reach these huge iron gates in front of the fortification and I try to batter at them with my fists to gain entry. I'm suddenly apprehensive, but I don't know why. My heart is beating so loudly that I can hear it in my ears. I look for my sword, but it has vanished and my horror rises even higher.

'I don't have a chance to beat on the gates for a second time. With much creaking, they open before I have raised my hand. To my left, a gatekeeper is standing, and he welcomes me with a broad smile. I remember him in so much detail that he seems more real to me than my own father. His livery is blue and very clean. Despite missing several of his teeth, this man is well kept, healthy and tidy. He raises his right hand and I notice he is wearing knitted gloves without fingers. He points across the courtyard towards the gates of the ruler's hall.

"*Ah, Macsen Wledig!*" he says. "*You are expected!*"

'I'm surprised that he should know my British name. But, in the way of dreams, I trudge through the snow to the hall to find that the door is opening as I reach it.

'Inside, I'm surrounded by soft light from the fire pit and the wall sconces. People are sitting at their ease on stools carved from solid timber and cushioned with golden cloth. The air is perfumed with the scent of flowers, so I can believe that spring has come to the winter landscape. But my waking self tells me that it's only the dream.

'Women are sitting and talking around the fire and its light plays on long curls and plaits of great complexity that are wound around their heads like crowns. Their faces and hands are rosy with warmth, while their lips and their eyes glisten with beauty. Even their dresses glow, so that I'm surrounded by nodding, brilliant faces moving in a perfumed breeze.

'Then I raise my dumbstruck eyes and I see this beautiful

woman. Oh, Caradoc! I have a Roman wife who has given me fine sons and daughters. And I'll not deny that I've married the daughters of princes and tribal chiefs across the Roman world. Thus, we secure our borders and build treaties that endure because my tribal sons will rule these far-off kingdoms for many ages after I'm dead and gone. But I swear to you that I have never seen a face more fair, a body more voluptuous and a smile so infused with innocence that my heart almost stops, right there at the fire pit.

'I am prepared to lay down my heart for her to trample on and will swear my soul to her for ever more. But, just when I am about to speak, the gatekeeper places his hand over my mouth and leads me away.

'I try to struggle with him, for the gatekeeper is frail and ancient, but all the strength in my body has bled away like snow in the sun. I can still hear the women as they carol like birds in consternation as if they want me to stay, but the gatekeeper's hands are like iron and I am whisked out to the castell gates and I am left in the falling snow.'

Maximus paused. 'One last detail is worth repeating, Caradoc. Eventually I waken and I am bathed in sweat. But, before I wake, the gatekeeper stares at me with pale-blue eyes veiled with milky growths that make him almost blind. But he smiles at me and speaks.

'"*You must find the lady and make her yours, although the wide world keeps you apart. God has decided, so your fate is sealed and, if you refuse to find her, your world will be swept away all the sooner and the sword of the barbarians will be raised over this land without hinder.*"

'Then he smiles at me and I awaken from my dream.'

Caradoc considered his friend's words. The Maximus who was sitting on his saddle to keep the cold off his rump was a man without much capacity for poetry in his soul, but his description of the castell had transfixed the Dumnonii king. But how could he reassure his friend?

'Your dream is lovely and it's full of promise, so why does it frighten you? I've never known you to fear anybody or anything, least of all some insubstantial thoughts that have passed through your mind in the depths of the night.'

Maximus raised his leonine head. Under his close-cropped cap of greying hair, his dark eyes seemed haunted.

'It won't let me be! Even fair dreams can become horrific if the damned things won't release you from their clutches. Could this dream be a message from God? Or the Old Ones whose spirits survive in the old stone monuments. I'm a plain warrior, but I have a sense that terrible things will happen if I don't find this woman. Can you help me?'

'I'd like to try, but I don't see what I can do for you,' Caradoc replied slowly. He tried to imagine his friend baring his heart to his colleagues and realised that Maximus was trapped by his own rank in the Roman hierarchy and the necessity to be strong and pragmatic at all times.

'Would you be prepared to come into the north and visit me in Deva after you've completed your task in Anderida? I know that you've been away from Tintagel for a whole spring and summer, but I assume that your lands have been in the safe hands of your second son during your absence. If you are prepared to undertake a journey into the north from Tintagel, you could provide me with a service that goes far beyond friendship. You would be able to search in places where Romans would be decidedly unwelcome. I've cut into my time by detouring here, so I intend to make the best possible speed to reach Deva. If you were prepared to visit me at my headquarters there, you could carry out a search along the western coastline of Britannia. In fact, my dream suggested that the afternoon sun was setting over the sea, so our castell could be located somewhere along the western coast of Cymru. Perhaps such a search will reveal some fortifications with young girls in residence. I understand that you have no reason to waste your time on my fancies, but I swear that I'll be forever grateful for any help that you can give.'

Caradoc gave a little sigh, because he had been looking forward to a pleasant winter and autumn in the peace and the remoteness of Tintagel, but he knew the challenge of this quest was already gnawing at his vitals.

'I have a daughter, Maximus. She is a lovely girl, but has not yet reached the age of womanhood. I love her to distraction. Her name is Endellion and she will be furious if I arrive home, only to leave immediately on another long journey. I will bring her on my journey to Deva because she has rarely travelled, other than a visit to Venta Silurum several years ago. To take my daughter, I will have to wait until spring is near. If you are still prepared to have me carry out this quest, I will do so.'

Maximus shrugged carelessly because the happiness of an anonymous girl-child meant nothing to him as long as Caradoc carried out his search and, hopefully, completed his quest. If Caradoc refused to depart before the arrival of spring, then Maximus would have to agree.

'Agreed, my friend. You'll know best how to handle a search such as this. You'll also understand the terrain and the people you're likely to meet along the way. I'll leave all the details to you.'

Caradoc's brows rose and Cadal felt his own fists tighten at Maximus's presumption. Roman arrogance never diminished.

'The night is drifting towards dawn and we have much to do in the cold light of day. We should try to catch a little sleep,' Caradoc suggested. 'We'll discuss the finer details before you make good your departure.'

Strangely, now that he was free to sleep, Cadal found his weariness was too great to let him drift off into nothingness. Instead, he found himself watching the full moon as it slid through the thinning cloud to bathe the poor, ramshackle ruin below it in a silvery light. For a moment, Anderida was silver-dipped and new, a wondrous place which had endless promise.

Then the moon was obscured by a finger of cloud and the illusion was broken.

The detritus of a battle is huge, messy and time-consuming. So many dead bodies pose a significant threat of disease in summer, meaning the dead must be burned or buried immediately. For several hundred Saxons corpses, incineration would be the only practical means of disposal.

But to burn several hundred corpses to bone and ashes required a huge quantity of timber. Much of Anderida had already been burned during the battle, but some dismantled huts, cottages and dried thatch provided a good basis on which to start building the separate pyres for the British and Saxon fallen. Caradoc sent a troop of cavalrymen into the forests to drag out dead trees to augment their supply of flammable material. Other warriors were given the task of building the large cairns on which the corpses would be placed.

The disposal of dead horses was a major concern. They were unwieldy and heavy to move, but they too posed a threat of disease. Cadal was given the task of dragging the dead steeds to a suitable depression away from the town where they could be stacked, incinerated and covered with sandy loam. Knowing the unpleasant task was essential, he set about it with a will.

Caradoc's role was more difficult. The Dumnonii king insisted that all pomp and ceremony should be given to these warriors whose ashes and possessions would be returned to their wives, parents and children. One wagon was allocated to this herculean administrative task, and a courier was sent, post haste, to Venta Belgarum and King Gwaun ap Mairtin, asking for seasoned sailors and labourers to transport the ceols, laden or empty, back to Portus Adurni. As this message implied that the army had collected a large hoard of booty, Caradoc was certain that his request would be answered with alacrity.

This cynicism prompted several tribal jokes between Caradoc, his son and the Dobunni king. All three agreed that the kings of the alliance would appear like magic to claim their share of the spoils of war.

After two days of assisting with the movement of the corpses, Maximus bid farewell to the Britons, after reminding Caradoc of his promise and assuring his friend that he was looking forward to seeing him in Deva. With a nonchalant blast from their battle horns, the Romans rode away, to begin their long journey to Deva and the latest chapter in their ongoing battles with the Picts.

Caradoc's men stripped the Saxons of any items of value or practical use. This grotesque task was dirty and frustrating, but another empty wagon was soon groaning under the weight of weapons, armour, furs and body jewellery. Still more were already packed with the looted wealth from the towns, villages and traders who had fallen foul of Ironfoot's marauders. Several others had been laden with dried foods to feed the Saxon enclave on the Albis through their long and bitter winter. Caradoc insisted on taking these spoils for the survivors of the Saxon attacks in Anderida Silva, who otherwise would probably starve in the coming winter. In a landscape thick with oily black smoke, the eyes and mouths of the Britons were assaulted by the vile smell and awful taste of burning death. Day and night, flames flickered on the landscape as timber and corpses continued to burn down to ash.

Even then, the task was unfinished. While the ashes left after the incineration of the Saxons and the horses would be dispersed by the autumn winds, the remains of their fellow Britons required more care and attention. The British bones must be gathered and pounded into small fragments, then collected, mixed with the ashes and stored in a series of gold-plated boxes that Caradoc had taken from the Saxon hoard of stolen treasure. As most of the dead were from the Dumnonii, Dobunni and Regni tribes, three large boxes were required. Caradoc predicted that some of the other kings might complain that such valuable chests should be allocated to only three tribes and he was already preparing a strong response to any dissenting comments. The work went smoothly, but no one who worked on the clean-up remained untouched by the experience. Each man carried a mental picture of some dead warrior or of a trivial incident that touched them personally.

Cadal stumbled across a particularly gruesome group of bodies that were clustered around, and under, a pair of dead horses. The find had touched his heart. It was obvious that two tribal horsemen had been ambushed by a group of five huge Saxons who had gutted the first rider's horse. The beast had fallen, trapping the first Briton under its flank.

A second Briton had ridden madly towards them in an attempt to save his comrade. Cadal could read the desperate speed in the splayed legs of his horse and the long scrape on its legs and side showing how it had been brought down from a long sword stroke, delivered from below. The Saxon who disembowelled the horse had died under its thrashing hooves with his long knife still gripped in his hands. Cadal could see the perfect imprint of the horse's iron-shod hoof in the very centre of the Saxon's forehead where it crushed the skull and drove shards of bone directly into the brain.

The second of the British warriors had fought hard over the prone body of his comrade, killing two of the four Saxons as he waged a ferocious struggle for survival, only to be cut down by an axe blow on the left side of his skull.

His comrade, the first Briton, was killed with a deep, contemptuous, slice to his throat that almost took his head off. However, before he died, he had taken one last throw of the dice. With the bottom half of his body pinned to the ground by the weight of his dead horse, and having only a short knife to protect himself, he struck upwards at his Saxon killer in a final act of defiance.

The knife blade was stained with congealed blood so Cadal checked the bodies of the two Saxons who had survived the initial attack.

The smaller of the two hulking Saxons had received a hideous wound to the eye socket. But the shortness of the blade had allowed the Saxon to live, despite the gross wound.

Then, with a grin of satisfaction, Cadal realised that the two remaining Saxons had been killed by a volley of arrows that had pincushioned them from a distance. He felt a grim elation that they had been denied a good death, for they had been executed by common Dumnonii archers. Peasants, one and all, had killed those proud warriors.

Cadal realised that this story was unremarkable, but it had been written in blood and human flesh. Like Maximus's dream, he would find that every night was a replay of the small skirmish that had killed all seven of these men. But, each time, he would search for some new solution that might save some British lives. Sometimes he despaired, and the Saxons survived and continued to kill, again and again.

For those men who were forced to bear individual and personal burdens, the week passed very slowly. But even the greyest of days comes to an end and the worst winters are always followed by a spring. At last, all the terrible tasks had finally been completed and the Britons departed in a long cavalcade that headed off into the west.

Llew halted his horse and looked back, although he had sworn to himself that he would relegate Anderida to the past. The Dobunni king had put away his youth in the fierce battles that had taken place at the eastern gate, the town square and the headman's hall. No longer a tyro, he had learned the intricacies of strategy at Caradoc's knee and he was grateful for the influence of that canny old man that would assist him when he planned his own battles in the future. The town gaped open like a ruined skull with the crown torn away. Several buildings to the south and west had survived to bake in the summer sun. Rain had yet to wash away the stains of fire and soot on any of the structures that were still standing. Piles of rubble filled those laneways where stone walls had collapsed and the black rafters were lifting their vertical skeletons upwards to the sky. Then, from the ruins, seemingly dead and stripped of all hope, movement flickered between the collapsed buildings and a closer examination told Llew that dogs and cats had emerged from whatever hiding places had protected them. Now, they sought food, digging into the midden near the edge of the swamp and around the cremation pits in the hope of tasty morsels.

Scavenger birds were also in evidence around the soft and muddy soil of that midden.

'The corpses of the villagers must have been hidden in there,' Cadal said to Llew as he halted his horse beside the Dobunni. Llew followed his pointing hand to the many predatory birds that were digging into the piles of garbage without fear.

'Do you really think so?' Llew asked him, dumbfounded at the thought that they had camped so close to a mass grave.

'I do,' the prince sighed. Then his heels dug into the ribs of his horse and the beast sprang away.

Llew also booted his horse into a canter and rejoined Cadal as the forest embraced and enclosed the cavalcade.

'We always wondered where the people of Anderida had gone,' Cadal mused in a depressed monotone. 'The only possible place was the town midden.'

'But from what we've seen, the Saxons don't care about any rites for enemy dead. Why would they have buried all those men, women and children?'

Cadal was angry. If any of the Saxons had still been alive, he would have enjoyed killing them all over again. 'They were as aware as we are of the diseases that come from rotting corpses. But they must have buried them in shallow graves because the dogs could still smell the meat. I suppose they'll eventually expose the bodies. Ugh!'

'If Maximus is the kind of man he appears to be, the birds and beasts will dine well on the Picts, Hibernians and Saxons in the north of Britannia. Let us hope that his sword remains sharp and true,' said Llew.

'Aye,' Cadal replied. Then both men fell silent, lost in their separate thoughts, as the long train of wagons and warriors worked its way along the tracks through the black woods. At least the forest shadows remained cool and comfortable as they headed towards Venta Belgarum and the callous greed of foolish men.

THE COASTAL ROUTE
FROM TINTAGEL TO DEVA

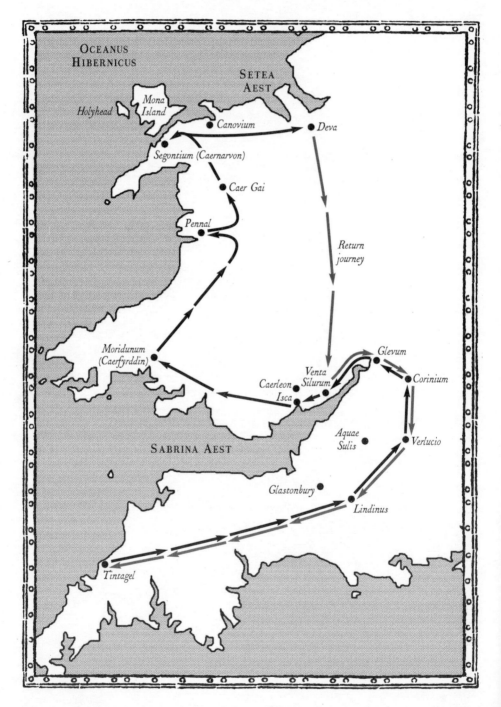

OCEANUS
HIBERNICUS

SETEA
AEST

Holyhead

Mona
Island

Canovium

Deva

Segontium (Caernarvon)

Caer Gai

Pennal

Return
journey

Moridunum
(Caerfyrddin)

Glevum

Venta
Silurum

Corinium

Caerleon
Isca

Aquae
Sulis

Verlucio

SABRINA AEST

Glastonbury

Lindinus

Tintagel

CHAPTER XV

A JOURNEY INTO TIME

By convention there is colour, by convention sweetness, by convention bitterness, but in reality there are atoms and space.

Democritus, Fragment

'The world is rarely as it seems, petal,' Caradoc warned his daughter, as she sat in the saddle of her quiet mare with a dreamy expression on her face.

'It will be exactly what I wish it to be,' Endellion replied distantly, playing with a drooping bouquet of wildflowers that had been picked from the hedgerows. With her long and slender neck, her head seemed to droop under the weight of long, unbound hair. The Dumnonii king was dumbstruck with pride in his changeling child.

Father and daughter rode at the head of their thirty-strong guard, a supply wagon and another heavy-duty cart that carried the essentials required by dignitaries for a journey of state. The guardsmen's cloaks, bright with the Dumnonii check, were a sight to be seen as the warriors trotted along, with their proud faces held high and their horses curried and buffed to a brilliant sheen. Even the horses used in the traces of the wagons were well presented, as befitted beasts used in the train of a major tribal king.

Ostensibly, the two Dumnonii aristocrats planned to visit the tribal centres of Gwent, Dyfed, Powys and Gwynedd. They would then move on to the Roman garrison at Segontium and, finally, the city of Deva, the neutral trading centre where the legions had guarded Roman interests in Britannia for hundreds of years.

Endellion's presence was explained as an opportunity for her to be seen by the local kings who might be prepared to ally themselves with the powerful Dumnonii tribe at some time in the near future. This ploy had worked well with the queen and Prince Cadoc, but Cadal remembered the pact between Caradoc and Maximus, so he was aware of his father's guile. In a private discussion with Caradoc, Cadal was particularly scathing in his arguments against his half-sister undertaking such a potentially dangerous journey.

'I've already made my decision,' Caradoc told his heir bluntly. His face was set in uncompromising lines. 'I made a promise to Endellion that she would be given a treat if she behaved herself during our absence in Anderida. She did exactly as I asked, so I'm keeping my word to her.'

'And what if one of the kings decides that she's perfect for his son? Do you plan to betroth her to one of the Cymru lords?'

Cadal suspected that a suggestion of marriage and an eventual parting from his daughter would enrage the old man. On cue, Caradoc's face reddened with temper and his eyes glittered.

'She'll not be promised. She's far too young!'

'That's nonsense, Father. Endellion is eleven now and she'll soon have her moon blood. She's almost ready to make her wedding vows. You can't lock her away forever.'

The king rose angrily to his feet. His forefinger poked at Cadal's chest until his son wanted to take the offending digit and snap it like a twig. As his own temper rose and he heard less and less of his father's tirade, Cadal decided to stop his teasing now he was certain that Endellion wouldn't become a pawn in Maximus's game.

He had been able to smile and wave as the entourage carried his sister away. Beside him, his wife and his mother gossiped about what kind of man Caradoc would choose for his daughter, for once in agreement over matters of dowry and suitability. Cadal shook his head at the strange thought patterns of women. His wife and his mother couldn't be more different in personality, but both ladies succumbed to sentiment, greed and gossip whenever decisions on the marriage bed were required. The queen had convinced herself that Caradoc had finally decided to see sense and would use this pretty by-blow as a useful tool to negotiate a profitable marriage.

The journey had started well, with the first destination being Llew ap Adwen's town of Corinium. But before they reached that fair city, so close to Cymru and its many castells, word reached them that Llew was visiting the small town of Verlucio with his wife. Verlucio lay a short distance off the Roman road leading to the north, but it was blessed with light forest, sweet water and flat agricultural lands. With a pleasant outlook, the small town was quiet and peaceful.

Llew proved to be the perfect host. His wife, Llian, was a red-haired beauty from one of the important clans of the tribe, but a woman who was reputed to suffer from extreme shyness. She avoided the company of guests to their town, a disability that must have been awkward for Llew, given that Corinium was situated at the crossroads of a major trading network, so poor Llian was occasionally forced to welcome her husband's guests in her soft, deprecating voice. Verlucio was the perfect haven for such a timid queen.

But Caradoc was soon to discover the reason for the queen's crushing shyness.

When they were sitting beside each other at the feast of welcome for the Dumnonii party, Caradoc had been surprised to notice that Llian's wimple covering her hair had slipped. He spotted many strands of grey in her dark-red hair, so wondered if her age was the reason no children frolicked in Llew's hall. The Dobunni king was childless.

More than one young ruler had found himself married to an older woman in the past, or had become embroiled in an ultimately childless marriage for the sake of close ties between neighbouring tribes. Usually, the king would cast off his older queen in favour of a younger, fertile woman once a little time had elapsed.

Ever the diplomat, Caradoc made a conscious decision to remain courteous at all times.

After several days of rest and entertainment, Llew suggested that Endellion might enjoy the exotic amusements on offer in Aquae Sulis, which was arguably the most Roman of all the trading centres in the isles of Britannia. Caradoc quickly came to the conclusion that his daughter would enjoy everything about this rich and important town.

So, on this leg of their wanderings, Caradoc had enjoyed introducing his lovely child to the wonders of Aquae Sulis, famed for its healthy mineral baths, its wealth and its epicurean delights. Endellion was charmed.

Several miles from the town walls, the thoroughfare had been widened, and the repairs to the road had been so expertly cobbled that very little shuddering and bouncing could be felt through the huge wagon wheels. Endellion's excitement mounted from the moment they reached the well-maintained road.

The usual outer settlements of houses and shops had sprung up outside the city's walls, no dirtier than those found outside any established Roman settlement. In fact, these premises were cleaner than most. The shop owners, common whores and housewives were clean, rosy-cheeked and were clad in neat Roman apparel, although their dress was a little old-fashioned. Even the finery of the gaily dressed whores filled Endellion with a delicious sense of guilty pleasure and envy.

Now that womanhood approached, Endellion had begun to interest herself in female adornment, so cosmetics were fascinating mysteries to be studied. Unaware of her father's intense scrutiny, Endellion raised her hands to her lashes to check their length and curl. One gloved finger rose to her lips and felt their dry texture after more than a week of travel.

Caradoc read the thoughts passing through the child's pretty head, and he was concerned.

The citizens' welcome to Caradoc's cavalcade was warm and open. As always, the whores attached themselves to saddle leathers and gazed up at the embarrassed faces of young warriors with practised innocence, but they refrained from screaming out any lewd invitations while they were on the roadway. Peasant women bearing baskets of steaming washing, or offering displays of vegetables for sale, gave smiling welcomes at the newcomers who set up camp in a grassy field outside the town gates. No town would ever welcome armed men within its walls, although Caradoc decided to take his daughter to one of the many luxurious inns that catered for noble travellers who came to Aquae Sulis to sample the healthy, life-giving waters.

Once a good establishment had been found and a comfortable night's sleep had blown away the worst exigencies of travel, Caradoc introduced his daughter to the wonders of a true Roman bath. Fortunately the most lavish bathing establishment provided a service whereby prominent ladies of breeding were able to bathe in single-sex comfort, with obedient servant girls to wash and dry their hair, fashionable manicurists to trim, clean and colour their nails as well as masseuses to oil their bodies and massage away the dirt and cares of the day. A visit to the baths could last for the best part of the day.

Endellion was in heaven. Once her nails were stained with henna, her hair was dried and dressed by skilled servants so that it cascaded down her back in a river of shining waves. She felt as if she had reached the heady excitement of womanhood.

Buffed, cleansed and tingling, Endellion was escorted back to their inn by Rowen ap Aidan, so that the royal visitors could dress in their best and present themselves to the magistrate of Aquae Sulis as a diplomatic courtesy. Endellion was almost sick with apprehension, for this meeting would be the first occasion on which she would be on public display. She was particularly fearful that her bucolic clothing would mark her as both a child and a provincial, even though their visit was scheduled for the late afternoon and formal dress wasn't required. Frowning, Endellion examined her woollen dresses and cotton shifts and cringed.

Fortunately, her father understood the feminine heart. While

Endellion wallowed in the luxury of the Roman baths, he had sought out a superior establishment that designed and made quality clothing for the Roman aristocracy of the city. The proprietor was an astute businessman who had no hesitation in pressing food and drink upon his noble guest in an attempt to separate Caradoc from a goodly number of his gold coins.

Of course, no time remained to turn swathes of beautiful material into suitable dresses for a young lady, but Caradoc knew that every seamstress or tailor possessed clothing that had been made for clients who belatedly decided that the finished products were less than flattering. Without hesitation, Caradoc asked to see some of these unwanted garments. Within moments, he was given access to a trunk filled with beautiful clothing of all cuts and sizes.

After a discussion with one of the helpful seamstresses in the establishment, Caradoc was able to find a number of suitable items, including one sea-green robe with an underskirt of pale lemon, with a dark green cloak to match, and arranged for their delivery to his lodgings. The proprietor of the shop was more than satisfied with the final price that Caradoc had agreed to pay. Now, as Caradoc watched his daughter discard one article after another from the pile of clothes she had brought with them on their travels, he could see that she was almost in tears.

'I don't have a single thing that is fit to wear at a social event,' Endellion wailed.

'Then it's a good thing that I conspired to find these foolish adornments,' Caradoc replied, as he placed each of the gaily wrapped parcels on her sleeping pallet. She threw herself onto the prizes with the voracity of an eager child.

'For me?' she breathed with mounting excitement. Her arms

were filled with shining fabric. 'Oh, best of all fathers. How could you have known?' Then she burst into scalding tears of relief until her father reminded her of the ravages that her tears were causing to her pretty face.

'Look at yourself, petal. Your eyes will be swollen and reddened if you aren't careful, so get yourself dressed so I can see how my choices suit you.'

Later, preening in her silver mirror, Endellion gained years in a moment as she leap-frogged from childhood into womanhood in the blinking of an eye. She pirouetted before her father so her new green robe belled around her narrow feet and Caradoc felt a bitter pang of envy for the inevitable man who one day would steal his daughter's heart away from him.

The business heart of the town, with its beautiful sandstone and marble buildings and tall, often naked sculptures rendered Endellion mute with amazement. Blushing, she turned away from brightly painted, marble sculptures of Venus, with her robe sliding away from a perfect, naked breast. Still more embarrassing were the carvings of the various gods, all proudly naked, and with their genitals exposed to the casual glances of the citizenry. Endellion attempted to keep her eyes averted. However, curiosity eventually won over embarrassment, so her eyes were soon darting from one beautiful public building, basilica or temple to the next. They roved too over the markets with their displays of luxury goods and staples.

Unfortunately, Endellion created her own small stir of interest as her beauty and colouring captured the attention of the most jaded male appetites. Her extraordinary hair, which hung loosely down her slender back, was bound at every hand-span by cuffs of silver.

Caradoc noticed to a trio of young farm labourers, probably

brothers, whose eyes had locked on his daughter as they dawdled over the task of carrying baskets of cabbages into the markets. With lewd gestures, the louts were mentally unbinding her robe from each shoulder and unclasping her hair from the virtuous cuffs. Caradoc almost dismounted to clout the youngest man for voicing his lustful thoughts, but he realised how foolish his actions would look to the crowd.

'I'd cause a scene in front of the peasants if I was stupid enough to say anything,' he murmured. 'Besides, Endellion wouldn't thank me if I made a display of her.'

'Sir?' Trefor inquired from his left side.

Caradoc winced, for he realised he'd been speaking aloud.

'I'm just feeling a father's concern, Trefor. I don't like the way those young bucks are looking at Endellion.' Caradoc pointed towards the farm labourers.

'Would you like me to discuss the matter with them?' the hunt-master asked, smiling with anticipation. The Dumnonii king trusted to Trefor's good sense, so nodded crisply.

Endellion, captivated by colourful songbirds in wicker cages for sale on one of the stalls, missed the entire discussion.

With a sharp heel in the ribs, Trefor sent his horse trotting towards the three young men who had resumed hefting the baskets of cabbages and were carrying them to a stall where an older couple were busily selling fresh vegetables.

Trefor deduced from the suggestive grinding of the youngest lad's hips and groin, as well as a series of obscene gestures made by the oldest brother, that these young oafs were making jokes at Endellion's expense. Caradoc rode on with Endellion and her three guards, while Trefor dismounted and approached the three braggarts.

'Can we help you, sir?' the second eldest of the brothers asked with thinly veiled sarcasm. He was superficially courteous, so Trefor addressed him in a like manner.

'I've been instructed to inform you and your friends that my master, King Caradoc of Tintagel, will be forced to teach all three of you to mind your manners if you continue to make jokes at the expense of Princess Endellion. She happens to be his daughter.'

'Says who?' the eldest brother snapped, without even a modicum of respect. 'We don't take orders from no blowhards, kings or no kings. So tell that to your master, whoever you are.'

'Yah!' the younger lad sneered in a sullen voice. The second son wisely decided to step back into the shadows where he could watch the action, as he tried to look impartial and respectful.

'I am Trefor, hunt-master of the King's Guard. You buffoons should remember my name, for I'll be the one who removes your fingers, one by one!' Trefor smiled engagingly and without threat. 'I'll also enjoy the process of teaching obnoxious oafs to respect their betters.'

He turned slightly and pointed directly at the eldest son.

'In your case, it'll be your prick that's removed. I doubt that it'll be a large task.'

Then he turned back to the youngest brother and picked him up by his shirt-front.

'As for you, I suggest you keep your pimply face out of our affairs and shut that vile mouth of yours. Do you understand? Good!' Trefor could have been discussing the latest horse sales for all the passion he revealed. But the middle brother recognised the iron in the captain's voice and he flinched away from Trefor's hard, unsmiling expression as he hurled the young lad back into the straw.

'You've done nothing to anger me – yet! I'd rather you did

nothing to alter this state of affairs, and cause me to change my mind.'

Then Trefor turned contemptuously and remounted his horse.

Within minutes, he had rejoined the column as it continued on its way towards the forum at the centre of Aquae Sulis. Endellion had been so engrossed in her surroundings that she failed to notice his absence.

The forum left Endellion breathless. She had visited Venta Silurum when she was a young child, but was unable to remember the half of what she had seen. Now, approaching adulthood, she could recognise the order, the cleanliness and the power that emanated from these public buildings, including a Christian basilica and a deserted temple that had once been full of those faithful to the gods of Rome. Within the temple precincts, the old ways weren't entirely dead. Someone had made a crown of fresh daisies and placed it reverently around the head of Jupiter, who was scowling down at foolish humanity from his position on an elevated plinth, careless of time and indifferent to the adoration of those who came to pay homage.

They halted and dismounted outside the old forum, now used as the council chamber for the administrators of this very Roman town. The small group was ready to present themselves to the town magistrate, his councillors and an avid group of citizens who had heard that an important tribal king from the south of Britannia was paying their town a social visit.

Trefor had carried in a small box made from scented wood that Caradoc had found among the spoils confiscated years earlier from Elphin, the outlaw. He had selected this particular container for its rarity and value. Inside the box, nestling on precious silk, were several rare shells that had been thrown up on the shores of the Dumnonii lands and remained miraculously unbroken. The largest, a conch shell with delicate spirals and a mouth of the most delicate pink, had been trimmed with a lip of the purest orange gold. More gold strengthened the point of the shell and had been applied in a filigree pattern along its back.

The smaller decorated shells waited to be presented too. When the trip had first been planned, Endellion had suggested them as excellent gifts for those dignitaries who offered hospitality to the party during their journey. With fingers crossed, Endellion hoped they would find favour with the sophisticates of Aquae Sulis.

They were met outside the building by a superior servant who introduced himself as Marcellus the scribe, the personal adviser to Marcus Gallus Felix, the magistrate of Aquae Sulis. Caradoc's eyes flared at a name that sounded pretentiously noble, so Marcellus unbent sufficiently to explain to this well-educated outlander that his master came from an aristocratic line whose branch of the family had gone into a decline, forcing the paterfamilias to engage in foreign trade.

Caradoc had no objection to aristocrats who chose to migrate to other lands if they could augment their impoverished family fortunes through doing so. He was eager to meet the man whose ancestors had shown such courage, and wondered if he would show such bravery if forced to face the same challenges.

'Quality, like water flowers, always rises to the surface. It makes itself felt in the most unpromising and brackish pond,' Caradoc murmured. Marcellus, taken aback by the king's poetic turn of phrase, examined the Dumnonii visitors covertly, for he was charged with giving his master a full briefing on the qualities of these barbarians.

The Dumnonii aristocrats were ushered into a large outer room with shuttered windows admitting air and light into the chamber. As they entered they became the centre of attention for the prominent citizens of Aquae Sulis and their wives; Endellion would have cringed under their cold scrutiny if she hadn't been wearing her new clothing which, Caradoc was happy to note, was the equal of any worn by the women present. He squeezed her hand and whispered some quiet advice.

'Stiffen your spine, my dear. Your birth is far better than theirs, so face them down.'

'I'll try, Father,' she whispered back. 'They are being quite rude, especially the ladies.'

'Aye, petal. Unfortunately, these people treat us as if we are provincial nobodies. Think of Tintagel and its strength, and then give them the most courtesy you can manage.'

A pair of large double doors opened sufficiently wide to allow a short, thick-set man to enter the antechamber. His sparse white hair was cut short and artistic curls had been arranged across his forehead. However, this foppish affectation was unable to weaken the effect of a pugnacious jaw, a firm mouth and two acute brown eyes that closely examined the newcomers. With a politician's easy smile and a smooth, outstretched hand, the man crossed the finely tiled floor to meet Caradoc. The Roman's grip was forceful and strong when he grasped Caradoc's wrist in the universal gesture of peace.

Marcellus stepped forward smoothly. 'My lord, Marcus Gallus Felix, Magistrate of Aquae Sulis, may I present Caradoc ap Ynyr, the king of the Dumnonii tribe, and Princess Endellion, his daughter.'

'Well met, Your Highness. I welcome you and your beautiful daughter to our city. I hope that our hospitality will meet with your satisfaction.' Caradoc was surprised at the warmth and strength in the gravelly voice.

Felix ushered his guests through the glittering crowd.

'Livinia, my dear, please introduce the fair Endellion to ladies of a suitable age, while I discuss private matters with my guest.'

An almost cadaverous lady swayed out of the crowd to usher Endellion away from the comforting company of her father. Endellion wanted to flee, but her father's advice stiffened her backbone. She accompanied the magistrate's wife to a corner of the room where she was introduced to a bevy of girls clad in robes that contrived to show more of their bodies than Endellion thought proper.

The double doors leading to the interior room swallowed Felix, Caradoc and Trefor, who had refused to leave his master's side. Endellion watched them depart with frightened eyes. She had been thrust into the company of young ladies who had been coerced into entertaining a young pretender from the backwaters of rural Britannia. Their mannerisms were affected and their expressions so patronising that she had difficulty controlling her responses.

'What is there to do in ... Tin ... Tin ...?' inquired a girl with an exotic hairstyle of delicately piled curls.

'Tintagel,' Endellion replied.

'What sort of name is that?' her sister, a girl in blue, scoffed.

'It's a Dumnonii word.' Endellion was trying her best to remain polite, but the young ladies continued their pointed and sarcastic questioning.

'So! What is there to do in your remote backwater of Britannia?' Livia, the girl with the curls, repeated. 'Do you dance? Or do you take lovers?'

'Certainly not!' Endellion protested and flushed delicately

across her high cheekbones. 'My father would kill any man who tried to touch me without his permission.'

'Gracious! How do you stand such bullying? You'll be telling us next that you weave and sew all day,' the girl in blue, Drusilla, smiled maliciously and then giggled behind her hand.

'I would *expect* my father to protect me from any unwanted advances. And what is wrong with the tasks necessary to maintain a good household? I expect to be a wife one day, so it's important that I have the skills necessary to supervise my servants.'

'My goodness, you really are a country mouse, aren't you?' Livia continued. 'And you have such interesting warriors to tend to your every need. She was eyeing Endellion's guardsmen with crude admiration.

Endellion was close to losing her temper.

'My father would punish me if I were to act like a whore, not that I would ever want to shame him. I wonder whether your father would wish you to sully his name, but perhaps you aren't as loved and as protected as I am. I'm sorry for you if that's the case. I'm the daughter of a king and I have been raised to act with propriety and to be generous to all the men and women who serve the members of the royal family. I would never tempt them to act in ways that would bring harm to their persons – never!'

'Are you calling me a—' Livia snapped, but Drusilla realised that her sister was treading on dangerous ground. She clasped Livia's hand in a vice-like grip.

'Don't bother with this provincial, Livia. Our father will be angry if we should get into a confrontation with one of his guests,' Drusilla hissed. 'As for you, young miss, I'd keep your opinions and your complaints to yourself, if I were you. The magistrate is our father and our bloodline goes back to the very beginnings of Rome. You do not count in Aquae Sulis, and you are only a guest in this house.'

Endellion stared at two pairs of cold eyes that seemed to strip her of her fine clothes so that she stood naked in front of their contemptuous smiles. She had never felt so raw or so alone.

Some deeply buried streak of obstinacy rose to the surface as her dislike for these girls reached its zenith and her palate tasted of acid. It brought with it memories of her childhood and stories of the decimation of her people that had been related to her by her old nurse. A sense of pride made her lift her chin.

'Beware whom you accuse of being a fool, a whore or a nobody. My mother is a servant of the goddess and my father is a king. In the fullness of time, mine shall be the womb that brings forth new kings ... and more than kings.'

Her eyes glittered like viridian prisms and she seemed to stand so tall that her shadow rose up the wall like a monstrous giant. Then, as suddenly as her strength had come to her, her shoulders drooped in defeat. Desperate, she forced back the tears that would only encourage these horrible girls to laugh at her.

Angry and upset, Endellion swept away. She hurried up to her guardsmen and fought to control her trembling lips. 'Please, inform my father that I will wait for him outside in the cool air,' Endellion told Rowen, who was standing beside the door. Rowen opened the door for her and followed her out into the night. Behind her, the room was suddenly silenced.

'Begging your pardon, mistress, but we can't permit you to wait alone,' Rowen insisted, but a tearful Endellion informed him that she had no intention of returning to the inner sanctum of the forum and her antagonists.

'What those women did to you wasn't right, Highness,' the

guardsman murmured. He handed her a well-washed length of cloth, obviously a neck scarf.

Turning away to allow Endellion some privacy, the warrior spoke from over his shoulder.

'I'll wait with you while the other guards speak with your father when he's completed his business with the magistrate.' He held his ground because he knew that her safety was paramount. He, for one, would not care to face Caradoc's wrath if the king discovered his daughter had been permitted to remain alone and unattended outside the forum.

'I understand your embarrassment, Lady Endellion, but your father would have the skin off our backs if you were left unprotected,' he explained slowly. It was Endellion's turn to flush with guilt. She brought her temper under control, blew her nose and attempted to compose herself.

Endellion had never been treated with such spite before, so she had no idea how to combat it. Instead of tears, she damaged the fine felt of her slippers as she kicked angrily at loose stones on the forecourt while pacing from one side to the other.

Suddenly, this beautiful city was no longer friendly or even particularly attractive. The buildings may have been constructed from finely dressed stone, but they seemed too close together. Endellion was used to the open spaces of Tintagel with its cleansing winds and the strong sucking ocean tides. Here, every nuance of her conversation was judged, so the simplest of conversations made her feel as if she was walking on thin ice. Not yet twelve, she was as yet powerless to find a witty phrase that could protect her in this undeclared class war.

The outer doors opened and Caradoc strode forward with his two guardsmen one pace behind him. Trefor brought up the rear, with the exotic wooden box still gripped firmly in his hands. Caradoc could see her wounded face, even from the far side of the broad forecourt.

Endellion ran straight to him and threw herself into her father's open arms.

Caradoc soon winkled out the details of the sordid insults directed at his daughter. As she spoke, the flood gates opened and the whole, vulgar incident tumbled out.

'There, there, petal. Let's return to the inn and climb out of these foolish clothes. We'll depart tomorrow, because the sooner we're out of this gilded whorehouse the better. It's sad that you've been treated so knavishly by those bitches, but I won't tolerate such rudeness.'

They were forced to wait for their horses to be brought back from the nearby stable, so father and daughter were still in the forecourt when the magistrate hurried out to discover what was amiss. Without hesitation, Caradoc described what had occurred, in the bluntest possible terms.

'Let me tell you, Felix, that I came to Aquae Sulis, and your hall, in the spirit of friendship. But my daughter, who is not yet twelve years of age, was subjected to the kind of treatment that she has been raised to reject. I had hoped to open trade negotiations between us, and to develop a pact that would ensure our mutual protection in times of attack but, apparently, your citizens want nothing to do with backward peasants from the British tribes. Terms such as *country mouse* and references to *provincials* are hardly descriptions that should be thrown at guests in any lands. Nor would I expect such talk from well-born ladies who see fit to imply that my daughter should cavort sexually with guards or servants. Is this how your daughters act in your house? There can be no justification, sir, for their manners or their actions.'

The magistrate spluttered and tried to apologise, while

Caradoc tapped his booted foot impatiently and wondered inwardly at the time it was taking for the horses to arrive.

'I admit that some people in Aquae Sulis have forgotten that they live in Britannia and not in Rome,' Felix began. 'In fact, all of us would be judged as provincials if we returned to Rome. I cannot express how sorry I am that Endellion has been upset, but I assure you that my daughters and my wife will discover the extent of my embarrassment as soon as I am alone with them.'

Somewhat mollified, Caradoc accepted Felix's apology.

'I've experienced the prejudice of some noble Romans in the past, so I'm very touchy in this regard. However, my good friend, the Comes Britanniarum, has changed some of my bias. As I told you earlier, we will be staying with Magnus Maximus in Deva for some weeks, but I anticipate we will pass through Aquae Sulis when we make our return journey to Tintagel. I hope that Endellion has a friendlier reception during her next visit.'

As they spoke, several boys ran up from the stables with the horses in tow, so Felix's final apology was brief and heartfelt. Caradoc left the magistrate with mixed feelings.

Before they left the inn the next morning, a messenger arrived with a gift for Endellion as proof of the city magistrate's regard. It was a large cloak pin set with a deep-blue stone surrounded by sea pearls. She sighed over the beautiful ornament, because she believed herself to be morally obliged to return it.

'Why, petal? I believe we should let the magistrate grovel a little. I spoke with the messenger who delivered this small trinket before I gave it to you and said everything that is necessary to express your thanks. Apparently, the whole villa is buzzing with rumour and innuendo at the punishment inflicted on the females of the magistrate's house. The gift of jewellery you received was intended for the magistrate's wife and had travelled all the way from Ravenna in Italia. He's struck his poisonous females in one of the few places where they can really be hurt, in their love of valuable and pretty baubles. Yes! You must accept this brooch, my girl.'

Shortly after sunrise, the Tintagel aristocrats rode out of Aquae Sulis to rejoin the rest of their party outside the gates of the city. As they passed the market place where farmers and their labourers were setting up stalls for the start of another day of brisk trading, Caradoc spotted one of the louts who had so annoyed him the day before. As soon as he saw Dumnonii warriors, he scuttled towards the farm cart like a scalded cat.

As Caradoc watched, the other brothers limped and shuffled into view, while painfully carrying a basket of carrots between them. Both men were battered and bruised, while the visible parts of their faces and arms were covered in networks of bruising, cuts and abrasions. As the bandage around his badly beaten face attested, the eldest brother would be unable to practise his lewd sneer for some time. His swollen, bruised and splinted arm showed further evidence of a serious fall or accident during the night. When the pair saw the Tintagel riders, they dropped the basket and scurried away as best they could into the safety of a nearby laneway.

They didn't look back.

Suddenly, Caradoc's day was decidedly brighter, so he shared a quick, knowing glance with Trefor. While the warrior's face remained bland and impassive, he winked at his master. Justice had been done.

The Dumnonii column wound its way through the towns of Cymru in a spirit of leisurely adventure. Only one incident rivalled their unfortunate experiences in Aquae Sulis, at least from Caradoc's point of view.

Endellion had visited Venta Silurum before, on the occasion of her brother's search for a wife, but she had been a child then. The soft green landscape outside the town, along with the imposing mountains in the background, appealed to the girl's sense of privacy and her love of beauty, so it was inevitable that she would enjoy their visit to this city that serviced the Roman camp that was home to the Dracos Legion.

For Caradoc, visiting Venta Silurum would always be a pleasant affair. He valued his friendship with his daughter-in-law Ardunn's parents, Aelheran ap Einion and Queen Aoifi. On several occasions, Caradoc had escaped there, ostensibly to make treaties, but actually for his personal entertainment. At times, the endless carping of Tegan Eurfron drove Caradoc to search for a convenient bolthole.

This visit had been comfortable and much had been made of Endellion's dark beauty. The royal family were also energised by the visit, so a hunt was organised along the fringe of the impenetrable Forest of Dean to celebrate this social event.

Under normal circumstances, the Tintagel column would have passed along the edge of the forest during the trek to Venta Silurum. But Caradoc had decided to follow the coastal road so that his cavalcade could avoid the dark wilderness that harboured all manner of beasts and dangerous outlaws. And so it was that the Dumnonii king could claim some familiarity with the terrain where the hunt would be conducted.

To ensure the success of the day's entertainment, the beaters had been arranged by King Aelheran, while Queen Aoifi had personally ordered an elegant repast for the guests. Against custom, the aristocratic ladies of the court had been given permission to take part in this particular hunt; however, most of the female guests refused to entertain the idea of killing any animal, least of all the pheasants with their magnificent tails or the quail that were so comical in their scurrying haste. Endellion, who was a keen fisherwoman and loved to hunt coney in the spring with a slingshot, asked her father if she could seek out a weapon and test her skills. Caradoc eventually agreed.

The great day finally dawned. Endellion was almost ill with excitement, for this hunt was the first real occasion where she could attend a private party among her peers. She harassed her father constantly with requests to check her sturdy clothing, jewellery and hair. Her maid, a plump little girl from the south-west, was as excited as her mistress, so the girls giggled together as Endellion showed her first appreciation for younger members of the opposite sex. Caradoc bit his lip to quell the smiles that his daughter brought to him through these innocent pleasures, even as he stifled a twinge of envy when he watched the two girls admire the fine legs and shoulders of a handsome young huntsman from the Silures tribe.

Finally, after much heartburn and nerves, Caradoc decreed that Endellion should wear her Roman cloak pin and the golden earrings that had been gifted to her on her tenth birthday. He vetoed the many rings she had jammed on every finger, by informing her that ladies never wore all their jewellery at the same time.

'Only a whore or a fool wears their rings that way. One set per hand is sufficient, because this item will show off the quality of your selection. Do you understand?'

Endellion looked down at her hands and then felt very grown up as she selected her gold thumb-ring shaped like a scaled fish.

'That's perfect, my sweet. You should also remember that

ladies of quality never push themselves forward. My pretty girl doesn't need to chatter to gain attention from young or old.'

So, mounted on shining horses, the Tintagel party joined the other invited guests and rode at a leisurely pace towards the margins of the large, spreading forest that was a source of fascination for Endellion, who had never before seen such huge trees so close up. On this occasion, she saw fields that were awash with blue and yellow flowers in among the viridian-green grass. Birds were singing in the coppices, while farmsteads seemed newly-dipped in sunshine, scrubbed clean during the overnight showers.

To the south, the waters of Sabrina Aest glittered in the perfect spring light. Unconsciously, Endellion began to sing in a sweet, high treble. Her song told a tale of a red vixen who hunts in the forest for food to feed her hungry cubs while the moon sinks towards the horizon. Even when she reached the final verse, where the vixen is bemoaning the loss of her mate in a sharp-toothed trap, the song continued to lift the spirits of those who heard it. The words seemed to promise that life-long love was not an impossible dream.

As the song reached its conclusion, Endellion sat quietly in her saddle. She was lost in her thoughts when the sound of clapping hands broke her reverie. Turning awkwardly, she saw a young man sitting on a large stallion, his blue eyes warm with appreciation. She blushed, unaware that she had been overheard by another member of the hunting party, and also because this young man was attractive.

'I beg your pardon, Mistress Endellion. My intention was to praise you, not to cause you any discomfort. I've never heard your song before and it's rare to enjoy a melody presented with skill and passion.'

317

'I am disadvantaged by you, good sir, for I'm a stranger to the land of the Silures and I don't know who you are. I know my singing voice isn't perfect, but I do so love the old country songs that my nurse sang to me when I was a child. To be honest, I didn't realise I was singing aloud.'

The young man smiled engagingly, while Caradoc watched the young man's face in an attempt to gauge his intentions.

'My name is Aeron, son of Iorweth, and I was born in Caerleon. My home lies a little to the west of Venta Silurum. Caerleon is a beautiful town and my father is the lord of all he surveys, although he bends his knee to his lord, Aelheran ap Einion. My mother, Eavan, is a sister of Llew, the Dobunni king, so my father plans to send me to Corinium to learn statecraft at my kinsman's knee. I have heard of you, Your Highness, from both my father and King Llew. They both speak of your strong arm and your unfailing sense of justice.'

Brought into the conversation with such grace, Caradoc was disarmed for a moment, but his natural suspicions soon returned.

'King Llew is a clever young man, I'll own, but he gives me too much credit. Your kinsman is an excellent person for any young man to emulate, so your father is a wise man. Nonetheless, I am surprised that your father never sent you to King Aelheran for your tuition and training.'

Caradoc spoke gruffly and was pleased to see the smile widen on young Aeron's face. Gracefully, the heir of Caerleon asked the Dumnonii king to share some details of the Anderida raid, and Caradoc practically purred under Aeron's acclaim. By the time the conversation ended, Caradoc's misgivings had been mollified by the young man's considerable charm. Only later did he realise that Aeron had not answered his question.

Caradoc was so taken with Aeron that he invited the young

man to ride with them, an invitation that the Caerleon heir accepted immediately. He pulled his horse aside so that he could ease it forward to ride on Endellion's free side. So far had Caradoc's opinion mellowed that he made no objection, telling himself that young people will always seek each other out.

'I disagree with you, Mistress Endellion, when you say that your voice is impure. I would never presume to guess at your age, but I'm sure that you're still growing. Your singing skill will continue to develop, but I believe that the most perfect and angelic voice will soon weary an audience if the singer uses perfect sound without deep feeling. I know that I felt sympathy for the vixen and her broken heart, although I doubt that foxes have souls that can be shattered.'

Endellion smiled shyly at his compliments, unsure if he was serious or not.

'Surely any creatures who can think must have souls,' she replied with downcast eyes.

'The Christian priests, including my own tutor, would tell you vehemently that Man is the only creature who was born in God's image. In fact, for Eve's sin, my tutor believes that women also lack souls.'

Endellion gasped at such an idea, so she looked to her father for confirmation.

'Aeron is quite correct, petal, when he says that many men of God share this belief. They are convinced that the female sex is the source of all sin, so women were sent into the world to tempt men.' Caradoc paused when he saw his daughter's horrified expression. 'Not all men of God are sensible. In fact, some are f— stupid.'

Caradoc bit back the expletive. However, he could have sworn that the lad riding with him had grinned for a brief heartbeat.

'If God is a truly loving father, he wouldn't have created Eve with sin inside her, for her fate would have already been sealed. Why would the Lord of Hosts entrust women to bear and raise the children of the future if they were so wicked? It makes no sense.'

'You are quite the little philosopher, Endellion. Your point is well argued!' Caradoc leaned across his horse to pat her face protectively. 'You can believe me, petal, when I say that no man will ever treat you like a sinner without a soul, regardless of whether he is a priest or a king.'

'Well said, sir,' Aeron agreed seriously. 'I've argued with my tutor, Father Peter, on many occasions over his stance against the other sex. I've also discussed his strange views with my father, but Father Peter is adept at flattery and at hiding the worst of his prejudices. He thinks of me as a boy rather than a man, so he's more careless of his tongue when he's with me.'

'Surely he realises that you'll take your place as the lord one day,' Caradoc answered.

'It'll be a long time coming. My father was betrothed when he was very young. Unlike most arranged marriages, he was captivated by my mother on sight. I was born when he was only sixteen, so he's only thirty-two now. He insists he's at the peak of his strength, and I don't deny it. My father is a remarkable man.'

Endellion, who had received a liberal education at Caradoc's behest, calculated that Aeron was only a few years older than she was and fast entering adulthood.

As Fortuna would have it, Endellion never had an opportunity to hunt, but she hardly felt any lack in her day. Once the hunting party had reached the outer edges of the Forest of Dean, villagers were waiting to serve as beaters and to help raise the pavilions that had been brought in a wagon for the comfort of the ladies. Sturdy blankets were laid on the bare earth, folding stools were unpacked and soon servants carrying large wicker baskets were presenting a feast sufficient to feed a whole village.

The men ate swiftly and with gusto, while the beaters headed out into the tangled, wild coppices that grew on the edges of the forest. A mood of gaiety and celebration prevailed and every man present felt his blood rise in response to the coming hunt.

The ladies' eyes shone at this variation from their normal routines and, although their work baskets had been brought with them in the supply wagon, they were already enjoying the conversations of like-minded women who saw each other only rarely. Soon, in a flurry of giggles and chatter, needles and thread were plied busily in prosaic mending, or in fashioning small items of clothing.

Endellion was welcomed among their ranks, although she possessed nothing to keep her fingers busy, but Queen Aoifi had brought a serving maid with her who was a noted player of the six-stringed harp, while one of the ladies from Magnis in the misty mountains drew out a simple reed pipe. The queen asked for entertainment as the fruit juices and the wines of the south were passed around.

Then, with a wicked smile, Aeron informed the gathered ladies that Endellion knew many of the old songs from the distant past. Once again, Endellion found herself flushing hotly and attempting to explain that she was far from expert.

'Nonsense, child! I sound like a crow when I try to sing and most of my friends lack any knowledge of the old songs, even if they have pleasant voices,' the queen explained in a no-nonsense fashion. 'We'll overlook any deficiencies in your performance if you'll be kind enough to entertain us.' A chorus of pleas followed from the ladies present, so Endellion mutely appealed to Aeron for assistance.

'Don't look to me, fair mistress,' Aeron answered with a charming smile. 'I think you sing very well, as I've repeated several times. Besides, I'll be out on the hunt, trying hard to kill something. I was just about to ask you to give me a token for good luck, as I'm not really expert on the hunting field.'

Endellion, embarrassed by the knowing smiles of the queen and her ladies, hastily rifled through her waist pouch in order to find something appropriate. All she could find was a plain black band of plaited leather that she used to tie back her hair when she was riding.

She held it out with an apologetic shrug. 'It's all I have, but it might bring you luck.'

With an ostentatious sweep of his arms, Aeron pulled back his russet hair and tied it with the band so that only the plaits at his forehead could swing free. 'Your token convinces me that I can now kill a boar or two in your honour, Mistress Endellion.' The bow he gave her was only slightly less than the obeisance he was honour bound to give to the queen. The women tittered in amusement.

As Aeron swung onto the back of his horse, he saw a simple tambour thrust into Endellion's hands by one of the women. Then she struck the tight hide with her knuckles to set the beat, and he heard her voice rise in the now-familiar tune about the hunting fox. He laughed with the pleasure of the day and the joy of being young.

Then he rode away in an exuberant trot that sent clods of earth flying from the hooves of his stallion. The sound of Endellion's voice followed him, light, airy and full of a peculiar female longing that nestled somewhere near his heart.

CHAPTER XVI

OF ARMOURED BOOTS
AND FAIR WOMEN

Who is she that looketh forth as the morning, fair as the moon, clear as the sun, and terrible as an army with banners.

The Song of Solomon, 10:10

'Endellion! Endellion! What am I to do with you?' Caradoc asked himself as his daughter lifted her woebegone face into the teeth of a light rain. They rode along a dilapidated track leading to the north, having left Venta Silurum, Caerleon and Caer Fyrddin behind them. Thus far, there had been no sign of the Castell of Maidens, so his daughter was driving him demented as she pined for a pair of fine blue eyes and a mane of russet curls.

'I never had a chance to say goodbye to Master Aeron ... and I don't even know if he survived his wound.' The last words were wailed and were followed by a bout of hiccups, as she tried to swallow her tears.

'The lad wasn't badly hurt,' Caradoc replied gently. 'Especially when you consider that he jumped onto the back of an enraged boar that had its mind set on killing King Aelheran who, I've belatedly discovered, happens to be his uncle. The lad has more courage than sense, but he only sustained a broken arm and the odd scrape and cut. He was a very lucky young man, so you don't need to maunder on as if he was close to death.

'Still, young Aeron did ask me to pass his apologies on to you. He was unable to return your lucky token, and he was quite vociferous in his belief that your charm saved his life. I had no idea what the boy was babbling about, but his obvious regard for you should make you feel a little less miserable.'

'I only gave him an old hair tie, because I had nothing that was more suitable. What will he think of me?' She hardly knew the young Silures nobleman. They had spoken for barely half an hour, yet Endellion was heart-broken by his absence.

Impatient with his daughter, Caradoc spat onto the verge of the roadway. Endellion was showing far too much partiality for this particular youth, a lad who might not reciprocate her feelings. The king leaned across the saddle of his horse to offer comfort but, if he had had his way, he would have preferred to shake her out of her misery.

'Even his mother didn't know how badly he'd been hurt. She asked *me*,' Endellion sobbed, wiping her tear-streaked face on her sleeve. Caradoc began to accept that this shared journey might be the last time he enjoyed any close contact with her. What could he say if Aeron ap Iorweth came to him with an offer of marriage for Endellion? The whelp's birth was no impediment. He was well placed to rule the Silures tribe through his father's status or, if Llew should die without issue, he could easily become king of the Dobunni through his mother's line. No, Aeron's birth was impeccable and the boy was everything he could ask for in a son-by-marriage.

'Damn the boy! Life was so much simpler before we met him.'

'You're being unfair, Father. I thought you liked Aeron?'

'I do! But you've only spent less than an hour in his company. You're far too young to have developed any affection for him. Besides, he's a young man rather than a boy.'

'What does that mean?' Endellion countered, her tears forgotten as the conversation took on a more adult tone.

'I'm afraid that young men fall in love very easily. Don't pout, petal. Aeron may be taken with you now, but his world is full of beautiful young women who are eager to attract such an eligible suitor. I'd not have your heart broken by a lad who is trying to take advantage of your innocence.'

'He's made no promises to me, Father,' Endellion said slowly. 'So I have no hold over him. However, some young people are capable of constancy, even men.'

'Hmmph!' Caradoc cleared his throat. 'I've seen many love matches and few remain deliciously happy. By the same token, many arranged marriages work reasonably well. In fact, my dear, we sometimes find we can be much happier if our heart isn't engaged by that of another.'

Father and daughter rode on in a frosty silence. Endellion had dried her eyes and was staring rigidly at the path ahead of her horse, chewing over her father's words and showing the first real signs of doubt over her feelings. Caradoc felt his heart melt. He relented, for she was far too young to be disillusioned by love.

'The lad did ask if he would be permitted to see you, when he recovers from his wounds. He's aware that he's too young to make serious choices about his future, but he has expressed a desire to become acquainted with your family and yourself.' As Caradoc spoke, Endellion's face broke into a glowing smile.

'Father . . .' she began, but Caradoc raised one hand to silence her slew of questions.

'I've invited him to visit Tintagel, once he's in good health and has taken up his position in Corinium. I told him he can come if he can be spared from his duties, and if he gains his father's approval. Does that news please you, petal?'

Endellion simply nodded, but this dull, grey day was suddenly brighter.

Caradoc had chosen not to mention Maximus's dream to Endellion for he was certain that the Comes Britanniarum would resent a young girl of eleven or twelve summers knowing the details of his intimate secrets.

Instead he had told her that the Roman had asked him to carry out a survey of fortresses along the western coast of Britannia and to provide an assessment of their effectiveness if the Picts and Hibernians were to unite and initiate a determined attack.

So, after a pleasant journey along the spectacular coastal road that took the travellers to Caer Fyrddin, they had been forced to forsake the coastline in order to reach Pennal on the western coast. There was only one negotiable track, which took them through remote and difficult terrain. Endellion had marvelled at the never-ending wonders of nature that seemed to appear before them at every turn.

'Now! Can we concentrate on the journey that lies ahead of us, daughter? The next major town we visit is Pennal, so we should arrive there in a few days. It lies on an inlet on the western coast of Cymru and I've been told that it's the site of a Roman fortress. The town is very small, apart from the fortress which only has a token force, now that so many troops have marched away to fight in the north.'

From the first days of their sojourn in Cymru, father and daughter had been awe-struck by the unusual features of this wild land. Caradoc had been amazed at the tidal surges that engulfed the great river at the very end of Sabrina Aest, a venerable and astonishing body of water. Now, at the furthest end of Sabrina Aest, which was visible from atop the first line of tall hills that loomed over Caer Fyrddin and the waters, this cleft in the body of Britannia was both beautiful and frightening.

Then, as they followed the road leading into the north, they discovered that the treeless hills were golden with gorse and blue-violet with heather. They had travelled without seeing another living soul for over half a day, yet sheep clung to the hillsides in quaint brown and white clusters. They had spied an occasional shepherd's hut from the road, but the bleak landscape brooded over the track. The land was silent and very, very empty.

Huge stones loomed out of the spring mists. These monuments weren't as impressive as the monoliths of the Giant's Dance but were still drenched with that *something* that raised the hairs on Caradoc's neck and sent Endellion's hair crackling and glittering with their power. In circles, rows, or ominously alone, these stones seemed to hide in every dell, as if they sought coolness from the hot sun. They sprouted out of meadows like mushrooms, they waited above headlands like sentinels that pointed towards the Pole Star and swirled with a superstition that could send maddened men running towards the cliffs and the black sea below. Cymru was filled with inexplicable wonder.

The Tintagel column was following a road into the north that led them to a range of mountains glowering over them. The Roman road was still holding together, but Caradoc winced to see the signs of decay nibbling away at its edges. The deterioration in maintenance along the thoroughfare pointed to a deeper malaise that was beginning to appear in the Roman provinces. Maximus had warned his friend that the Western Empire was struggling, decaying at the centre from greed, ennui and viciousness, while younger and more vigorous tribes were waiting on the fringes to feast on Rome's leavings. Sooner rather than later, the sporadic attacks on Rome's possessions would turn into waves of ravening savages screaming for Roman blood.

'And what will happen to us?' Caradoc asked into a stiff wind. Ahead of him, Endellion missed his despairing comment. He bit on his lip. Why spoil her innocent pleasure with his old man's fears?

But my daughter may need to survive the death of an empire. And what will happen to her children? Will she lose sons to the collapse of the Roman Dream?

'All things die!' His clever mind came to the inevitable end of all philosophies. 'The weak give way to the strong and the young replace the old. I had hoped to die in the peace and harmony where I spent my youth.'

Endellion was waiting for him with the sun behind her. Somehow, the road had made a gradual turn and he hadn't realised the change of direction. His daughter was now a silhouette against a sun that was sliding down towards the sea.

Caradoc shook his head to clear it, then rode towards his daughter and the black shape of her mounted figure became clearer. The green shade of her eyes seemed even deeper when he reached her and the light inside them seemed to crackle with something he didn't understand. Then, behind her, Caradoc could see a wide sweep of sea below them. Its colour, too, was a deep grey-green, with a border of black weed that made a clear line between the earth and the sea.

Endellion shook her head like a young horse and her hair

flew out from her shoulders. Her eyes were strange and fey.

'The strangest thing has just happened, Father. I fell asleep in the saddle.'

'What are you talking about, Endellion?' She failed to answer. Father and daughter rode down the slow, steep slope to the sea and a small fishing village that hunkered on the very edge of the land.

She extended her left hand and Caradoc sensed that she wanted him to hold it between his own scarred palms. He obliged her, so she clutched at his right hand as if it was her lifeline.

'I've occasionally fallen asleep in the saddle, especially if I've become exhausted after a long battle or I've been weak from loss of blood.' Caradoc laughed. 'Trefor can sleep almost anywhere. I've seen him fall asleep on bare earth, in snow and in sleet. I can swear that I once saw him doze all night in the fork of a tall tree. Why shouldn't you fall asleep if you're tired?'

'But I had the dream again, Father,' Endellion whispered fearfully.

Caradoc's heart sank. His daughter hadn't been troubled by night terrors for nearly six years and he had hoped that she had outlived her strange aberration. He looked at her suspiciously. Had she experienced that first rush of moon-blood that marked her entry into womanhood, and not told him?

Red-faced and embarrassed, he asked his daughter the intimate question, while wishing that Tegan Eurfron or Ardunn were here to handle this awkward intrusion. Endellion blushed as hotly as he did, but she answered him fairly. She admitted asking the Silures queen for advice when the first gouts of dark blood had come, for she was terrified that she might be dying from some unknown illness.

'Why didn't you come to me, petal? We could have discussed this matter together.'

She shrugged. She lacked the words to explain the secret, mortifying horror that she had felt as she realised the implications of her step into adulthood. Oh, how she wished that she was still a little girl and could remain ignorant of her body's ebbs and flows.

She diverted the awkward conversation towards shallower channels. Like her father, she had heard that priestesses had often-times found their power after womanhood came upon them and blanched at the thought.

'I dreamed that a wagon came down this road, heading for Caer Fyrddin. A woman was holding the reins, Father, but she wasn't a peasant. She was wearing a strange, silver necklace and she was frightened of something. I knew that this was one of those dreams where I was the watcher and no one could see me, so I rode as close as I could to the wagon.'

'What else did you see? Was the wagon alone on the road? Are you sure it was here?'

'Aye, Father. That's why it was all so strange. There were several wagons, accompanied by mounted servants and a warrior guard, so the woman was someone important. She had a young girl with her. The young girl was pregnant, Father, and she was very, very angry with someone or something. I could see that she was furious with her mother, her world and all thoughts of happiness. It was as if I could see inside her head and what I saw there was murderous and maddened. Then I woke.'

'It's not the dream that's frightened you then?'

Endellion shook her head and her father could tell that she was herself again, as if by sharing the substance of her vision, she was able to banish the things she had seen into the mists of memory.

'Forget the dream, petal. A long time ago, I was told by one wise woman that time sometimes ripples like a ribbon that is blowing in the wind. Past, present and future are very close together for an instant when this happens. Perhaps you dreamed something that has happened, or is yet to happen at some time in the distant future. I cannot tell. I'm a plain man, and I'm not used to the world beyond us. But I know that your mother could sometimes see things that would come to pass. I can't pretend to understand your dreams, darling, but I want you to promise me that you'll speak to no person, other than me, about any night terrors that visit you, for the ignorant may decide you're possessed by a demon.'

Endellion's eyes were very wide. 'Am I going mad, Father? Am I a witch and accursed by God?'

'No! Never! You just have a special way of seeing life on some occasions, that's all. But others might not understand, so we'll keep your dreams as a secret between us.'

Endellion nodded happily, as if a huge weight had been lifted from her shoulders. Her father was the fountainhead of all wisdom, so she accepted his explanations and was comforted. She leaned across and kissed his leathery cheeks with a sweetness that made his mouth dry. She smelled of flowers and sunshine, and all light seemed to be trapped inside her midnight hair.

Spring had fled and summer had begun, but if Caradoc had hoped for sunny days and clear skies, then he discovered that Cymru had an unpredictable climate. Storms came unseasonably and split the sky with jagged lightning, lashing winds and, after the thunder had ceased to shake the straining earth, rain poured out of the heavens in huge, splattering drops.

All too often, the Dumnonii party was delayed or forced to scurry for shelter in a cave, huddled against the side of a cliff, or in the decrepit barns of local farmers. After Pennal, which had revealed nothing of any importance to their search, except the decaying hall of a drunken Ordovice chieftain, the party had been forced to turn inland again, heading towards Segontium by way of Caer Gai, a long-abandoned Roman fortress.

Caradoc occasionally flayed himself for bringing his daughter on this mare's nest of a journey although she never complained, even when she was soaked to the skin and forced to sleep under the wagon or beneath an inadequate roof of tree branches. Her natural strength and ebullience served her well, so she sang with gusto, regardless of the weather.

The mountains rose beyond the beaches in peaks that raised their heads higher than anything the Dumnonii people had ever experienced in the south. Mists surrounded the grim valleys where narrow, swift-flowing rivers wound sinuously over pebbled beds. Here, the earth was bare and the soil was barren, so the small farms clutched at mountainsides and valleys with desperate fingers and sheep with long coats and black faces clung to the slopes with unnatural skill.

The winding track took the column along the valley floors, splashing through the shallows where fords gave them easy crossings, and weaving their way along goat tracks that had never known the tread of Roman boots. On several of the steeper inclines, Caradoc was forced to pray that the wagons would not have to be lightened, so the horses could drag them to the tops of hills. The weight and strength of the guardsmen became an essential element in their successful progress through this horrendous terrain.

Caer Gai was spectacular. The Roman fortress was little more than a ruin, having been abandoned by its garrison years earlier. A tarn of a most unusual colour, as if the moon had been captured in its depths, filled a large hollow between the hills, while the local peasants lived much as they had done for a thousand years or more. Their round flint and thatch huts clustered like limpets at the bottom of the Caer. When Caradoc tried to speak to these small, dark people, they looked at him blankly, as if they understood nothing he said.

Endellion thought Caer Gai was a wondrous place, but her fits came closer and closer together to haunt her, awake and asleep. That night, as the members of the column were drowsing in their tents on the hard earth, Endellion had another frightening dream from which she awoke screaming.

'What's happening?' Caradoc panted. Woken from a sound sleep, he threw himself out of his tent with his sword in his hand to find himself surrounded by his guardsmen. They were dishevelled and half-awake, but were armed and ready for what could have been a surprise nocturnal attack.

Endellion sat on her rumpled blankets, her pupils dilated.

'I saw . . . I saw . . .'

Caradoc pushed his way into his daughter's small tent after ordering his guard to stand down.

'What did you see, Endellion?'

'I saw a woman with hair down her back like white ice. She was standing over there, beside the tarn.' Endellion waved her hand towards the lake with a hint of panic in the gesture. 'She was holding a huge sword . . . so big that she could barely lift it.

'The blade was bloody in the light as she handed the sword to a man standing beside her. The sword was beautiful. It was adorned with gems and gold, Father, but I could smell the blood on it. I was glad when the warrior swung it around his head several times before casting it into the water. The blade seemed to sing as it sliced through the air. Then the man released it and the weapon sailed upwards for some distance before it fell, point first, into the depths of the lake.'

'Could you hear their voices?' Caradoc asked, wide-eyed, as he waited for her response.

'I could, Father. There were names mentioned, but I didn't recognise them.'

'Tell me what your heard. Perhaps the names might mean something to *me*.'

'I thought the woman was called Nimue. Such a strange name! And she wept for a man called Myrddion, who was dead. As for the sword, she said it was far too dangerous to fall into the hands of strangers, so they sent it to the lightless depths of the lake. Do those names mean anything to you?'

Father and daughter looked at each other, their faces blank and uncomprehending.

'No, petal, they mean nothing to me. Perhaps, one day . . .' Caradoc began.

'Yes! One day,' Endellion agreed, as another memory returned.

'I also saw piles of bodies . . . so many, and the crows, the ravens and the shrikes were feeding on them. They were Britons, Father! Thousands of them.'

Caradoc stroked her head, thrusting down his alarm at the sudden return of her fits.

'Why are these dreams coming to me, Father? What have I done that I should see these things? They make no sense! Is God trying to punish me?'

'No, darling girl,' Caradoc soothed. 'I don't know why you've been chosen, but your mother had the Sight and I've no doubt that she passed it on to you. I'm more worried that the guardsmen might talk among themselves about what they've seen, and then pass their gossip on to others. There are so many people in this world who fear what they can't understand.'

Endellion curled up on her blanket and turned her face away from her father. Caradoc felt more impotent than he had ever been in his life. He loved his daughter with an old man's last passion, so he suffered from every blow that struck at her and he wished with every bone in his body that he could cleanse her mother's poisoned birth-gifts from her blood.

But if wishes were horses, then beggars would ride.

The camp gradually settled back into a semblance of peace and quiet, but Endellion remained awake. She could hear the sounds of men sleeping around her by their snores and the small noises from restless bodies. A small slice of her leather tent remained open, so she could see a tiny triangle of white stars from her travelling pallet.

With little effort, the faces of strangers came to her. Three in particular remained in her memory. The woman with white hair; a thin ascetic scholar of a man with long black hair streaked with a swathe of silver on his right temple; and another woman with blonde curls and cruel eyes. All three came into her tent to gaze at her, smile and then turn into smoke. Endellion bit her lip in awed terror.

Like the little boy who called *wolf*, she was fearful of screaming and waking the whole camp. She had no intention of allowing vulgar gossip to mark her as a crazed-woman.

Dawn finally arrived. Tired and fretful, Endellion was grateful for the clean, empty light and vowed to sleep lightly in the future.

The track from Caer Gai to Segontium and Caernarfon was the least-navigable of all the roads traversed during their journey. Caradoc frequently cursed Maximus who had laid this pointless task upon a friend. Was Tintagel suffering in his absence? Disastrously, Endellion's mental fits had returned during their passage through this strange, wild country that was still a stronghold of Celtic magic. Disconsolate and miserable, Caradoc blamed himself for the length of their journey and its failure to achieve anything important.

With the exception of her night horrors, Endellion's health had flourished from her exposure to sunshine and fresh air. Pale freckles criss-crossed her nose and lent additional charm to her features, while the rays of the noontide sun had kissed her shoulders and cheekbones with the sheen of warm gold. She had become thinner with exercise and her emergent womanhood, but her budding breasts, narrow waist and long legs gave her strength and athleticism. Her beauty had grown, but she was earthier and warmer now than the elfin creature that had left Tintagel a season earlier.

The northern path taking them through the landscape was so wild and empty that an occasional shepherd's hut was the only sign of human habitation. The path ran beside narrow streams that became fast-running torrents in minutes after short bursts of heavy rain. In the waters, leaves and flowers that Endellion had dropped were quickly carried away, while every step taken by their horses must be carefully chosen in case a traitorous stone should tilt under their weight. Any slip could break bones or kill. Above the column, a series of peaks were crowned with melting snow and grey with thunderheads.

Caradoc craned his neck to look up at the terrifying mountains and hungered for his own wild shores. The winds that howled, the peaks that beetled over them and the dislodged boulders that rattled and roared down the mountain slopes threatened to put their foolish journey into perspective. The earth of Cymru had no love for the temerity of ant-like humans who tried to exist on its flanks. As his cynical nature won over his excitement at seeing Maximus again, Caradoc wondered at how easily he had been dragged into another man's dreams. Cadal had been right. Why had he brought Endellion into this alien landscape? Caradoc had planned this journey as a jaunt for his personal pleasure, but the gods of Cymru had decided to remind him how ineffective he really was.

The track branched into two on the banks of a widening river that cascaded from the tallest mountain, gaining volume and strength as it tumbled into the north and travelled onwards to the distant sea. When the party finally came across a shepherd's hut that showed evidence of recent habitation, Trefor hunted out a laconic herder who told Caradoc that the left-hand path would lead them to Segontium, so the Dumnonii party headed along its rutted surface.

Eventually, the track reached the sea and then turned in a southerly direction along a wild coast where an island brooded across a grey and dreary strait. Something about this body of water made Endellion feel sick and dizzy, so she turned her face away from the sea towards a hill and a widening road that led to a Roman fortress. The road ran as straight as a sword blade and she noted that the palisade on the crest of the hill was the conventional four-sided, walled compound aligned in the direction of the rising and setting sun.

'We'll stop here for a short while, Endellion. I don't suppose that this Roman fortress is our castell, but the commander may know where the local chieftain makes his home. Wait here with the wagons, and I'll return shortly.'

Caradoc thrust both heels into the ribs of his stallion and trotted along the road leading up to the fortress. Trefor and Rowen rode off after him, while Huw stayed behind to supervise the guardsmen and the wagons.

As if by magic, several children appeared from a small group of peasant's houses on the far side of the road.

Endellion waved at two of the smaller boys who were watching her with serious eyes. Surprisingly, the smallest one waved back after a short pause for reflection.

Despite Huw's protests, Endellion dismounted and walked towards the peasant children.

'You're pretty!' the older boy said with a slow, nervous smile. The younger boy wordlessly nodded his agreement.

'Good morning, boys. What are your names?'

The two boys looked at each other for confirmation and, although no words were exchanged, some kind of communication seemed to have taken place.

'I be Merfyn and he be Dalias,' the older boy said carefully, so Endellion curtsied as if they were important men. Both urchins flushed under the grins on their faces.

'Do you know where the local chieftain lives, boys?' Endellion asked.

'Yes!' the eldest boy replied with a little hiss. 'But we don't goes there. No one goes there but the high ones.'

'The high ones? Do you mean men and women like my father and me?'

'Yairs!' said the smallest boy, while staring defiantly at his brother. 'Pretty ladies be there!'

'How do we get there, boys?' Endellion asked, her right palm itching when the older boy cuffed his brother for his presumption in speaking out of turn. She knew she'd get nowhere if she frightened or angered either of them.

The youngest boy stared at his brother malevolently and then pointed down the muddy track that led along the southern coast.

'Thank you, boys,' Endellion responded with a smile. 'You've both been very helpful.'

Hurrying to the wagon, she found the wooden box in which the last four shells nestled forlornly. Because of the debacle at Aquae Sulis, the insults that had wounded Endellion and the strained relationship with the magistrate's family, no further gifts had been given out, by Caradoc's express orders. With a silent prayer that her father would forgive her, she took the two smallest ones and hurried back to the boys.

'I want to thank you for your help, boys. You've been very nice to me, so I've selected two gifts for you. These baubles are very special. The shells come from a faraway place where the sea is wild and strong. I am Princess Endellion, and I live in that place.' She placed a shell, wrapped in a small square of silk, into each boy's dirty hand. Their eyes became saucer-wide and they would have given the gifts back, but Endellion waved their protests away.

'Hush! You'll make me cross if you refuse my gifts. You must run back to your mother and give her these valuable gifts for safe-keeping. You mustn't tell anyone else but her, because they could be stolen from you. Run home now, because my father is coming. Run!' The two boys scattered like startled rabbits, but Endellion still heard the last of their wondering chatter.

'She be a fairy! She must be,' Dalias shouted at his brother, who threw a quick glance back over his shoulder.

'Nah! She be a princess,' Merfyn retorted, as they disappeared into a field of long grass that was taller than they were. Only their voices marked their movements as they continued to squabble their way across the fallow land.

The boys had no sooner disappeared than Caradoc, Trefor and Rowen appeared and pulled their horses to an ostentatious halt. Caradoc tried to spring from the saddle, but he only succeeded in making an awkward dismount.

'Damn my hips! Old age is a bugger,' he snarled, before adding, 'Sorry, Endellion! I sometimes forget that you're here.'

She pointed down the track in the direction the boys had indicated. 'I believe that's the way to the fortress,' she said knowingly. Am I correct?'

'Aye! The officer in charge of the garrison wasn't particularly forthcoming, even when I invoked the name of Maximus, but he grudgingly informed me that the British fortress is further down the southern coast. He assured me that it's about half an hour from here by horse.'

He flashed a quick smile at Endellion. 'I'm rather partial to thoughts of sleeping at the castell if we can reach it by nightfall. But perhaps you'd prefer to rest here for the night. We could then arrive at the castell in the morning, after we've enjoyed a good night's rest.'

Endellion guessed that his swollen joints must be hurting a great deal.

'Two young boys were kind enough give me directions to the fortress. I'd suggest that we ride on now, Father, so you can rest in a real bed for the night, if the lord of the castell offers us some hospitality. I yearn to sleep on a real pallet, with proper wool-filled pillows.'

Endellion felt guilty that she was pressing him onward when he was in pain, but she had been worried about Caradoc's health for some time. Her father needed rest and she would ensure that he would get it at the castell. If the local chieftain was so unobliging as to send them on their way, then he would learn that the daughter of this king would not be gainsaid.

While she prattled, Endellion watched her father covertly.

The old man was still wincing after his awkward leap from the saddle, but he was far more cheerful since learning that they were within easy riding distance of the elusive fortress.

'Why was the Roman officer so uncooperative?' Endellion was curious because, in her experience, Romans had always been polite to her father, not only because of his rank, but because of his evident gravitas, a quality Romans admired.

'I can understand his bad temper. Every available Roman soldier has been sent into the north to fight the Picts and the Hibernians, but he's been left here in command of a skeleton force. He feels resentful about the orders he's been given, but someone must be delegated to protect the Roman fort during the absence of the legions.'

'If I were a Hibernian raider, I would strike here,' Endellion mused as she glanced to her right where the grey straits linked the island of Mona to the mainland.

'Then it's a lucky thing that you're Endellion and not a raider, isn't it? Don't you like Segontium, petal? You keep staring at that island like it's going to bite you. It's only earth, sand and salt water, regardless of its foul history. The local population still despise the Romans because of their actions long ago when they slaughtered the druids.'

'That explains why I can smell blood in the air,' Endellion replied, as she firmly closed her mouth and refused to say another word. Caradoc was grateful for her restraint.

The column rode into the afternoon, jaunty despite the palpable measure of gloom that rose out of the straits like a very old curse. Caradoc passed the time away by telling Endellion the history of Mona Island and the murders of the druids who had sought refuge there.

The sun in this northern tip of Cymru sank slowly into the

evening sky with a bloody cast that overcame any beauty in the day. Endellion refused to acknowledge the thoughts and images that tumbled into her head and was determined that she would enjoy this last part of their long journey. They would soon reach Deva and then, after a short visit, they would head for home. Caradoc had drawn a map in the dirt the night before, so she had seen by the light from the fire how a road ran from Deva to southern Britannia in an almost straight line. With a brisk effort on the part of the cavalcade, a journey that had taken many months to reach Deva along the coastal route would only require a few weeks of relatively comfortable travel for the column's return to Tintagel. Endellion yearned for home, but Caradoc had assured her that if they were unsuccessful in their current search at Segontium, there was only one more location that could satisfy the strange and elusive task that Maximus had asked of them. Only Canovium remained, if this Ordovice fort was not the object of Maximus's search.

Once again, they had no real difficulty in getting directions to the British fortress. The road branched, so Caradoc led the wagons along the fork heading inland towards the same glowering mountain that had seemed to block their path into the north. A line of smaller hills descended to the sea along its flanks.

'Your eyes are younger than mine, petal. Can you see this mysterious fortress?' Caradoc asked. But as she opened her mouth to reply, Huw shouted a sharp warning.

Caradoc's attention was alerted to a contingent of horsemen galloping towards them.

As swords were drawn from scabbards, the Dumnonii column came to a halt and prepared to take up defensive positions along the track on which they were travelling. Then, at a sharp order from Caradoc, the warriors rested their swords on their shoulders or across their pommels to await orders.

'They're Britons, Father. I can see their plaited hair and checked cloaks. They must be from the Ordovice tribe.'

Caradoc stared into the cloud of low dust and clods of earth as the troop approached. The Ordovice cavalry divided into two lines of horsemen as soon as they came within arrow-shot of the Tintagel column, before sweeping around in a spectacular movement that surrounded the Dumnonii in a circle of drawn weapons.

Caradoc raised his hand and gestured to his warriors that they should maintain their positions and protect Endellion and the wagons. His daughter could see a slight dewing of nervous sweat on her father's face, but his profile remained calm as he walked his horse to meet the obvious leader.

'Do you usually greet travellers with drawn swords? I am King Caradoc of the Dumnonii tribe, travelling from Tintagel in the south to Deva in the north. I am accompanied by my daughter, Princess Endellion. In Deva, I will be the guest of the Comes Britanniarum, Magnus Maximus, who is my very good friend. I learned that a local king ruled this section of coast, so I deemed it a courtesy to visit a fellow ruler before we turned the heads of our horses towards Deva, and the end of our journey.'

The captain of the local Britons ostentatiously sheathed his sword, although Caradoc noted that the encircling horsemen remained at the ready, with their weapons drawn.

'I am Barr, Commander of Cavalry for my lord, Kynan ap Meriadoc, who is the son and heir of Meriadoc, the Ordovice lord of Caernarfon. My master has bid me to welcome all men of good will and invite them to share his master's hospitality, or to repel any strangers who come into our land with evil intentions. Since you are a king, as you say, I will assume you have no base designs on Ordovice security. Where is your home, so I might introduce you appropriately to my lord and master?'

Caradoc refused to rise to the bait of Barr's clipped voice and the underlying threat in the officer's expression.

'As stated, I am Caradoc ap Ynyr, the king of the Dumnonii tribe and I rule many broad acres that stretch from Isca Dumnoniorum on the southern coast of Britannia to the impregnable fortress of Tintagel on the western coast. I wish to visit Meriadoc and his son in the spirit of co-operation, trade and friendship. These are wild and dangerous times, Master Barr, so it behoves all men who love peace to work together if we are to bring prosperity to our lands.'

Barr inclined his head courteously, but Endellion noticed that his eyes were hooded, so Caradoc's impassioned words had washed over the Ordovice warrior like so much weed-choked water. Perhaps close proximity to Roman might had insulated this particular British king from any need for alliances or friendships with his peers. Time alone would tell.

With columns of Ordovice cavalrymen on either side, the Dumnonii cavalcade set off along the track that would take them to the still-invisible fortress. A heavily-forested area crowned a low hill overlooking the sea and, as the cavalcade gradually climbed upwards, a settlement became visible. Small farmsteads were clustered along the lower sections at the base of the hill. Then, on the slopes of the rising terrain, the Dumnonii visitors recognised tradesmen's huts while closer to the crown of the hill, a number of shop fronts and dilapidated markets jostled for prominence.

Finally, as they topped the last rise, the fortress appeared. Above them, massive wooden palisades surrounded a structure built entirely from timber. Whole tree trunks had been used in its construction so that it seemed to rise organically out of the forest. These sturdy fortifications were deeply embedded into the top of the sloping hill. Despite its vulnerability to the effects of fire and burning, this fortress would be extremely difficult to attack.

As the column approached a deep ditch that had been dug to surround the whole stronghold, the local population stopped working on their fields or vegetable gardens to gawp, to call out words of greeting to friends in the cavalry or to exclaim over the unfamiliar sight of Caradoc and his beautiful daughter. Few diversions came to Caernarfon, so strangers in the town were a welcome distraction.

They passed through the thick gate as it slowly swung open. Heavily reinforced with broad strips of beaten iron, the gate could resist battering rams for some time, even the heavy-duty machines used by Roman engineers.

Beyond the fortified walls, more timber buildings of both one and two storeys rose upwards, their construction so foreign in structure and design to the roundhouses of Britannia that a Roman influence was clearly evident. The space within the compound was limited and the hooves of so many horses kept inside the ramparts had chewed the bare earth into a mass of drying mud.

The party picked their way across a tiny forecourt before halting in front of a rectangular building shaped like a Roman basilica. Caradoc noted that an invisible curtain of vigilance hung over the visitors, as if the men who manned this fortress were expecting an imminent attack.

'This place cannot possibly be the important fortification described by your Roman friend, Father. You told me that Master Maximus spoke of a powerful castell with great gates. Look at it, though! The horses have spread dung all over the forecourt, so I'm sure that every person who enters the master's hall must track horse manure in with them. And the hall itself! It's crude and it doesn't instil a sense of pride. It's almost as though the fortress began its life as a temporary camp and developed over time. I doubt anything here could be of interest to a military commander such as Master Maximus. Besides, he must have seen it on many occasions.'

Caradoc's eyes shot a sharp warning towards his daughter. Part of him was proud of her incisiveness and acumen, because many of her observations were correct. But it wasn't a woman's place to offer unsolicited advice. Besides, Endellion was still unaware of the true purpose of the journey that had been undertaken on Maximus's behalf.

'Shhh, Endellion,' Caradoc warned, but his common sense told him that Maximus's dream was false, or Caernarfon wasn't the site of the castell containing the lady of his dreams.

As Caradoc gazed at the huge timber fortress, an elderly man came through the rough doors that led into the interior of the hall. He walked with the aid of a tall staff, because an old wound had caused his leg to heal at an awkward angle. The man's face remained tanned and firm, and spoke of a life spent in the outdoors. He wore the black and yellow checked cloak of the Ordovice; his curly black hair hung down his back in a mane that rivalled Endellion's, and the overall impression of the man was one of vigour, power and experience.

'My master, Caradoc ap Ynyr, and his daughter, Endellion, are from Tintagel, the Dumnonii fortress on the western coast in the south of Britannia. We are journeying into the north to meet with Flavius Magnus Maximus in Deva and discuss matters of mutual interest,' Trefor explained as he stood to one side to introduce the Ordovice steward to his king.

'My master has taken the opportunity of travelling to Deva to meet and greet those kings of Britannia whose lands lie along our line of travel. My master's daughter, Princess Endellion, journeys with him as proof that he has no ulterior motives, merely a desire to promote peace and communication between the tribes.'

The older man introduced himself as Sion Cripplefoot, steward of King Meriadoc. He was unimpressed with Caradoc's credentials, but remained courteous.

'You may come in, King Caradoc . . . along with your daughter and one guard. You understand that matters of security preclude us from allowing fighting men into the hall and the presence of our king.'

Caradoc waved away the steward's concern and called on Trefor to accompany him. Together, Caradoc and Endellion stepped up to the door, with Trefor behind them.

The doors opened with an alarming creak of iron hinges.

The Dumnonii aristocrats stepped into the deep gloom of a room lit only by clerestory windows, a narrow strip of apertures near the roof line that allowed the fading afternoon light to enter. The windows also allowed smoke to escape from the hall, in an attempt to keep the air sweet and clean. Several wall lamps lit the interior, but the weather was too warm to make a fire comfortable. Caradoc was led to a partially visible group of people seated at the far end of the room. He sensed the small movements of armed men behind them, while his daughter chose to stare into the dimness where she could see some twenty warriors in various stages of readiness as they stood or sat near the entrance to the hall.

Although the room was stuffy with afternoon heat, Endellion shivered and pulled her cloak around her.

In a ringing voice, Sion introduced the visitors to Meriadoc and his son, Kynan ap Meriadoc, plus a number of lordlings whose names were quickly forgotten by the Dumnonii aristocrats. Lamplight illuminated the faces of the only two men of any importance within the room.

'Curtsy low to both the king and his son,' Caradoc ordered in a soft undertone. 'We'll be the epitome of good manners until such time as we know exactly who these people are.'

Obediently, Endellion cast back her cloak and sank almost to the reed-strewn floor in a deep obeisance. The two Ordovice looked on with approval.

'Sion, ask Lady Elen to attend to us so she can offer hospitality to Lady Endellion,' Meriadoc ordered in a voice that was febrile and thin. Caradoc flinched at the mention of a woman's name. Was this Elen a wife? A daughter? Could this unprepossessing hall in a small forest along the Cymru coast actually be the fulfilment of the dream of Maximus?

Meriadoc was a man in his forties who displayed the ruins of what had once been a powerful physique. He was very tall, a good hand taller than his largest warrior and, like his servant, Sion, he had a full head of vigorously curling hair. His face, under his youthful hair and long, warrior plaits, was haggard from illness; the high cheekbones, broad forehead and determined chin shone whitely like exposed bone in the light of the lamps. His shoulders were huge, but his skeleton seemed to thrust through the heavy wool of his robe as if all muscle and flesh had been eaten away by disease. Caradoc could see that the loose skin over the man's face and hands were yellowish with sickness. His long, stained fingernails clutched at his heavy robe as if he was suffering from the cold.

By contrast, his son was shorter, but his energy and vitality seemed to light his face from within. He was in constant motion as his fingers, booted feet and mobile eyebrows moved and jiggled with a life of their own. His hair was lighter than that of his father, but it curled with the same vigour. Caradoc saw that Kynan's carefully trimmed locks and shaven face indicated a Roman influence.

But in the young man's eyes he saw a *something* lurking there in the clear brown depths, as if a great pike was swimming in them, hunting restlessly and hungrily. Caernarfon would never be enough for this young man; Caradoc promised himself that he would never allow himself to trust Kynan ap Meriadoc.

Caradoc and Endellion were offered stools. Then, once they were comfortably seated, cups of wine or beer, as well as platters of fish, meat, fruit and nuts were proffered for their enjoyment. Endellion nibbled on an apple. Too fastidious to grease her hands and her chin with fat, she was loath to pull a leg off one of the roasted chickens, despite their delicious smell after the long journey from Pennal on dry rations. She was also conscious that Kynan was openly staring at her across the tabletop. Caradoc was talking policy matters with the Ordovice king, but he also saw the calculating gaze of Meriadoc's heir and his lips tightened.

Just when Caradoc was sure he would disgrace himself with a temper tantrum aimed at the arrogant young heir, the situation resolved itself when a group of young women entered the room. The girl who led the group into the hall wore a gown of pale-blue wool that swept along the grimy floor as she glided over to her father, bent over his aging form and kissed his pale cheek.

'King Caradoc! Lady Endellion! Allow me to introduce my daughter, Elen, the Flower of Caernarfon,' King Meriadoc announced with a fond smile.

The girl nodded her head and curtsied neatly to each of the

guests, giving Caradoc and Endellion the exact measure of respect to which they were due. Endellion felt a sudden surge of dislike at the smug expression on Elen's pretty, vapid face.

Forcing down her antipathy, Endellion smiled and curtsied in turn, exaggerating each action so it was a caricature of respect. Elen's sense of importance was such that she accepted the fawning of the Dumnonii princess as her due.

'I am very pleased to make your acquaintance,' Elen responded diffidently as she seated herself next to her father. Then, with a vivid smile, she instructed her ladies to prepare a plate of the most succulent portions of food on the table. As she began to eat, with some refinement, Endellion had the opportunity to gaze around the hall and assess its features, while her father was dragged reluctantly back to the conversation with the Ordovice lord.

But while Caradoc kept his eyes deliberately bland and unaware, privately he was amazed at what their long journey had unearthed.

For Elen was surely the subject of Maximus's quest. She was beautiful in a ripe, very feminine fashion, having womanly hips, a tiny waist and breasts that were large, firm and well shaped. Even Trefor was captivated by her generous body, while every man in that dim hall allowed their eyes to caress her voluptuous curves. Elen, aware of the effect she had on men of all ages, smiled knowingly as she felt the Dumnonii party examine her with approval.

Elen's hair was a rich, russet shade with tawny highlights, and fell as straight as a spear shaft to her knees. Her eyes were the same brown shade as Kynan's but they had a yellowish cast that made Caradoc think of a lynx he had once seen as a mascot of one of the Roman legions. Every gesture and expression underlined Elen's absolute certainty that she deserved the worship of all men within her ambit.

Ignored, Endellion chose to watch the Ordovice beauty surreptitiously, rather than add to her already overblown vanity.

And so the twilight moved on towards darkness, while Elen continued to preen. Kynan stared and undressed Endellion with his eyes, while Meriadoc struggled to find the strength to speak of matters of state with King Caradoc. Stuffy and dirty, the hall smelled of old bones, wet dog and something vaguely unhealthy, so that Endellion longed to scrub her hands clean in the nearest bucket of water once the kings had concluded their conversation. On cue, Elen ordered Sion to show their guests to the rooms that had been hurriedly prepared for their accommodation.

Outside, the moon was rising in a scarlet haze. As the Dumnonii aristocrats followed Sion, Endellion longed to run in case Elen's shadow should pursue her. It was only when the door of their spartan room had closed behind them that Caradoc's daughter had the courage to take a deep and cleansing breath.

The cloth on the bed was dingy and smelled vaguely of damp, but neither father nor daughter cared. Caradoc had travelled many miles, almost half the length of Britannia. He had searched for a dream, but had found an enigma. Had he begun something he would regret? Or was he simply a vessel in a larger plan that would become clearer with the passage of time? Caradoc faced up to his uncomfortable bed with his bared sword close to his arm and prayed that he, at least, would be spared from dreams.

CHAPTER XVII

FORTUNE'S FAVOURITE

Man, you have been a citizen in this world city. What
does it matter whether for five years or fifty?

Marcus Aurelius, *Meditations*, 12:36

The wedding was neither large nor ostentatious, although the
bride had wished that the ceremony was more elaborate. Elen
had dreamed that she would wed a great man, a coming man,
and now she stood in all her considerable finery beside the
Comes Britanniarum who was fresh from his great victories over
the Picts and the Hibernians.

Yes, Elen loved pomp and display, so a large group of tribal
kings, local dignitaries, prominent citizens from the Roman
cities and celebrated military personnel were all present at the
specific invitation of the Roman commander, along with their
servants, guards and advisers, but a surreptitious glance at Elen's
discontented face revealed that she was far from happy.

The difficulties of providing accommodation and hospitality
for the variety and number of important guests were such that
Maximus decided to hold the wedding ceremony in Deva. In

any event, the Comes Britanniarum had no intention of being too far distant from his troops in case the defeated Picts should try to regroup. Elen accepted this sensible arrangement with smiles but, within, she seethed with fury.

This rage was mitigated when she gazed upon her husband's emotionless features. Undoubtedly, he was a handsome and powerful man, one who would advance high in the world outside bucolic Caernarfon, Segontium and Deva. He had been frank with her, so he had told her of his Roman wife and adult children. But Elen knew men instinctively. Any Roman wife would be aging, but she was still young. She was happy now that she had remained virginal, knowing that Maximus would prize her inexperience. Yes, a clever girl could supplant a distant, middle-aged Roman wife.

The service, conducted by the legion's priest, was long and sonorous. Elen had been decked out like a small doll of painted gold and white wood, much like the carved Madonna she had once seen in a church in Deva.

Her silk dress, shot through with gold thread, had been bought at great cost from a Middle Sea trader. Her arms tinkled with gold bangles, and heavy earrings dragged on her ear lobes. Still more chains and necklaces hung around her neck with her bulla, for in this Roman birth gift, Meriadoc had chosen to follow the traditions of his long-dead Roman wife. With her arms filled with a sheaf of wheat for fertility, perfumed with costly nard and with her eyes outlined with kohl, she was comely, distant and as still as any ancient goddess. Even her nails had been polished and tipped with golden tracery.

The wedding ceremony was soon completed and her husband heaved a great sigh of relief. Within minutes, the bridal procession filed out into the forecourt of the small church and strolled onto the parade ground where the Roman troops were on display, filling the wide space with the glister of armour and the scarlet of their cloaks.

Then the cry went up. It was a lusty cheer at first, replaced by almost inaudible words that grew clearer and louder as a thousand masculine throats roared out the salutation

'Hail, Maximus . . . Imperator. Hail Maximus . . . Imperator.'

One of the men marched from out of the ranks. He was a veteran officer, his skin burned to the colour and texture of old leather by many hot suns. His hazel eyes, in nests of thin white wrinkles, were steady and open.

The old warrior carried a crown of dried grass, woven so that the withered stems marked this simple object as the most precious gift that a Roman warrior could ever receive. The Grass Crown, given to generals by their subordinates, told all and sundry that Maximus was deeply beloved by his legionnaires.

Few men had ever been presented with the Grass Crown and even fewer had lived long enough to enjoy the honour, for their popularity brought sudden death to them. But Maximus was now being gifted with his own opportunity to curry favour with Fortuna and carve his name into the ranks of Roman emperors for all time.

He tensed as he stood beside Elen, every muscle on alert. He paused to think as he considered his options. To take the Grass Crown from his troops was to declare war on the Emperor Gratian and attempt to usurp him.

He would be pitting his strength against the might of Rome. But this chance might never come again.

In the crowd behind him, Caradoc strained to see his friend's face and prayed that Maximus would reject this honour that could bring them all to ruin.

Time seemed to stop as Maximus continued to think.

The outstretched hand held the crown proudly and Caradoc remembered Saraid's warning, offered so many years earlier at the Red Wells. The words began to echo through his head as he stared at his friend from the steps of the church.

'In years to come, a cool head will be needed or disaster will destroy the isles before their time.'

Caradoc had thought he had forgotten that disturbing night, although his dearest love, Endellion, had been sired then. But nothing had been forgotten, not even the husky web of Saraid's voice.

'He is destined to wear the imperial wreath.'

When Saraid had predicted a glorious future for Maximus, Caradoc had yet to meet the Roman who would later become his friend. Over the years, he had chosen to deny Saraid's quiet voice. But Saraid had insisted that Caradoc must keep the Roman close to him.

'Regardless of the temptation, you must never leave your ancestral lands, not for him and not for the sake of any kin.'

Other parts of the prophecy were swept back from the deepest recesses of his memory, but they seemed to speak of a later time. Even the need to share the prophecy with his son was finally remembered; he prayed that Maximus would reject the Grass Crown so that the details of his sin with Saraid and the conception of Endellion could remain his personal secret.

But even as he prayed, he knew Maximus could never resist such an honour.

Caradoc sighed as Maximus stepped forward and bowed his head to the hard-bitten veteran, who with due solemnity placed the crown upon Maximus's close-cropped head.

Then, as Maximus straightened to his full height, the veteran bowed and sank onto one knee. 'Hail, Maximus! Imperator! Hail, Maximus! Imperator!'

A thousand throats repeated the call. A thousand soldiers kneeled in the forecourt and offered their homage, while a thousand swords were unsheathed and raised towards the noontime sun so that the blades ran with golden light.

'Hail, Maximus! Imperator! Ave, Maximus!'

And Caradoc felt a coldness that bit right through to his heart.

Several months earlier, the Tintagel cavalcade had reached Deva to find that the city had been transformed into an armed camp in support of the Roman soldiers who were fighting in the north. The city, which was even more Roman than Aquae Sulis, was now defended by several units of citizen soldiers who had been given the task of maintaining good order and discipline.

The Tintagel troop had been halted at the city gates. Here, Caradoc's temper began to chafe as he was forced to answer a barrage of unnecessary questions. Even the invocation of Maximus's name couldn't allay the suspicions of one ludicrous officer in full armour who was burdened by so much flesh that he couldn't strap his breastplates together. Ultimately Decius, come to investigate the fuss, convinced the zealous gatekeeper that Caradoc was no imposter.

Eventually, with a promise to share a drink with Decius in the very near future, Caradoc and the rest of his party were permitted to enter the city.

Deva was a compact city, as befitted a Roman garrison. As the wagons made their way along the road parallel to the wide river, they could see the shops, houses and business establishments that had been built on the slopes adjacent to the deeply eroded river banks. Endellion was quick to realise that Deva possessed all the essentials necessary to maintain a high standard of living, at least from a Roman point of view. Baths were situated near the forum, a military hospital was centrally placed and a neat amphitheatre had been built on an area of flat land near the river where it would not be damaged by rising floodwaters.

Caradoc found a clean, well-appointed inn near the forum where he was prepared to house his daughter. Fortunately, his men could be accommodated in the large well-ventilated stables, while comfortable quarters were provided for Trefor, Huw and the rest of the guard's officers. Then, once the servants had stowed Endellion's maid and her baggage into a secure room on the second floor, father and daughter descended to the dining area in search of a meal.

Meanwhile, a courier from the military headquarters in Deva arrived with a message from Maximus informing the Dumnonii king that the Roman was unavoidably detained in the north. The war against the Picts had reached a critical point and Maximus was unable to give an exact indication of when he could return to Deva. Caradoc concluded that he would be forced to wait there for the entire summer if Maximus couldn't achieve a miracle victory, so he decided to return to Tintagel while leaving a detailed message for his friend. In this way, Maximus could make his own decision as to whether he wanted to act on the information provided.

When Caradoc discussed his options with Endellion, she offered a surprisingly common-sense solution to their dilemma.

'We should wait here for a few weeks, Father. We both need to rest and I, for one, would like to reacquaint myself with the sheer pleasure of sleeping in a comfortable bed. If we must go before his return, you can leave a written communication with his subordinates that tells him what you gleaned during our journey through Cymru. Ideally, he can do what he should have done if the Picts weren't killing our people in the north. He can come to us.'

Endellion had noticed the signs of extreme weariness in her father's face and body during the past month and become increasingly alarmed. Caradoc was an old man now, and had the swelling disease in most of his joints, making every day of riding agony for him. Endellion decided that her father would luxuriate in the baths, a place of pleasure, where he could enjoy massages and receive treatment from the healing waters that would rebuild his strength.

Caradoc quickly agreed, which told Endellion that he also knew his health was failing. With each keeping their own secrets, father and daughter decided to allow Maximus four weeks to make good his return to Deva.

The baths worked their magic on Caradoc's protesting muscles, although the public pools lacked the enervating minerals of Aquae Sulis. Still, after five days, the king was walking easily and happily accompanied his daughter on the shopping expeditions that all girls love. Goods from all over the Roman world filtered through Deva's warehouses, as well as the better trade goods from Britannia and Hibernia. Soon, Endellion had almost filled one of the wagons with bolts of cloth, silk, linen and other exquisite treasures from the East, as well as gifts for her family and friends in Tintagel.

Also, Caradoc found his friendship with the Comes Britanniarum won him invitations to dine in the homes of prominent citizens. His nights were kept pleasantly busy. After initial feelings of repugnance at reclining to eat, Endellion learned the correct protocols and was soon smiling her way through a series of invitations. As for the vast meals and the many courses devoured, she only had to nibble a little and plead a cultural inability to eat large amounts of food.

'Use your wits, girl. You just need to remain charming and complimentary. There's no need for either of us to change the customs of a lifetime.'

Endellion made a point of wearing her Roman brooch to every social occasion. Fine clothes and good jewellery made an impression on her Roman hosts, so she worked hard to keep up her appearance by urging her maid to experiment with a wide variety of hairstyles. From the time she mounted the steps of each mansion, she ensured she was self-effacing, compliant and eager to please. For his part, Caradoc was satisfied with the plethora of complimentary comments that Endellion earned from the sophisticated citizens of Deva.

'You've managed to raise a fine girl,' one smug wine importer, Castor, informed the Dumnonii king after the ladies had retired and the men had been left to their hard drinking and serious conversation.

'I, for one, wish my daughter showed the same good manners and charm,' a fish-trader, Gallus, added. 'She has a good brain and seems to understand the rudiments of local politics. She'll make a good wife to some young man and I'll tell you straight, if I had an eligible son to offer you, I'd snap her up in an instant. Who cares about dowries?'

'Aye, gentlemen,' Caradoc smiled, and blushed with pleasure. 'I must admit that this visit to you fine city has changed my little girl into an accomplished young woman.'

'Are there any signs of a suitor on the horizon?' Gallus asked with a wide, gap-toothed grin. 'She's a beauty and young men set store by the looks of a woman. I tell them often enough that it's character traits that count, but what lad listens to old men when pert breasts and a lush mouth are on offer?'

'You're an old goat, Gallus,' Castor joked and punched his friend's forearm. 'You'd walk over hot coals to find a pretty girl with pert breasts who'd even look in your direction.'

'Who are you calling an old goat? I've seen you at the baths, ogling the servant girls. You'd disgrace yourself thoroughly if you could, Castor, but Sofrania, your wife, would string you up by your balls.'

Caradoc, worried that this disagreement might become serious, especially with men who had been imbibing freely, brought the conversation back on track.

'My girl has one suitor of note and he's a young man of pleasing appearance, which hasn't hurt his chances with Endellion. Best of all, he's the possible heir to two kingdoms. He's a nobleman of the Silures tribe and his father rules in Caerleon. It's famed for its natural beauty, so I'm sure you know the city well.' Both businessmen nodded, because they had extensive trading links with the town.

'His mother's brother is the king of the Dobunni tribe and this ruler is, as yet, childless. Actually, he's been married near to ten years, since he was fifteen, so perhaps he's impotent. A pity, because Llew is a good lad and a warrior of some competence.'

'You have all the luck, my friend' Gallus said enviously. 'You're fortunate to have a suitor who could become a king via each of two routes. That would surely be a coup for Endellion, and for you. She'd reside close to Tintagel, which would give pleasure to your wife.'

'Actually, my wife is not Endellion's birth mother and, while I'm sure she's fond of my girl, she wouldn't pine if Endellion was far away. I, on the other hand, would be desolated. Listen to my words of woe! I'm turning into an indulgent old man now, and I'm barely fit to hold a sword.'

Both businessmen examined his sharp eyes, the barrel chest and the huge, sword-scarred hands. A man less feeble, given his age, would be hard to imagine, although the swollen joints in his fingers betrayed his advanced age.

'Somehow, I don't think many of your enemies would consider you were feeble. If I may presume on our friendship, could I ask when you were last in battle?' Castor poured another glass of wine for his guest.

'It was well over a year ago. We were forced to teach some Saxon raiders that our coasts were dangerous places to visit. Their widows and children will still be weeping, so we'll not see any more incursions for a few years. But, give them a little time to forget their losses and the bastards will come back again.'

The Romans gazed with admiration at this man who'd been forced to fight for the security of his people in his old age, marvelling that he was still capable of such an effort.

'So you have the same problems in the south as we do?' Gallus asked, as Caradoc felt the mood darken perceptibly in the room.

'I'm afraid that the whole of Britannia is under attack,' Caradoc said. 'Savages hover around us, just as they do in the rest of the Roman world. They are ready to invade our shores as soon as the Romans depart, and I'm convinced that the Roman senate and the emperor will leave us to our own devices in the fullness of time. My friend Maximus believes that Rome is decaying from within, torn apart by greed, ennui and reckless ambition. Yes, my friends, you'll be deserted as much as I will be if the legions should leave us. Can you transplant yourselves to Italia? This is the only land I understand, so I'm stuck with it.'

Castor and Gallus looked grave. Both men had been born in these isles, as had their fathers; where could they go if the legions deserted Britannia? More to the point, what country would accept them? Both men were realists, so they examined their hands, their rings or their togas, anything but permit Caradoc to see the bleak fear that permeated their bitter prospects for the future.

'I understand,' Caradoc said, as gently as he could. 'So we will all face the future together, my friends, for my land is also your land.'

'Aye!' Gallus answered, with some bravura. 'Together or apart, the Romans and the British tribes will face the same fate. Better to be united, don't you think?'

Glumly, all three nodded.

'I heard some gossip today from one of my friends in the militia,' Castor said with a sudden grin. 'It seems that a despatch arrived from the north this morning that spoke of a great victory to Maximus. He has trounced the Picts – again! And one of his columns ambushed a party of Hibernians and sent them to perdition – again! It seems that your friend crushes his foes whenever he meets them. He has such ability that he is able to mount campaigns on a number of fronts, so he is probably one of the greatest military commanders of modern times. The gossip from the courier spoke of the high regard with which his men hold him. There is talk that they intend to offer him the Grass Crown.'

'The Grass Crown?' Caradoc was aghast.

He had a vague idea what this honour meant, so he knew that Maximus would be elated at the prospect. But would he accept such a gift and use it to wrest the throne from the legitimate emperor? Maximus was Hispanic, so he was more Roman than the Romans in his attitudes and desires. Would he risk everything for the crown?

In a heartbeat, Caradoc admitted to himself that Maximus would.

'What would such an honour mean to us?' Castor muttered, his face paling a little under the mellow light of an earthenware lamp.

'He will take the legions and as many of our young men as care to follow him to Old Gaul, where they will do battle with the empire's defenders for the throne,' Caradoc answered. 'One ruler will live – and the other will die.'

'Then we must pray to the gods that Maximus has a talent for survival,' Gallus murmured.

'Aye! And that he has the ability to know his own limitations,' Caradoc added.

Maximus returned in a cloud of late summer dust with his beloved *cataphractarii* trailing behind him. Along with the rest of Deva's population, Caradoc watched a spectacular approach at full gallop that barely paused for the town's gates to be opened before the mounted warriors swept into the central square. Caradoc waved to his friend from the steps of the legion's hospital while mulling over the vagaries of fate. He had planned to leave Deva on the very next morning and now, here was the great man himself, newly arrived with his usual display of elan.

Maximus threw himself from the saddle of his pure-white horse, which had become one of the Comes Britanniarum's affectations. Aware of the noble figure he cut, Maximus raised his muscular arm and the crowd quietened immediately.

'With the grace of God and the strength of our ancestors, we have succeeded in destroying the armies of the Picts and the Hibernians. They have departed from our lands.'

The crowd embarked on an orgy of celebration while Caradoc returned to the inn on unwilling feet. Sooner or later, Maximus would send for him. What could he say to deflect a force of nature? This man's stature was growing before Caradoc's eyes, as if his friend could feel himself becoming a god. Was Maximus so reckless?

Fortuna gave freely, but she could just as easily take the gifts away.

Later, Maximus discovered that his earlier dreams were largely true. He glossed over the long months that the Tintagel party had spent on his quest with a practised smile and cursory thanks before interrogating his friend for hours on everything that the Dumnonii could recall of Lady Elen, her male relatives, the family's steward and the fortress at Caernarfon.

'Could you have met King Meriadoc when you were posted to Segontium twelve years ago?' Caradoc asked.

'Yes, I believe I did. I recall that we invited him to a banquet in the barracks. He came, but I had no idea that he had a daughter. In any event, she would have been little more than a babe at the time. Nor did I consider his wooden palisades at Caernarfon to be a castell. Did you?'

How very like Maximus to throw any omissions back onto the shoulders of others. 'No, I saw Caernarfon and its accompanying village, but I never thought of it as a fortress, though I suppose that, technically, it is one.' Caradoc wanted any decision involving the Roman to be made by Maximus himself.

Subtlety was always lost on the Comes Britanniarum, so Caradoc was certain that the Roman would be off to Caernarfon as soon as his role permitted him to do so. But all that Caradoc wanted from life was an opportunity to lie in his own bed in

Tintagel, with his own sky and his own sea wrapped around him.

The wagons were packed and the party was ready for departure the following morning, so Caradoc half expected his friend to take the time to visit their inn and to wish him well. Thus when the innkeeper came to inform him that a visitor was awaiting the king in the dining room Caradoc assumed it was Maximus warming his backside beside the fire pit.

He was wrong. The red cloak worn by the waiting man deceived Caradoc's old eyes for a moment, but then he recognised the white hair and knew that Decius had come instead.

'Decius! I imagine you bring word from Maximus. Sit down, old friend, and share a jug of wine with me. We can be comfortable while I discover what your master requires of me.'

Decius had the grace to flinch a little at these words. 'Not as such, my lord. But he asked me to give you this box and to ask a small favour of you when you return to the south.'

The old retainer looked profoundly embarrassed, as if he had betrayed his master by the simple expedient of confirming Caradoc's suspicions. Once seated with the wine, Decius handed over a plain beech box that was remarkable for its fine proportions and its exquisite smoothness. Caradoc opened the lid carefully, noting that the hinges were tiny and beautifully wrought, and inside, wrapped in fine wool, discovered a striking torc, or necklace.

Made of gold, the torc had been fashioned to sit around the base of the throat and was delicate enough to suit either a man or a woman. The two twisted ends, designed to sit above the collarbone, had been shaped to resemble two fish. Enamels of various blues and greens created the appearance of scales while the eyes were small green stones inlaid into the design, so that each fish stared out at the world, its jaws gaping and its gills extended.

'This bauble is far too valuable to be given away with such casual generosity.' Caradoc put it back into its box and carefully closed the lid. 'Is it Hibernian or Pict?'

'I believe it's of Hibernian origin,' Decius replied drily. 'Please take the bauble, my lord. It would be better in the hands of someone who can treat it with respect; if you don't accept the gift, it will be melted down for the value of the gold and the jewels. That would be a waste.'

Caradoc thought for a moment. 'Very well, I'll take the torc and give it to Endellion, my daughter. It can be part of her dowry, if she doesn't care to wear it. You may tell your master, if he asks.'

Decius drained his mug and grinned ruefully as Caradoc refilled it. 'I'll be falling-down drunk at this rate, sir. I just can't drink like I could in days gone by. *Anno Domini*, I expect! Ah, well! Old age eventually comes to all of us.'

Caradoc, looking resigned, flexed his swollen fingers and agreed. 'What does your master want of me? It's best that I know.'

'Well, sir, he has some kind of plan in the making, but he doesn't bring me fully into his calculations. However, I know him too well to be deceived after all these years. He's very interested in the success of the pact you made with your local kings in the south of Britannia. In particular, he'd be obliged if you could use your influence to praise him to your fellow kings and, if needed, to convince them that they should unite behind him. I believe he intends to make a similar pact with the local kings in the north. All that he asks is that you should shore up your alliance with your southern friends and ask them to become a part of a larger coalition.'

'Aye, Decius, you can tell your master that I'll speak to the local kings and I'll praise his successes and his abilities in glowing terms. Anything else would have to be assessed at some future time, once Maximus has decided on a course of action. Of one thing I am certain: Britannia depends on him for its continued survival.'

'Ah! We can wish for the wind, but there's no guarantee we'll get it. My master has high ambitions, perhaps too high, but I'll follow him, regardless of what path he travels.' Decius laughed with little mirth, aware of his master's strengths and weaknesses. 'He'll have what he wants and count the cost later.'

'Aye!'

Both men sat quietly and stared into the fire pit with hooded eyes. Both knew how little they could do to change the fate of Magnus Maximus, the self-proposed overlord of Britannia.

'Tell me one thing, Decius,' Caradoc asked. 'For many years now, I've been haunted by the death of Elphin, the outlaw chief, when first we all met all those years ago. Do you remember?'

'I could never forget him, sir. I knew you saw me when I spoke to him, and I must confess that I was surprised when you didn't tell my master what you had seen. Ask what you want, my lord, and I'll try to answer you fairly.'

'Did you give him some poppy juice in wine to hasten his death?' Caradoc's voice was quite neutral.

'Aye! Crucifixion is a cruel death and should only be reserved for the worst felons and curs. We didn't know much of Elphin's history, but he showed us that he was a brave man and a true warrior. He deserved better than to be blinded by sodding crows while he was still alive. He thanked me, sir, and told me that he wished me a clean death when my own time came.'

Decius snorted, sorrow and regret in his watery old eyes. 'My master should have given him a better death, because to drag out Elphin's execution was petty and shamed my master, rather than the victim. I decided to redress that wrong.'

Caradoc leaned over and patted the old warrior on the knee. 'You did what I wished to do, but I lacked the courage. I didn't speak to Maximus of what I saw that day because I agreed with your actions. I must tell you that I've puzzled over that death for years and all the time the answer was so simple.'

'Most things are, in the end,' Decius replied and continued to stare into the fire, pondering his fears of the disaster that might bring his master to a terrible fall.

While Caradoc and Endellion were speeding back to Tintagel, freed at last from the demands of friendship, Maximus turned his face towards Caernarfon. Time was very short. He, too, had heard what his troops planned to do, but when word of his victories reached Rome, he would be recalled to fight on some other frontier and would lose the initiative. He must marry and tie himself to Britannia as its overlord. An heir would be even better. Then he could embark on his campaign to become the Roman emperor.

Maximus could feel the weight of the purple draped around his body and could imagine the shape of the golden leaves as they were balanced on his forehead. A Grass Crown from his subordinates was a great honour, but it was ephemeral and a nothing when compared with the golden diadem. He was prepared to die to achieve that goal.

Maximus felt no shame at using a young girl he had never met as a pawn. She would provide the firm base from which he could snatch his desires, though she would never rule beside him in Rome. No matter how beautiful and accomplished this girl might prove to be, she lacked the birthright to become an empress.

His mind ranged over the waters to his uncomplaining wife, Theodora, who lived in Augusta Treverorum and endured his constant absences. She had followed him for many years, like any good Roman wife, during that long period when he had been passed over for promotion by lesser men, but he had difficulty in remembering the face and form of the girl he had married. Strangely, he could clearly recall the features of his two daughters and his son, Victor. Theodora had done her duty by him impeccably and had even found a good match for his eldest daughter, Victora. Yes, Theodora would become the empress when he finally arrived in Rome.

Maximus thought with satisfaction of his daughter's new kinfolk. Theodora had brokered a match with Ennedius, the Proconsul Africae, and the lass had already produced a son, Petronius Maximus, whom he had never met. His own son grew tall and talented with exemplary military skills. If Maximus had been other than an over-ambitious gambler, he would have been content with the gifts he had already received from Fortuna's Wheel.

But ambition and resentment grated together like large grinding stones that rolled around in his gut. Gratian, ruler of the Western Roman Empire, had sneered at him and had used his talents wastefully along his northern borders, had refused to give Maximus the recognition that he craved. To strike back at Gratian would fill the aching void that lived within him, although he would never have raised a hand against his kinsman, Theodosius, who ruled the Eastern Empire in Constantinople.

But, in the meantime, Elen must be used to cement his position as the unquestioned king of Britannia, the High King of Kings. Caradoc's hunting skills and tenacious spirit had found her for him and the Roman congratulated himself on having such a friend. Caradoc would play a major part in his plans, a critical part; a trusting fool he might be, but he was always a man of honour and gravitas.

So, as autumn stripped the trees bare and hastened the harvesters in the wheat fields, Maximus rode out of Deva with much pomp and ceremony to find himself a wife.

From the muddy, leaf-strewn track below the fortress, Maximus decided that Caradoc's warnings had been wise. The seat of King Meriadoc was unimpressive and the old king was little more than a grey shadow in his dismal, rain-drenched hall. Even Maximus's most fervent attempts to be conciliatory and complimentary were thwarted by the cold hearths, the king's hacking cough and the well-judged rudeness of Meriadoc's son, Kynan ap Meriadoc.

The Comes Britanniarum felt the devilry rise in him, allied to a sense of wonder, from the moment the gates of Caernarfon opened and Sion, the steward, stepped forth to greet him.

Sion was nothing like the gatekeeper of his dreams, except for his eyes. Maximus looked across at the king's hall and transposed stone for timber in his imagination. There it was – the exact copy of the structure he had seen, night after night. Suddenly, Sion's cool features matched the gatekeeper of his dreams in inscrutability, as the Roman felt the feather-like touch of Fortuna.

He dismounted, and then dropped the reins for others to take up. Around him, his guard snapped to attention in full battle order and the eyes of Sion and Kynan, who had come out to greet him, snapped with displeasure.

Good! Maximus thought triumphantly. Let them feel fear, as long as they obey me.

'No armed men are permitted to enter the hall of my father. Disarm your men, Master Maximus,' Kynan ordered.

But Maximus had practised rudeness with more able men than Kynan would ever be.

'My guard never disarms unless they're dead, Kynan. As you can see, they are very much alive. I am the Comes Britanniarum and I have no interest in harming your father. There are mutual enemies aplenty to keep our swords red with blood, without turning on each other.'

Kynan coughed as if to cover a curse-word. Yet he capitulated, stepped aside and ushered Maximus and his guardsmen into his father's hall.

The guardsmen entered directly behind Maximus, who ignored the Ordovice warriors and stalked towards the old king who was seated on his wooden stool with his shoulder wrapped in a blanket to prevent any chills from reaching his old bones. Behind their master, the Roman guards marched in three lines across the hall, their senses alert for movement. Outnumbered, the Ordovice warriors looked to Kynan for orders and received no response.

'Who comes to my hall with such an impressive guard? For a moment, I thought that the emperor of my youth had come out of Eburacum to pay me a visit. I forget his name,' Meriadoc said in a voice that was fretful, yet excited.

'I am the Comes Britanniarum, Magnus Maximus, come to meet your daughter, the fair Elen. I have heard of her beauty and I wish to see if the rumours do her justice.'

Start this campaign as you mean to finish it, Maximus's brain whispered inwardly. Around him, a hum of comments and exclamations rose towards the rafters like the twittering of so many birds.

'Elen? What could you possibly want with my daughter?' The king's voice was querulous with illness.

'If she is the one I seek, I wish to marry her and make her the wife of the king of all kings in Britannia. I am also known by the name of Macsen Wledig and I have determined to throw my lot in with the fates of the British people, for better or for worse.'

'Fetch Lady Elen!' Meriadoc ordered, wincing, before sinking back on his stool.

'Father . . .' Kynan protested, but Meriadoc waved away any further discussion.

Maximus chose to be solicitous for the welfare of Meriadoc, as if he was a son by marriage already. He poured a mug of wine from a crude carafe on the king's table and offered it to the old man, whose hands were trembling. In the presence of such decrepit old age, Maximus felt a shiver of disgust. Better to die with a sword in your hand than to rot away like this.

Maximus had little softness in his nature; most decidedly, he did not believe in love at first sight.

Then he saw the face of spoiled, self-centred Elen, and magic flooded through his body.

Emotionless and uncaring men such as Maximus sometimes fell in love for the first time during their middle years with a sudden madness that seemed to make little sense. And so it was when Magnus Maximus gazed at the sullen face of Elen. He was to become her slave, at least for a time.

On Elen's part, she saw a man in his late forties who stood tall and proud in the insignia of a senior Roman office; gold decorated his body, which appeared hard and muscular from his sturdy, polished half-boots to his bared head of thinning hair. His jawline was firm and determined.

As she sank into a low curtsy and her eyes rose to meet his, she almost faltered in her graceful bow. The Roman's eyes devoured her so intently that the air seemed to be charged with lightning.

The rest of the negotiations passed as if they were part of a dream sequence. Maximus was indifferent to the dowry or to any stipulations that King Meriadoc demanded as a part of the bridal contact. Indeed Maximus waived the dowry entirely and agreed to build Elen her own villa or palace at a location of her choosing. Meriadoc was actually shocked when the Roman agreed to the most ambitious and outlandish demands without any quibbling.

'I don't understand his reasoning, daughter, but Maximus is determined to have you as his bride. He will settle an obscene amount of wealth on you, if you should bear him a son, but even a daughter will make you an extremely wealthy woman. You've done very well, Elen.'

'But I haven't done anything at all. I don't know him, Father. I'm not sure I want to marry him.' Elen was utterly bewildered. 'He has sworn that he loves me and that God, or the old gods, had planned our marriage a long, long time ago.' Maximus gave her an impression of being a very abrupt lover. He had kissed her hand briefly and had bathed her with an intense and demanding look that spoke of ownership and physical desire, rather than the purity of marriage. She had been both attracted and repelled, until she felt an unexpected heat in her loins.

'You will belong to him for the rest of your days, Elen. Regardless of your thoughts on this matter, the Comes Britanniarum isn't the brand of man who will ever relinquish what is his. You must take no lovers and you would be advised to tread carefully, my dear.' Meriadoc's withered hands had clasped hers and she recoiled.

'No one can own me, Father,' she protested, but her father forced her to listen.

'This form of marriage involves ownership, Elen. You cannot expect a noble Roman to treat you any differently because you're the daughter of a king. You may believe that empresses can do as they please and that Roman matrons disport themselves in a scandalous fashion. Not so! Maximus is a military man and he will not tolerate such behaviour from his wife. You can expect to have your throat cut without pity if you should ever embarrass him.'

Eventually, displeased with each other, father and daughter parted, but they were unsatisfied, for Meriadoc had already decided to accept Maximus's offer of marriage.

And so, with almost indecent haste, Elen was married in the spring, despite her protestations that she had barely enough time to prepare her bridal clothes. The kings of Britannia travelled from their halls to attend the event, certain that they stood on very edge of a great and ennobling adventure. Caradoc was accommodated at the same inn that had showed him such excellent hospitality on his previous visit, but Endellion stayed in Tintagel on this occasion. Instead, Cadal was invited to meet the man whose guidance he would be forced to accept once his father had gone to the shades.

'You'll see your fellow Britons on their best behaviour at this event,' Caradoc warned. 'I wouldn't believe what anyone says for a moment. I'd recommend that you always judge them by what they do, rather than what they say.'

Cadal sighed with frustration, for he lacked the talent for subterfuge that his father seemed to possess in such abundance.

'But you must watch Maximus even more closely. You saw his approach to war at Anderida. The man is a realist and he's practical. They're great talents, my son. His flaw is his hubris, his certainty that he was born for a great purpose and a determination that his name will live forever.'

'I thought he was your friend, Father. Yet you speak as if you dislike him.'

'I do and I don't!' Caradoc sighed with deep regret. 'He's my friend, but he could very easily have us at war with Rome. You must be careful what you say around him. Don't commit yourself, or the Dumnonii people. Be on your guard . . . always.'

The wedding feast was intended to be splendid, so excellent wines and plentiful food loaded down the long tables in one of the great halls of Deva. The bride and groom sat at a small table on a dais at the head of the room, Elen's face as pale and as still as a graven image.

Beside her, still wearing his grass crown with pride, Maximus sat at his ease and lounged back on an armed chair with the same nonchalance he would have shown on a Roman eating couch. In deference to the number of guests and the obvious cultural differences, the wedding feast was presented on long tables with benches for seating, rather than the traditional furniture used in the Roman triclinium.

Wine and beer flowed like water and the roistering guests became noisier and more animated as the afternoon lengthened. Even Meriadoc seemed re-energised by the marriage of his only daughter. When he shakily rose to his feet, the room initially exploded with laughter, followed by advice offered on his daughter's good fortune, given Maximus's reputed physical endowments. Finally, Meriadoc raised his wine cup, and the hall slowly came to a ragged silence.

'Master Maximus, fellow Britons and Romans, and all men of good heart. I ask you to join with me in a toast,' Meriadoc began. 'Today we have seen a great honour bestowed on our Comes Britanniarum with the presentation of the Grass Crown. But we have the power to offer an even greater honour to my esteemed son-by-marriage. Now, after experiencing repeated attacks from the north, the west and the east in recent years, we find that we are in great need of a warrior who can protect us with wisdom and force of arms. Our Roman friends refer to this protector as the Dux Bellorum. But such a leader would be powerless if we, the kings of the tribes of Britannia, did not support and obey such a commander.'

Several heads nodded, although one or two of the kings listened with stony faces.

'If we wish to ensure the security of our realms, we must agree that our Dux Bellorum would, in effect, become a high king. During my long reign, I have watched our people come to rely, more and more, on the might of the Roman legions to guarantee our security. But the Roman influence is receding with the passage of time and there are strong indications that Rome will abandon us in the years to come. Her future lies in Italia and the lands on the continent.'

The old man paused to husband his strength.

'You may argue that each time the Picts, Hibernians and Saxons have attacked our shores, our Roman friends have defeated them. Lord Maximus has been sent to Britannia twice. But how many citizens and warriors perished during his absence from our shores? A thousand? Two? Ten? Such deaths have cost us dearly, so surely we'd be safer if our war leader was here permanently, to protect us from the very first landings by those savages who intend to ravage the British homeland.'

Around the table, the kings were covertly examining each other's reactions as they were forced to admit that Meriadoc's claims had some validity. They knew that burned villages, acres of stolen or burned grain, orchards and fortresses had all been laid to waste in the most recent raids and every spring brought some incursions from small, opportunistic groups of warriors bent on rapine and pillage. Fortunately for Meriadoc, the kings who had been part of Caradoc's southern alliance were the first to raise their hands and speak in favour.

'We agree wholeheartedly that Maximus should be invited to become our Dux Bellorum. We must have an impartial protector and Britannia must learn to speak with one voice. Let us invite Macsen Wledig to be our first High King.'

The swell of comments and shouted responses was joined by a barrage of cheering as those kings of tribes with the most to lose in the recurrent raids raised their voices in acclamation.

Caradoc sighed again as Maximus rose to his feet, bowed low to Meriadoc and raised both hands to exhort silence. Like all skilled orators, Maximus waited until the wedding guests settled.

He'll take it, Caradoc decided. He won't be able to resist. He'll use his achievements in Britannia to convince us to install him as our protector and then, in short order, he'll use that achievement to elevate himself to the purple.

'Friends, kinsmen and loyal lords of Britannia! Meriadoc does me too much honour. I am fortunate to have joined a tribe by marriage that is as strong and as dedicated to its people as the Ordovice of the north-west of Britannia. We have done much in recent years to rid ourselves of common enemies, so I have been grateful for the opportunity to serve the Britons in the role of Comes Britanniarum. However, much more needs to be done and I fear for Britannia's future if we continue to defend ourselves as a divided and splintered group of small, independent kingdoms. If even one of you should fall, the rest will quickly follow. Rome is in turmoil and its rulers could decide to retreat back to the continent in the near future. You would then be at the mercy of your traditional enemies who will come to your shores in a flood. I understand that some of you might be offended by Meriadoc's proposal. Perhaps I would feel the same, if I stood in your boots. I propose that we meet in one week to discuss this matter. The future of Britannia is a matter for cool and reasoned heads rather than impassioned and self-interested decisions, made on the emotions of the moment.'

'Clever sod!' Caradoc muttered.

'If you choose to extend this honour to me when next we meet, I will be honoured to vacate my role as a servant of Rome and become the figurehead of your resistance to evil. Such a trust should not be given or taken lightly, so let us eat and drink now and we shall put all thoughts of such matters of state away until the cold light of day permits us to consider the course of action for Britannia and its people.' Then Maximus offered a toast to the beauty of his bride while smiling down on her upraised face with a warmth and pride of ownership that could easily be mistaken for true love.

Around her, the room spun in a frenzy of eating, drinking and talk as the kings ignored Maximus's exhortation, as he knew they would. Yet they would weary of the subject within days and would then be more than half-inclined to see the Roman firmly ensconced in his new role.

Caradoc was certain that, somehow, Maximus had engineered Meriadoc's proposal and had already achieved the desired result, with Caradoc's assistance. Before him, the Comes Britanniarum's path to the purple was straight and true and Magnus Maximus was on his way.

The night had held no surprises for Maximus, at least concerning his father-by-marriage, who had proved to be an easy man to gull. His son was a different proposition. Kynan hadn't hesitated to voice his protests to his father, but Maximus bore him no malice. After all, a brother-by-law who happened to be the High King of Britannia would prove advantageous to Kynan, once the young man followed Meriadoc onto the Ordovice throne, so the prince would soon learn the error of his ways. Maximus gained some enjoyment by niggling at the young man's ego by using the Roman equivalent of his name, Conanus, which Kynan hated. Maximus always apologised with sincerity, but evil humour danced in his eyes no matter how contrite he sounded.

But Elen proved to be a welcome surprise, one that he had not anticipated.

Maximus's wedding night had been a revelation. He had crossed the bedchamber threshold expecting very little enjoyment from a virginal and inexperienced bride.

Without doubt, Elen was virginal, but her lack of experience would not last for long. Unlike many of her sex, his bride responded immediately to even the most casual of touches.

He had expected inexpert and frightened responses to his caresses in the darkness, so a swift slaking of his desires in her flesh had been planned, to be followed by a triumphant night of excellent sleep. Now, his interest and his libido were piqued by curiosity as he began to explore her body in the lamplight, while enjoying her reaction to his unfamiliar caresses.

She shivered when he kissed her throat where the veins and arteries were closest to the skin; she moaned in surprise when his thumbs first teased her hardened young nipples, and she tried immediately to become one with his body in the most charming and inexperienced fashion. When he stroked her belly and delicately licked at her thighs, her whole body arched as it responded to his slightest touch. Elen surrendered to the touch of an experienced lover with an eagerness that spurred him to exercise every element of his own self-control, as he tutored her in her first lessons of Eros.

As he smoothly entered her flesh, Maximus marvelled at how willingly she had surrendered to his ardour. The cold part of his brain that was rarely overwhelmed had enjoyed toying with her inexperienced body and mind, as he drove her to the peak of passion and then permitted her to slide back to the desperate longing of unfulfilled sexual arousal. She moaned, she begged and she tried to arouse him in turn with quickly learned caresses.

But, even as he luxuriated in his power over her and was pleasured by the blind madness and longing of her half-closed eyes, she found the secret spots on his flesh that ignited the slow-burning force of his own passions until he was as lost as Elen; he could no longer resist her and he drove her into her scented pallet as both enjoyed their release. Sated and panting, he lay upon her sweating flesh, desperate to catch his breath and recapture that god-like sensation of triumph.

Thoroughly dishevelled and with badly bruised lips, she smiled at him like a contented cat. She stretched every muscle under the heavy weight of his body and nestled her head into the pillows so he could rest his head between her soft breasts.

'My lord,' she whispered, once she could speak without panting. 'Was that what all men seek of women? Did I pleasure you?'

'Aye, girl! That was exactly what all men strive for, but so few women are able to give. Yes, you have pleasured me greatly. And what of you?'

This last questioned surprised him. He hadn't asked for a woman's approval since he was a callow, seventeen-year-old youth who'd been taken by his uncle to the best whorehouse in Egypt.

'I feared I would die, my lord. I thought you would kill me with pleasure,' she murmured with a small giggle that caused his body to twitch against her thigh.

She gasped with a courtesan's honed insight. 'Will our love always be so . . . ?'

'Ah, wise one, a woman can give and take pleasure a thousand times and yet, like a sweet spring, her waters will never run dry. I fear I'm an old man and I'm unable to find the energy to meet your needs as well as I should.'

He cupped her heavy breast in one hand and toyed with it, sucking on the nipple like a selfish infant until he felt his desires start to build once more. Surprised, he kissed her swollen lips and played with the hairless, shaved mound of her secret places.

'I could not imagine a more passionate lover, my lord. But I know so very little of how to pleasure you as you deserve.'

'I will teach you, little Elen.' He laughed suddenly. 'You're a surprising gift that Fortuna has given to me.' Then he ceased to think of anything at all.

When he finally slept, he dreamed of a throne of gold and stirred in his night imaginings as he sought her breasts with the eagerness of a child.

Elen smiled.

Who would have thought that she could hold the soul of the great Maximus in the palms of her narrow hands?

CHAPTER XVIII

A LONG TIME FOR WEEPING

We make war that we may live in peace.

Aristotle, *Nicomachean Ethics*, Book 10

Two brief and busy years passed, creating a whole new way for
Britannia's governance, and Caradoc had been in the thick of it,
his gravitas covering him with an aura of wisdom and invincibility.

As always, the High King moved with the speed of his beloved
cataphractarii. Before Elen could become truly comfortable in
Deva, Maximus whisked her away southward with a large
contingent of his troops, as he prepared for another spring and
the inevitable Saxon Summer with a new flood of invaders from
the north. Elen wept copious tears over the separation from her
father until, in a fit of temper, Maximus decided that she could
stay behind and rot in Segontium, if that was her preference.

Aware of her error, Elen slid back into her husband's good
graces, using seduction and apology in equal measure although,
inside, she raged at his apparent indifference. For his part,
Maximus had gambled that his wife would soon come to heel.
While his need for her grew more powerful with each passing

day, he feared that his fondness for her could drive away the God-given chance to gain his heart's desire.

In one fast swoop of the Roman eagle, Meriadoc had lost both children, for Kynan was lured into Maximus's service as a captain of the native cavalry, having decided, belatedly, that his future lay with the Roman who had won the heart of his sister.

Maximus's sense of urgency was so acute that their supply wagons were forced to move at speed, so extra carthorses had been requisitioned and regular harness changes made to maintain the column's brutal pace. Maximus, his troops, his engineers and his wagons charged down the straight Roman road through the belly of Britannia, towards a destination where Elen would be friendless and alone.

At Corinium, the road split into two with one branch heading towards Calleva Atrebatum while the other took travellers to Sorviodunum. Maximus sent a courier to Tintagel with an invitation for his old friend, Caradoc, to meet him at Venta Belgarum. The excessive pace made good by the column and problems with communications, supplies and vehicle maintenance necessitated a one-night pause at the comfortable court of King Llew, who remained a loyal supporter of the Roman High King and an emerging strategist of note. This comfortable evening was spent in Llew's scriptorium with a flask of red Spanish wine, numerous document scrolls and Llew's kinsman, Aeron ap Iorweth, who was kept busy taking copious notes of their discussions.

The next morning, when Maximus awoke to the first rays of the sun, the hollow in the bed next to him was already cold and empty. He searched impatiently for his wife and eventually found her in the latrines where she had been vomiting uncontrollably. Maximus's immediate emotion was one of intense irritation.

'How long have you been ill, Elen? Damn it, woman! You'll hold up the journey if you can't travel. Of course, you could stay here for a few days until such time as you're feeling a little better. I'll leave a small detachment of warriors for your protection and, when you've recovered, they can escort you to Venta Belgarum.'

Elen stared up at her husband in horror.

'No, husband! No! I *must* travel with you. I'll be well again as soon as the nausea passes,' Elen mumbled through her stiff, pale lips. Then, another paroxysm shook her. She retched miserably until Maximus took charge of the situation and carried her back to her pallet.

Ignoring Elen's increasingly loud protests, Maximus called for a physician to ascertain what ailed the queen, all the while chafing at the delay.

The physician was a small, hook-nosed man with the very dark complexion of one of the sons of Abraham, so Maximus's opinion sharpened with age-old prejudice. Unafraid, the physician stared into his untrusting eyes after he had made a diagnosis within moments of being led to his patient.

'You're to be congratulated, Your Highness,' the physician stated baldly. 'Your wife is very well. She's a fine, buxom lass who will bear a healthy child. Make sure she drinks boiled water or milk and eats nothing before noon, other than finely sliced fruits.'

'Oh! So that's it!' Maximus replied blankly. 'I understand now. Thank you, Master Physician. I should have recognised her condition for myself, if I hadn't been so anxious to depart from Corinium. Is it safe for Her Highness to travel?'

The physician smiled sleekly. 'She's very strong and healthy, so she could walk to Sorviodunum if she had to, morning sickness or no. You're a fortunate man, Your Highness.'

Maximus's nerves were twitching with irritation over the unforeseen delay to his travel plans, but he still sent the Jew off with several gold coins for his trouble. A generous reward was expected from one such as the Comes Britanniarum, and he was pleased at the show of avarice in the Hebrew's eyes.

Despite having fathered children in the past on both sides of the blanket, Maximus was mildly pleased with the news of Elen's pregnancy. The existence of a potential heir was an essential ingredient if a High King was to rule Britannia in perpetuity.

But when Elen was informed of her condition, she was thunderstruck. 'I don't want to be pregnant and I refuse to become fat and ugly. Do you hear me, Maximus? I don't want a brat crying night and day or chewing my breasts until they're flat old dugs. I don't want your baby!'

Furious, she turned on her husband.

'It's your fault! You don't love me, or this wouldn't have happened.' Then she pounded on her husband's chest in frustration.

Sadly, no one had ever explained the mechanics of procreation to her. So Elen had gone to her marriage bed with complete ignorance of the consequences of sexual congress.

Llew's queen, Llian, tried to reason with Elen.

'Your husband won't care for any changes in your body that don't meet with his desires. He'll cherish you as the mother of his heir and you'll become beloved of the British people if you choose to obey his wishes,' Llian explained. 'It's your appointed task to bear the child who'll help to make your people safe.'

Elen threw herself onto her bed and kicked the covers violently. 'I don't want to be pregnant. I want it killed! I want it killed!'

Queen Llian retreated towards the door with both hands

pressed over her ears. When she was safely outside the room, she pushed her back against the wall for support while she thought of what could be done to placate this silly creature. More than anything else, she wished fervently that she could have changed places with this ungrateful pig of a girl who didn't deserve the gift of motherhood.

Inevitably, Maximus heard of Elen's tantrum and her uncontrolled display of temper, and finally showed her his true nature. By the end of the meeting, she was shaking, pale with terror and speechless with pain.

The Roman's message to his wife had been agonisingly simple. 'You will cease all unseemly behaviour instantly, woman. Do you have any desire to sit beside me on the throne of Britannia and, in the fullness of time, to wear the purple? You have made demands that are not negotiable. You're proving to be a disgrace to your family, a slight on your tribe and a travesty of womanhood.'

Maximus's eyes were cold and pitiless. His lips curled with disgust.

'I've heard that you want to kill my child? Well, woman, at this moment, you'd be dead if you weren't carrying that child. I'd have strangled you as soon as I entered this room.'

'You wouldn't dare!' Elen hiccupped in her distress. 'How can you threaten my person? I'm the daughter of a *king*.'

'The lowliest servant in Rome would stand higher in the social world than the daughter of a king in a backward pocket of land such as Cymru. You don't matter a jot, Elen. I could have married other suitable women and any of them would have been less trouble than you. I should give you to my soldiers for their sport but, at the moment, too many people know you're pregnant. Perhaps I'll still hand you over to my men after the babe is born. Your future attitude will determine your chances of survival.'

Elen threw herself at her husband, snarling and spitting, and sank her teeth into his forearm, grinding them together until her mouth filled with blood.

He cursed and struck her hard on the side of the head with his closed fist. Then, with blood streaming from her mouth and running down her chin like a harpy, she came at him again with her long nails extended to rip out his eyes. So far, Maximus had been careful to stay his hand for the sake of the unborn child, but his rage began to rise like a tide of volcanic lava.

He hit her again, but on this occasion he used all his strength. Her eyes glazed as she took the blow on her jaw, so he picked her up and threw her onto their bed until her senses returned and she began to spit and curse like a camp follower. He flipped her body over so that she was lying on her belly, and tied one arm to the bed head with his neck scarf. Then he tore her robe along the hem to provide a tie for the other hand, although he was forced to sit astride her upper body to secure her to the bed. Another strip of cloth tied each ankle firmly to the foot of the bed on each side.

Spread-eagled and unable to move, Elen was finally at his mercy. He regained his feet and stood beside the bed so she could see him. Then the High King deliberately removed his heavy leather belt and held it loosely by the buckle.

'I've decided to be merciful. I had intended to cast you out and be rid of you, but you may thank the Dobunni queen for my change of heart. Llian explained that you have been raised without the influence of women, so I'm prepared to put your wilfulness down to ignorance. Be warned, Elen, that there will be no repetition of this shameful behaviour. I won't hit you with the buckle of my belt on this occasion, because I don't wish to scar you. But it's best that you remember your lessons, young woman, or you'll be doomed to suffer, again and again.'

Although she cried and begged after the second stroke of the leather belt, Maximus struck her ten times until her flesh was swollen and her skin had broken.

'I'll send your nurse to tend to your needs. You will keep our discussion private, but the number of strokes will be doubled if you speak of this punishment with others. Do you understand me, Elen? Answer me.'

'Yes! Yes! I understand.'

'Good! You're supposed to be a queen, woman, so you will learn to do better in the future,' Maximus retorted in a quiet voice that was almost sympathetic.

As the Roman passed through the doorway, Llian pressed her body against the adjoining wall. Quietly and fearfully, she scratched at the door and then entered the room to repair what other fools might well have broken, and to ensure that the world would continue to turn.

Venta Belgarum seemed to shudder in the spring warmth as the Roman commander came to the city to change its destiny forever. Gwaun ap Mairtin gathered his aged wits together and met Maximus at his gates, accompanied by his only living son, Gethin. Obviously apprehensive, Gwaun greeted Maximus as a brother, pressing the Roman's hand with his own age-spotted and sweaty ones. Maximus flinched away from those importunate fingers, without bothering to hide his distaste.

'My home is yours, Your Highness, so I bid you welcome.' Gwaun's querulous voice was that of an old man, one who no longer had the will or the strength to rule.

'My thanks go to you, Gwaun,' Maximus answered diffidently. 'My wife is with child and will need to be nurtured in the future.

May we speak once I have billeted my men? I have a proposal to place before you.'

Gwaun discovered, once Maximus had turned Venta Belgarum into an armed camp, that Maximus had no intention of presenting a proposal. A fait accompli was a better description of his actions. Gwaun's venerable, two-storeyed wooden palace had been taken over by the Roman commander and his staff, while engineers had commenced detailed planning to turn the ancient tribal centre of the Atrebates into Maximus's personal domain. A larger hypocaust was the first item to be designed, to replace Gwaun's small bathhouse. With typical Roman speed, bricks were ordered, metal work was commissioned from the smelters in Calleva Atrebatum and roof tiles were purchased from local potteries. Within weeks, the whole structure was being renovated and new construction work had begun.

Gwaun, appalled, was unable to find any way to stop the tidal wave of Roman efficiency.

'Why do you need my palace, my lord? I don't understand,' he asked diffidently, while desperately trying to keep his voice steady and strong.

'I expect to put down another Saxon advance within weeks. As we mount our defences, I propose to call for tribal troops to join me in a major campaign against a common enemy. It is unfortunate, but I need a central rallying point that lies close to Londinium where our galleys are berthed. Venta Belgarum is also a place from which I can strike at any point along the south-east coast with relative ease. You are a man of sense, Gwaun, so I expect you to be sympathetic to Britannia's strategic needs. In simple terms, I selected Venta Belgarum as my command centre because of its proximity to the southern ports.'

Maximus scowled with irritation that he should be called upon to explain his actions.

He gestured towards the dilapidated hall. The surfaces of the building's interior were obscured by layers of grease and a scum of straw and household dirt that was generations old. Even the tiled floor, a masterpiece of its kind displaying a design of fish, bright coral, shells and blue water, was heavily chipped.

'But I don't understand! What is my part in this grand plan?' Gwaun's younger self would never have permitted such arrogant behaviour by this usurper.

'I have no wish to supplant you and yours, friend Gwaun. You are the king of the Atrebates tribe and that status cannot change. Your son, Gethin ap Gwaun, will rule on that distant day when you breathe your last. Nothing has changed, except you are graciously allowing me to use your hall while I am conducting a war that will ensure the security of Britannia.'

Gethin plucked up his courage and strode forward to the table where his father and the High King were seated. Although near to thirty, he gave the appearance of being far younger. He was unpopular with the citizenry, mainly because his eyes were weak and he was inclined to stare fixedly at people or objects as he tried to make sense of the blur in front of him.

Gethin tried to bring Maximus into full focus.

'My father is at a loss to know where he is to go, Lord Maximus. At his age, you are asking a great deal when you instruct him to uproot himself and his whole family, servants and all, to move to some other place. He needs more assurances from you, and your assistance.'

Maximus managed to disguise a sudden flash of temper at being questioned, but he impaled Gethin with his autocratic stare. 'I have given some consideration to the needs of your father, as well as the needs of the citizens of Britannia who will rely on us to keep them safe during the coming summer. Your father has been a loyal king and his support was pivotal to my success during the early years of my reign, so I have set certain plans in motion. Through war and disease, the line of the local ruler of Clausentum and Portus Adurni has died out and his heirs have either perished or been dispersed. I have sent my engineers to Portus Adurni to ensure that the facilities in Gwaun's new hall will be of an acceptable standard for him. The city already possesses a fine hall and commands an excellent view of the island of Vectis and the sea.'

'But what if Father doesn't want to live in Portus Adurni or Clausentum?' Gethin demanded pugnaciously, although he knew in his heart that his father was a beaten man.

'Your father may live anywhere he likes, although Venta Belgarum has no other suitable palace. I suppose he could build another—' Maximus began, but Gwaun rose to his feet, while leaning heavily on his cane.

'Never mind, Maximus!' Gwaun said before turning back to face his son. 'No more, Gethin. I appreciate your kindness, but you have no hope of changing what is meant to happen. It's time to hold on to your intemperate tongue, my son, and help me to organise the movement of our family and servants.'

Then Gwaun saw a flicker in Maximus's blank eyes and he sighed deeply.

'Of course! You will also want my servants. I fear the older slaves will not choose to serve you, so I beg the right to take my elderly retainers with me. They'll be of no use to you.'

'There's no need to beg, Gwaun. Make a list of the retainers you require and present it to my servant, Decius.'

The effrontery! The gall of this man who chose to treat his

father like a foolish old servant whose usefulness had come to an end!

'Thank you, Maximus. May an old man offer a word of advice to an erstwhile friend?'

Maximus nodded, his impatience clearly written on his face.

'Beware of overconfidence, my king. Our desires do not always make something so. To our cost, fate sometimes plays tricks on us by offering trifling gifts of success. We are then emboldened by Fortuna's favour and we think the goddess is ours to manipulate as we choose. But she is a fickle and mercurial bitch and she'll remove every favour as quickly as she has granted it. Beware, Maximus, in case she entraps you.'

Maximus stared fixedly at Gwaun, his expression unreadable. His restlessly tapping foot was the only sign of any reaction to the old man's speech. 'Don't worry about me. I have no intention of tempting fate.'

Gwaun permitted Gethin to assist him to walk, although the king's old legs seemed to gain strength as he slowly limped out of the hall.

'The usurper will be dead in less than five years, my son. I hope the air in Portus Adurni really is clean and healthy, because I intend to live long enough to hear reports of his death. Remember, only a fool dares to use the gods for his own advancement.'

'I hope you're correct, Father, for my palms have been itching to strike him across his self-satisfied face. He'll lead us to disaster, if he has the chance.'

'Or he'll bring us glory! But the gods will not be mocked, so how can we know their true purpose? I know that you follow the Christian faith and your Jesus exhorts us to avoid pride. Perhaps he is here for some noble purpose that none of us can know.'

In perfect accord, father and son left their palace and their town without argument. The people of Venta Belgarum noticed their departure and many whispers wound through the Atrebates lands that their king had been banished by a man who had been Gwaun's friend. Without raising his voice, or his hand, the old king did more to shake Maximus's throne to its foundations than a thousand troops could ever have managed.

So Gwaun watched, and waited, and prayed for a very long life.

Caradoc arrived one month later to find that renovations were in full swing at the hall and in the palace. Maximus was absent, trouncing several Saxon fleets that had landed, one to the north of Londinium, and the other near Dubris. Caradoc surveyed the stirred-up anthill of workers who were setting new shutters into the walls of the hall and enlarging the baths. Further alterations were taking place in Maximus's apartments where glaziers were installing a number of thick glass windows.

'Where's Gwaun?' he asked Decius, who had been left behind to oversee the renovations. Decius gave a casual shrug, but he avoided the eyes of the Dumnonii king.

'We have received word that the Saxons will be making major incursions into the south-east during the coming summer and my master decided that he needed a capital in the south. King Gwaun found himself unable to refuse the wishes of the High King.'

'And Gwaun agreed? Where did he go?' Caradoc paused in his questioning when an ominous possibility crossed his mind. 'Is he still alive?'

Decius looked quite shocked. 'Of course he is, sir. King Gwaun has taken his whole household to Portus Adurni where my master has organised a modernisation of the palace. He took his older retainers with him, but it wasn't practical to take them all, considering that there are already servants in residence at his new hall.'

'How unpleasant for King Gwaun to lose his ancestral hall. Are there any other surprises that I might discover during this visit?'

Decius looked far happier as he led Caradoc to a renovated room at the back of the living area of the largest structure. The walls had been freshly lime-washed, and one of the servants had found an old, crazed pot with a broken handle and filled it with flowers. This small spot of colour gave a jaunty appearance to the pale room while a row of windows with new shutters flooded the small space with light and air.

'It may be a small room, but it's one of my favourites,' Decius said carefully. 'I presumed you wouldn't want to feel as though you were hemmed in, after having spent so much time in Tintagel. I remember your home well, sir. I've never seen a bigger sky or quite so much sea. I hope you'll enjoy your visit to Venta Belgarum.'

With a pang, Caradoc recognised that the rough, humorous Decius had vanished into the past, and a servant had taken his place. Where had the faithful decurion gone?

Caradoc muttered a polite reply and sat on the end of the pallet while Huw laid out his saddlebags and unpacked the contents. Once everything had been squared away, Huw excused himself and showed his master an even smaller room across the corridor where he would be sleeping for the duration of their visit.

'The men are billeted in either the warriors' quarters or in the rooms attached to the stables. If you wish to meet with the other kings as they arrive, I'll escort you to the hall. Otherwise, I can organise meals to be delivered to you from the kitchens. They are some distance away, so I can't guarantee the food will stay hot. You know how to find the bathhouse.'

'Aye, Huw! You look after me very well, my friend. All the kings are coming, you say?'

'Yes, my lord! Or so the gossip from the kitchens tells me . . . You, more than anyone, should know that servants know everything, even the slaves,' Huw added with a sly grin.

'Especially slaves!' Caradoc agreed. 'It's their way of taking their revenge on their captors. Listening at corners is so easily done in a big house, isn't it?'

Huw laughed as he disappeared into his own small space to rest, before coping with the demands of the coming evening.

'Well, well, well!' Caradoc spoke aloud. 'What's Maximus up to? He never does anything unless there is some purpose to it.'

Then he lay down on his bed and, swearing that he'd only close his eyes for a moment, he permitted the darkness to embrace him.

Over the next week, as other kings appeared at Venta Belgarum, Caradoc was kept busy. Everyone was talking, talking, talking. What were Maximus's long-term plans? What was Emperor Gratian up to with his ever-increasing demands for extra taxes? When would the Roman troops be paid? The legionnaires were mumbling in discontent over delays to their pay from their masters in Rome. And a senior officer, a member of the hated Alan tribe, had arrived to squeeze more funds out of Britannia and to determine whether there were any further areas where administrative savings could be made. The Romans based in Britannia were sullenly unhappy and so, too, were the local landowners and traders. The British world was ripe for change.

'What's going on?' Caradoc demanded of Llew ap Adwen, when he arrived in Venta Belgarum with young Aeron ap Iorweth in tow. The younger man had grown in both stature and gravitas since Caradoc had first met him, so the old king was becoming increasingly fond of the emerging young strategist from Caerleon, and trusted both Llew and Aeron sufficiently to share his intimate thoughts with them.

'The Western Roman Empire is in trouble,' Llew replied. 'Whispers arriving in vessels from the Middle Sea suggest that Gratian has only a loose hold on the reins of power and he has surrounded himself with Alans, Scythians and Ossetians, who are all hated by the population of Rome. Although many of these new men are stern Christians, they run roughshod over Roman citizens and are intolerant, ambitious and grasping. Romans are very touchy about their status as men born in the City of the Seven Hills. Rome has become a woodpile of inflammable emotions, so even we barbarians on the far frontiers are being dragged into a mess created by Gratian.'

'Do you think this feeling of dissatisfaction stems from him?' Caradoc asked, his amazement clear.

'So we're being told,' Llew retorted, but he slowly winked one eye. 'The walls have ears in Venta Belgarum, and some of our masters seem to discover everything we say.'

Caradoc airily waved away any fear of spies with a casual flick of one hand. 'I don't believe fear is the motivation for this . . . this edgy feeling, as if we're all standing on the lip of a precipice and someone behind us is pushing us closer and closer to a long and fatal fall.'

'Sir,' Aeron interrupted quietly. 'I believe that our High King is readying himself for something far larger than another Saxon Summer. I've been called to Venta Belgarum by personal invitation on the strength of my skills with scrolls. I believe he intends me to record certain events, whatever they might be.'

'Maximus is making sure that his role in history will be recorded so that his status in the world can be glorified for ever. My old friend has always seen himself as Fortuna's darling, a man who was born for a great purpose.

'I fear he may drag us into some form of disaster just to realise his own grandiose vision of how he sees himself in the flesh. He is a man for whom power is a poison. Given time, it will kill him.'

'I pray to God that you're wrong,' Llew responded thoughtfully.

'Aye! On a happier note, have you met the queen on this visit?'

Both men expressed their eagerness to offer their congratulations to the newly impregnated young woman, but Caradoc explained that she had been suffering from morning sickness.

'It keeps her close to her apartments.'

'At least the High King seems to cherish her,' Aeron said carefully with a face that he kept deliberately blank.

'So it appears,' Caradoc replied, but his acquaintances noticed that he was biting his thumb in that tell-tale gesture that they recognised.

'His crown is established in her body,' Llew observed.

'But Maximus has yet to order the making of that crown. Does he consider the role of High King as his penultimate goal? Or does he reach higher?'

'How high can his ambitions reach?' Aeron asked with a dawning horror.

'You are beginning to see the fears that have racked me for some time, but his ambitions will come to nothing without us. Beware, my friends! The two dice of Julius Caesar have not yet been thrown by Maximus, so fate will surely surprise us in the months to come. In matters such as these, wise men do best when they speak little, but watch everything.'

After several such conversations, Caradoc settled down to a prolonged period of waiting. Maximus moved at his own speed, so mere mortals would be forced to wait on his decisions.

So, summer came and had almost fled while a continuing state of inactivity, impatience and growing doubt prevailed over the king's halls.

Still Maximus did not return.

Caradoc was surprised when a servant girl approached him as he rested in his small garden outside the hall to consider the beauty of the cherry trees, watching the drifts of early-falling leaves while sitting on a mossy stone seat in his quiet corner.

'Master, the queen has requested that you visit her this afternoon. She has need of your wisdom.'

Caradoc wondered what that foolish, outspoken and vain young lady wanted of him. He had shown no preference for her company and very little respect during their few meetings over the last two years. Nor had he made any secret of his belief that such a mismatched marriage had little chance of happiness.

With Huw's assistance, Caradoc took pains to look more presentable than usual before he arrived at the doors leading into the queen's apartments. An Ordovice warrior stood at attention in the corridor to ensure the queen's safety, although why Elen would need protection within the palace was beyond Caradoc. Nevertheless, he submitted to a very thorough body search before he was ushered into the perfumed bower where Elen spent every day cowering in fits of fear, illness and despair.

The woman who greeted Caradoc was old, weathered and obviously very martial in her desire to keep her mistress safe and happy. Except for this elderly woman, her old nurse, and a single servant girl, Elen was alone in the well-appointed four-roomed apartment. Bowls of dried rose petals sweetened the air and all the shutters were thrown open to capture the cooling breezes from the sea.

Elen entered and as Caradoc sank to his knees in front of her, he winced at the changes that less than two years had wrought on this abrasive beauty.

Elen was very thin, except for the obvious hard ball of her pregnant belly. Her collarbones were prominent and sharp, as were her cheekbones. Elen was still lovely, but her beauty was worn down and almost ethereal, as if the infant inside her was sucking the life out of its host. Caradoc's face became grave and he found himself bowing a little lower than normal, out of sympathy for the young woman.

With a graceful wave of her hand, Elen indicated that he should sit and then sank onto a couch. For a few moments, the silence stretched out between them, creating an awkward space that the king would have liked Elen to fill. Over the years, he had discovered that impatient conversationalists always tried to fill the void, so he had learned a useful store of information by the simple device of waiting for them to speak.

'I suppose you've wondered why I've asked to see you,' Elen began tentatively.

'Yes, my Queen. Although I admit that an old man is very gratified to look upon your youth and beauty. I'm flattered to receive your request for a visit.'

She smiled wanly and her pale lips seemed to flush a little.

'You're far too generous with your praise, King Caradoc.' The silence dragged out again and Elen cleared her throat. Caradoc waited.

'I've been trying to find some polite way to make a personal request of an extremely sensitive nature. You'll probably think I'm mad, but I'm concerned about my babe. I truly don't know what to do, King Caradoc, or I wouldn't have come to you for advice. You're my husband's oldest friend in Britannia, so I can't hope for you to take my part. Still, everyone says you're a fair and honest man. I'm forced to trust you because my life depends on your silence.'

Damn! Caradoc thought. She's having trouble with Maximus and she wants to drag me into it.

'The people who sing my praises are very kind, but not very accurate. I'm a simple man, Your Highness, but I believe I'm trustworthy. If I give my word, I do my utmost to keep it.'

'So? Can I trust you, my lord? I will die if you should speak out about this meeting.'

Caradoc was biting back an urge to make a dismissive comment when he suddenly realised that tears were beginning to roll down her cheeks. But the queen made no sound. Wordlessly, she wiped her streaming face on her sleeve and rang a little bell on the table beside her couch.

Within moments, one of the older servants entered the room, so Caradoc was certain she had been waiting with her ear pressed against the door.

'Yes, Highness?' the servant asked, and then noticed the tears. Clucking her tongue like an indignant hen, she stared at Caradoc accusingly before taking Elen into her arms.

'There, my lovey, there's no need for those tears. If the king has distressed you, old Bregeen will send him away so you can be comfortable again.'

'Oh, Bregeen, King Caradoc hasn't done anything to upset me. I'm just tired. But I really need to speak with the king, so could you arrange some of those little fish cakes that I like? And I'd also like a hot tisane to settle my stomach.'

'You'll be having some warm milk for the infant, some sliced apple for you and some fish cakes for your guest. You must do as you're told, or I'll send King Caradoc away.'

Caradoc nodded amicably. Elen understood her nurse's nature as well, so she consented.

'You'll be having some beer, Master Caradoc?' Bregeen asked. He thanked the old servant, and he and Elen sat in companionable silence as they waited for the refreshments to arrive.

Once the food and drink were spread before them, Elen regained her composure and returned to the sensitive conversation.

'I know that what I am about to say could easily bring about my ruin, but I've decided that I must place my trust in you. I have to put my faith in someone and my father always insisted that you were an honourable man.'

'I thank you for your kind words, Highness,' Caradoc answered carefully.

'My husband is an ambitious man, as I'm sure you're aware. No one could know Maximus well without recognising the forces that drive him onward,' Elen began.

Caradoc nodded, because this piece of information was hardly contentious.

'He has decided to go to war with Rome. Oh, he hasn't said as much, but I've heard his orders to his troops and I've been forced to listen to his fury over Gratian's demands. He is sure that he'll be recalled and sent to a far outpost of the empire where he'll be beyond the reach of those troops who are loyal to him.'

'I've heard of the troubles that exist between the emperor and his troops in Britannia. But there is nothing I can do to influence Maximus once he makes up his mind on a course of action. Your husband has a forceful nature.' Caradoc smiled gently.

'I've become afraid for my child, Caradoc. If I've gone, my babe will become a tool in the hands of powerful men, ambitious men who'll try to steal the throne of the High King the moment that my husband leaves these shores. My father is too old and too far away to provide any protection that might become necessary. My brother will leave with Maximus, of a certainty. As Maximus's oldest friend, I am begging you to protect my child, regardless of what arrangements my husband might want to make with you.'

Caradoc was stunned. He had expected any number of requests, but acting as regent for her unborn child wasn't one of them. In effect, that was the demand she was making of him. His mouth gaped open and he was forced to think quickly.

'I'm far too old to be of any real service to you, Highness.'

'Is there another among you who holds the trust of the tribal kings?'

'Llew of the Dobunni is a man of impeccable honour.'

'But he has no children. He and his wife lack the experience to raise a child, least of all one who is destined to become important in these lands. While Llew is a trustworthy and honourable man, he lacks your reputation for calm, common sense and your dedication to the future of a united Britannia where all the tribes are equal.'

'There must be someone else,' Caradoc complained, after he had been silent for a few moments while he reviewed all the tribal kings and their suitability to provide the service requested.

'What I'm asking of you might never happen,' Elen added. 'I could be wrong in my assessment of what Maximus plans to do in the days and months ahead.'

She smiled wanly. 'But I don't think so! Maximus is a cruel man, one who doesn't care for this babe except as cement that will solidify his path to the throne that he craves. I'll only see him rarely once he leaves our shores, and I fear that my lifespan will be short, even if I should survive the birth of my child.'

'Such fears are always a part of pregnancy, Highness. I believe that Maximus will prove to be a loving husband and father after your babe is born, for he will have pushed back the Saxons and stabilised his throne. Let's wait and see. I believe that all will be well.'

Elen shook her head. 'No, Caradoc. I know better now, even if Maximus should make a pretence of love. I've only lived for eighteen summers, but I've come to learn my husband's true nature. He's your friend, but I wouldn't expect you to know him as I do. Your experience of me tells you that I'm just a foolish girl, and you are justified in having this opinion, but I've learned the hard way that I must be a compliant wife. I'm not complaining. I chose my fate, but my child is innocent of any crimes.'

'Come, my dear! Maximus is a complex man, but he's not deliberately cruel,' Caradoc said soothingly.

Instead of replying, Elen rose and permitted her robe to sag at the back, while clutching the heavy folds of fabric to her breasts for modesty's sake. She turned so her back was bared to Caradoc's gaze.

Caradoc recoiled in shock. Her beautiful, alabaster skin was cut with scarred flesh wounds which had barely healed. Repeated blows with some type of whip had left her back as a symphony to pain.

Gently, he lifted her robe back into place and patted the girl's shoulder, stunned. The marks on the queen's back were evidence of beatings that must have been inflicted over several months. Elen cradled her belly protectively and Caradoc realised the queen was only a few months from her travail. These beatings must have taken place during her pregnancy.

With a sickened heart, the old man fell down on one knee. Of all things, he had never expected this of Magnus Maximus.

'I have no sword to swear upon, so you must take me at my word. If Maximus departs for Gaul, and if he leaves you behind, I will protect your child with all the strength of my tribe. Whether you live or die, I will hold to my word. So I swear!'

'Thank you, King Caradoc. I understand what I am asking of you, so I am very grateful.'

They spoke for a few more moments. Then, saddened and sickened, Caradoc carried away her secrets and a determination to redouble his efforts to discover the plans that were formulating within Maximus's devious mind.

The weeks passed slowly, while life continued within the gilded halls of Venta Belgarum.

Maximus returned to Venta Belgarum at speed, his cavalry strung out in formation behind him.

Even before he spoke to the kings who had assembled in Venta Belgarum, couriers were sent out to those tribes who were without representation at Maximus's command centre giving notice of the High King's intentions. Finally, late into the twilight at the end of an inauspicious day, the visiting kings were called to a meeting in the great hall.

Refitted, repainted and freshly gilded, the hall was bright with the pennons of the various tribes. Lamps shone over fine clothing, the armour of the Roman guards and the gems of the tribal kings who had donned the regalia of their office. Once they had assembled, the only sound came from the fire pit where logs were crackling and exploding.

'Greetings, Lords of Britannia. I realise that some of your peers have been unable to make the long journey into the south to attend this meeting, but I have sent messages to all the tribes of Britannia, including yours, to call for a levy of all single men of courage to come with me on a quest that will teach the Emperor of the West that we will no longer tolerate his greedy taxes or the sycophants who have been appointed by our masters in Rome to lord it over those of us who are not Roman by birth or breeding. Britannia will cast off the yoke that holds us down, and we will cease to be slaves to Rome's caprices and win us the purple and our security for as long as I am your High King.'

The kings murmured thinly like the leaves in a wood when wind starts to blow.

'We will be gone before the spring comes again! Winter will soon be here, so we have only six months at the most to set our plans in stone, since time and fortune will not wait for us. Our hearts, our strong right hands and our well-honed swords can make us safe from the upheavals that will soon come out of Rome and its corrupt bureaucracy. I expect that you will follow my leadership by sending those of your warriors who volunteer to join us, plus an agreed levy of supplies. In return, you will gain your freedom from the Roman yoke. Think on that! No more obscene taxes to be spent by a bloated bureaucracy in other parts of the Roman world. Who are the patriots in this room? Who are those men who love their lands and their tribes above their personal ambitions? Now is the time when all must stand and be counted.'

The kings looked at each other, and then gazed surreptitiously at their High King. How could they refuse? Under the spell of those cold eyes, their manhoods shrank in fear. Waving one hand at Aeron, Maximus called on the kings to make their marks on a long Latin document which Caradoc scanned when he had the opportunity. The pact between Maximus and the vassal kings was clear: they would provide all possible support to the High King, in both men and supplies, to facilitate his attack on the Roman emperor, Gratian, and the Western Empire itself.

Caradoc signed. He cursed himself inwardly for his cowardice, but he swore that none of his kin would go to Gaul with his friend. If Saraid's old prophecy was correct, anyone who went with Maximus would never return. Remembering her warning, Caradoc felt a flood of gratitude for her ancient gift. Her message was so clear and complete that he couldn't deny its meaning, even if his common sense told him that such prescience was not possible.

The kings either signed their names or made their marks under Aeron's guidance. No matter how long it took, Aeron read out the agreement in detail and showed each man his name, including the space where he had to give an indication of his consent. As Caradoc expected, none of the tribal kings had the courage to deny the High King his victory. Caradoc was relieved, because he realised that his friend would probably bring some form of retribution to the tribes of any recalcitrant ruler.

The entire court at Venta Belgarum was waiting now. Winter came and the short days dragged until they seemed as long as any in midsummer. When winter was at its coldest, Elen went into labour and the midwives were called. After Caradoc's long search to find her, the dreams, the portents and the changes that had embraced Britannia, the young queen's death was an anticlimax. Though Maximus sent for an army surgeon from Londinium, even the fastest horses were defeated by the distance between Venta Belgarum and the city on the Tamesis River.

When the hard-faced Roman physician arrived, Elen had

drawn her last breath some hours earlier, having slid gratefully into death from exhaustion and haemorrhage. With Caradoc holding Elen's hand, the inconsolable Bregeen had used a small sharp knife to slice the birth canal open so she could draw the babe from her mother's body before both mother and child perished.

Maximus had insisted that Elen's screams would be such that he couldn't bear to listen, so Elen was forced to face her travails alone. Out of pity, Caradoc allowed himself to stand in Maximus's stead.

Caradoc looked down at the large baby girl, who was veiled in her mother's blood, and he prayed sincerely that this child would transcend her ugly beginnings. Elen now seemed less flesh than the wooden carvings of the Madonna in the church beside the town square – just as she had been since her wedding day.

Maximus entered the room as the babe was being cleansed by the servant. He was followed by Kynan, who made a guttural exclamation when he saw that his sister was awash in her own blood and sweat. For a short moment, the room was silent except for the sound of a slow drip of blood from the saturated pallet. Then Maximus came back to his senses as a mental door clanged shut inside his head, and his face set in an impassive expression.

'And the babe?'

'A girl-child, Maximus! She is very strong and vigorous, although this good woman was forced to pluck her from Elen's dead body to save the babe's life.' Caradoc's voice and expression reflected his weary acceptance of Fortuna's unfairness.

'You're here, Caradoc? I didn't realise that Elen was an intimate of yours. My, you do get around, don't you?' Caradoc's hackles rose.

'I resent your implications, Maximus. Elen was lonely and frightened about her coming ordeal. She believed our friendship wouldn't be compromised if she asked me for some advice about children in the presence of her servants.'

Caradoc's gaze was fixed on the Roman's face; Maximus broke eye contact first.

'I'm sorry, friend, but most men would have thought as I did, if only for a short moment. I'm sorry that I wasn't present for the birth of my child, but time doesn't stop for me. The army has asked me to take the purple and I've accepted their offer. We sail from Londinium in two weeks.'

Caradoc was forced to bow deeply to hide the anger that flashed through his eyes. Saraid's warnings were becoming reality; even the immature Elen had made an accurate assessment of the Roman's character.

'I fear I'm too old to join you, but I'll come to Londinium to speed your departure. Young Aeron is dear to my daughter, so I'd ask that you do your best to avoid getting him killed.' This weak attempt at humour brought a fleeting smile from Maximus.

'Aye, Caradoc, I acknowledge your years, but a troop of Dumnonii warriors has volunteered to serve with me in Gaul. Your assistance is needed here in Britannia, where you will be performing matters of state for me.'

He turned to face Elen's servant.

'Woman?' Maximus shouted at Bregeen, who jumped nervously.

She hurried towards him with the freshly swaddled baby cradled in her arms. 'How may I help you, my lord?'

'Give me my daughter,' Maximus demanded, as he took the child from the nurse and laid her on a part of the bed that wasn't stained with blood. After unwrapping her, he carefully examined her wriggling body. Then, satisfied, he rewrapped her with the efficiency of an experienced parent and returned her to Bregeen as the baby began to wail.

'She will join the family of God on Sunday. Her name will be Severa, for my maternal grandmother.

'When I am gone, I propose to leave the running of Britannia in the hands of two regents. King Meriadoc must be one of them in honour of his granddaughter, if only in name. I doubt that the king will leave his castell of wood and survive even a short journey.'

Caradoc nodded, although he failed to see the logic in this appointment.

'I need safe hands to care for my realm and my daughter during my protracted absence. What safer hands can there be than those of King Caradoc, a man recognised as the most competent ruler in Britannia? When I return, I will find everything as it should be and, in return, I'll ensure that your Aeron remains safe.'

Caradoc protested. He was too old, too weary and unwilling to spend his last years away from his beloved Tintagel while caring for another man's daughter. But Maximus refused to listen. He countered each argument as if he was planning a war and, eventually, Caradoc ran out of excuses.

As his master had planned, Caradoc was now the virtual High King of Britannia. He might not wear the crown, but he would be wholly responsible for the safety of the isles until Maximus returned.

That is, if Fortuna permitted Maximus to return.

MAXIMUS'S CAMPAIGN IN GAUL AND ITALIA

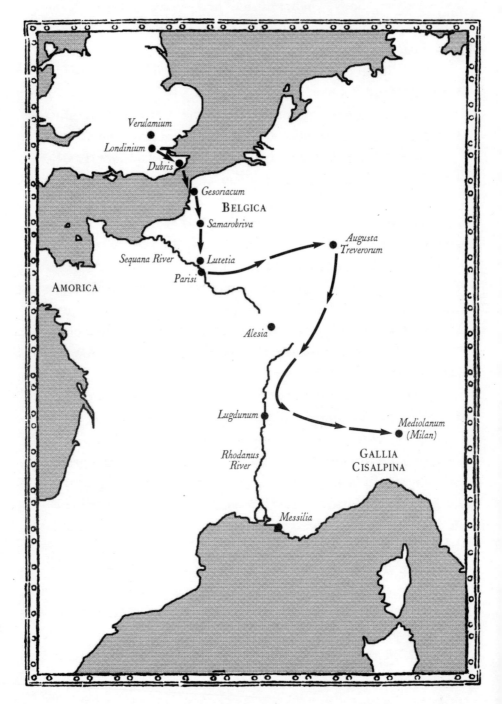

CHAPTER XIX

THE EMPEROR OF THE WEST

Whom the gods love dies young.

Menander, *Dis Exapaton*, fragment

Londinium crawled with traders, flocking to vessels of all sizes as they manoeuvred up the tidal Tamesis River, a brown, turgid flood that was too deep and too wide to be easily forded. Roman engineers had built a simple wooden bridge close to the walled fortress that had been laid out in the familiar rectangle, with four gates pointing to the north, south, east and west. A large island in the centre of the Tamesis was a hive of activity around the last of the supply and war galleys, and the workshops that lived off the maintenance of these vessels. A system of pulleys drew clean water from deep underground, for who could trust the many streams that fed the main watercourse? These streams were bordered by thick, tidal ooze, exposed daily, that was carefully explored by the poor for any largesse that the river might bring. Reeds choked many of the watercourses and those close to several of the British villages were fouled by discarded rubbish in the mud, derelict timber and crushed vegetation.

Fortunately, winter had frozen the smaller watercourses and the insects of summer temporarily vanished with the intermittent snow and cold winds.

The landscape was flat and deceptively gentle, but solid Roman buildings created a sense of order in a place that had few natural advantages, except for the remarkable river. The sea was some distance downstream, but large seagulls flew in each morning to feast on the various middens, sitting in neat rows on any fences until strangers passed by their feeding grounds.

Caradoc stared at the cobbled streets which, blessedly, kept his feet out of the mud. Somehow, he had expected more of the largest of Rome's settlements in Britannia. The town had an unfinished appearance for all that it possessed all the comforts of civilised life, such as baths, an amphitheatre and communal fountains. There were few administrative buildings of note, because Verulamium, a nearby settlement to the north, was the town where the public service and the bureaucracy had been established. Londinium was a trading and communications centre and all the roads in the land led to her busy heart. Some smaller, native townships also clustered around the skirts of the town, and a fortress that was no longer fully manned.

Maximus had requisitioned the lion's share of the soldiers and supplies from the garrisons that made up the Roman presence in Britannia. The British kings had been required to supplement these forces with a large contingent of young warriors, along with all the weapons, horses and other accoutrements needed to maintain them through a long and gruelling campaign. Londinium was bursting at the seams as the galleys were loaded and quickly despatched to make the short dash across the Litus Saxonicum to Gesoriacum. Caradoc looked on with regret. Would the legions ever return? Or would this expedition to the continent mark the beginnings of the non-Roman Britannia that was bound to come?

Endellion had insisted on accompanying her father, for she feared that Aeron might never return. Two years had wrought many changes in her appearance, and she now had a natural sophistication that many young girls lacked. She had also taken to staining her lips a deep pomegranate red, although Caradoc objected to this show of vanity.

'I have a pale complexion, Father, so I simply add to what God provides,' she responded.

Walking with Endellion was always an unnerving experience for Caradoc. Other older men stared at him with drooling envy and tried to fathom how such an ancient could attract such a beautiful young woman, while younger men stared at Endellion, undressed her with their eyes and tried to understand what she could possibly see in such an elderly man.

Now, Caradoc and Endellion stood among a large crowd of well-wishers waiting for one last glimpse of their loved ones as they embarked. The river bank was packed with crying mothers, wives, lovers and children, while still more parents pressed gifts upon their sons or strung flowers in chains around their necks or the heads of their kinsmen. Nor were the Romans ignored, for many had British wives and children.

Suddenly, Aeron appeared on the bank and then eased his way politely through the crowd until he reached Endellion's side.

'My lord, may I speak with Endellion before I'm forced to embark?'

Caradoc nodded and moved back a little way to give the young people an illusion of privacy. Aeron lost no favour in Caradoc's eyes by asking the king's permission to speak with his daughter. On the contrary, Aeron always treated his elders with respect, whether they were powerful or not. The thought of such a brave and promising young man dying to further Maximus's ambitions was a greater source of annoyance to the Dumnonii king than he could readily explain.

Caradoc tried hard to ignore the whispered words between the young lovers, but he couldn't help himself.

'See, Endellion. My master has surrounded himself with a huge army so, as his scribe, I'll be with him at all times. I'll be perfectly safe while I'm performing this role! I doubt that I'll even be allowed to hold a sword,' Aeron explained. He was trying his best to avoid touching Endellion, although her closeness was intoxicating. Her perfume made his head spin.

'The emperor will have far more men than Maximus, so I'm afraid that none of you will return to Britannia,' Endellion whispered as slow tears ran down her face. 'You must promise me that you'll take care.'

Aeron took Endellion's hand, as he tried very hard not to overstep the bounds and compromise her. He kissed her soft palm and breathed in the scent of her body.

'I promise that I will return, Endellion. I swear on the life of my mother that I'll return to you, and then I'll beg King Caradoc for permission to marry you.'

As her eyes filled with tears, Endellion threw her arms around his neck, prompting Caradoc to take half a step forward before he stopped himself. He realised that other couples were embracing around them, so no one would notice his daughter's behaviour.

Don't be cruel, Caradoc, a small voice told him from within. She may never see him again. The voice sounded so much like Saraid's throaty contralto that Caradoc felt his lips tighten. In unspoken approval of their embrace, he turned away from the young couple to give them some privacy.

'I shouldn't be touching you,' Aeron whispered into Endellion's hair.

'I don't care what anyone thinks. I'm hand-fasted to you forever, Aeron,' Endellion told him calmly. 'If you should be killed, I will die unwed. I love you, now and forever.'

'Please, Endellion. I couldn't bear it if something happened to me and you spoiled your life over a memory.' Despite his words, Aeron held her even tighter as if he could breach her skin, and her flesh, to become one with her.

She covered his mouth with hers. In a chaste but passionate embrace, they stood in their own private silence until the sound of brazen horns called the troops to their boats.

'It's time to go, son. Release him, Endellion. Don't make his departure harder for him than it already is. Chin up, girl, because you're the daughter of a king.'

Caradoc took Aeron's hand and felt the young man's vitality surge through his blood.

'Take care of yourself, my boy! If you should fall, Endellion will travel to Hades to bring you back to this earth, just like the lovers in the old legends. Besides, my daughter will keep her word on her future intentions and I am relying on you to give me grandsons.'

'Aye, my lord, for that is also my intention. I ask you to take good care of Endellion, for she's not as strong as she thinks she is. I'll send a report to you in Venta Belgarum whenever a courier is available to bring messages back to you.'

Then, with lagging steps, Aeron joined the other men on the wharf who were waiting for the small boats that would take them out to the galleys that were holding position in the channel.

The tide had turned, so it was time to go.

Father and daughter stood quietly and watched for the whole afternoon as the boats carrying the Roman expeditionary force slipped down the Tamesis in ragged formations. Like gulls at rest on the tidal flow, the galleys slid along the soupy, brown flood along whose river banks oak trees threw out green flags of new growth. Caradoc was overcome with sadness as he watched the departure of the flower of Britannia's young men, the new blood that would replenish the land; Maximus was taking the hopes of Britannia with him on his ambitious journey.

Caradoc would still have strong sons by his side, for both Cadal and Cadoc had acceded to their father's wishes and remained at their posts in Tintagel. But tribe after tribe had been deserted by virile young men who sought adventure, spoils and power with the charismatic figure of Magnus Maximus.

As the sun set in the west, the last of the galleys slid around the great turn in the river as it headed out to the open sea. Then darkness and distance stole away their last views of those stately vessels. Endellion began to cry in earnest, so all her father could do was hug her tightly and remind her that he was still the rock on which her hopes were built.

To Caradoc
King of the Dumnonii tribe, and Regent of Britannia
Hail and Blessings
With the approval of my master, Magnus Maximus, I write to you to advise you of the success of the united forces of Britannia in the fields of Gaul.

We landed just south of Gesoriacum and were immediately welcomed by troops from the army of Emperor Gratian who had deserted the emperor. These warriors offered their services to Magnus Maximus in order to swell our ranks. Buoyed by this influx of numbers, Maximus moved with his usual speed to strike deeply into Gaul as he headed towards Parisii.

As we passed through the province of Belgica, the population welcomed us as we marched, while towns such as Samarobriva opened their gates to us without incident.

I have been kept busy recording every detail of our advance because Maximus expects that he will prevail and will become the Emperor of the West. He has told me on numerous occasions that he has been selected by God to save the Roman Empire and its people. He becomes more god-like with every milestone that we pass, but I can attest to his sincerity. I never noticed before that your friend was over-religious, but perhaps he can feel that circumstances are massing behind him.

We move quickly now. Maximus has promoted a man from the ranks to take his place with the *cataphractarii*. He is called Andragathius and this soldier is the new master of horse. In your absence, Maximus puts much faith in him and often discusses strategy with him. I fear my lord makes a mistake, for Andragathius is hot-headed. But, for the moment, he says what Maximus wants to hear.

We will reach Parisii soon and Maximus will then hope to engage Gratian's army. It must be massed somewhere ahead of the line of our march. Maximus must know but, as always, he remains silent about his battle plans. I will learn his secrets when he has succeeded.

One final matter of interest will amuse you, my lord. My master has adopted the nomen of Flavius to celebrate his elevation to the rank of emperor. His men insisted and he agreed – with some pleasure.

I beg you to give my regards to Endellion and I ask you to assure her that I continue to take good care of my health. I hope you are also in good spirits and your family continues to flourish.

I remain your most loyal servant,

Aeron ap Iorweth

Secretary to Flavius Magnus Maximus

Caradoc was much amused by Aeron's sharp and sardonic inclusion. He could imagine the boy's voice as he drily proclaimed that Maximus had placated his troops by reluctantly adopting the nomen of Emperor of the Western Empire. Caradoc continued to chuckle and, eventually, his daughter came to him with a plea to read Aeron's missive, which she afterwards refused to return.

Six months passed and very little happened. Caradoc tended to worry and pace the forecourt at Venta Belgarum, while the servants and guards who inhabited the palace would laugh kindly at Caradoc's careworn face and his inability to keep still; but they appreciated his halls of justice where he dispensed the law to arguing farmers, citizens and warriors with fairness and blunt toughness.

Within months, Magnus Maximus had become a rather exciting memory, a dream, as was the time before the Roman when King Gwaun had judged their petty squabbles. These were the days of the Dumnonii king and the peasants hoped his benevolent rule would never end.

Across the Litus Saxonicum, deep into the landscape, the

warmer months were beginning to fade and Maximus realised his army must reach Parisii and defeat Gratian before the onset of the coming winter. The great forests of the province had been cut down for lumber during the time of Caesar, but pockets remained, as dense as in primeval times, so an army could surround Maximus and crush his fledgling force before he knew they were there. The army that had left Britannia had seemed huge at the time, but in these vast plains, cut by farms and long-civilised by the Romans, their numbers were dwarfed by the surrounding terrain. For a short moment, Maximus felt overwhelmed and lost sight of the throne of Rome at the end of his journey. The thread of his life trembled.

Then his hubris reasserted itself. He could not fail, as long as the stars shone and the moon rose at night.

Andragathius was instructed to send out scouts to reconnoitre the terrain ahead of them and to gain intelligence on the size and disposition of Gratian's forces. Maximus was aware that the Sequana River lay ahead and Andragathius's warriors had given him reports on Parisii and the Matrona River that fed into the Sequana.

Maximus's force made a cautious turn eastward when the leading troops made contact with a deep tributary that flowed down from the north. His scouts were fortunate enough to find one section that was sufficiently shallow for his army to make a crossing, but the need to secure the terrain on the distant bank and facilitate the movement of troops, horses and vehicles ate up valuable time. Maximus chafed with impatience, for he could feel time running away like dried sand though his fingers. The stress of maintaining an air of invincibility wearied him, but the troops took their lead from the Roman commander's inflexible face, so he made sure that he appeared to be on his guard and full of confidence.

That night, the army made bivouac in an area of heavy forest some little way from the small town of Lutetia. For security's sake, and until the scouts made their return, Maximus ordered his troops to camp without fires to ensure that the small town, whose lights were just visible in the distance, would remain ignorant of their presence.

The night was dark and the moon was hidden behind dense banks of cloud but, mercifully, no rain fell to make conditions difficult for the soldiers and warriors who were trying to sleep under the stars. With a single, shrouded oil lamp, Maximus pored over crude maps of the area as he searched for a suitable site on which to confront Gratian, but his head felt thick with an emerging headache and his eyes were gritty with weariness. He would have remained hunched over his camp desk for hours, but Andragathius slid into the tent.

'The scouts have returned, my lord,' he said. 'Do you wish to see them immediately?'

Swallowing an impatient retort, Maximus nodded and demanded a full report from them.

'Lord . . . Gratian's army has finally taken the field. They have set up camp to the east of Lutetia and are without fires to mask their size. However, we were in positions where we could overlook their bivouac and were able to make rough estimates of the size of their forces. We are outnumbered, probably two to one, but these calculations don't include Gratian's troops who are manipulating the siege machines. I formed the opinion that these devices will be useless to Gratian, if you can select the right terrain for the battle.'

'How many native centuries has Gratian assembled?' Maximus demanded. He knew that many were likely to change sides, especially if they hadn't been paid for some time. On the other hand, the elite troops such as the Roman Guard would never desert him if they had declared themselves for their emperor. Similarly, mercenaries such as the hated Alans, who had been conscripted into the forces of Rome, would remain loyal to the very end.

One of the British scouts gave a reckless laugh and stepped forward to speak. 'I estimated that there were near enough to five native centuries. I couldn't tell what tribe they came from, but they seemed well disciplined and competent when they prepared their bivouac.'

'Thank you, gentlemen, you may rejoin your troops.' Maximus's fingers traced his rough sketch of the land between his present position and Lutetia. Outnumbered and unfamiliar with the countryside, he had lost the advantage, especially as Andragathius informed his commander that a troop of Alan cavalry, the hated favourites of the emperor, had also been seen among the force deployed against him.

'I can depend on your *cataphractarii*, can't I?' Maximus demanded.

'Unto death, my lord – and beyond,' his master of horse assured him.

'Then rest, Andragathius! Tomorrow we finally go to war . . . and Fortuna will decide who takes the day.'

To Caradoc
King of the Dumnonii tribe, and Regent of Britannia
Hail and Blessings
I trust this missive finds you and Lady Endellion well? Please assure her that I continue to take care and I hope to see her very soon.

But I digress. This missive is to inform the kings of Britannia of the great news. Our High King is now the Emperor of the West in all but name. Yes, such an elevation is amazing, so perhaps Fortuna does choose her favourites. Maximus has rejected the old gods since his elevation, and has embraced his Christian background with a fervour that borders on obsession.

I speak frankly to you because I am reasonably certain that Maximus will not be concerned over the contents of this document. He trusts you implicitly and he is aware that correspondence flows between us from time to time.

At any rate, we waited for dawn in the forest north of Lutetia, which is less than an hour's ride from Parisii. I found myself sweating with nervousness. Gratian's army was very large, but many of its parts were tribal, including a contingent of cavalry that was almost exclusively Alan, the hated tribe that has won so much favour with him. The Alans come from the desert beyond the Middle Sea and the fertile rivers, the Tigris and the Euphrates, so they have little in common with us, except for their religion. They are almost fanatical in their devotion to the Christian God.

I have digressed again. Parchment is very valuable, so I will continue my tale.

Once the sun had crept over the horizon, we emerged from the forest and marched towards the enemy encampment, for Maximus had determined that he would prefer our enemy had the river at their backs in this largely flat landscape. Our army was very steady from the outset, with the Roman foot soldiers in the vanguard and our cavalry hovering on the wings on each flank. Maximus's strategy was clear and simple to put into effect. He would depend on his battle-hardened Roman soldiers to attack the centre of Gratian's less experienced troops, for fighting vicious enemies along a frontier, such as the north of Britannia, is far more difficult than keeping the peace in settled provinces such as Belgica, Celtica and Cisalpina. Then, according to Maximus's strategy, the wings of native cavalry would enclose and smash the enemy. The plan was solid and could easily have succeeded, but all such planning became moot. Fortuna had one more surprise for us all.

Caradoc put down the long densely written scroll. His old heart had stirred as he read the preliminary events leading to this major battle, but because of his aging sight he required the deepest concentration to do so.

The door to his private rooms opened with a clatter as Endellion rushed in like a small storm.

'Has Aeron written? I heard a courier had come so I hurried to discover if he carried any news from Gaul. Is Aeron still well? I've been ever so worried, Father, because I started having those dreams of hooded men being strangled with silken cords. I've become certain that disaster has been following the High King like a pestilence. Oh, please tell me.'

'Silence, girl! How can I read this scroll if you gabble at me like a vulgar fisherwoman in the marketplace?' He continued to grumble as he squinted at the letter and tried to make sense of the small, tight writing, until Endellion could no longer bear his slowness.

'Allow me to read the scroll, Father. Just sit back on your stool and rest because you'll probably need to explain parts of it for me.'

She took the scroll over to the window with her thumb

marking the spot where Caradoc had stopped peering at the document. Her heart in her mouth, she scanned the previous section rapidly, but then a slow smile gradually replaced the frown of just a few moments earlier.

Once she reached the desired part of the document, she cleared her throat and began to read in a clear and pleasant voice.

"'Maximus was eager to learn whether Gratian planned to use archers, so we halted about fifty spear lengths from the enemy. Most Roman commanders consider the bow to be a barbarian weapon, but Maximus has learned the tactical advantages of archery from his many years on the frontiers. We discovered quickly that Gratian had a small troop of archers but they were kept at the rear, mainly as a defensive weapon against our cavalry. Maximus immediately ordered our bowmen to advance to positions where they could defend our flanks and nullify Gratian's cavalry.

"'Both armies were poised like wild beasts that fight for the amusement of crowds. We waited for the order to attack, but the command never came.

"'Suddenly, the Roman soldiers at the centre of Gratian's army sheathed their weapons and lowered their standard. Then, using a white flag, they fell out of the ranks in disciplined rows. Several of their officers approached Maximus slowly as he sat astride his tall white horse, and they swore allegiance to him, declaring him to be the new emperor.

"'The remaining native troops were thrown into total disarray. Most surrendered their arms immediately, but the contingent of Alans stood firm. No man should question their courage, regardless of how roundly they are hated as a race. Maximus loosed his own cavalry to crush them, along with the bulk of his centre troops. They were ably assisted by those Romans who rebelled against Gratian, who annihilated the remnants of Gratian's army in short order.

"'Gratian was forced to flee the battlefield, in company with his senior aides and those confidantes who contrived to escape the slaughter that followed.'"

Endellion's voice shook. 'In my dream, I saw a man in a litter who had been gutted like a fish. He was wearing a purple toga so I suppose he was a Roman noble, but it didn't seem real. Now...'

'Yes, girl! It's all too real when it's written on parchment, isn't it? Read on, my dear! So far, our High King seems to have won a stunning victory.'

"'I was in the commander's tent when Maximus called his master of horse and two other cavalry officers into his presence. They were ordered to track down Gratian and return him to Maximus for punishment. If the emperor couldn't be taken alive, then my master wouldn't weep if his head alone returned to face the consequences of his actions. We heard no more of Andragathius, Conanus or Crucius, the third man, for many weeks.

"'We marched east towards Italia and the road before us was empty of any threat to Maximus. We paused at Augusta Treverorum and Maximus was briefly reunited with his wife. She is a great lady, but quite old and very grey. Surrounded by his daughters, his wife and his son, Flavius Victor, Maximus was suddenly an aging man in his fifties, well past the age of great deeds. I must admire my master for his power that charms us into believing that he is both young and a brilliant warrior, when I have never seen him raise a sword. How odd the power to charm can be.'"

425

'Read ahead of me, Endellion. I'd like to mull over Aeron's words before reading on. Your young man weaves a compelling story, and I'd swear he has something of the poet in his tongue and his fingers. I'm tired, my dear. If you can keep the scroll safe, I'll return to it in a few hours. For the moment, I must think a little and have some sleep.'

Augusta Treverorum was a small town where the church was the centre of daily life. Theodora, Maximus's Roman wife, was a woman of famed piety and discretion, but long years alone had worn her down, so that her thin Roman nose seemed even longer than he remembered. Maximus greeted her with wary affection, gripping her shoulders in a brotherly fashion and kissing her chastely on each cheek.

'I'm pleased to see you looking well and healthy, husband,' Theodora said bluntly in an aggressive tone that was unfamiliar to him. Maximus assumed that her new assertiveness had developed from the management role that she had been forced to maintain over his estates outside the town. She had also successfully married her daughters to men of significant status and substance, adopting the role of paterfamilias with consummate ease. Maximus tried hard to hide a twinge of irritation as she took control of the conversation.

'You also look well, my dear. As my letters indicated, your negotiations for the marriage of our daughter to Ennodius were skilfully handled.' He stumbled as he tried to remember which daughter had been married to the proconsul of Africa.

Had he been able to read Theodora's mind, Maximus would have been shocked. The girl who had longed for romance and who had fallen in love with a handsome Hispanic officer regretted her long celibacy. When she looked in her silver mirror, she knew that she was a dried-up husk of a woman who would never again experience the passions that had once flushed her handsome face with such rich colour.

He doesn't need me, she thought with some regret. He never has. But he's come to me because he's on the brink of becoming the emperor and he needs a wife with an impeccable reputation and lineage. She sighed.

'Any child of mine will be happy with her lot because she's been trained to understand her duty to her husband and her family. Still, I'm pleased that my girl is now in Africa with her husband. She will be safe there.'

'What does that mean, Theodora? Do you expect me to fail in my ambitions, now that I have so nearly achieved my goals? I can swear that I won't!' His lips twitched with a brief smile as he considered how out of place Theodora would be in the vast, echoing corridors of power in Rome.

'I'd expect you to succeed as long as you act in the best interests of the people of the west, your loyal followers and your family.'

'Spoken like a true statesman, my dear! You've said one thing, but you mean something quite different. Have I been all that unsatisfactory as a husband?'

Maximus exerted his charm to convince her of the purity of his motives. Yes, he needed her, especially considering the stiff-necked moralistic bastard who was sitting on the throne in Constantinople. Theodora had always represented the finest characteristics of Roman womanhood and Theodosius had always liked her.

Her stiff back relaxed a trifle, so Maximus took her hand, while ignoring her dry, papery skin and the first age spots that marred her flesh. Briefly, he thought of Elen.

Husband and wife had parted amicably, but warily. Pleading the need to be ready to march at short notice, he returned to the army bivouac on the outskirts of Treverorum. In a tent of significant grandeur that had once belonged to Gratian, Maximus consulted over his maps and documents as he tried to determine the best route to follow for his approach to Italia. He concentrated on the comfort of his army and kept himself apart from his family and the town dignitaries. Wisely, he ensured that all merchants were paid for food and supplies taken in his name, so that the citizens of the town lauded his forbearance. He won a large number of friends, simply by using Gratian's discarded war chest to pay for the needs of his army.

On a Sunday when the bells were calling the faithful to prayer, word reached Maximus that a small troop of horsemen was approaching the bivouac at speed from the south.

He dressed carefully, choosing full armour and his red cloak, for he felt the tide turning once more and sensed that Fortuna's eyes had focused on him again. He left his tent with his guard snapping at his heels with their usual strict discipline. Decius had spent days polishing armour and honing his master's weapons so that Maximus would appear like an emperor-in-waiting. The old soldier also ensured that the guard were as busy as he was, mending their cloaks and cleaning every inch of their accoutrements, including the armour of their horses.

'Our master is judged by you, lads, and by your discipline and appearance. Those fat-arses in Rome think we're all filthy barbarians. Which we are, but we don't have to look like them. A little elbow grease won't hurt us and our master will benefit from your appearance. Be ready, boys, for you can't know when a little play-acting might serve Lord Maximus well.'

When Maximus left his tent on that momentous day, the

guardsmen fell in behind him in perfect, shining rows, as neat and polished as parade-ground soldiers.

The small troop of cavalrymen approached the picket lines at a trot. The coats of the horses were running with sweat and foam marked their mouths and chests. The rest of their powerful bodies, their armour and their saddles were covered with dust from the roadway.

As the riders dismounted, Maximus tried to discern who they were beneath the thick coating of dust that covered them. One man took off his helmet and shook his head and Maximus recognised Elen's brother, Conanus. Then with brusque hands, the other officer took off his cloak and shook it vigorously until clouds of fine road-dust filled the air. Andragathius had returned at last.

'I assume you have found the erstwhile emperor for me, gentlemen? Where is he?' Maximus asked curtly.

Andragathius took a bag that had been looped over the pommel of his saddle. Maximus noticed that this side of the horse was caked with something sticky and was immediately alerted to the bag's gruesome contents.

'I have the honour, master, to introduce you to Emperor Gratian!' He abased himself to the victor of the Battle of Parisii as he dropped the bag's contents at Maximus's feet.

Gratian's head spun out from the leather container. Blood and serum had dried in the curled, foppish hair and the face still showed the grimace of fear and surprise that the emperor had worn when Andragathius had leaped out of a woman's litter that had carried the assassin to the flaps of Gratian's tent. In the blinking of an eye, a quick knife stroke to the emperor's throat, followed by another to the belly, left the emperor dying on the ground. Yet another knife stroke killed his closest guard who had been caught flat-footed by the ruse. Suddenly, Andragathius was wielding the dead guardsman's sword and the litter bearers had pulled out concealed weapons and attacked those servants and protectors who were within range of their murderous blades. Within a minute, the guards had thrown down their arms and begged for mercy. Gratian's corpse was lying in the dust, his blood running down a hollow on the roadway. He had been entranced at the prospect of a pretty face and a lush body, one of the oldest tricks used to snare men who possessed gross appetites for sex. Ultimately, Gratian had died because he was a voluptuary.

After removing the corpse's head, Andragathius had showed it to the one hundred men who had ridden off with Gratian, and then given the warriors the choice of making their way to Maximus's army at Treverorum or falling back to Rome and pleading for mercy from the senate.

'We don't care what you do. Our master will be coming to Rome anyway,' Conanus shouted, so all the enemy troops could hear him. 'You can choose to serve the new emperor or you can die on the outskirts of Rome. The choice will be yours.'

Then the officers and their two warriors had taken Gratian's horses and ridden away.

At Treverorum, Maximus tried to hide his excitement as Conanus bowed low and presented him with the golden wreath of oak leaves, which Maximus immediately placed over his short hair. Around him, his guard snapped to attention and the soldiers watching began to cheer, spontaneously uplifted by the thrill of the moment. Maximus raised his fist in salute, so the army cheered more loudly as more and more of the troops came running to join the impromptu victory celebration.

Once the melee had settled down and Maximus had returned

to his tent with his two officers in tow, he heard the story of the ruse that had taken them into the heart of Gratian's bivouac. He listened to their story of betrayal with obvious pleasure, but one question teased at his mind. 'How did you manage to meet up with Andragathius?' he asked Conanus. 'When you left the battlefield, you were heading in a different direction.'

Conanus had changed very little in the three years since Maximus had first met him in Cymru. His face was sullen most of the time, as if he resented most aspects of his life in the Roman army, yet he had volunteered to sail with his brother-by-law, even after his sister, Elen, had died. In truth, Conanus understood Maximus as few men ever had and he was sensibly determined to make a place for himself that was free of his father, the damp vales of Cymru and the brooding warrior-culture of the west.

'I followed Gratian's trail for some time, but I lost his spoor two days after leaving Parisii. However, I could tell he was heading east at some speed, so I followed in the same direction. I eventually heard word of him at Alesia where one old man agreed to speak with me, after some encouragement, about Gratian's escape route.'

Maximus avoided asking about the fate of the old man and urged Conanus to continue.

'I was advised that Gratian intended to turn south and head towards Lugudunum once his column reached the Rhodanus River. We hurried after him, although we seemed to be heading away from Italia. Nevertheless, we persisted. Gratian was leaving a trail of unpaid and frightened peasants behind him, as well as ravished women, so we knew we were hot on his trail. At the same time, I realised then that I hadn't given any thought to how we would separate him from his large guard after we caught up with him.'

'Was he at Lugudunum? That's a major centre.'

'No. Gratian had already departed by the time we arrived, but I learned that Andragathius had followed Gratian's trail by a roundabout route that started near Parisii. We caught up with Andragathius in the river valley. He was chasing after Gratian when the emperor made a run toward Gallia Cisalpina. This escape route would have taken Gratian through the mountains and into Italia. From there on, you know what would have happened.'

'You've always been a clever and sneaky bastard, Conanus. That idea of taking him for a fool with the litter was a stroke of genius.'

'Thank you, master. I've learned a great deal since entering your service.'

The two kinsmen circled each other like wolves and watched every movement and expression in their battle for ascendancy.

Maximus knew that this conflict had to be won without violence, so treachery must play no part in Conanus's demise. He must be left alive until such time as Maximus was safe. Both men smiled at each other and pretended they were playing a harmless game, but the battle for the purple was heading towards its ultimate conclusion.

'"In Treverorum, Maximus planned to push us towards the frontier, passing through Alesia and Lugudunum and heading towards Gallia Cisalpina. Through the impossibly high mountains, a pass led to the river lands of northern Italia, so our master decided this would be our route. Each day, he scanned the roadways to the south and the east, hoping for signs of movement – anything that indicated that Gratian had been found.

'"When his scouts had not returned, Maximus worried

constantly and pored over his maps and plans every evening. So we were all very relieved when word came that some of the scouts were returning on the southern road to Treverorum.

"'Andragathius and Conanus had stumbled across each other during their search for the fleeing emperor. I had been instructed to carry a message to Maximus's wife during the afternoon when they returned from their mission, so I was absent from the camp and I missed the presentation of Gratian's head and crown to our king. However, our king took great pleasure in telling me the whole tale of Gratian's assassination in all its gory detail. Maximus even removed the head from its bag so I could examine it, and I was surprised by how ordinary the features of the dead emperor had been. Even his brow was surprisingly low, although I would never suggest that this part of his physiognomy was a sign of Gratian's lack of intellect. My master had made no attempt to clean the head, so it stank of corruption and the thick, congealed blood that had dried in the head's snake-like curls. I swear, my lord, that Maximus gloried in the condition of that head and the crown that came with it, which he rarely took off for that whole afternoon.

"'I expected that we would stay in Treverorum, now that Maximus had achieved his purpose, but our king was like a horse, freed from both saddle and bridle and now able to run where he chose. No human hand controlled the reins of Maximus's actions. The king ordered camp to be struck the next morning and we made haste directly towards Italia.

"'We reached Lugudunum with Maximus's usual speed, where we learned that Gratian's son, the second Valentinian, had fled by ship from Italia, obviously bound for Constantinople. Anyone but Maximus would have permitted Valentinian's mother and his siblings to depart with him, for the boy emperor was only twelve. But our ruler is not a generous man, so he couldn't permit the fledgling heir to the throne to foment revolt from across the sea. By his actions, I learned much about our High King's character, for he rewarded Andragathius by sending him to Massilia. Andragathius's orders were to take ship immediately and head for the Ionian Sea to block Valentinian's escape. Few of us believed that Andragathius could succeed in this endeavour, considering he was so far behind Valentinian's ship and would need to sail around Italia to reach Valentinian's departure point. But Maximus was determined and Andragathius always obeys his master, even at the risk of his own life. Such blind loyalty is a little frightening, when examined closely. Andragathius's devotion is complete and unthinking. He never asks for explanations: he simply obeys.'"

'Father?' Endellion paused in her reading, looked up from the parchment and bit her thumb in concentration. Caradoc smiled to see his own affectation repeated by his daughter.

'Yes, lass? What troubles you?'

'Who is this Andragathius? I don't remember him among Maximus's warriors, and you've never mentioned him as one of the High King's confidantes.'

'I recall him dimly, from Maximus's second campaign in the north. He was a fellow Hispanic and distinguished himself by obeying Maximus's orders with no regard for his personal safety. You would call him an ugly man, Endellion. I remember very startling amber-yellow eyes and a scar from a sword cut that crossed his face from ear to ear, a wound that left his nose misshapen.'

'He sounds like a loyal subordinate, Father, but I still can't recall him. Maximus always chose officers who were of use to him. I regret sounding critical, but the High King was your oldest companion and still conspired to use you. At least your thoughts were your own, so Maximus valued your advice. This Andragathius seems to be a follower who cannot think for himself.'

Caradoc sighed and smiled. 'All true, daughter, but I can't help liking Maximus, despite his flaws. He never tried to hide what he was, so I can't make the excuse that I didn't know his intentions.'

'So this Andragathius is a tool, nothing more,' Endellion decided with youth's arrogance. She sought out her place in the parchment.

'As are all servants of the great ones, my dear. We'll find that Maximus will prove to be a great ruler. For my part, I prefer to be a man rather than a god or a hero.'

Endellion stared at her father for a moment, but he had taken care to hide his eyes from her acute gaze. Thwarted, she read on aloud.

'"My letter grows over-long.

'"We have reached Mediolanum in the rich lands that are crossed by the great rivers in northern Italia. Our master is waiting outside the city for a company of priests and Roman aristocrats who wish to parlay with us. Everyone in camp is on edge, although we pretend that we fear nothing while we follow Magnus Maximus, the rightful master of Rome and all her provinces. I am a little afraid of our situation, far from the sea and many miles from friendly faces, although our army has swelled with recruits who have come from all over Gaul and Hispania. They give us hope, for the empire has been needful of change for many years, as it groans under the arrogance of Gratian's Alan allies.

'"We have heard that an army has been hastily cobbled

together under the command of a general from Constantinople called Flavius Bauto, a kinsman of Theodosius. Ambrose, the bishop of Mediolanum, has also put himself forward to broker some kind of compromise that will satisfy Theodosius and Maximus, but rumour whispers that Theodosius is under attack on his northern borders and will probably try to make a treaty with our king, if Maximus is inclined to be reasonable.

"'I fear that reason is one word that Maximus refuses to recognise.

"'Maximus has asked me to record all the discussions with Ambrose, so I must cease writing this missive at this time and arrange for a courier to forward the scroll to you.

"'Be sure that I will honour my friendship with your daughter and, if I should survive this campaign and return to my homeland, then I intend to ask for her hand in marriage. I hope you will look favourably on this union.

"'I remain your most loyal servant,
Aeron ap Iorweth
Secretary to Flavius Magnus Maximus'"

Aeron's letters raised more questions than they provided answers, so Caradoc suffered fits of curiosity and dread that made him feel ill when he tried to understand. Did Maximus rule in Rome? Or had his ambitions come to nothing in Mediolanum? The silence was grim and complete. Both father and daughter watched the road from Portus Adurni for any sign of another courier, but no more long and informative parchments came, covered economically with spider-fine black Latin so that not even a tiny portion of the valuable space remained unused.

Nor did gossip filter across the Litus Saxonicum to warn them what had befallen Maximus and his army. The world, it seemed, conspired to deprive Caradoc of information. So, with nerves stretched, he waited impatiently for any news, any information at all that would end this agony of indecision. Spring passed into an oppressive summer, and autumn arrived with good harvests.

In Caradoc's hall of justice, traders still squabbled with citizens, questions of inheritance caused family disputes and arguments over property boundaries occupied much of Caradoc's time as he exercised his conciliation and arbitration skills. The servants of the hall at Venta Belgarum became accustomed to the wakefulness of their Dumnonii master, so the patterns of waiting became normal in a world that would never again be wholly settled or fully comfortable.

BARBARIAN INCURSIONS
INTO NORTH-WEST BRITANNIA

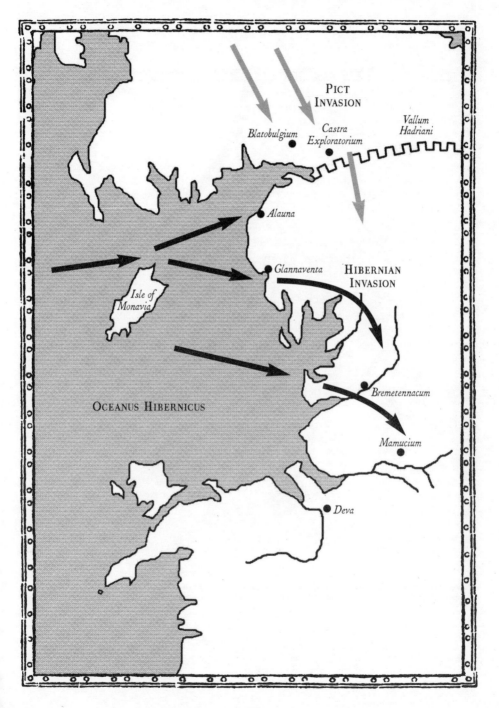

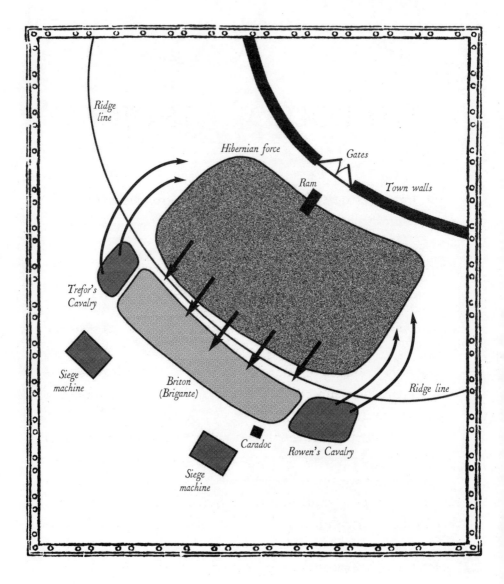

Ridge
line

Hibernian force

Gates

Ram

Town walls

Trefor's
Cavalry

Siege
machine

Briton
(Brigante)

Ridge line

Caradoc

Rowen's Cavalry

Siege
machine

CHAPTER XX

THE ROLL OF THE DICE

On him does death lie heavily who, but two well known
to all, dies to himself unknown.

Seneca the Younger, *Thyestes Chorus*

Six months of silence followed the delivery of that very long
missive that had set his daughter to weeping and fits of crazy
happiness by turn. Six months with no word!

The days stretched on and another year came. With the spring
weather, the Picts and Hibernians took advantage of the Roman
absence to set the north-west coast of Britannia aflame.

The Picts burned the towns and villages between the walls, as
they continued on their murderous way until their arms could
barely lift their weapons. Their enmity was fuelled by hatred and
revenge, because the blue-tattooed warriors could never forget
that Roman Britannia had once been their home. The heat of
their resentment had never cooled, although centuries had
passed since the Britons had first begun to drive them northward,
and then the Romans had penned them beyond the Vallum
Antonini. Now, Castra Exploratorum and Blatobulgium were

burned to their foundations as the Pict army swept over the Vallum Hadriani and flooded into the wealthy flatlands.

Meanwhile, the Hibernians had been biding their time. The narrow straits of water that separated their homeland from the fat towns of the Brigante tribe were easily crossed by the raiders. Using their ungainly ships, they ranged up and down the central coast where they sacked and destroyed churches, monasteries and nunneries, targets which were notoriously easy prey because the religious communities were unwilling and unable to protect themselves. Alauna, Glannaventa, the island of Monavia and as far inland as Bremetennacum and its convenient river all felt the scourge of Hibernian attacks.

But Caradoc had not been idle. Although his time as a warrior was over, his skills as a strategist had saved Deva from being sacked when he levied the tribes of Britannia from one end of the land to the other and led a relieving force against the invaders.

Caradoc's considerable powers of persuasion forced the tribes to deplete their already dangerously low reserves of warriors. He would have taken old men and boys into his army if he had to; always pragmatic by nature, the king knew that half the success of any battle was based on the size of the army that took to the field.

Meanwhile, he sent a courier to Maximus, explaining bluntly that the situation in Britannia was grave.

To Flavius Magnus Maximus
High King of Britannia and Master of Gaul
I extend my greetings and salutations to my Master and Friend on your successes in Gaul.
Unfortunately, your old enemies have seized the

opportunity made by your absence to ravage your kingdom. The damned Picts and Hibernians have robbed your cities, towns and villages of your gold and taken many of your citizens as slaves. Your return is vital, if there is to be anything of Britannia left for you to rule. Our need is urgent, as I am only one old man and I fear I am no Magnus Maximus.

Your daughter, Severa, thrives and is well.

I trust this missive finds you successful and happy, but I wish I could send better news that will speed you home.

As always, I am your loyal servant,

Caradoc,

Regent of Britannia, and King of the Dumnonii Tribe

With his old bones aching from the rain and cold air, Caradoc observed the still-smouldering outskirts of Mamucium. His army had headed at speed for this industrial complex after the Hibernians mounted a major attack on the lightly defended centre in their search for an easy victory over the Britons. Now, trapped within the walls of their town, the British tradesmen, metal-workers and citizens waited for the inevitable breach of their defences and the reprisals that would soon be inflicted on the population.

Although Caradoc had almost killed his rag-tag army during a forced march to the town, his inexperienced warriors had no time to rest and recuperate. To make things worse, continuous rain had fallen throughout the whole journey and his men were bedraggled, hungry and miserable. As he and his officers stood on a small hill overlooking the township, the cold downpour showed no signs of stopping.

Thick, sticky mud made any movement slow and difficult. To

fight in such conditions was tantamount to breaking the swords of his tyro troops and sending them unarmed against savages who lived by the fruits of rapine, pillage and murder. Throughout that first night, Caradoc puzzled over the terrain, struggling to find an edge that he could exploit.

Initially, the only advantage that his army had over the Hibernians came about through a conundrum that the raiders had inflicted on themselves. They had not expected Caradoc's relieving force to arrive so quickly, so they found themselves sandwiched between Mamucium's protective wall and the encircling relief force and thus forced to face their British enemy on two sides. Not that the Hibernians were particularly worried. So far, they had experienced little opposition and the absence of the Roman army emboldened them.

Meanwhile, inside the low walls of the town, the population had been given new hope by the arrival of the British column, though their plight remained dire. Rocks, hot oil, sewage and well-aimed arrows were rained down on unprotected Hibernian heads with renewed catcalls and raucous jeering.

But the Dumnonii king remained patient, although the novice warriors in his force were eager to charge directly at the raiders and blood their swords for the first time. Fortunately, Caradoc's head was cooler and his views prevailed. The impasse that followed their arrival was broken by occasional skirmishes and much shouted name-calling, but the weather ensured that the two armies must wait for a more auspicious day before battle commenced.

'The old fox is up to something,' one white-haired grandfather muttered as he leaned on his spear. 'Caradoc has never done anything that wasn't aimed at victory.'

'How would you know, old man? Caradoc lets old farts like

you come on these jaunts so he doesn't feel so ancient himself.' The younger man who spoke was heavy-set and mature, but walked with a limp. In the past, such a warrior would have been rejected because of his disability, but Caradoc was desperate enough to take any volunteer who could carry a sword.

'When I fought at Anderida with King Llew, I weren't much younger than I am now, so don't take my white hair for any indication of my sword play. I came out of that charnel pit alive and I tell you that Caradoc doesn't fight until he finds a lever that will give him an edge. He's a leader with respect for the lives of his men.'

'Aye. But if we aren't prepared to fight, those Hibernians will burn Mamucium to the ground,' the younger man retorted. 'The old king is the regent for Macsen Wledig, so he's still in command. His pride won't let him lose, but he's become very cautious in his old age. He knows that the time is fast coming when his army will be forced to fight.'

'Damn! It's raining again and the mud's just getting stickier. Caradoc won't attack the Hibernians while the weather's against us, unless he's got some secret plan. But, then again, them raiders won't be too interested in crossing swords with us.' The old man winked and pointed to four heavy wagons that were slogging through the sticky terrain towards the British camp. 'Those wagons might explain why we've been sitting on our arses for two days.'

'What are you talking about?' the younger man snapped as his eyes scanned the draught horses that were straining between the traces. Whatever was carried under the oiled covers was extremely heavy.

'I saw two couriers ride out at speed before we were even halfway to Mamucium. At the time, it were long before we knew that the weather weren't going to break. I wondered what Caradoc needed from Deva that was so important. I've been thinking on it, and I'll bet my left ball that those wagons contain some of them siege machines.'

'Siege machines? Are you wanting in your wits, old man? The Hibernians aren't under siege.' The younger man prodded at the mud with the shaft of his spear.

'But they would be, if Caradoc tried to encircle them raiders,' the old warrior replied dourly. 'Of course, we'll probably be dead if they were to attack our piddling little army before we were ready to contain them.'

'We'll see what happens, old man,' the limping warrior snapped. 'You might be right, but I doubt that Caradoc is daft enough to bring large siege machines into this much mud.'

As the miserable day continued, Caradoc's warriors realised that the old man had, in fact, been so wanting in his wits that he had sent for two of the Roman siege machines that were stored in Deva. Apart from ropes, these machines required little maintenance, but they had been unused for almost a century and few men were familiar with their workings. While there were some doubts as to the king's sanity, he had given a great deal of thought to their usefulness in the coming battle.

The old man had sent for the weapons as soon as his forward scouts gave him a description of the barbarian siege that was building at Mamucium and the terrain that surrounded the town. Fortuitously, the commandant in Deva had anticipated the Briton's needs to perfection and had despatched two of the smaller machines, catapults that could be easily manoeuvred by a squad of two engineers with forty warriors to provide the manpower. Now that the machines had arrived, they could be assembled on the lee side of a low hill that hid them from the prying eyes of the Pict warriors.

The two additional wagons contained extra rope, spare parts and a supply of nails, scrap iron and timber, ammunition that would be invaluable when the battle commenced.

A night of frantic energy followed the machines' arrival at Mamucium. Only two men among the warriors in Caradoc's command laid claim to any knowledge and understanding of their assembly. To make matters worse, it soon became evident that the two young engineers had exaggerated their own skills.

During the wet hours that followed, the pair tried to make sense of the complex siege machines. Caradoc became an essential presence at the site, for he provided the clear thinking and logical thought processes needed in the absence of drawings or plans. Eventually, by trial and error and the expenditure of much imagination, the two catapults were finally assembled. Then, as morning came and Caradoc ordered the covered torches to be extinguished, he prayed to God that this gamble would actually work.

As the dawn brightened, the old king ordered that a trial should be carried out. With their metal baskets filled with heavy stone and small lengths of timber, the engineers test-fired the machines in directions that couldn't be seen by Hibernian observers. Caradoc had no intention of giving advance warnings to an enemy who believed that the Britons feared their superior numbers. Worse still, advance knowledge could allow the Hibernians to mount a pre-emptive strike.

At first, the catapults failed to fire. One collapsed when the ropes winching the basket frayed and snapped; the load tilted as it fell, so one unwary warrior was crushed under heavy rocks.

Like an angry snake, the traitorous length of rope sliced through the air and cut more men down in its wake.

Ignoring the recriminations and human damage, Caradoc instructed his men to replace all the aged ropes with spares. Part-way through the process, the second catapult was found to have a broken wooden strut, so timber reinforcing was bolted onto the wooden crosspieces and, for added security, the king ordered metal braces to be fixed to the frame.

As the work progressed and his men learned to treat the catapults like dangerous and unpredictable animals, Caradoc occasionally stared down the road towards Deva.

'If this war was a Greek play, the gods would send Maximus down the road with reinforcements at the very time when my spirits are at their lowest ebb,' Caradoc mused to himself. 'But today isn't a Greek play.' He took pains to check the mechanisms of both catapults closely before proclaiming himself satisfied.

The time had arrived to draw together the various elements of Caradoc's plan. First, small trees and shrubs, scrap timber, straw, old tents and anything that could provide traction over the mud must be laid along the paths that the machines must follow as they were dragged up the rain-sodden incline.

'You understand your orders, Huw? The Brigante volunteers are ordered to position themselves halfway up the hill, with their weapons facing towards Mamucium. They are tasked to protect the siege machines that will be on the top of the hill behind them. The Hibernians will be forced to fight their way up the slope when they mount their attack. Position a cohort of our southern troops, under your command, behind the Brigante to reinforce the entire line. Our numbers are limited, so I'm hoping that the Brigante warriors can hold their own.'

'I live to serve, King Caradoc,' Huw replied with a cheerful grin. As one of Caradoc's most loyal followers, the king could depend on him to carry out his instructions.

His next set of orders were for Trefor and Rowen, who had been given command of the two cavalry columns on the left and right flanks of the main defensive line. 'Your warriors must understand that their role is to encircle, contain and funnel the enemy towards the centre of our defences. The Hibernians must be massed towards the ridge line where they can be crushed by the siege machines in a confined space, whether they like it or not. Finally, the cavalry must cut down any raiders who try to escape from the trap.'

Both officers nodded and headed off towards their respective wings, both exuding confidence as they sauntered away.

As they set off, King Llew joined Caradoc, but his expression reflected his confusion.

'The walls of Mamucium will provide the rear of our trap, Llew,' Caradoc explained. 'The raiders will see our troop movements along the ridge line and will realise our numbers on the ground are stretched thin in the centre. They will consider that we are vulnerable at this point, so they'll mass for an attack on the narrower parts of our defensive line at the centre, expecting us to mount a counterattack from the wings and the flanks. We'll do exactly that, but we'll do it at a time of my choosing. Do you have four sensible young lads who are fleet of foot? They'll be needed to relay my orders at speed to our commanders on the front lines.'

Llew stared out at the proposed field of battle and he noted the Brigante foot soldiers as they moved into their defensive positions. From his position on the ridgeline, Caradoc observed the first part of his strategy set in train as if he was some kind of god who could stare down at the living chessboard of the grimy town and the two armies jockeying for position in front of the town gates. Once the central troops were in position, he ordered three of the couriers to run to the front lines to inform the commanders that they could anticipate an enemy attack once the first siege machine was fired.

'Boy,' Caradoc ordered the fourth lad, who was barely twelve years of age. 'Tell the Roman officers at the catapults to move them up onto the ridgeline. Run!'

The lad sprinted down the slope of the hill to where each of the catapults was standing on its wheeled chassis.

Caradoc was fascinated by the ingenuity of the teams whose sole task was to position the catapults, for he knew that victory would ultimately depend on them. Mercifully, the hill's gradient was slight. Brute strength, determination and stubbornness won the day and, eventually, the catapults were ready.

The moment they were, the excited courier was instructed to relay Caradoc's order that the catapults should be anchored to the earth with ropes attached to sharpened stakes. Stripped to the waist, men laboured under a pale sun that had emerged from behind clouds, Caradoc watching as his orders were obeyed. The baskets were filled and prepared for firing.

As they massed before the city gates and stared up at the ridgeline, the Hibernians could clearly see the huge, insectile forms with long legs that were poised to leap down on them.

'On my order – fire!' Caradoc shouted.

The levers and ropes were released and the rubble sailed into the air in a high arc to smash into the very edge of the raiders' position, scattering those men who remained untouched.

'Calibrate the sights so the target is moved four spear lengths to the right. The range can remain the same as the current setting.' Caradoc issued his orders without taking his eyes off the milling and disorganised raiders whose mass seemed to be swirling aimlessly at the town gates.

Reloading was faster than he had expected, for the crews became more and more adept as they familiarised themselves with the complicated firing mechanisms.

'Fire at will,' he shouted, and then the real carnage began.

Caradoc had an intimate knowledge of war, but he was unprepared for the damage that catapults could inflict on human beings. Men died in ugly piles of smashed flesh. When old chains, nails, timber spikes, scraps of iron and shards of broken pottery were added to the rocks in the baskets, these manufactured missiles stabbed, speared, impaled and lacerated the assaulted flesh that had once been human bodies.

Confused, maddened and terrified, the Hibernians attacked the centre of the British line, but such was their fear and confusion that the raiders seemed unable to develop a concerted assault that would maximise their numerical advantage. From his vantage point, where the catapults continued to rain their murderous fire into the melee, Caradoc was amazed to see that his barrage had suddenly turned the Hibernian attack into a complete rout. Only later would he discover that three of the Hibernian commanders had disobeyed every law of battle by standing arrogantly together to discuss various aspects of the British lines and the coming battle. They had been cut to pieces in the very first volley.

Leaderless, the raiders finally used a large wedge of men to press against the elongated line of Brigante warriors, causing it to bulge ominously. Another courier was despatched immediately to Rowen, who was ordered to use his cavalry on the left flank to charge into the press of men. As confusion reigned and the raiders moved away from the town gates, the catapults ceased to rain death down on the enemy. Their bloody work was done.

The battle seesawed back and forth, but the Britons had the advantage of a cool brain atop the hill. The end had never been in doubt from the time that the catapults came into play and the enemy commanders had been killed in the first sortie. Arthritic, aching and sick at heart, Caradoc presided over the victory with cold mental strength, but his personal vitality had been eroded. Cold and shivering, he huddled into furs brought by Llew's men, for he refused to leave his command post until the Hibernians were dead or had escaped towards the sea.

Later, he was carried from the field because his legs would no longer hold him upright, leaving Llew to assume the duties of the victor and preside over the grisly clean-up. Caradoc had achieved his last miracle. But still Maximus did not come.

Although the battle against the Hibernians was decisive, the Picts continued to rampage unchecked throughout the north. Britannia was teetering on the edge of defeat.

The courier rode two of his three mounts to death as he hastened north to Deva with a message for the regent. Mud-splattered and swaying with exhaustion, he could barely lift himself out of the saddle on arrival, but to fail in this task was unthinkable.

Caradoc was abed and fretful from a bone-deep weariness. Weeks in the saddle and constant exposure to the elements had taken an inevitable toll on the old king's reserves of strength, so he yearned for the luxury of complete rest. Tintagel was a distant dream, something barred to him because of his foolish devotion to what he saw as his duty. He faced the wall in misery, while his head was elevated on pillows in an attempt to ease the strain on his aching lungs. His pain was such that he cursed the day he had invited Magnus Maximus into his home and into his heart. Endellion met the courier at the entrance to the villa where Caradoc was ensconced, having reached Deva with Severa, for whom she had become a surrogate mother.

'I will take you to the regent but your message had better be important. He's been ill and I'm reluctant to disturb him.'

The courier bowed so low that his plaits almost swung to the tiled floor.

After he had scrubbed off the worst of the mud that spattered his face, she led him to Caradoc while issuing ultimatums along the way.

'My father is just beginning to heal, so don't tire him out. He's an old man who has just fought a hard and hazardous campaign against our Hibernian enemies, so he mustn't be disturbed. You can be assured that I'll become very angry if you distress him.' With a flourish, Endellion opened the door to the sickroom. Caradoc looked up from the scroll he had been trying to read.

'It's an honour to stand in your presence, Regent Caradoc. My name is Glanmore ap Niall, once of Gwent, but now the personal courier for Emperor Maximus of the West. I bring you his warm greetings and his thanks for your efforts on his behalf. He bids me to tell you that he will be arriving in Deva by ship within days, if the good Lord so wills it. His troops are already marching overland to scour out any threats that might exist within his kingdom.'

'Emperor? At last! So my old friend has achieved his heart's desire after all this time,' Caradoc murmured. 'Endellion, fetch some wine and food for our young friend. He's famished, and he must be weary if he's ridden all the way from Dubris in such miserable weather.'

'Father?' Endellion tried to interrupt and ask about Aeron, but her father hushed her by placing one swollen forefinger over her lips.

'Enough, young lady. Where are your manners? Young Glanmore is obviously exhausted, so you must remember the rules of courtesy.'

'Of course, Father. Excuse me, Master Glanmore. I will return with refreshments in just a moment. But, please, can you give me some word of Aeron?' Although her speech was conciliatory, her eyes flashed lightning bolts towards Glanmore ap Niall in an obvious desire to know if her man was in Maximus's boat and heading for Deva. The young man responded with an an apologetic smile.

'No, mistress. Aeron has been ordered to remain in Treverorum to finish a series of important scrolls.'

Endellion's face fell and she had to stifle a sob.

'But he told me to tell you that his feelings have not altered and he will come as soon as Maximus agrees to release him.'

Endellion ran from the room with her face buried in her skirts.

Caradoc immediately sat up in his bed and impaled Glanmore with his dark eyes.

'I haven't heard a word from Maximus for nigh on eight months and that message was old when we received it. Quickly, young Glanmore! How did my friend become emperor?'

'Firstly, Your Highness, you mustn't be deceived by his new title of Emperor of the West. My master, Flavius Magnus Maximus, is angered by his newly negotiated position, but Emperor Theodosius himself offered my master a working compromise that couldn't be refused. Maximus's lines of communication and supply were overburdened and he could see that any further engagements in Italia might last indefinitely, especially with Emperor Theodosius's tacit support for the claims of the boy-emperor, Valentinian.'

Caradoc nodded. He knew that compromise and consensus were sometimes thrust upon unwilling leaders, who occasionally must accept that half a loaf was better than no bread at all.

'Anyway, the Empire of the West was ultimately divided in two. Predictably, Theodosius lost nothing, while Valentinian relinquished those parts that were slipping beyond his control.'

'So the plot between the two emperors was successful, although Maximus did gain at least half of what he had originally desired,' Caradoc said reflectively. 'They have treated my friend like a simple, ambitious and vulgar servant who is grasping for a position that is far above his station. Am I correct? Let me guess at the lands that were ceded to Maximus. Gaul to the lands of Germania, plus Hispania, Britannia and selected parts of Africa: those sections of the Empire that are already under threat or are largely agricultural in nature. Except for the odd lead, silver and gold mine, little of great worth has been lost. The frontier is expensive to guard, so Maximus has been being treated as Theodosius's fool while Valentinian retains Italia and the riches of Africa. Does Maximus understand what his kinsman has done?'

Glanmore's face flushed an ugly shade of beetroot.

'After the initial elation, Maximus realised that he was very much the junior partner in this triumvirate of emperors, and was secondary to a boy of tender years. He's not happy, but he has spent the best part of this year shoring up his borders, developing useful trade and military alliances with his near neighbours in Germania and creating a court of justice in Augusta Treverorum.' The young man flashed a deprecating smile. 'Yes, the town has been renamed, just as Maximus has adopted the new nomen of Flavius to reflect his newfound position.'

'Is all well with the native troops? I often think of my Dumnonii volunteers and how they fared once they left their homeland.'

'Aye! They do well, and they now possess lands of their own in Gaul. The native troops have been given the lands known as Armorica, which men now call Brittany in the local tongue, although that language might not last too much longer.'

Glanmore noticed Caradoc's raised eyebrows, so he hastened to explain.

'Conanus has sent the young lords of Britannia to lands which have been equally divided between the tribesmen who served under Maximus. The men have been encouraged to wed local girls, but Conanus is a stern and embittered man who seeks to create a new Britannia in the old lands of Gaul. I can't say I agree with his brutal methods, even if they are successful.'

At this moment, Endellion entered the room with Severa running along in her wake. A servant followed, carrying a loaded tray that held beer, platters of cold meats and other delicacies, all designed to tempt Caradoc's indifferent appetite. Endellion poured the beer and filled plates for each man while little Severa looked at them all, wide-eyed.

'Please continue, Master Glanmore. I'm very sorry to have interrupted you.'

'Conanus's solution isn't a fit topic for the ears of ladies,' Glanmore began hesitantly.

'Don't pay any mind to my daughter. I'm happy to say that she's as tough as my old riding boots,' Caradoc urged. 'How does Conanus hope to end the use of the local language?'

'Why, he simply ordered that every woman who marries into

the tribes will have her tongue removed. As women usually teach their children to speak, our language will quickly become the dominant language that is spoken in Brittany. Those servants who refuse to speak our language will also lose their tongues.'

Even Caradoc was struck dumb by this brutal and simplistic solution to the problem, so he rapidly changed the subject. 'What does Maximus require of me?'

'He requires a detailed account of the disposition of the tribes of Britannia, their effectiveness and your plans for the future of these lands. He sent me in great haste so you would have a full report prepared by the time he arrives. The emperor wishes to return to Gaul as soon as possible, so he plans to crush the Hibernians and the Picts so profoundly that they will think twice before they attack again, even if he must pursue them into their homes.'

Caradoc nodded slowly, while Endellion's expression was thunderous. In Maximus's place, Caradoc would require the same information, for more than two years had elapsed since he had last been in Britannia. 'What changes has Maximus wrought in his new lands?' Caradoc asked mildly. 'I always believed that he would make an effective emperor.'

'Aye, he is!' Glanmore said enthusiastically, pleased to have avoided any further contentious subjects. 'He has made a number of treaties with most of the northern tribes who had cherished ambitions of invading the Roman lands. As friends, these tribes have now been drawn into Maximus's kingdom and have provided several centuries who serve in his armies. Trade links have also advanced the interests of the barbarian tribes and the minorities in Gaul, while Hispania and Britannia are expected to pay less onerous taxes for protection. Maximus has enforced order along the frontiers, and has reorganised the provinces as part of this imposition of order, rewarding the native troops who have shed their blood for the empire. In a short time he has become a popular ruler, even within the ranks of religious zealots, for he has taken pains to protect the church from charlatans.'

'I'm amazed,' Caradoc admitted. 'Maximus never seemed very religious to me.'

'Aye! But he takes his position as the titular head of the Church very seriously. He has executed one group of heretics who used so-called magic to strip the credulous of their coin. Maximus discovered that this trickery was based on ventriloquism. Some of the churchmen disapprove of his methods, but my master is the very first emperor to execute felons for heresy against the Church.'

Glanmore was having difficulty keeping his eyes open now that he had eaten and drunk his fill. When he stifled a jaw-breaking yawn for the second time, Caradoc halted the conversation and insisted that Endellion arrange for the courier to be taken to a warm bed.

Later, Endellion returned to her father's room where she discovered he was alert and a healthier shade of colour had returned to his face.

'Can you believe it, Endellion? I'm not surprised by Theodosius's chicanery, although Maximus's position must have been tenuous if he so readily accepted their offer of compromise. However, the successes he has gained have given me some hope. Maximus may yet save the west from the barbarian threats, if he can convince the British tribes of the north and the north-east to accept a role under the rule of a high king who would ensure their long-term welfare. He may still be our saviour.'

'I hope you're correct, Father, but I'm amazed that such a man could accept the poor bargain that leaves his ambitions in the hands of a boy. I hope you're right.'

'You're speaking my secret thoughts aloud, Endellion. Could Maximus accept half of the Western Empire? And could he effectively rule his kingdom from Augusta Treverorum rather than the Palatine? I've never seen either place but Maximus's dreams were always bigger than one man's body could contain. I must be old and near to death, my dearest, because good news makes me afraid. I believe I'll pray on this matter before I sleep on it.'

Endellion stared at her father with alarm. Perhaps he could feel that death was approaching and his work was not yet completed.

'Sleep now, Father, for tomorrow you must prepare your responses to our master's request. I'll send a scribe to you as soon as you have broken your fast in the morning.'

You'll soon see your friend, Father, so rest well, she thought to herself. Perhaps Glanmore is wrong and Aeron has come to Britannia with Maximus. I hope so. If he has come here, I'll do everything in my power to ensure that he stays with me for ever.

Where he can come to no harm, she added. But she lacked the courage to speak aloud, for her father had enough worries without her weird and formless fears for the future.

But I am afraid, her racing mind continued, once she was alone in her room. There's a smell of blood in air, and I sometime wish my father had never met Magnus Maximus.

Outside, a fresh sea wind came with more rain in its wake. As the first drops began to patter on the roof, Endellion heard the voice of the Mother speaking to her.

'It's too late,' the voice cried. 'Far too late!'

She buried her face into the bedclothes and tried to sleep.

* * *

Three days passed and the weather steadily worsened, despite a general understanding that spring was supposed to be a time of clear skies, new growth and rebirth. Under leaden skies and gripped by unseasonal cold, Deva shivered and sniffled, so its inhabitants avoided the streets.

In the fine villa loaned to Caradoc by grateful citizens, the hypocaust ran night and day to warm the cold tiles and create a pleasant fug of steam in the baths. Caradoc's lung infection improved markedly, but it left him with a nasty headache and a red nose. His swollen joints caused him considerable pain, although his daughter pressed small doses of poppy juice onto her patient to ease the crippling agony. The old man prayed for warmer days but, as time drifted by in illness and inactivity, his temper was sorely tested.

The galleys came at noontime, swooping along the river with a deadly grace. Five of them rounded the bend in the river and their oars drove them, straight and true, towards the docks and the amazed crowd that quickly gathered.

'Maximus has returned,' the whispers began and soon swelled into a roar of relief and excitement. 'Maximus has returned and our troubles are over.'

As the galleys approached the wharves, the oarsmen were ordered to reverse their strokes, a movement which acted as a brake and permitted the vessels to slide seamlessly into their berths. These graceful manoeuvres seemed to have been made without effort, but those seamen among the observers understood the discipline, training and expertise required. No sooner had heavy ropes tethered the leading galley to the mooring rings than an imposing figure in a familiar red cloak leaped onto the wharf with athletic grace.

Those citizens who saw the emperor on that memorable day would later swear that he appeared taller, stronger and more impressive than mere mortals. His hair was grey now, but it only added to his dignity without any suggestion of aging. His easy movements were free and youthful and his muscle tone remained supple.

As soon as the galleys began to disgorge men, supplies and the emperor's horses, Maximus stepped forward to greet a welcoming committee of nervous councillors and Roman officials from the garrison, all of whom were resplendent in their togas and chains of office.

'Welcome back to Deva, sire,' the chief magistrate proclaimed in an anxious rush. 'The citizens wish to offer their felicitations on your well-deserved elevation to the throne and to express their gratitude at your return. They also wish to express their hopes that you will drive the Pict usurpers from our lands. Thanks to Regent Caradoc, we have survived attacks from a large force of Hibernians who were eventually destroyed in a battle at Mamucium. King Caradoc has been our saviour and led our forces to a great victory, but he has been ill in recent weeks. In his absence, King Llew of the Dobunni tribe leads the combined forces of Britannia's tribes against the Picts. Our northern enemies move further south with every passing day, but we hope that your arrival will see them sent back to their hovels in the north – never to return.'

Maximus broke into the magistrate's elaborately constructed speech with obvious impatience and demanded to be taken to Caradoc's villa.

Endellion, with Severa holding her hand, met the emperor at the forecourt of the villa. The little girl, now a happy four-year-old, was very shy and appeared to be younger than her years. Her small, triangular face was plump and a little vacuous in expression, a mask that the young girl could hide behind.

As Maximus strode towards the waiting ladies, Endellion eased Severa into an awkward curtsy. 'I bid you good day, Majesty. I am Endellion, daughter of King Caradoc. This young lady is your daughter, Severa, who has come to meet her papa.'

Maximus was bemused for a moment, but then he bowed cursorily. 'I have heard much of you, Lady Endellion, and I can now understand why your father has always guarded you so zealously. I would like to compliment you on taking such excellent care of my daughter.'

'Such duties are hardly onerous, Your Majesty. Severa is an intelligent, pretty and good little girl.' She turned to face the young child. 'Welcome your father, Severa,' Endellion ordered kindly, because she could feel the child's terror through the vice-like grip of her hand.

The child curtsied again. 'Welcome, Father,' she whispered. Maximus also bowed, obviously feeling on edge in the presence of this child who represented his complex plans to win the purple. As he looked into her frightened eyes, he remembered the expression on Elen's terrified face when she had been beaten. Could the child in the womb identify the hands that gave out such pain to the mother that had carried her? The emperor felt a frisson of superstitious anxiety.

He loathed feeling guilty, so his manner became increasingly forbidding. Sensing his mood, Endellion called Severa's nurse to take the child away to the nursery while she conducted Maximus to Caradoc's bedchamber. 'My father is still very weak, Majesty, so I beg you to remember that he has spent his strength in your service. He won the field in your name at Mamucium with a heavily outnumbered force. He was forced to fight with an army of tyros and old men. Unfortunately, the rigours of conducting the campaign in terrible weather conditions left him with a weak chest and severe pains in his joints. He's been prepared to serve you to the death, my lord, for he has always been your most loyal friend.'

Other than a tightening of his short upper lip, Maximus was silent, so, thoroughly rebuffed and put in her place, Endellion led the emperor and his guard to Caradoc's door.

'I wish to see my friend alone. Wait outside,' the emperor ordered his guard – and Endellion. Then he opened the door without knocking and closed it firmly behind him.

Inside the airy room, Maximus put on his conciliatory face, smiled and advanced with his arms outstretched to show his affection. In response, Caradoc smiled with sincerity, although Maximus failed to recognise the reserve in Caradoc's expression and body language. He inquired briefly about Caradoc's health before giving praise to his regent for the decisive victory at Mamucium.

'You always were a fox, Caradoc. The Hibernians must have been amazed when they saw the two siege machines on the ridge above them. I can't recall those catapults having been employed in living memory. Anyway, who'd have thought to use such weapons against an aggressor? They're meant to batter down walls and defences, not strike down massed groups of warriors.'

'They did very well against human flesh,' Caradoc answered and watched his friend's face as he laughed at the regent's black joke.

'I'd like to have your assessment of the situation,' Maximus ordered, having been in the room long enough for the niceties to have been covered.

Caradoc complied succinctly, while presenting Maximus

with a section of parchment at the end of his report to confirm the details he had provided. Because of the scarcity of parchment in Britannia, Caradoc had ordered one of the missives from Gaul to be scarified and scraped clean, which allowed his priest to use it as a totally new document. He resented having to use such a precious material for something that was essentially a memory guide for the emperor. But he knew his friend all too well; the discussions would have been interminable without a written record, because Maximus was pedantic and questioned and probed at every discussion point.

'I've heard of your successes in Gaul, my lord,' Caradoc said carefully. 'It seems as though your gamble was successful, at least on the surface.'

Maximus nodded. Some refreshments had been delivered to the room, so he did the honours, pouring wine into the glasses provided.

'You've achieved your ambition, my lord, and few men can boast of such achievements.' Caradoc's grin belied his inner caution. Perhaps his friend would soon be forced to enter another world that was far removed from Britannia and the Britons.

As Maximus considered his answer, Caradoc realised that their fleeting moments of honesty had been rare, but the emperor had never been capable of anything more intimate. The Dumnonii king was the only man who had ever breached Maximus's preternatural reserve, even if only momentarily. For the first time, Caradoc felt genuine pity for this powerful and uncompromising man who never accepted his own inadequacies.

'Theodosius trapped me,' the Roman finally admitted, and Caradoc realised how hard these words were for a man like Maximus to admit.

'Theodosius has trapped many brilliant men over a long period of time. He's survived and prospered in Constantinople where he is surrounded by men who would assassinate him in an instant. I can still recall the execution of his father, a man who could truly boast of raw strength and ability. The son overcame that disaster to become Emperor of the Eastern Empire in his own right. There's no shame in being outmanoeuvred by such a consummate survivor.'

Caradoc tried to be gentle, but every word seemed to drive a nail into Maximus's heart.

'I could see his intention from the beginning, but my hands were tied. His own empire is vast and he has massive armies at his call. My forces will always be limited because of the nature of the frontiers and the need to be constantly on my guard against invaders. Young Valentinian was sneering at me, even as we stripped away half of his kingdom. I was nothing but a posturing fool to him – yet my birth outranks his and Theodosius's. There's no chance of a workable triumvirate developing on such a shaky foundation. I had hoped for more, but they have no respect for me. And I have none for them!'

'So? Does it really matter what they think of you? They'll change their tune when the Dacians or the Huns attack their borders. Sooner or later, Valentinian will have to eat dirt to get your help. You know what I'm saying is correct, so you have to let the petty insults float over you. You've handled far worse.'

For the life of him, Caradoc couldn't explain why he spoke so passionately to his friend. Maximus's expression was dour and he remembered how often the Roman had complained of being overlooked for promotion. These old angers continued to fester; Caradoc could recognise the burning hurt and dissatisfaction that lay within him.

Once again, Maximus changed tack.

'At any road, my old friend, I'm working on a solution to the problems of reigning inside a triumvirate.' His wolfish smile seemed to split his face. 'Don't look so alarmed, Caradoc. I'll only be shaking up the insulting complacency of Valentinian and his advisers. Mind you, I'll probably be shaking up Theodosius as well. I have some useful allies in the north who might provide some surprises for him.'

'You must beware, Maximus,' Caradoc warned. 'Rome has survived because it has a structure that has lasted down the centuries. It would be very hard to overcome the obstacles that would be placed in front of you. Even the rank incompetence of Gratian couldn't bring the city down. Any man who tried to take her would feel the weight of a thousand years of history collapse on him. You don't know the terrain of Italia, because no attacking army has set foot on its soil for many centuries. Please don't tempt the fates, Maximus! I have very few friends in this world and I'd like to keep the ones I have.'

'Don't worry, Caradoc. I don't plan to invade Italia. I'm not an idiot, so I would never act until I was absolutely certain. But before I can do anything in Rome, I have some Pict warriors to slaughter along my northern borders.'

As the Roman continued to scan through the parchment, some forgotten detail reasserted itself in his memory. His brow furrowed.

'Caradoc? May I ask another favour of you? I trust it won't be too onerous.'

'The last time I agreed to assist you, I ended up as a regent and acting as the High King of Britannia,' Caradoc laughed wryly. 'Very well! Ask away!'

'Decius has come with me, but he's very ill. I believe he's

dying. I couldn't refuse him, because he'd have tried to follow me by himself and he'd have perished in the wilds of Belgica. Would you be prepared to care for him here until such time as I return?'

Caradoc's breath caught in his throat. Maximus was speaking of Decius as if he was a faithful old dog who'd become a nuisance. Yet Caradoc was almost certain that tears threatened to spill out from behind the emperor's traitorous eyes.

'Of course! Decius is a friend, and he will always be welcome in my house.'

'Good! Good!' Maximus surreptitiously wiped his eyes when he thought his friend wasn't watching. 'I'll send him on his litter this evening.'

Nothing more on the topic of Decius was said; a long discussion on the current campaign followed, during which Maximus picked his friend's mind clean of every piece of useful information. Only when the emperor had left the villa to make his preparations for his journey into the north did Caradoc have any real opportunity for reflection.

The evening began to lengthen. Caradoc staggered out of his bed and cursed his weak legs and the pains in his ankles, before pulling on a robe and taking up the sturdy staff that Endellion had found for him. As he gripped it with both of his crippled hands, he reflected that the simplest dexterity was beyond him. He thought of Decius and was saddened.

He was forced to order several servants to leave him to his own devices before he reached the forecourt and the small orchard of fruit trees below it. He sought out a stone seat where he could watch the sun on the horizon, hear the din of warriors from the roadway beyond the villa walls and smell the fruit blossoms in the sweet night air. Such a scene of peace should have eased his worried mind but, instead, it provided an ironic backdrop to his doom-laden thoughts.

The clouds were edged with fire as the sun approached its full extension. Why was Maximus so obtuse? He had an opportunity to create a huge empire, one that would be mighty in the future but, instead, he looked backwards and yearned for a throne that had lost its validity. Caradoc had never seen Rome and he had no desire to visit its seven hills. All that he had been told, and all that he had seen of invading barbarian tribes, told him that the Roman world was heading towards its death knell. If the emperors refused to adapt to the new world, they would be swept into the past.

Could Maximus succeed in his crazy quest? He would try. But Theodosius would never permit such an attack on the status quo to be successful, and Maximus would go into the shades.

No! If Maximus attempted to attack Rome, he would inevitably fail. And if he failed, the world of Britannia would shudder to a stop. There would be no going back and the life that Caradoc loved so much would be finished.

As pink and white blossoms fell about him, Caradoc considered the strange nature of love. He didn't love his wife, or even either of his sons, although he was very fond of them. Only Endellion had shown him what love could be.

Likewise, his Roman friend had wed twice and had fathered many children, but he had never demonstrated love for any of them. Only Decius, a worn-out decurion who had served him for decades, could draw a tear from the hard heart of Magnus Maximus.

'What fools we are,' Caradoc murmured. 'We live without the warmth of human contact for so long.'

The sun sank below the horizon and the light began to fade.

But Caradoc continued to sit quietly in the encroaching darkness. His mind was leached of all thought as he absorbed a beauty that he could barely see.

The darkness was complete when Endellion's servants finally found him and returned him, kindly but firmly, to the prison of his bed.

THE BATTLE OF THE SAVE

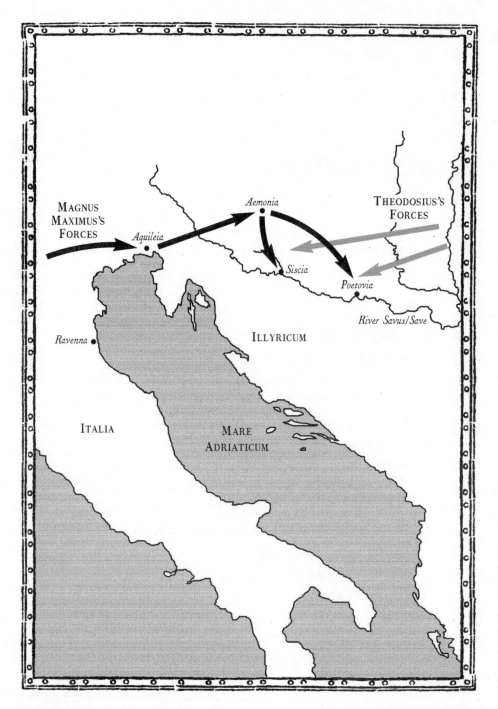

MAGNUS
MAXIMUS'S
FORCES

Aquileia

Aemonia

THEODOSIUS'S
FORCES

Siscia

Poetovia

River Savus/Save

Ravenna

ILLYRICUM

ITALIA

MARE
ADRIATICUM

CHAPTER XXI

THE SCORPION IN THE NEST

A man's character is his fate.

Heraclitus

The months and years were running quickly together as the tide of human affairs ebbed and flowed while Caradoc continued to sicken. Decius had travelled back to Tintagel with the Dumnonii king, for he stubbornly refused to die until his master returned from his travels. Nothing had been heard of Maximus, or Aeron, and no more long letters had come either to trouble or ease the minds of those who waited at the fortress. Endellion grew pale from the many duties and concerns that occupied her, in addition to caring for two old men. Meanwhile Severa began to grow tall and willowy, and traces of her father could be seen in her wilful strength of purpose. The little girl took to spending her hours with Decius, who told her many stories about her father and her mother.

Endellion spent her free time in her father's rooms. His body betrayed him gradually, but his mind remained sharp and, when he was awake and in his full wits, father and daughter would speak quietly together about any number of topics. Both cherished these intimate and intensely-private times. Endellion would read to Caradoc from a never-ending supply of manuscripts; sometimes she managed to beg, borrow or steal a manuscript that was totally improper for any young woman to touch, least of all to read. In the long evenings, she would occasionally speak with Decius and she observed his stubborn hold on life; something of Severa's obsession with the old man had captured Endellion's empathy.

'Can't you see, Endellion?' Caradoc asked. 'God has sent Severa to Decius to give some meaning to the last dregs of his life. Meanwhile, she learns all the good, the brave and the noble in her father's history. Yes, Decius no doubt makes his master seem a far better man than he could ever hope to be, but think about the situation in which she finds herself. She has no mother, no father and no kin, now that Meriadoc is dead. Kynan is far away in Brittany, so he will never return to these lands. Without Decius, how would she have learned the history of her family? Who would give her a sense of belonging?'

Endellion was struck by Caradoc's explanation. She had never possessed a mother, but she had never felt the lack because Caradoc had told her everything she had ever wanted to know about Saraid. Once Caradoc went to the shades, she would be as alone as Severa.

'Yes, Jesus has sent Decius to give Severa a special gift. I can see that now.'

As he slept under his furs in the snug heart of his fortress, Endellion looked down at her father's shrunken form and knew she was presiding over the death of one of the great British kings. She understood that others would come in the future to rival Caradoc's achievements. However, few would be as reasoned or as tolerant. Where Caradoc had walked, life had flourished. If he killed, he did so with cold precision and without the rejoicing that some men felt. Whether history remembered him or not, a man such as Caradoc would remain rare.

'Why are you spending so much time with a husk of a man? You're young, Endellion, and I'm poisoning your youth.'

Caradoc's voice was so faint now that she could barely hear him and the huge bones of his face had pushed through his age-thinned skin, so that only his spirit seemed to light him from within. She kissed his hand and he felt her silent tears on his skin.

'I can't rest if you won't go outside and spend some time in the sunshine. Fetch me some wildflowers and return to tell me everything you've seen that interests you. I long for the open air. I also hunger to go riding, but I know such pleasures have now gone forever. Please obey me, daughter. After all, I'm not likely to run off in your absence.'

'You would, if you could. You'd order one of the servants to carry you outside and they'd obey anything you asked of them.'

'I promise that I will obey, but only if you'll agree to rest and spend a little time walking along the clifftops. Would that be an acceptable bargain, Endellion?' Endellion knew she was being outmanoeuvred, but she ceded the field of battle to the old campaigner and promised that she would stroll along the cliffs.

On the sheer precipices of the mainland, the long grasses had been flattened by the winds that blew in from the ocean. Yet wildflowers still nestled among the grass, where they were protected by the long, hardy fronds. She set to work and quickly gathered a large bunch of them, filling the basket that she had hooked over her saddle.

Then, in the beauty of the soft, warm afternoon, she rode down to the causeway and dismounted. The tide was out, revealing shiny-black rocks, limpets and small stretches of sandy gravel, where seagulls squabbled and fought over tasty shellfish morsels. Endellion sat on a drying rock and watched their antics for several minutes. Then she clambered down onto the narrow beach, tied up her skirts and began to hunt through the crevices and spaces under the rocks in the hope of finding something unusual that would amuse her father. Pieces of timber, splintered remains of ships, had found their way onto the shore, reminders of human frailty in the face of the ocean's eternity.

Several broken shells came to light, but Endellion discarded them as being too damaged. She discovered one rock pool that was protected by a small crab, which she eventually caught and moved into another pool so that she could search through the dark recesses of its home for sea treasures.

Her strong fingers explored deep into the rocky extremities of the pool and, finding nothing, she continued to rake through the sand and the pebbles. The waters clouded immediately, but she suddenly felt something hard as she probed with her forefinger, and managed to get a grip on a smooth, egg-shaped object. Elated, she drew out her prize.

At first she believed she had found a pretty pebble, except that something about its slick surface was unlike that of any she had ever seen. She held the object up to the light.

Unlike normal stones, even fragments of quartz, it wasn't quite opaque. With the light behind it the stone was a pale, crystalline green with dozens of tiny bubbles trapped within its depths. Endellion turned it again and again until, partially obscured by the strange bubbles, she discerned a minuscule leaf buried into the stone's heart. The tiny veins, the vivid green of the upper side of the leaf and the silver of its underside, told her immediately that what the sea had given her was a plum-sized egg of green amber.

Her heart beat quickly and she would have returned to Tintagel immediately, but her curiosity impelled her to search a little further. She discovered no more pieces of the rare amber, but treasure trove still existed in the pools. The skeleton of a fingerling, still intact; an unbroken, brown and white shell scraped clean by the waves; a single, stained tusk as long as her hand and, finally, a piece of driftwood tortured and shaped into a spiked crown by wind and water were retrieved by her busy hands. Eventually, satisfied with her search, she took all the trophies back to the fortress. Her legs were very weary by the time she reached the forecourt, but she had little time for weariness. Caradoc was waiting.

The long twilight filled Caradoc's room with a soft glow. Light bounced off the waves and limned the underside of the low clouds that filled the western sky, while Caradoc had arranged for a silver mirror to be mounted so he could observe the world outside the unshuttered window. As Endellion entered the room, her father was turned onto one side so he could watch a group of fishermen at work. Once their fine nets had sunk to the bottom, the two men in each boat would draw up the load of captured fish by hauling on ropes attached to the weighted outer edges of the nets.

'Look, Endellion. They've caught a bumper crop of fish.' Her father knew she was there, although he hadn't turned his head to acknowledge her presence. She went up to the end of his bed and gazed out of the window at the wild scenery below the ramparts of Tintagel.

Because of the shape of the bay, the causeway and the headland, the waters were often very rough and dangerous, especially when strong, offshore winds blew. The local fishermen were always alert for changes in the weather; rips and rogue currents were known to drag careless fishermen far out to sea, a journey from which they would never return.

On this day, the waters were relatively calm. But, despite this, the catch that was dragged into the boat was landed with much more difficulty than usual. This exceptional cast of the net would provide the fortress with food for many months to come, Fortuna having favoured the fishermen for one particularly auspicious afternoon.

Endellion placed the wildflowers she had collected during her stroll in vases, then seated herself on a stool beside his bed and offered her trophies, one by one, to her father. Caradoc's eyes sharpened with pleasure and he handled each still-damp object with surprising dexterity.

Each item received his full attention, but Endellion had left the amber egg until last. As soon as she placed the cool shape into his hands, she saw Caradoc's face begin to glow with genuine appreciation as he raised the egg up to the window so that the setting sun could illuminate it from behind.

'You're a truly fortunate young lady, daughter. Green amber of this size is very, very rare and to have a leaf trapped within it? . . . What a wonderful prize! How did you find it?'

The story of her discovery, and their discussion on the quality of each item, took up the entire space between dusk and darkness. Caradoc listened like a child, asking the occasional question that helped him to visualise the place where the amber had made its final home.

'I'll have an exceptional jewel made from this stone so that you'll have something special to remember me by once I make my final journey to the shades,' he told her. 'Leave your gift from the sea with me and I'll return it to you shortly.'

Endellion obeyed and another day sank into the sea in the strange and surreal silence that had ruled over Britannia since Maximus had ridden away a year earlier.

In the dead hours before the dawn, death comes quietly to carry away the souls of the sick and the feeble. On this night, Severa wakened, teased by an awkward presentiment of trouble, before hurrying down to Decius's room.

The old man was barely breathing so, panicked, the child ran pell-mell to fetch Endellion. A quick glance at his blue lips and nails and the slowness of his breathing told Endellion that the end was in sight.

With Severa's aid, Endellion carefully lifted him so that he was almost sitting upright.

Decius opened his eyes as they raised him. He stared into one of the dim corners of the room and moaned in alarm. Severa gripped his hand tightly.

'So . . . it is true,' he panted. 'The dead come . . . to take . . . their killers . . . into . . . the darkness.'

'Fear no dead men or frightening tales, Decius. You have acted with honour for all of your life. You'll be judged by that honour,' Endellion whispered in his ear, and watched as his panic settled.

'No!' Severa moaned. 'Please don't die, Decius. Who will talk to me about my father? Who will care for me?'

'Lady Endellion . . . will do all . . . that's right.'

He seemed to sleep for a few moments and then, just when

his breathing slowed dangerously, he snapped awake again. Severa dipped a piece of cloth in cool water and raised it to his mouth. The ancient, wizened lips sucked weakly on it.

'Lady, will you pay . . . the Ferryman for . . . me?'

'Of course, Decius. All will be done as you would wish.'

'Tell my master . . . to beware. Tell him . . . I loved him like . . . a son.'

Endellion promised to do so. Then, without fanfare or trouble, Decurion Decius, Roman officer and loyal friend, died with a smile on his face.

In the silence that followed, Severa burst into tears. Endellion embraced the child with all her strength.

'Hush, Severa. You owe more to Decius than weak and sickly tears. He would want you to ensure that he goes to his gods like a warrior and a man, rather than a helpless weakling. He was a warrior, so you must take the place of your father, his leader and master.'

Severa had learned much at Decius's bedside. Her small hands tried to tear her robe from neck to waist in the old expression of grief. Endellion had to help her.

'What must I do for Decius?' Severa asked.

'Go and find your nurse, the cook and the other serving women and tell them that Decius has died. Ask them if they will lay out our friend.'

'What will they do to him?'

'Why, they'll wash him and clean him, and then brush his hair to make him look his best. After that, we will place some coins in his mouth that will be used to pay the Ferryman, so he can cross the River Styx and enter the shades. You can help, if you wish. I know Decius would be honoured for your help.'

Comforted, Severa considered what had been asked of her. Then, with a silent nod, she trotted from the room.

Endellion sighed in distress. She found that she was weeping, less for Decius than for Caradoc, who was also close to eternity. Then, in case Severa should catch her with red eyes, she pulled herself together and began to straighten the soiled bed.

Tegan Eurfron passed Endellion in the corridor the next morning, after visiting her husband just before dawn. Her face had long submitted to age, assisted by a perpetual frown of dissatisfaction.

'You, girl! How is the king really faring? What does he speak of when he's rested? I can't get a lucid word out of him, so I've come to think that he's deliberately ignoring me. Oh – I told him about that old Roman's death. He was quite upset.'

Damn, Endellion thought to herself. This stupid woman hasn't an iota of tact or common sense. But now was hardly the time for an argument.

'He's quite worried, Your Highness. He fears for the future of his tribe if Maximus should fail in Gaul, emperor or no. Also, he was very fond of Decius, so his death has come as a shock. I believe my father is forcing himself to stay alive until he hears word of his friend's exploits in Gaul.'

'Surely not! Caradoc has never been maudlin before,' Tegan Eurfron frowned, and then remembered how worry could cause lines on her face. 'Please inform me if there is any change in his condition. His family should be at his side if his health worsens.'

'You'll be the first to know,' Endellion agreed, but she would have preferred to keep his family as far from Caradoc as possible. They always managed to upset her father, but the queen and her sons had an expectation that they would care for him at the end of his life. Up until now, the family's many duties, and their belief that Caradoc would live for ever, had allowed Endellion to spend as much time in her father's company as she wanted.

Two days later, after Decius's body had been laid out in Tintagel's chapel, a courier arrived and demanded permission to see the regent immediately. Endellion would have refused, but a small voice in her head warned her that such an act would be a betrayal of her father in every way.

The courier was exhausted. He was also carrying a wound along the shoulder of his sword arm and was brusque to the point of rudeness.

'I have come, sire, at the bidding of Aeron ap Iorweth, who wishes you to understand the situation in Gaul.'

In response to Caradoc's brisk nod, he accepted a glass of wine to wet his throat.

'My master, Maximus, invaded Italia last year in the summer. He quickly took Mediolanum and imprisoned the bishop, who remained loyal to Valentinian. We were heartened by the ease with which we defeated the local troops, so Maximus planned to extend his land grab as soon as winter was over. The weather was particularly harsh for months, but I've come to believe that we should have taken the initiative and marched on to Rome. But Maximus had already planned his attack strategy in full. We threatened Rome yet did not take it, a feat which was well within our power.'

'Explain!' Caradoc panted, breathing so heavily that Endellion insisted on raising him in his bed with extra pillows and dosing him with a little herbal stimulant before the courier was allowed to continue.

'Maximus has divided his army into three parts, but he still commands the larger part of the force. His brother, Marcellinus, commands a small, mobile force that Maximus has tasked to harass the enemy before the larger force makes contact. In this way, Maximus can assess their strength and their responses. At the same time, Maximus's fast cavalry has been placed under the command of Andragathius, who has vowed to smash any force that moves against his master.'

'Where is Valentinian?' Caradoc asked, his mind still working like the commander and strategist that he had always been. 'Has he holed up in Rome?'

'Not he! We caught up with him at Mediolanum, but he managed to break free and escape with a fast troop of guards and ran for Ravenna. According to our scouts, he travelled through Illyricum to meet with Theodosius, who has offered him assistance and vowed to protect him from all harm. Maximus is furious, for he has lost the initiative. However, he was still holding his ground when I was instructed to travel to Tintagel at speed. Perhaps he will cross Italia and enter Illyricum to confront his enemies.'

Caradoc visibly winced at the suggestion.

'Why have you come to me?' Caradoc asked, knowing that Maximus must be in a desperate situation to warrant a request such as the one that was coming or he would not have sent a courier on such a dangerous mission to Britannia at a time when he was fully engaged in a complex battle for survival in Italia.

'The Franks, under the command of Marcomer, have picked this time to foment a rebellion in Northern Gaul. They have put Maximus's supply lines, his rear and the flanks of his army under threat. This situation cannot be allowed to continue. I have been to Armorica and Conanus has sent his remaining reserves to the northern frontier, although most of his men had already left with Maximus's main force. We are in desperate need of your help. Any troops available must take ship for Gesoriacum immediately. They must assemble and march to Nemetocenna, where they will join with Conanus's forces and send the Franks back to where they came from. We need one thousand men – immediately!'

Caradoc snorted with disappointment and anger.

'Look at me, young sir. I am unable to feed myself, let alone hold a sword or mount a horse. How could I raise a force of warriors from my sick bed?'

The courier, Varrus, set his face into stern lines. 'All men listen to Caradoc. Not all your young men went with my master when he departed Britannia after killing the Picts. You have sons and you can send messengers to the other tribes to levy an army. I have been instructed to demand that you call your eldest son and do as I say. Your loyalty to your High King is being tested, King Caradoc.'

'Leave me be, while I consider this matter,' Caradoc ordered in a voice so faint that only Endellion could hear him with ease. 'Daughter! Send for Cadal and Cadoc! Meanwhile I will think on what has been said.'

'But, sir. I don't think you recognise . . .'

'How long has it been since you left Mediolanum, Varrus? At a guess?' Fuelled by his anger, Caradoc's voice had gained a little strength.

'I left in the spring, at a time when my master was making plans to march towards Aquileia. I have been seeking aid for my emperor for more than ten weeks.'

'Thank you for your truthfulness. Now, leave me to think and to speak to my sons. Endellion? Show this young man to his accommodation, and we will speak further on this matter in the morning.' Caradoc paused. 'One more question, young man! Did Maximus ask after Decius, his servant?'

Varrus looked puzzled, as if he had no idea who Decius was. With a little prompting from Endellion, however, he finally recalled the existence of the old decurion.

'Maximus's old servant? He made a nuisance of himself when he insisted on continuing in the service of my master beyond the time when he was still of any use. Why would the emperor ask after him?'

Caradoc looked pained, but Endellion permitted herself a mirthless smile as she ushered Varrus out of the king's bedchamber.

'No reason at all, Master Varrus. No reason at all,' she answered him, before shutting the door firmly in his face.

'You can see in that young man's attitude the best and the worst of Magnus Maximus. *Out of sight is out of mind!* So, as much as it pains me, we will act in a similar fashion. It's time now for the Britons to plan for their own survival.'

Caradoc refused to say another word, so the courier was forced to accept Endellion's hospitality until such time as the king informed him of his decision. Endellion sent word by servants to fetch Cadal and Cadoc, and ensure that they presented themselves to their father in his rooms.

Before Endellion permitted them to enter, she explained the situation to them, especially Varrus's demands for troops to relieve Maximus's northern frontier from the threat of a Frank invasion. She also explained the manner of Decius's death, and how Maximus's indifference to the loss of his servant had upset their father.

'Your father will want to discuss his decision with you before he makes it, my lords. He's near to death and the worry alone could kill him, if he becomes overexcited. I've given him as much stimulant as I dare. The healer explained to me that too much would likely bring his diseased heart to a stop. I've also fed him poppy juice in his wine, which has made him very tired. Rest would help him to survive this shock, so don't keep him awake for too long. Varrus will have to wait for an answer – I don't think he's earned the right to ask anything of us that we don't wish to give.'

Cadal pressed his sister's hand and found that it was trembling. 'Thank you for taking such good care of Father and protecting him from this courier. It's a pity that I wasn't present, for I'd have thrown him down the steps to the causeway if he became too obstreperous.'

Endellion allowed the two men to enter their father's apartment. She followed them and stood in one of the corners while Cadoc searched for more oil lamps and used his flint to strike a spark and set the wicks alight.

Caradoc awoke with a jerk. Endellion moved straight to his side, lifting his frail body so he could sip at the cold spring water with which the fortress was blessed.

'So you've come, my boys. Has Endellion told you what that damned courier demanded of me?' The two younger men nodded and the king sighed with satisfaction.

'I won't permit either of you to travel to the continent. Nor will I countenance more of Britannia's precious youth spilling their blood in Gaul and Italia to win a throne for another man. Many years ago, Endellion's mother warned me that this day would come and that I must resist all blandishments to strip our land bare of the last of our warriors. Varrus will have my permission to enlist any Romans who wish to travel to Gaul, but I'll not allow him to recruit British warriors to his cause.'

This long speech exhausted the old man, who coughed weakly until Endellion gave him a little more water.

'Maximus made a command decision to march towards Illyricum, which is in the north of Greece, boys. There's no reason you should have to live and die in these foreign lands, nor any logic that could persuade me that any of my young men should perish in outlandish places so Maximus can achieve the throne on the Palatine.'

'Surely the people of Britannia owe something to the High King, especially if he is in personal danger?' Cadal stated. Caradoc realised that his son's sentiments were those of a loyal man who had known Maximus since the long-past battle for Anderida.

'I'm forced to make a decision, my son. Should it be Maximus or Britannia? We've given all we can to Maximus's cause, without stripping the tribes bare. To send more of our men to die in places that are far removed from their ancestral lands would be a fool's errand, one that would damn us to a slow decline until the Picts, the Saxons or the Hibernians finish us off. No, Cadal, I will not do it. After all, what would Britannia gain for such a sacrifice? Very little, as far as I can judge.'

The following morning, Caradoc said as much to Varrus, flanked by his sons for support.

'My loyalty and my duty must be to my lands, my tribes and my kinfolk. You are free to petition the tribes yourself, if you so wish. You won't receive any interference from me, but I'll not send a single man across the Litus Saxonicum for doubtful reasons.'

Varrus was furious beyond any thoughts of self-preservation. His intemperate words washed over Caradoc, causing the old king to wince, until Varrus found a new coin in the pouch attached to his belt. He threw it down onto the table, where it rolled to a shaky stop near Caradoc's hand. The king picked it up and stared at the face of Maximus that had been impressed onto the coin.

'Keep the image of your one-time friend to remember what he looked like before treachery brought about his demise. It's a silver coin of value, so it will pay for whatever food and drink I have consumed in this place. I'll leave now and I'll not wish you a good day.'

As Varrus stormed out of the fortress, Caradoc sat in his chair and turned the silver coin over and over with his fingertips. The profile of Magnus Maximus looked out at the world, as young, as vigorous and as indomitable as he had been when Caradoc had first met him at the top of the cliff stairs at Fortress Tintagel.

'Pray Maximus isn't finished. Pray that he prevails over Theodosius because, without him, we may be lost.'

Cadal looked down at his father's face and, for the first time in his life, saw that his father was weeping.

'You will take my place at the interment of Decius, my son. He asked Severa if he could be buried on the headland overlooking Tintagel, so he can remain on guard while he waits for the return of his master. I've ordered that a monolith should be brought from the broken cliff face near the village to mark the last resting place of a brave and dutiful servant.'

Cadal felt ill from his recognition of his father's impending death. He cursed Varrus and he would have cursed Decius, but he saw the respect and misery on Caradoc's face. He slowly nodded.

'Aye, Father. I'll ensure that your orders are carried out in accordance with your instructions.'

'Remember too, Cadal, to bow your head to the decurion. Decius was a true man.'

Time passed as slowly and as ponderously as the indrawn breath of a dying man. Tintagel held tight and prayed for the peaceful passing of its old king. In her ceaseless efforts to protect him, Endellion became so pale and thin that it seemed as if the next strong wind might blow her over the battlements.

She looked out over the road leading down to Tintagel for so long that she no longer bothered to scan its empty, dusty spaces. Autumn had come and winter was sniffing at the heels of hurrying farmers who were trying to complete the harvest and prepare the fields for the spring that would follow. Long-dead grass crackled under her boots when she walked along the clifftops, as if the frost that encircled her wasting heart was also holding the earth in thrall.

When he appeared, the horseman was almost overlooked in the ennui of the fortress. He must have reached the outskirts of Tintagel fishing village before the arrival of nightfall and had slept out on the bare earth after finding some fodder for his horse, his lifeline to survival. What happened to him was of less importance than his mount. Every fibre of his emaciated frame sent him towards the fortress he had never visited and did not know because he could only rest once he had completed his sworn duty.

The horse slithered on the icy surface of the causeway and only just kept its footing. The servants who ran to help the rider noticed a shaggy coat that hadn't been curried or brushed for many months, although it still retained some fat under its bay hide.

The rider was another matter. Too weak to climb the steps leading to the forecourt, he was winched up by an ingenious rope and pulley mechanism installed for the movement of supplies. Barely conscious, he was taken to a lower room where the herb woman examined him. 'This poor boy isn't ill. He's just exhausted after many months of travel. He's starving.'

The visitor's face was covered by a beard that obscured his features. His dusty hair was knotted and needed washing and brushing, while his skin was grey with the dirt of many roadways. Curious, Cadal came to view this wild man who had appeared out of nowhere without warning. The prince noticed that his clothes, although they were worn, faded and very dirty, were of good quality.

Having reached his goal, the vagabond fell into a deep and restless sleep. His carers tried to wash what they could reach of his body, until they stripped him bare of clothing that was so threadbare the material fell apart in the hands of the servants. Cadal stared down at the man's unfamiliar features and wondered why he had come to this lonely and distant place.

'This mystery man has been burned by suns that are far hotter than ours,' Cadal remarked to his brother as they sat down to eat their evening meal. 'But we'll have to wait until he recovers before we can discover who he is.'

That same night, Endellion was wakened by her father's servant with word that Caradoc was scarcely breathing after slipping into an unnatural sleep. The servants felt certain that he would never waken, and were already weeping. She rushed to his room, while sending for the herb woman, the queen and his sons as she ran through the halls.

Father's time has come! Somehow Endellion couldn't understand the words that echoed through her head. He'd been ill for years, but he had always rallied. Suddenly, she was very much alone.

She felt like an intruder in the sickroom as each of Caradoc's kin paid their respects and took their leave of the indomitable old man. The only real sounds in the room were the heaving and rattling noises that came from the king's chest. Feeling more lost than she had ever been before, Endellion waited until a weeping Tegan Eurfron was helped from the sick room by Cadoc. Then she moved forward to kneel beside Caradoc's unconscious form.

'What will happen to me, now that you're about to leave me, Father? How will I live?'

Out of self-pity, Endellion had voiced her misery aloud. She felt a warm presence beside her and Cadal's heavy hand fell reassuringly onto her shoulder.

'Out of respect for Father's intentions, Endellion, I will honour his wishes. He loved you and he will expect me to care for you,' her brother assured her. 'Look to me for support, Endellion, for I'll not permit anything to happen to you.'

Then brother and sister looked down at their father and the tears began to flow. While they had been speaking, Caradoc ap Ynyr had passed into the shades. In an anticlimax that bore no similarity to his turbulent lifetime, he had relinquished his spirit peacefully, certain that Endellion would be cared for and that he had carried out his duty to the best of his abilities. Both siblings' hearts were lighter to see that the pain and suffering had been wiped from their father's face so that, once again, he looked young and free. This strong face had seen the best in Magnus Maximus and had acted as the emperor's regent. His huge heart had held Britannia together in those times when the darkness had hovered on the horizon.

Caradoc ap Ynyr was finally dead and his struggles with his old friend would now be a thing of the past.

* * *

The official period of mourning that followed was accompanied by visits from most of the local kings of Britannia or their representatives. Many duties softened these miserable days of mourning, not least the humdrum, prosaic necessities that convention demanded of kinfolk.

As Caradoc's heir, Cadal's duty included clearing the detritus of his father's private life once the funerary rites had been completed. The new king felt a need to present a brave face during the performance of this sad duty, so he asked Endellion to assist him with the delicate task of distributing his father's personal effects. The love that father and daughter had shared entitled her to this one last chance to say farewell to the great man.

Then, as Cadal cleared Caradoc's possessions from his clothes chest, he found one last gift that had been wrapped in fine cloth but not yet presented to its intended recipient. In almost-illegible script on a piece of valuable parchment, with what must have been an excruciatingly painful hand, the old king had written a message to accompany the gift:

For Endellion, my daughter – her wedding crown

Somehow, in secret, Caradoc had set his smiths to work on a delicate task, much like the golden shells that had been wrought so long ago for the kings of Britannia. The piece of driftwood found at the water's edge had provided the base of a crown, embellished with yellow gold and silver, as were some shells, a spiralled whale-tooth of ivory, the entire skeleton of a fingerling, delicate traceries of golden weed and, in the very centre, a huge amber egg surrounded by gold and silver wildflowers. Endellion held the parchment to her breast and cried in earnest.

Meanwhile, the fate of the comatose man who was lying in a small room on the lowest level of Tintagel Castell was all but forgotten. He had sickened after his arrival and had wandered through night horrors in his delirium. At first, the servants who were charged with caring for the stranger had feared for his life but, eventually, he woke on the very day of the king's cremation. In his weakness, he was as light and as pale as sea mist and as insubstantial as a wight.

'I must speak with Caradoc, the regent for Magnus Maximus,' he said urgently to the first servant who entered his room, as he tried to rise to his feet. Light-headed, he could barely stand upright as the servant tried to explain that the master had passed into the shades.

'I'm sorry, sir, but such a meeting is not possible. If you look out of the window and across to the headland, you can see King Caradoc's funeral pyre. He passed into the shades on the very night that you arrived at Tintagel.' The stranger tried to position his body so that he could see the tower of timber.

'Do you wish to watch the ceremony that will soon take place when the fire is lit, sir? I'm sure no one would object if you watched from a seat in the forecourt.'

The stranger smiled up with heart-stopping charm and gratitude. 'Such kindness would place me forever in your debt, good sir.'

Two servants helped the stranger out to the forecourt and placed a stool near the ramparts where he could sit and view the massive funeral pyre. Across the causeway, if he had been able to move himself, he could have seen Decius's monument on the opposite headland, the place where the decurion's spirit looked out towards the sea in a fruitless wait for his master.

Caradoc's body, under a coverlet of fur, had been placed at

the very top of the pyre and made ready for the torch. Above the fur, the king's hands gripped the hilt of his sword upon his breast. The dead king appeared like a carved image on a sarcophagus, distant and impassive in the realms of the dead.

The sick man had no sooner seated himself than the fire had been lit in each of the four corners by Caradoc's male kinsmen. Soaked in fish oil, the timber flared with an audible whoof and the crowd below stepped back from the sudden heat of the conflagration. The stranger's eyes swept the crowd and, eventually, he was forced to stand and move to the edge of the battlements to observe the tiny figures on the headland that seemed to have been frozen in exaggerated expressions of grief. Leaning against the stone half-wall, the stranger watched the whole ceremony as the pyre collapsed and continued to blaze fiercely. Then, as the twilight began to lengthen into dusk, the inhabitants of Tintagel began to move back towards the causeway as they mourned the loss of their king, the man who had been the bulwark of their lives for so many years.

Why Endellion should suddenly chance to look across at the cliffs as she was returning to the castell was a mystery to her later when she attempted to make some sense out of this strange, strange day. She had stared at her feet throughout the entire cremation ceremony with her head shrouded in a thin black veil. Suddenly, as she was crossing the causeway, the edge of the veil had blown away in the breeze to sail off like a pennon of sorrow. She leaped high to catch it, and raised her eyes in an attempt to snare the frail piece of errant material that was slipping through her fingers.

Then, she saw the figure of a man who was standing high above her.

And she knew!

The stairs seemed impossibly high and faint in the half-light, but Endellion wormed her way through the guests like an eel, racing up the uneven steps with all of youth's fervour. She had not seen him for seven years, but she had dreamed about the set of those shoulders, the colour of that russet hair and the shape of that forehead for every day of that interminable, lonely time.

Aeron ap Iorweth had finally come home.

THE FAMILY TREE OF
FLAVIUS MAGNUS MAXIMUS

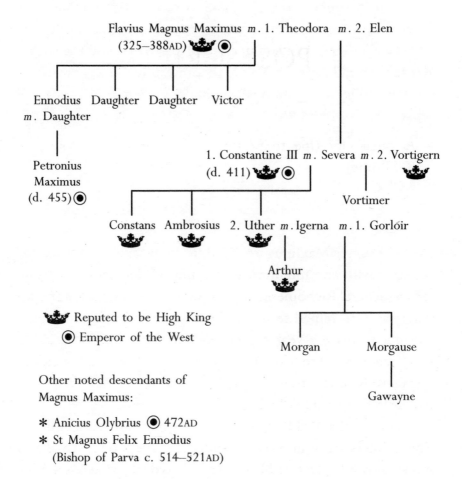

Reputed to be High King

Emperor of the West

Other noted descendants of
Magnus Maximus:

* Anicius Olybrius ● 472AD
* St Magnus Felix Ennodius
  (Bishop of Parva c. 514–521AD)

nb. While many of these people are historical figures, the destruction
of the Roman Empire and the wars of the Dark Ages ensured that
some later figures fall into the ranks of legends. We will never know
for sure if historians and academics, who wrote a century or so after these
huge figures are rumoured to have lived, were accurate in their details.

POSTSCRIPT

A venal city ripe to perish, if a buyer can be found
(Of Rome)

Sallust, *Jugurtha*

Flavius Magnus Maximus marched into Illyricum in the heat of summer with the intention of cutting off Theodosius's army, led by General Richomeres, a dour general from Constantinople who was determined to break the siege of Italia that Maximus had put in place a year earlier. Andragathius and Marcellinus had been ordered to take their commands to Siscia and Poetovio respectively, with orders to trap and encircle Richomeres in an iron grip that couldn't be broken.

The heat of a Middle Sea summer made movement difficult. The soldiers' armour was scorching to the touch, while the horses also suffered terribly inside their oxhide protection. Eyes were gritty from sun-blindness and dust, and even those men born in Italia suffered under the flail of the abnormal heat. The land was barren, bereft of shade and glittering from shale and stones that reflected the summer glare.

On the third night of their forced march, Aeron, the secretary to the emperor, took a rare opportunity to speak frankly with his master. Previously, they had enjoyed insufficient time for the luxury of conversation, even on those occasions when Maximus permitted such familiarity.

'I know you're weary, Lord Maximus, and you require nothing of me apart from my writing skills, but I'm moved to ask permission to speak on a matter concerning the safety of your army.'

'You may speak, Aeron, but get on with it. I want to sleep while time permits,' Maximus snapped. His gaze roamed around the campaign tent, anywhere but into the eyes of his secretary.

Since Decius had been left behind in Britannia, Maximus had felt unaccountably cut adrift in time. No one would dare speak bluntly to him and he was unable to trust the opinions of his officers.

Only Aeron, the scribe, offered some honesty. So, although Maximus seethed with impatience, he permitted the Briton to speak his mind.

'I'm moved to ask whether it's wise to divide your forces, my lord? I've seen and learned much from King Caradoc's strategies, but I can't understand why you've adopted such an unusual one. I'll need to understand your thinking on these matters if I'm to complete your history.' Aeron knew he was gabbling but his honesty was such that he couldn't still his tongue.

'I've watched as you fought battles across the known world, my lord, but your brother is a relative tyro as a commander. Andragathius is an experienced officer, but he is more successful when he is following the orders of a more imaginative superior. Neither man is a Caradoc, and definitely not a Maximus.'

Aeron could see that Maximus's face was reddening with temper, but something prevented him from following a more prudent path.

'We could easily be cut to ribbons if the battle goes wrong.

You've asked me to keep meticulous records of your campaigns, sir, and I've done as you asked. In the way of these things, I have learned much by watching you carefully, but you would never follow such a course in your usual approach to an important battle. Never!'

The emperor turned and knocked his chair over in the process. His rage was a living thing, but Aeron suspected that much of it was a pretence, designed to deflect further unwanted questions.

'Let me tell *you* something, *Master* Secretary. My father was Flavius Julius Crispus, who was executed on a false charge when I was an infant. I was raised on the estates of Theodosius Major in Hispania, a place where I could be kept under the close observation of my masters.'

'I don't understand, my lord. I thought your brother was younger than you. I'm sorry, but I don't see the reason for such behaviour.' Aeron was beginning to fear for his safety as Maximus whipped himself into a furious tantrum over old wrongs.

'I'd forgotten that you British are ignorant of Roman history and family lines. Marcellinus is my half-brother. Crispus, my sire, was the lesser son of Constantine the Great. I am the Imperator's grandson and the politics were such that I should have been murdered when my father was executed. I don't know if Theodosius Major was part of the plot to clear the way for other men to rule, but he was also executed for his pains. I should have become emperor in Rome and Constantinople but for the dirty tricks of lesser men. The throne is mine by right, so Theodosius Minor and Valentinian will remove me any way they can. Theodosius must know my history, and he won't permit me to live. I can sit and wait for the strangler's cord, or I can take the initiative. I've never been one for waiting.'

Aeron opened and closed his mouth several times, but he had nothing further to ask. So many details had fallen into place in the puzzle that was Magnus Maximus, even the venom of Theodosius Minor, which had always seemed odd to a clinical mind like Aeron's. The secretary had found the answers to his questions.

Likewise, he now understood that Theodosius would never acknowledge Maximus's parentage. He, and his line, would be carefully and coldly removed from life so that the Throne of the East, in Constantine the Great's city, would remain in Theodosius's hands. Even Valentinian was likely to have a short and unhappy life, for the Emperor of the East was a man with a cool brain who was totally uninterested in sharing power.

'You have my permission to add those details to your history if it suits you. Should I live, it won't matter a damn. If I should die, Severa is the only child of my blood who is safe. Britannia is her prison now, but it is also her bulwark. I'd like to think she will survive me, but Fortuna seems to have turned her face away from me.

'Go away and sleep, Master Secretary. You can be sure that I'll keep you alive for as long as I can. I owe much to Caradoc, so I trust your continued survival might ensure that something of my life will be remembered.'

Aeron had no choice other than to obey.

The army of Flavius Magnus Maximus came to the River Save in a heatwave that made the air, the grass and the trees tinder dry with the scorching breath of a particularly vicious summer.

The land was flat and featureless, so the army of Theodosius could be seen long in advance of their arrival before the lines of Maximus's formations in their extended battle plan. To his surprise, the enemy was moving at some speed, seemingly content to fight with their exhausted men and horses. Maximus lit fires that burned through the dry, brittle grasslands, but the wind turned and he was forced to withdraw.

The battle that followed raged for hours. Maximus used every skill at his disposal but fate and luck had both turned their faces away from him. Time and time again, victory was almost in Maximus's grasp but, in the cruelty of history, the general of Constantinople eventually won that bloody and wasteful day.

Hun warriors, who were the implacable enemies of the Western Empire, had been induced to throw in their lot with Theodosius and Valentinian. Huge sums of gold had changed hands and land was promised, as well as noble positions in Rome's governance if the Hun was prepared to send in their cavalry. No opposing army had ever defeated them on horseback, for their superior skills allowed them to fight with the reins between their teeth, a talent that left both hands free to use their light and deadly bows during a battle, even at close range. Maximus had no answer for such a terrible weapon and he watched in a fug of impotence as his troops were cut to pieces. The flower of Britannia's young men died on that distant field with the river at their backs, along with the soldiers from the last of the massed Roman armies. Rome would never again have so many foot soldiers at her disposal.

Ultimately, Aeron dragged the wounded Maximus from the field, whipping their horses and forcing the shattered emperor to ride in a daze of pain and defeat. Like thieves in the night, they travelled until the sun rose, and then slept in hiding until night came again. Maximus rode, slept and talked like a man in a waking dream. Sometimes, he spoke of his sons and daughters and how Valentinian would kill them all, if he could capture them. Occasionally, he wept for Elen, but he was mostly silent, tormented by unspoken possibilities.

When they reached Aquileia, Maximus refused to run any further. Surrounded by the remnants of his guard, he refused to budge, although Aeron used every argument at his disposal. Here, they had hidden in a copse on the outskirts of the city for three days, knowing that the local population was aware of their presence, until Andragathius rode into their encampment. There were only six men in his wake.

Like Maximus, Andragathius had discovered the skills of the Hun cavalry when he faced them at Siscia. Boxed in by the Hun cavalry and unable to assist Maximus who was many miles away at the river, Andragathius had fought like a lion, but had been forced to order the retreat. On the grisly road leading back to the Save River, where the corpses of thousands of his fellow Roman and British warriors were rotting under a pitiless sun, Andragathius flagellated himself for his inability to keep his master safe. When a courier arrived to inform him that the emperor's brother had been defeated, captured and executed at Poetovio, Andragathius's grief was a living thing. He would have fallen on his sword, but his master still lived, so he rode on in a fruitless search that eventually led him to Aquileia.

So, as the light had fled, Andragathius fell onto his knees in the dust beside the campfire, where Maximus rested on a large stone and stared blankly into the dancing firelight.

'I have betrayed you, my lord! I have lost the battle of Siscia and our troops have either been slain or have fled. I stayed alive only to bring you the news that your brother was executed at Poetovio, on the orders of Theodosius. With your permission, I wish to ride back until I reach his army and search for honourable death.'

'No!' Maximus's hoarse voice sounded as if it had come from the bottom of a tomb. 'You have yet to complete a task for me.'

'Anything! You only have to ask.'

'Take my secretary away from this place and lead him through the mountains to Gallia Cisalpina. He must live, do you hear me? Our lives mean nothing! But it is vital that Aeron should escape and remain alive.'

'I am at your command, my lord,' Andragathius murmured through unshed tears. 'Secretary! Gather together your scrolls and your chattels. We depart within the hour.'

'No! I can't just leave, my lord. I'm bound by my oaths to you, and I don't intend to dishonour those vows for any reason,' Aeron began, but Maximus rose to his full height and gripped his secretary's cloak at his throat with one strong right hand.

'You will take all the scrolls that are in your saddlebags and collect the others that were left behind at Augusta Treverorum. Give my best wishes to my wife and tell her to protect herself by any means at her disposal. I'd prefer you didn't leave her to die unwarned because you have some foolish idea of honour and valour. Once you have completed this duty, you will remove all your notes and histories from these dangerous lands and return to your home in Britannia. You shouldn't let all this death be for nothing.'

'But what of you? Will you try to return to Augusta Treverorum?'

'Me? I'm already dead, Aeron, and there is no place in this world where I could expect refuge. I intend to go to Aquileia and wait for the jackals to arrive in the best inn in that miserable city.'

Aeron opened his mouth to speak again, but Maximus had turned away, ordering his guard to give Andragathius and Aeron the two best horses they had as spares for the journey across the mountains.

'Come now, or I'll be forced to tie you to your own saddle,' Andragathius urged. 'You will obey my master's orders without argument or you'll make the trip in an undignified position.'

Aeron took one more moment to kiss his master's ring, and then Andragathius dragged him away.

And so the long, unbearable journey began.

As promised, Andragathius took Aeron to the road leading to Lugudunum. Once they had reached the top of the pass, the vast network of Roman roads lay before them, straight and true.

'Any of the guardsmen who wish to remain alive can accompany you, but I intend to ride south to the Middle Sea,' Andragathius said. 'There, I will decide how best to end my life. As we've been travelling, I've concluded that I rather like the idea of drowning. Valentinian and Theodosius will never gain satisfaction from displaying my body to the peasantry as they did with Marcellinus at Poetovio. No, I will do my best to rob them of that small satisfaction. I can't take anything else from them. If I hurry, I can join my master's spirit as it wings its way to Paradise. Ride hard and fast, so that my lord's family has some chance of survival. I've left a store of supplies on your packhorses that will help your return to Britannia. One final word of advice! Avoid towns, hamlets and companions on your journey to your homeland. Trust no one! It's likely that Theodosius will have assassins ranging far and wide for those of Maximus's friends who have escaped the emperor's net.'

He paused and then shot Aeron a fleeting smile intended to thank the young man for his service to Maximus. 'Ave, Secretary. If your history should mention me, please say that I died without fear.'

Speechless, Aeron sat mutely on his horse as all but one young boy chose to ride with Andragathius to whatever death he selected. Their decisions made, the Romans trotted away with defiant grins and in a mood that was almost cheerful. Perhaps it is only when our choices are taken from us that we achieve a true measure of freedom.

And so the last remnants of Maximus's army rode into the south, free from the cares and guilts of their world and the lesser men who struggled to survive in it.'

The lad grunted, but his vacuous blue eyes that were so like marbles told Aeron that he was either a simpleton or the battle had robbed him of his wits. He rode, he spoke and he performed the small actions of living without thought or emotion as if he was sleepwalking in the sunlight. Pleasure and pain both seemed beyond him.

The two men travelled down the hills and turned to the north in a silence that was complete and beyond argument. The younger man followed without thought, doing whatever Aeron ordered.

At Augusta Treverorum, Aeron retrieved his scrolls, parchments and notes, sealing them all into a large, waterproof trunk which he tied to the back of one of the packhorses. The boy who travelled with him had already decided to stay in the town; Aeron had been glad to see the last of him. As for Theodora, wife of Maximus, his audience with her had been odd and ambiguous. She had allowed herself to weep several tears, but then her face had cleared.

'I will go to a nunnery with those of my daughters who are unwed. Given time, we will dedicate ourselves to God. If we do this, Valentinian might spare our lives. My son will be taken to safety, if I can persuade my cousin to take him. Perhaps I might still save us all, if God is kind. As for you, young man, you must flee as fast as you can. Friends of my husband will be hunted from sea to sea, so you must avoid towns and live off the land, if you can manage it. For now, take whatever supplies you might need from my kitchens to tide you through your journey.'

'I am in your debt, my lady, so I will pray for you every morning as I go on my way.'

She looked at him steadfastly, but without any emotion. 'Do you understand the dangers of hubris, young man? I hope you will never experience what hubris did to my husband and what it can do to all the great ones of this world.'

'Aye, my lady. I do understand. I've seen much during my travels.'

'Then go with God.'

She turned away with a stiff back so she wouldn't have to watch his departure.

And then the long journey home began.

Weeks earlier, Maximus had stood in his full regalia in the forecourt of the governor's villa. Valentinian and Theodosius were present, as was the general from Constantinople and officers of the guard, fine in their golden armour, their horsehair plumes and their impassive northern faces.

On Theodosius's order, Maximus's uniform was stripped from him, exactly as the clothing of his kinsman, Theodosius Major, and his father, Flavius Julius Crispus, had been removed when they were humiliated and executed in earlier times. His sword was broken, although the fine blade resisted their attempts to destroy it.

'You can execute me, but you can't rob me of my title as High King of the Britons,' Maximus croaked. 'That title was never yours to give, so I will die with standing that remains the equal of yours. Remember that, Theodosius, after I go to the shades. No matter how long it takes, I will be waiting for you beyond the veil.'

'I prefer to worry about the here and the now,' Theodosius retorted, his good humour undampened by Maximus's bluster. 'You have brought your execution on yourself.'

'Better men than I have died thus. I will try to think on immortality as I choke, and I'll wonder which of us will be remembered after the passage of time.'

Then the executioner looped the silken cord around Maximus's head and the delicate, strong threads cut off the High King's windpipe. Although his body tried to remain still, instinct betrayed him and Flavius Magnus Maximus perished in his own piss and shit, as all executed men do, even if they have stood as high as the gods themselves.

Theodosius and Valentinian congratulated each other and went in to dine as the dead emperor's head was removed, to ride back to Rome on the point of a standard.

The rain came later and sweetened the forecourt, although the servants had washed away the last remaining traces of Maximus.

Few mourned and, within six months, very few remembered.

AUTHOR'S NOTES

This novel is about two great men, two warriors who actually lived in the dying days of the Roman Empire as a huge bureaucracy began to jerk and stutter as the cogs broke, one by one. But not for nearly a hundred years! The Roman way of life endured even after the body and brain perished, although men refused to believe that a long-enduring, magnificent culture could ever cease to exist. When Magnus Maximus came to Britannia for the first time, the empire was fatally poisoned, although its rulers still squabbled over its still-breathing corpse.

My two protagonists, Caradoc and Maximus, have little in common, but both men have the seeds of greatness as well as flaws that limit their importance. Had he lived, Maximus might have saved the whole empire, or at least held off its demise for another century. The emergence of the concept of a High King is fascinating, given the Arthurian legends, and the odd links with those legends which exist in Roman historical records to tease us with the possibility that truth shines through the legends as well.

I have always loved symmetry and, given my desire to understand the blend of history, myth and legend in the Arthuriad, I found the story of Maximus very satisfying. After Maximus, the records become sketchy and, by the middle of the fifth century, only fragments of evidence remain. The bulk of writings have virtually vanished, destroyed by war, barbarian invasions and some despotic rulers within the British establishment.

The position and historicity of Ambrosius, Uther Pendragon and Arthur on Maximus's family tree are problematic, as are the family members of Maximus himself. I have chosen to accept the versions that make sense out of the world I am trying to create. What I have learned during my research is how cataclysmic the removal of the legions from Britannia really was, in that it contributed to the piecemeal destruction of a civilised people by the Anglo-Saxon invaders who took their place. This wanton destruction was, perhaps, the way of the world, but for anyone who is interested in the history of Britain, the gaping hole in the existing records is a great loss. All we can do to fill it is to try to knit together a plausible history from the fragments that remain.

King Caradoc of the Dumnonii tribe must have been a remarkable man to be so trusted by such a hard-headed, practical commander as Maximus. I have tried to bring him to life sympathetically, since he is so pivotal to the ancestry of King Gorlois of the Arthurian legends.

If you should find that there are too many wars in my history, all I can say is that constant warfare was the lot of the disorganised kingdoms of the period. I have invented some of the family members of the various rulers, but most kings would have very few heirs to replace them because of infant mortality and the violence of the times in which they lived.

I have also drawn on *The Dream of Macsen Wledig* for inspiration.

Rome didn't die overnight. Something so vast doesn't perish suddenly. As a matter of record, her last Roman emperor was Flavius Petronius Maximus, grandson of Flavius Magnus

Maximus, whose rule has gone down in history for its brevity and violence. I was delighted to discover that Theodosius and Valentinian failed to eliminate Maximus's influence, so several very prominent men were later to claim him in their ancestry.

As far as history allows us to know, Maximus seems to have been the first king of a united tribal structure, but others may have existed in earlier, unrecorded history. For all that, we can certainly say that he was the first High King to use his status as a springboard to achieve his Roman ambitions. As an emperor of sorts, Maximus will remain an enigma.

I have enjoyed researching the last years of Roman Britain and have been fascinated by the ease with which it is possible to place Arthur into the post-Roman world. When I address the task of stitching history, myth and legend together, I am always tempted to believe that there may be some truth lurking in the murky, indistinct world of what is inaccurately labelled Britain's Dark Ages. Surely some truth must lie among the fragments, even if they are exaggerated by time and poetic licence. And when they fit together so well, as in the history of Maximus, any sensible person must wonder where the truth lies.

The reference to Maximus's father as a descendant of the Great Constantine was utterly fascinating. How entirely apt and neat is this possibility? Unfortunately, so much doubt and ignorance is part of the great man's early life that we will never know if Theodosius was a practical man, eager to rid himself of a legitimate emperor.

As for Elen, she is mentioned in a remnant from the period as a wife of Maximus. Certainly, marriage to native women, especially the daughters of barbarian kings, was a frequent custom because this system bound tribes to Rome through bastard children who were cherished because of their link with the all-powerful legions. To become High King, Maximus would have had to take a suitable wife from a tribal, aristocratic family.

Some characters are entirely my own, most notably Decius and the lovers, Endellion and Aeron. I enjoy trying to capture the correct flavour and customs of the period by my own creations. They frequently speak with my voice.

Unfortunately, few facts are clear after Maximus, although the Romans were not quite finished with Britannia. Nor was Severa, or Sevira, quite lost in the annals of history. She appears out of the shadows for brief moments, permitting me to almost catch the shape of her face.

But that is another story.

M. K. Hume
June 2015

GLOSSARY OF PLACE NAMES

Alauna	Maryport, Cumbria, England
Anderida	Pevensey, East Sussex, England
Anderida Silva	The district surrounding Anderida
Aquae Sulis	Bath, Somerset, England
Augusta Treverorum	Trier, Germany
Blatobulgium	Birrens, Dumfriesshire, Scotland
Bodotria Aest	Firth of Forth, Scotland
Bremetennacum	Ribchester, Lancaster, England
Caer Fyrddin	Carmarthen, Carmarthenshire, Wales
Caer Gai	Llanuwchllyn, Gwynedd, Wales
Caerleon	Newport, South Wales
Caernarfon	Carnarvon, Gwynedd, Wales
Calleva Atrebatum	Silchester, Hampshire, England
Canovium	Caerhun, Conwy, Wales
Castra Exploratorum	Netherby, Cumbria, England
Clausentum	Southampton, Hampshire, England
Corinium	Cirencester, Gloucestershire, England
Cymru	The Celtic term for Wales
Deva	Chester, Cheshire, England
Durnovaria	Dorchester, Dorset, England
Dyfed	A kingdom in the west of ancient Britain
Eburacum	York, Yorkshire, England
Forest of Dean	Gloucestershire, England
Gallia Cisalpina	Province in France
Gesoriacum	Boulogne, France. Also known as Portus Itius by the Romans
Glannaventa	Ravenglass, Cumbria, England
Glevum	Gloucester, Gloucestershire, England
Gwent	A kingdom in the west of ancient Britain

Gwynedd	A kingdom in the west of ancient Britain
Hibernia	The ancient name for Ireland
Hispania	Spain
Isca Dumnoniorum	Exeter, Devonshire, England
Isca Silurum	Caerleon, South Wales
Litus Saxonicum	The English Channel
Londinium	London, England
Lugudunum	Lyon, France
Lutetia	Small town near Paris. Now part of Paris
Mamucium	Manchester, Greater Manchester, England
Mare Hibernicus	Roman name for the Irish Sea
Massilia	Marseille, France
Mediolanum	Milan, Italy
Menai Straits	The body of water between Wales and Anglesea Island
Middle Sea	The Mediterranean Sea
Mona Island	An island off the western coast of Britain
Nemetocenna	Arras, France
Oceanus Atlanticus	Atlantic Ocean
Parisii	Paris, France
Pennal	Machynlleth, Merionethshire, Wales
Portus Adurni	Portchester, Hampshire, England
Powys	A kingdom in the west of ancient Britain
Red Wells	A legendary well in modern-day Somerset, England
Rhodanus River	Rhone River, France
Samarobriva	Amiens, France
Segedunum	Wallsend, Tyne and Wear, England
Segontium	Caernarfon, Gwynedd, North Wales.
Sequana River	Seine River, France
Sorviodunum	Salisbury, Wiltshire, England
Tintagel	A fortress in Cornwall, England
Vellum Antonini	The Antonini Wall
Vellum Hadriani	Hadrian's Wall
Venta Belgarum	Winchester, Hampshire, England
Venta Silurum	Caerwent, Monmouthshire, Wales
Verlucio	Sandy Lane, Wiltshire, England
Verulamium	St Albans, Hertfordshire, England
Vindo Cladia	Badbury, Wiltshire, England

GLOSSARY OF BRITISH TRIBAL NAMES

Atrebates
Belgae
Brigante
Catuvellauni
Coritani
Cornovii
Deceangli
Demetae
Dumnonii
Dobunni
Durotriges
Iceni
Otadini
Ordovice
Regni
Selgovae
Silures
Trinovantes